From Ireland With Love

Liz Hurley was a finalist for the 2021 Romantic Novelists Association Debut Romantic Novel Award for *A New Life for Ariana Byrne*. She writes exciting and heart warming stories that will make you cheer and laugh. Her heroines are overflowing with grit, gumption and good old-fashioned gorgeousness!

D1494085

Also by Liz Hurley

The Hiverton Sisters

A New Life for Ariana Byrne
High Heels in the Highlands
Cornish Dreams at Cockleshell Cottage
From Ireland With Love

Liz Hurley

From Ireland with Love

hera

First published in the United Kingdom in 2021 by Hera Books

This edition published in the United Kingdom in 2023 by

Hera Books
Unit 9 (Canelo), 5th Floor
Cargo Works, 1-2 Hatfields
London SE1 9PG
United Kingdom

A CIP catalogue record for this book is available from the British Library.

Print ISBN 978 1 80436 343 0
Ebook ISBN 978 1 912973 78 1

Look for more great books at www.herabooks.com

Printed and bound in Great Britain by Clays Ltd, Elcograf S.p.A.

I

Chapter 1

The wind began to pick up in earnest as the walkers headed briskly across the field to Hiverton Manor.

'Do you think we'll get ahead of the rain?' laughed Ari.

Hal turned back to her with a grin on his face and Will on his shoulders. 'If we were in Cornwall, we'd already be wet!' He tugged on the boot of his little rider. 'One last charge at Daddy and Leo before we get inside?'

Will roared out, pumping his fist in the air, and Hal pretended to be a mighty war horse as he galloped over to Seb, who had Leo up on his shoulders. The two men ran in small circles whilst the boys tried to hit each other.

Pointing to the child in her sling, Ari called back to Rory. 'You know, as soon as Hector is big enough he'll require a battle horse as well. Are you up for it?'

'Lassie, I've been a donkey, a dragon and even the Loch Ness Monster for my brother's lads. It will be my pleasure. If my back hasn't completely died by then.'

As she looked at Rory, Nick couldn't imagine such a vital man ever having a bad back. Tiny Clem had fallen in love with a giant of a man. He looked the sort that could probably pull up a tree by its roots. Of the three men, he was definitely the broadest, clearly a very hands-on sort of farmer.

Paddy and Clem were bringing up the rear of the group. 'Are you looking forward to when Eleanor will be demanding shoulder rides?' said Nick to Paddy.

Paddy smiled at her tiredly. 'Yes and no. I love being with her like this.'

Like Ari, Paddy had her baby strapped to her in a sling – country living made a mockery of prams.

'Although at the moment I could do with a rest. We were up all night with her crying. I don't know where Hal finds the energy.'

Nick watched as her other two brothers-in-laws pretended to be horses, their little charges shouting with excitement from their shoulders. Like Rory they were good-looking and tall if not quite so broad, but it wasn't any of their looks that appealed to Nick. It was how the three men seemed to enjoy each other's company and how well they had joined the family. She had always feared one of her sisters marrying a man she didn't like, and indeed when Ari married Greg, her first husband, all the sisters had been appalled. Poor Ari, unexpectedly pregnant, said yes when Greg proposed. On reflection Nick felt a tiny bit sorry for Greg as well – after all, he had done the decent thing. It was just that the decent thing was also the wrong thing, once again proving that the road to hell was paved with good intentions. His sudden death had been a blessing for all. Well, nearly all.

'Why are you laughing?' asked Paddy.

'Bad thoughts. Ignore me. Here, can I carry Eleanor? Give you a rest.'

Paddy thought about it which surprised Nick – for her to contemplate it Paddy must be really tired, because she knew Nick wasn't a baby person. Pets and children were the very pinnacle of chaos.

'No, I'm grand. We're nearly there anyway.'

Looking ahead Ari, Clem and Aster had already reached the back door and were chatting to Dickie.

'By the time we join them, everyone will have their boots and coats off, the fire will be lit, the kettle will be on and we can just sweep in and put our feet up.'

'The Queens of Sheba!'

Nick stopped and curtsied towards Paddy, who grinned and began to curtsey back, but Eleanor began to grizzle. Nick put her hand out and gently held Eleanor's little chubby fist.

'I meant you as well, little one. We three shall all be the Queens of Sheba.'

As they got closer to the back of the house it began to rain. Paddy tried to keep Eleanor protected from the elements, but the heavens had properly opened. Everyone else had now disappeared inside but a back door opened, and Hal came running out towards them carrying two umbrellas. He had already taken his coat and boots off and was now getting his socks wet as he ran across the lawn towards them.

Laughing and gasping from the sudden downpour, they all piled into the house. Hal peeled his socks off and then grumbled about the cold flagstones. As he went off to grab another pair of socks, Nick and Paddy laughed as they heard him shout to Seb that he needed to install under-floor heating. Rory then shouted back that he needed to stop being a great southern Jessie. He might have got away with the jest but for the disembodied voice of Clem who reminded him that he had just installed a heated driveway. As the ribbing and the conversation continued loudly across many rooms, the twins headed towards the large sitting room where a fire was blazing, and the other three sisters were already enjoying hot drinks and were cuddled down into various armchairs and sofas.

Hector was building bricks on the rug in front of Ari but other than that the room was still and quiet. Nick smiled and relaxed.

'I know,' said Aster, 'a moment of calm. Isn't it lovely?'

'Enjoy it while you can,' said Ari. 'Seb is washing down the dogs, Dickie is feeding the boys and Rory is getting changed, I think.' Rory had been playing tug of war with Leo and Will and had somehow managed to lose and fall in a muddy puddle – to the boys' great entertainment.

'You know, I think he fell in the mud deliberately?' Ari smiled as she shook her head and continued trying to account for where everyone was. 'What's Hal up to?'

'Changing Eleanor and then they'll come and join us. He might see if she'll sleep,' replied Paddy hopefully.

The door opened and the girls smiled as Dickie came in. She was the only other person who had known their mother and they would regularly plague her for tales of her as a young girl.

'Ariana, I've taken the boys to bed. Their heads were nodding as they drank their milk.'

Ari looked at her wristwatch. It was three o'clock now, they would probably sleep for an hour which suited her perfectly. She had every day to spend with her children but opportunities to spend time with her sisters all together were few and far between. It was only because Aster was about to go travelling that they had all found a free weekend before she left. Ari couldn't help being uncomfortable that Aster was going so far away for so long. Seb pointed out the time would fly by, and that she would do better being worried for the countries that Aster visited.

'You know, Aster,' Ari addressed her little sister, 'you could always get a secondment to work with some of Nick's contacts. They're always looking for computer whizz-kids.'

Aster groaned. 'It's not going to work, Ari. I'm serious, I just want to play and explore. I want a change.'

Aster had got a first class Honours degree in Classics from Cambridge. It came as barely a surprise when they discovered that she had also been taking a degree in computing sciences and got a first in that as well. Aster was the brainbox in the family. She didn't get bored as such, but everything interested her, and she always wanted to know more.

'I plan to really sink my teeth into Greece and Italy. Imagine the triremes sailing out of Ostia, picture Plato striding around the Agora. I might call in on Otto and Louis.'

'You'll need to be quick; I think they're planning a trip to India before they return to Scotland for the summer,' said Clem, who had first encountered Otto in Scotland, running the family castle. Both women were creative geniuses who knew their own minds, they were both stubborn and had clashed almost immediately. It wasn't until Otto was reunited with the love of her life that she had begun to mellow and enjoy life.

For the past year Otto had been living something of a peripatetic life and hadn't yet decided where it was she wanted to settle. *So long as Louis is by my side, what do I care where I am?* The woman was a nightmare, but Clem missed her when she was away.

Nick sat and watched her sisters chat, gently mocking Ari for trying to divert Aster. She wriggled her toes in front of the crackling logs and enjoyed the moment. After all that they had been through, these moments were more precious to her than any portfolio or asset. The girls had grown up with next to nothing, just the love of their family, and when their parents had died even that was destroyed. It had been a gruelling childhood, but they had got through it together and now life was good.

The door opened and Seb walked in with the two dogs at his feet – they promptly rolled over Hector's wooden tower. Seb leant across and gave Ari a small kiss, then sat on the floor with the little one and started to rebuild the tower. The two dogs were scolded and told to settle down in the corner. The problem was that Hector had the best spot in front of the fire guard.

'Dragon, away,' and Ari pointed her finger to the other side of the room. Both dogs stood up and headed over to the far side. Dragon looked over her shoulder to see if Ari had changed her mind and then realising she hadn't, decided to make the most of the warm spot by the radiator. She looked at Ari reproachfully as she discovered it was cold, but Ari didn't appear to be paying attention, so the dog sighed and lay down.

A moment later Rory – carrying Eleanor – and Hal joined them bearing a teapot and a cafetière and refilled everyone's cups. Nick shook her head, so much for peace and quiet.

'What was that look, Letta?'

The others all looked over at her as Aster asked her question.

'Do you know, I miss hearing Letta,' said Ari.

Rory was sitting on one of the armchairs drinking a cup of Darjeeling, trying to decide if he liked Clem's latest fad. He wasn't convinced. He glanced across at the sisters.

'Who's Letta?'

'Nick is,' said Aster. 'Her full name is Nicoletta. Dad used to call her Nick and Mum would call her Letta. I don't have many memories of them, but I do remember that and how they would sing the two names. *Nick knack paddy whack* and *Alouette, gentille alouette.*'

The sisters laughed, remembering the songs, and joined in with the children adding to the noise. Dragon took her moment and slunk quietly closer towards the fire.

'Anyway,' shrugged Aster, 'I don't hear Letta enough so I like to use that name whenever I can. You don't mind, do you?'

'Not in the slightest. I like it as well. It was just you know, being called Nick in the financial market's never hurt. It's a lazy and sexist stereotype but one I was happy to use to my advantage. Still, people seem to find other people having more than one name confusing.'

'It is a bit, though, isn't it?' said Rory again. 'I mean, all of you have multiple names. I know women often change their surnames when they get married but you five are also Byrne or de Foix as well as Hiverton.'

'Strictly speaking,' said Seb, 'only Ari is Hiverton. The others are of the Hiverton family. Like the Duke of Norfolk, there is only one person that could be called Norfolk. It's a title as much as a name and only one person can have it.'

'Yes, and that's bossy pants over there,' teased Aster.

'Okay, but you all also have various forenames. Paddy is also Holly McDonald.'

'That's just a work thing.'

'Nick here is either Nick or Letta.'

'Both diminutives.'

'Clem is Clem, Clemmie or Clementine.'

'You forgot "Bloody Hell, Clem".'

'That's not so much a name as a daily cry.'

Clem threw a cushion at Rory which made the dogs look up in readiness for a pillow fight. One stern look from Ari and they lowered their heads again. Now that Ari had noticed Dragon, she had to move back to the cold radiator.

'Anyway, you can talk, Rory,' said Clem. 'One day you'll be Invershee, just like Ari is Hiverton. Plus you call me Bo.'

'I know, it's just you all have so many names it gets confusing.'

Aster poured a cup of coffee and brought it over to Rory.

'Here,' she said handing him the cup, 'and if it helps I'm just Aster. Short, sweet and uncomplicated.'

That caused everyone to laugh so hard that the dogs got up and started to bark. Hector, surprised by the sudden noise, began to cry.

Nick smiled to herself; Hector was a child after her own heart. She decided that now was probably a good moment to try and calm everyone down.

'That magazine article came out yesterday, by the way.' She rummaged in the bag. 'They've actually written a lot more about the family than I wanted, so I've got you all a copy.' She handed each sister her own copy of *Financial Focus*, the City's leading financial journal. Cressida was the editor and a friend of Nick's. She had asked if Nick would be happy to feature in an article, given her recent rise in profile. Nick had reluctantly agreed, and a particularly hopeless reporter had come over to interview her.

Now the article was published Nick vowed never to be interviewed again. In fairness, it wasn't appalling but she had been hoping for something that focussed on her business and the family's charitable enterprise – which it did, but at least a quarter of the copy focussed on the rags-to-riches aspect of their family and the sisters' private lives. Frankly, she was embarrassed to have allowed this breach into their privacy.

'Oh my God, Nick, where did they get this photo from?' shrieked Paddy in delight. 'You look like some ball-breaking dominatrix.'

When Nick had first started out she'd had a professional head shot done. She wore thick black-rimmed glasses; her then short hair had been slicked back and she wore a pin-striped suit. She liked the photo a lot, it portrayed confidence. She looked like every other stockbroker and most importantly, if you saw her in the flesh you wouldn't recognise her. She knew she came across as a dry old stick but that didn't really bother her. Growing up with her more flamboyant sisters she never felt the need to sparkle. It looked too much like hard work. She'd rather just beaver away in the background.

'I like this bit,' said Ari reading it out loud. '*De Foix Investments also caters to a different sort of investor. In Byrne's own words, "I felt that the stock market can seem too off-putting for a large sector of the community. For those that didn't grow up with money or for people within certain social groups, it really seems like it is for the rich only. I wanted to reach out to people from all walks of life." That really sums up your ethos.'*

'I guess,' shrugged Nick. 'I just wish she had reported more about the charity as well.'

The Five Sisters Charity helped people into jobs or to set up their own business. It also offered support and advice for those struggling with the welfare services, and recently had started to help small community ventures.

This was definitely a passion project and one Nick could talk about for hours.

'Instead, it just keeps harping on about how I brought down the Bank of Harrington's which everyone knows I didn't.' She waved the magazine in Seb's direction, drawing him into the conversation. 'Even your brother didn't actually do it. Harrington's were responsible for their own failure. George and I merely asked a few questions.'

'And the financial industry is all the better for it,' replied Seb. 'No one needed another run on the stock market. Even if it did cause a few issues for those of us that had invested in Harrington's.'

Hal winced. His was one of the families that had almost gone under, but he agreed with Seb, none of that was Nick's fault. He raised his cup in her direction.

'This bit is good as well,' called out Paddy. '"*Of course there are risks everywhere but I wanted to get away from the idea that various socio-economical groups don't like risk. They do – they're human after all. They just didn't know how to get in. So I set up a small company that offered business services, financial advice and money growth. All on a microscale, but I loved it. This is what money is for. It's about changing lives. It's about feeding ideas and watching businesses grow.*"'

'That is so you!' continued Paddy. 'Why don't you like this article? It seems really well balanced and ever so positive?'

Nick winced. They hadn't got to the part where the article wandered off into their private lives. 'Carry on reading.'

'Hang on,' said Clem in an outraged voice. 'Paddy, have you read this bit? It's completely unfair. *Abandoned by her muse just as her career began to take off*. You never abandoned me. I have NEVER felt that way. Who wrote this drivel? Nick, you didn't say that, did you?'

'Of course she didn't, Clem,' said Paddy. 'Stop being so touchy. Journalists will write any old tosh. You know that.'

'Oh dear,' said Ari. 'They do love this from-a-city-estate-of-broken-bottles-to-a-country-estate-with-a-title angle.'

'We grew up on a terrace street. Hardly an estate,' said Aster.

'Not as sexy though, is it?'

'Oh, and look the journalist has trotted out the rich-girl-falls-for-penniless-Irish-student. *A hospital porter, doing the best he could for his family. Did Lady Elizabeth ever regret her decision?* Bloody hell, that's a bit rich.'

'Don't they mention Dad's work as an artist?' demanded Clem. 'Nick, why didn't you tell her how talented Dad was?'

Nick sighed; it was all this sort of guff that had really wound her up when she'd first read the article. The sisters knew the truth of their upbringing and it really wasn't anyone else's business. Especially if they were going to misinterpret it.

'Of course I did. I even showed her shots of some of his pictures on my phone.'

'Well, she hasn't mentioned them?'

'And?'

'Well, all I'm saying is maybe you forgot. Maybe you didn't think it was that important.'

'This shit again!' Nick put her cup down. Maybe it was time to go. She had been really disappointed by the article and now Clem was winding her up with the old you-only-care-about-money crap.

'I don't know what's wrong with you sometimes, Clem. You know damn well that Nick would have been singing Dad's praises to the rafters,' admonished Ari.

'Has it never crossed your mind how proud I am of your talents? You and Dad always had that in common. But oh no. You have to trot out the whole money-grubbing Nick routine.'

'That's not fair. I didn't say that.'

'As good as,' Aster joined in.

'But that wasn't what I meant.'

'So what did you mean when you said *I didn't think it was as important*?' challenged Nick.

'Maybe she meant not important in the context of an interview about your business achievements,' said Aster and Clem pounced.

'That was exactly what I meant. I know if I was talking about my business it would take me ages to say how important your skills were to the company. And they are. They are essential. I'm really sorry, Nick.' Clem jumped up from her sofa and came and settled herself down by Nick. 'I didn't mean to make you feel bad. I'm a stupid idiot. Forgive me?'

Nick glared at her briefly then gave her a hug. She knew she was genuinely contrite and was acting from a position of deep insecurity. Honestly, Nick sometimes felt that she was the big sister, not Clem. The awkward moment passed, and they finished browsing through the article.

The three men looked at each other, Rory casting his eyes to heaven. All of the men had found it was safer to step back when the sisters were having a spat. Any time they had tried to get involved, the girls had rounded on them and then the row just escalated and spread out. Rory came from a large family and was used to sibling blowouts. Those same fights tended to make Seb yearn for the rare moments when he and his brother and sister were all in the same country at the same time. Hal, however, as a single child, found them deeply unsettling and Paddy would have to regularly convince him that the family wasn't, despite all appearances to the contrary, tearing itself apart.

Eventually the clock chimed the hour and Nick sighed. It was time to go.

'Okay. That's me.'

'Do you really have to go? You were the last to arrive on Friday.'

'Sorry, Ari, there's a lot going on in the markets at the moment and I have a 4 a.m. call tomorrow morning.'

'Ouch, poor you,' said Seb sympathetically. His brother, George, was also a city trader and ran his own investment company. Seb knew how hard his brother worked but like Nick, he thrived off the adrenaline and odd hours.

'Why don't you stay for supper,' tried Ari again, 'then head off?'

'Because then I won't have an early night. And I'll be groggy all day tomorrow and you know I don't like to start the week groggy. You know me, plan to succeed.'

The girls all laughed at Nick's self-deprecating joke. Nick was a stickler for planning ahead. She regularly had to deal with their gentle mockery, but life was so much easier if she didn't have to think about what to wear or what to eat. Every day, all the mundane stuff had been planned out and laid down the night before so that she could focus on work instead. She knew the efficiency could sometimes make her seem a bit boring, but she didn't care – she just wanted to spend time thinking about stuff she enjoyed. And that was her job. Popping the magazine back in her bag she asked if anyone could run her to the train station.

'Me!' said all four of her sisters, and a lovely warm feeling hugged her. She loved them all so much and wished she had been able to spend more time with them. But loving them also meant looking after them and running De Foix Investments properly. Nick looked across at Paddy, who kept glancing anxiously over at Eleanor on Hal's lap, and made her mind up. Her twin needed a break, even a tiny one, and she hadn't spent much time at all with Paddy since Eleanor arrived.

'Come on, Padster, what say you and I have a tiny road trip?'

Paddy beamed excitedly and stood up and smiled at Hal. 'I'll be about an hour; can you hold the fort with Eleanor until then?'

'I think I can manage a baby,' drawled Hal.

Which was precisely the moment that poor Eleanor began violently throwing up. Paddy ran across the room and was now using her pashmina to try and clean up Eleanor's face but as the baby threw up again she and Hal rushed out to the bathroom. The dogs ran forward excitedly until Ari barked at them and sent them to their beds. Nick looked on in horror.

'Were the dogs about to eat the vomit? This is definitely my cue to leave.'

'And mine,' declared Clem with the same look of disgust on her face. 'Come on, I'll drive, and I can apologise again for being a thin-skinned eejit.'

Chapter 2

As the car tore through the miles, the sisters chatted about how everyone was doing. The family seemed to be on an even keel, although Clem and Nick both agreed that Paddy looked under the weather. The conversation moved on to their respective businesses and Clem mentioned a type of muslin that she had been researching that was no longer made. As she explained the handmade process, Nick nodded along. This was Clem's passion, not hers, but she didn't want to sound totally bored.

'That's incredible, sounds hugely labour intensive – no wonder they stopped making it. The costs must be prohibitive?'

Clem's knuckles tightened on the steering wheel.

'I wasn't suggesting we do it. Don't worry, the coffers are safe.'

Nick stared ahead into the dusk. If Clem wasn't driving she thought she might have slapped her. Instead she counted to ten.

'Is this your idea of an apology?'

'What!'

'Doubling down and continuing to denigrate me about the finances?'

'Well, I was just trying to talk to you about something I was interested in.'

'And I was just trying to join in with the conversation. I know bugger all about fabrics and fashion, but I do understand business and finance, so I was trying to contribute.'

'I thought you were trying to stop me.'

'You thought?' Nick rolled her eyes. 'Did you think for longer than one knee-jerk second?'

'Oh, crap.' Clem flicked on the indicator and pulled over into a layby and burst into tears, apologising as she did so. Through the tears, the *sorry*s and the hugs Clem explained how terrified she was that her new collection was boring or derivative or too ambitious or dull. Plus, she had an idea for a new venture, and she was getting overwhelmed. Nick had seen Clem like this before.

'You know what this is, Clem. It means you have something major on your hands. It's always "go big" or "go home" with you, and you *never* go home. Come on. I'll drive and you tell me what you have in mind.'

The girls swapped seats and Clem began to tell Nick about her new idea. Whilst she talked, Nick's mind started to run, thinking about ways in which the scheme could be funded.

'I think we can support this. It sounds excellent.'

Clem looked at her in surprise and then let out a deep sigh. 'It probably won't make any money.' The admission was wrung out of her.

Nick looked across at her and smiled. 'No, I shouldn't think so, it doesn't sound at all like a profit-making venture, but this potentially has a huge community impact. Besides which, art for its own sake is important.'

'Do you really believe that?'

Nick let out a deep sigh. She loved Clem so much, but she was hugely self-centred when she was tired.

'Oh, Clem, how could I not? You really do say the most hurtful things at times. I sometimes think you must view me as the most awful greedy person in the world. And don't hug me,' she laughed, 'I'm trying to drive. Look, I meant what I said back at Hiverton. I have always been so jealous and in awe of your talent.' Nick added in a tired voice, 'What do *I* do?'

'You make money! You are the ultimate Rapunzel. I haven't a clue how to do that, all I know is how to spend and consume and—'

'Create. You create and it's wonderful stuff. So just understand that, and stop punching down on us lesser mortals. It hurts.'

As the journey continued they talked at length about their childhood and their parents and their feelings, until the car pulled into Norwich train station.

'We haven't talked like this for a good few years,' said Nick.

'I don't think we've ever talked like this. And I'm sorry for it, I've been a total arse this weekend.'

Both girls climbed out of the car and Nick picked up her overnight bag and laptop case from the back seat.

'Yes, you have, but I still love you.'

'I love you too. Now go get your train before we embarrass ourselves further.'

With a big hug they said goodbye and then Nick turned and walked into the station.

–

By the time Nick got home she felt rested after the noise and chaos of a family weekend. She felt buoyed from being with them all but now the silence was like a cool duvet on a hot night. Her new apartment had been found for her by her assistant, Daisy Halls. Daisy had great contacts within the property world and when she heard her boss was looking for accommodation closer to Canary Wharf she put her feelers out. The modern serviced flat in the heart of Canary Wharf was far more than Nick had anticipated but Daisy explained that they had had a problem letting it due to a fatal incident; now the rent was dirt cheap. Having investigated the fatality and discovered it had nothing to do with the apartment itself and everything to do with too many pills and powders, Nick said yes.

Now she closed the door behind her and placed her laptop on charge at the table so it would be ready for the early meeting. Even with an early start it was too soon to go to bed, so she got changed and left the silence of her flat, heading back into the bustle of a London evening. After all the noise of her family she wasn't quite ready for the peace of her apartment. With the sounds of their singing and laughing still carolling around her head, she ran along the lanes and across the parks as she relived the weekend. It had been really good fun. The rows and the vomiting were just the price of a large family, it had always been the case.

Eventually, she tired herself out and made her way back to the apartment. She threw the running kit into the washing machine with her weekend clothes, and placed her trainers by the front door. She showered, followed by a light supper and then laid out fresh running clothes for the following morning. Having set her alarm, she headed off for bed, and lay there. Half an hour later she was still wide awake and thinking about her running kit. Annoyed with herself and her sisters' teasing, she threw back the duvet and grabbed the kit that had been draped over the back of an armchair and shoved it back in the drawer. Satisfied she went back to bed. Half an hour later she got up again and replaced the outfit on the armchair.

Who cared what her sisters said, this worked for her. Finally, with a smile, she fell asleep.

Chapter 3

Nick woke up and looked at the ceiling. It had been two months since she had last seen any of her sisters and she missed them. Paddy and Eleanor seemed to be constantly ill at the moment, Ari was tied up with the family, Aster was abroad somewhere, and Clem was miles away in Scotland. Every time any of them had tried to meet up, one of the others had had to cancel. Nick had been planning to come and see Leo and Will in their school play but then an oil tanker had crashed into a major harbour wall and the world held its breath to see what would happen to the oil price. It definitely wasn't a day to be sitting in a school hall watching a bunch of six-year-olds re-enact the discovery of the North Pole. Stretching, she got up and walked across the polished wood floor and showered. This wasn't how she wanted to spend today and for the first time in a very long time she felt flat.

Heading to the wardrobe she opened the right-hand door and pulled out a hanger at random. This side of the wardrobe was workwear. Furthest to the right were the most formal outfits, clothes for presentations and meetings, the left-hand side had the more casual office wear. Had she opened the left-hand door she'd have revealed her non-work gear: some jeans, the odd polo dress and at the far end a few fancy frocks for special occasions.

Looking back over the past few months Nick wondered if she shouldn't check the outfits for cobwebs.

Of course today she could walk into the office starkers. She could tell everyone it was her birthday suit. Smiling to herself, she pulled on one of her more relaxed work outfits instead. It was going to be a busy day at work and the stock markets didn't care about birthdays. In a defiant gesture she grabbed a red singlet from the casual side of the wardrobe and wore it under her white blouse, which she left unbuttoned.

Grinning to herself, she headed off to work.

-

Pushing back from her desk, Nick poured a glass of water and looked out the window. There were so many people milling around down there. Her offices were in one of the smaller towers in Canary Wharf. Wherever she looked were gleaming buildings of steel and glass, new cathedrals to the new religion. In the distance she could see parks and trees and on the horizon the rolling hills. She didn't have any views of the Thames; those offices were on the other side of the tower block. That would have been far beyond her price bracket. In fact, this set of offices were also beyond her price bracket, but Daisy had said she knew the developers and they owed her a favour.

Nick did feel a little surge of pride whenever she invited clients here and could see they were clearly impressed. Deep in her heart, though, she'd much rather be back in the City. Those who worked in Canary Wharf viewed it as the new focus of the British financial market and it certainly looked good. But anyone who knew anything, believed that the British financial soul resided in a small square mile in the heart of London. Locals knew that London, the huge sprawling capital, was a town; the City itself was the small area around the Bank of England and St Paul's Cathedral. Nick loved it there, she would far rather be a little mouse running along the stone pavements and worn, sooty brickwork than a bird looking out over the wider horizon.

Laughing at her fanciful notions she decided to get back to work. She needed to keep an eye on the bigger picture *and* understand the tiny micro-movements that could destabilise entire economies and she wasn't going to do it with her head against a window.

–

Daisy leant in around the door smiling. 'I'm heading home now unless you need anything?'

Nick looked at her watch in surprise. She had got engrossed in an overseas news story and had lost track of time.

'No, I'm grand. I probably won't be long behind you.'

'Good call. Any plans for this evening or the weekend?'

No one in the office knew it was Nick's birthday; she liked to keep her personal life out of the office. She didn't object to the others bringing in cakes and celebrating but it didn't suit her.

'Catching up with friends this evening, then tomorrow I'm going to see how far I can cycle in a day.'

Daisy groaned as if that sounded awful. 'Rather you than me. Me and the girls are heading into town tonight. Maxine is flying to Berlin tomorrow so we're giving her a proper send-off. Then tomorrow I shall lie on the sofa all day regretting tonight and on Sunday, Jamie and I are going over to his folks', where no doubt I'll have to listen once more about how they used to own half of Kent, how children are such a blessing, and hear news of how successful their daughter is.'

Nick laughed. 'Sounds like fun. Try not to kill her. I couldn't run this office without you. Plus I don't think prison scrubs would suit you.'

–

With Daisy gone Nick started to make notes about next week's focus and set up some alerts in various news outlets. She always liked to keep abreast of world affairs and had a few markers in place that she felt would be good barometers for the feel of the market. Sometimes people did things that felt slightly out of place and Nick liked to examine them until she figured out the underlying cause. Most times it was just down to simple human capriciousness but sometimes it was driven by intent. On those occasions Nick could make a killing anticipating which way the stock market would react, either moving money in or out.

As she pushed back from her desk she stretched and then surprised herself by sighing. Admittedly today hadn't gone as planned but it couldn't be helped. Being an adult was about facing things, being excited or upset was for children. Wasting her time sighing about a miserable birthday was silly. But still she couldn't help but feel sad.

She switched off the computer, pulled her waste bin from underneath her desk and put it to one side for the cleaner. Then she left her office and headed into the team's workspace and started to put out all their bins as well. As a teenager cleaning offices on a nightshift, she remembered with surprise the first time she cleaned an office where someone had done the same kindness for her. That simple act saved her time and also made her feel part of the team – someone 'saw' her. Now every night she did the same thing for her contractors. She could have asked her staff to do this, but it was a little ritual that she liked to do herself.

As she passed Gyeong's desk she saw the bin was already to one side, Gyeong had been doing this since her first week of employment. That simple act, unasked for, had earnt Gyeong a small pay rise. When she questioned Nick about the pay rise, Nick told her what it was for. Nick was amused to watch as the rest of the team asked Gyeong why she put out her waste basket and she explained. Some followed her example for a week or two and then forgot, others didn't bother. Nick noticed that Gyeong didn't mention that she had received a pay bump to anyone. Nick hadn't told her to keep it confidential, but it amused her that she had. Well, everyone had to have an edge. In fact, thinking about it, Gyeong was nearly as private as Nick was. When she had started working for Nick her CV had been alarmingly vague, but Nick needed staff and the woman proved her worth quickly. That said, Nick knew nothing about her history or her social life, and the fact that occasionally she could spot a trend in a new market was almost suspicious. But that was what she was paid for.

As she rode down the lift with the other commuters Nick smiled to herself. All these hundreds of lives, all ebbing and flowing, like little shoals of fish in the mighty Thames. She watched as some women swapped high heels for trainers, but she was already in flats. At five foot ten, she had no need for added height, plus they were uncomfortable and rubbish to run in. She laughed to herself, remembering Clem sprinting after a night bus once in her high heels, throwing chips at it and swearing like a sailor. She hadn't caught the bus and Ari had made her pick up all the chips. Well, Clem may live and die in her high heels, but Nick preferred more sensible footwear.

As she started to walk the short distance home, she dialled Paddy.

'Hey, Nick!' Hal's face greeted her cheerily. She loved her brother-in-law but the fact that he had answered her twin's phone probably meant she was asleep.

'Happy birthday! Let me go get Paddy.'

'Don't wake her if she's asleep.'

'Are you mad? It would be more than my life's worth – you two have been missing each other's calls all day. I know how much she wants to talk to you. Hang on now.'

Nick waved briefly at the concierge as she entered the building and climbed up to the second floor. As she entered her flat she waited as she heard Hal gently whisper to Paddy and her sister's groggy reply.

'Happy birthday, Fartface!'

'Happy birthday, Ugly. Asleep before six? You are old!'

'Hang on, let me go into another room so I don't swear at you in front of Eleanor.'

'Is she asleep as well? Where are you?'

'We're down at Cockleshells. We came down last night so I could wake up here. I went for a swim whilst Hal looked after Elly then we all went out for a sail, followed by a beach picnic on a cove you can only get to by boat, so we had the place all to ourselves. Then we came back here and whilst Hal cooked supper it looks like me and Elly fell asleep.'

'Oh God, that sounds perfect,' sighed Nick wistfully.

'Almost. I just kept missing you. Where are you, is that your new place?'

Nick had been in the flat for almost a year but none of the sisters had visited it. It was a one-bed and whilst Canary Wharf was a great location for work it wasn't great for rendezvous. When they came to London everyone headed to the Kensington property instead.

'Yep, back home now. And yes, sorry I kept missing you. I had loads of meetings today. And then your phone kept going out of signal, although now I understand why.' Nick paused and sighed. 'I've missed you too.'

'Next year let's have a joint party and invite everyone? Have you heard from Aster today?'

'No, I got a card and a text message. I'm not convinced she's in Europe anymore though. I think she might be somewhere in Asia.'

'Aster in Asia. What will the stock markets make of that?'

'No idea but if the news starts reporting insurrections or land wars, at least it will confirm her location.'

Both girls laughed at the idea of their little sister wandering the globe putting things right as she saw fit. As they had both spoken to Ari and Clem they discussed their lives as well and agreed that all seemed to be very well in the family.

'Actually, there was another reason I wanted to talk to you.'

'Beyond telling me I'm the prettier twin?' laughed Nick.

'Yes, silly, you know that already.' Which made Nick laugh again. They weren't identical twins – Paddy had been a catwalk model, a regular on the cover of *Vogue* and *Vanity Fair*, but she still maintained that Nick was prettier. 'No, what I wanted to tell you was why I've been so ill recently.'

'Are you okay?' asked Nick anxiously.

'Yes, of course I'm okay. Don't butt in. I just wanted to share this with you first. I'm pregnant.'

Nick looked at her sister's shining face and felt her heart swell with happiness for her.

'That's brilliant news! Congratulations. You'll have to put Hal back on the phone so that I can threaten him to take good care of you.'

'He doesn't know yet.'

'What? Why?' Nick was instantly alert to a problem. Hal doted on Paddy, and Paddy worshipped the ground he and Eleanor walked on. Why hadn't she told him yet? Unless.

'You know.'

'Twin Thing. I know.' Any big problem or momentous piece of news they always shared with each other first. Even when they were squabbling or not talking to each other, as was often the case growing up. But when something major happened, Twin Thing came into play.

'Well, go and tell him now. And happy birthday. I love you.'

'I love you too. Wait, you haven't told me your plans for the evening. How are you celebrating?'

'Later. Go talk to your husband. I won't be responsible for a single second of delay. Love you.'

Laughing, Paddy hung up first and the flat fell back into silence.

Nick switched on the speakers and put on some Vivaldi. The bright happy tones matched her sister's mood. She wandered into the kitchen and chopped some veg for a quick prawn stir-fry. Next she changed into her running gear and headed back outside. This was a routine that she liked on a Friday night. During the week she often worked late into the evening and could only fit a run in during her lunch hour. On Fridays she would leave around five, head home, prepare her food, then run, come home, shower, eat and relax.

Tonight she ran with Vivaldi and she smiled as she thought of her sisters, and of Aster starting a small land war in Asia. And she was going to be an aunt again. What a fabulous present.

Back in the flat, she showered, then changed into the pjs she had already laid out. The stir fry hissed and spat, and she wondered about having a glass of wine. Mr Fanshawe, the family solicitor, had sent her a bottle of red as a present and whilst Nick didn't know the first thing about wine she knew that it would be a good one. However, if she was cycling tomorrow she wanted a clear head so ran the tap instead and settled down to an evening playing cards online with a bunch of strangers.

As birthdays went, this one was pants.

Chapter 4

Across town and back in the heart of the City, two men were plotting. Paul and Adam Harrington were enjoying a whisky in their private club on Pall Mall. The air was thick with cigar smoke – although now illegal indoors, the club kept its conservatory doors open and used that to define this section as an outdoor area. All staff had to sign non-disclosure agreements for all aspects of their work here. They had zero protection. Discretion was the prized jewel and members still behaved like it was the fifties. Of which century was uncertain. The brothers loved it.

After a filling lunch they were now drowsy with contentment. Adam had had the foie gras, naturally – he wasn't as keen on the taste as he was in knowing that he was keeping alive the demand for the product. Too much of society just caved in at the first mention of apparent cruelty and he was proud to push back. He was frightened of horses so didn't ride but supported an Englishman's right to hunt. He didn't even care about the arguments put forward for pest control; quite frankly, if a man wanted to hunt for the sheer sport of it then why not. It was important to maintain the status quo when it ran in line with his world view.

Paul was his younger brother and not as clever. Approaching his fortieth birthday he was disappointed with how his life was panning out. He had expected to retire by now but with the collapse of the family bank the year before all long-term ventures had had to be postponed as the business scrambled to recover from the blow. Along with their middle sister the brothers were now in charge of the day-to-day running of the Harrington companies. Without the easy money from the bank all three had had to work harder.

Paul had always boasted that a company like Harrington's pretty much ran itself. He was just there to put forward a good face. Success breeds success and he felt it was essential that his contemporaries saw the holidays he took, the events he frequented and the charities he donated to as part of that affirmation of his company's success. The fact was the taxpayer often footed the bill for the holidays written off as business expenses, the charitable donations were only ever announced rather than delivered, and the events were usually coerced invitations. Everyone knew that having a Harrington at an occasion was a sign of investors climbing on board. In the past year though those invitations had dwindled.

'Christ,' muttered Adam. 'It's Jack Heacham.' The brothers smiled as Jack approached but failed to stand up.

'Adam, Paul! Long time no see. We missed you at the gala last week!' Jack's soft Texan drawl had a way of making it to every corner of the room. A certain stillness developed as conversations paused to overhear the exchange. The family's disgrace had caused fury and glee in equal measures across the City.

'No time for play at the moment, Jack,' said Adam. 'Too busy looking at new markets.'

'Well, some of us have to work, I suppose,' laughed Jack good-naturedly, fooling no one.

'We'll see you at the Open next week, though. Surely you can spare the time for a round of golf?'

Harrington's had sponsored the golf Open for the past twenty-four years and there had been big plans to celebrate their twenty-five-year partnership with the prestigious event. The golfing federation, however, had terminated their sponsorship. It had been hugely embarrassing to the brothers, but their father had pointed out that they didn't have the bloody money anyway.

'Do you honestly think we'd show our faces there?' said Paul, quick to anger.

'Of course. How forgetful of me. It would be embarrassing,' said Jack sympathetically.

'That's not what I meant at all,' spluttered Paul. 'The way they turned their backs on us was bang out of order.'

'Oh yes, of course,' said Jack apologetically. And having achieved his goal of needling Paul into an outburst he returned to the rest of his group as they moved through to lunch.

'Why do you always rise to the bait?' asked Adam. 'You make us look foolish. It you can't say something smart, shut the fuck up.'

Paul shrugged. He was used to his brother's attitude. As the eldest, Adam always led the way.

'So then. Everything's in place?' he asked. Ash from his cigar fell onto the carpet. He tapped it again to make sure nothing landed on his shirt then took another puff.

'Yes. Within the next week things should start to roll out. It's been a long time setting this up, but my God I'm looking forward to watching her fall.'

The Bank of Harrington's had collapsed due to financial irregularities. The bank had borrowed too much money and had over-extended its credit past the point of being able to repay its debts. The family blamed its traders, they blamed the market for not supporting it, they blamed the regulators that prosecuted it and closed it down, but most of all they blamed the two people who first noticed the bank's precarious position. George Flint-Hyssop, and Nick Byrne. George was widely tipped to one day be the governor of the Bank of England so they couldn't go after him. Nick Byrne, however, was a young woman, wet behind the ears with minimal connections and resources. She might have had a title, but she didn't know how to use it and she hadn't yet cultivated decades of goodwill or blackmail to protect her. It was her that they were going after. The fact that she and George had saved the City from an even greater disaster had Harrington's continued to trade unnoticed was neither here nor there. Adam and Paul had been embarrassed and inconvenienced and someone was going to pay.

'And that will be the end of Nick Byrne and De Foix Investments?' said Paul.

'With what we've pinned on her, she won't stand a chance.'

Chapter 5

Nick opened her blinds and looked at the wind and rain tipping it down. So much for accurate weather forecasting. Nick could tell which way entire countries would react to world events, but whether it would rain the following day seemed to elude the good folks in the Met Office. All her cycling gear was already laid out but now her heart wasn't in it. The weather was atrocious.

She made her bed then showered. As she stepped out she looked at her hair gel and realised she probably needed to bin it. Now that she was growing her hair long, she no longer used so much product. Instead, she grabbed a hairband to pull it back off her face and popped in her contacts.

One of the things that bugged her about her new apartment was the lack of radiators – there was nowhere to hang her towels and wet clothes. Instead, she draped it over a hook and wondered for the umpteenth time what was so special about underfloor heating. It seemed extravagant and impractical. She appreciated the efficiency of design, and the fact that her flat walls were unimpeded by lumpy bits of metal. But nothing beat a radiator for hanging wet socks on, or for snuggling up against with a book in hand and a mug of hot chocolate.

In the kitchen she looked at her soaked oats and the banana ready to be sliced into the porridge for breakfast and then saw the bottle of red wine. To hell with it, her twenty-eighth year was going to be different. She was going to shake things up. She poured herself a glass and put some bacon under the grill. Two glasses of wine later and one bacon butty, her body decided that it didn't like things to be shaken up and she found herself back in the bathroom vomiting.

Back in the kitchen she poured the rest of the bottle down the sink. She might live alone but that was no call to act like a stereotypical single white female with a drink problem. Hell, she may as well install the cat now. Nick took some aspirin, a pint of water and changed into her cycling clothes.

As she opened the main door she wondered about the wisdom of this idea. She looked at the rain, and then thought back to the flat with the blond furniture and the empty walls. Swinging her leg up over the saddle, she set off heading east. Her initial plan had been to make it to Orford Ness. She and Paddy had been there once on a school trip and it had rained then as well. There wasn't a chance of making it that far today though, with the wind and the late start, but she'd still be able to get out of the city and stretch her body and her mind. Nick had only got into cycling in the past few years, but she loved the speed that she could achieve just through using her own body. It reminded her of when she used to run downhill. That same giddy sense of being only a step away from flying.

The roads were quieter than normal, it being a Saturday and the weather being so foul, but she smiled and nodded at the other cyclists and joggers that were out making the most of their day. One of the gutters ahead had become blocked and a large puddle spread out across the road. Checking behind that there were no cars she pulled out into the middle of the road to avoid it. Out of nowhere a car swerved alongside her, its strident horn sounding over the wind. She didn't know if the car clipped her wheel but in that instant she lost control of the bike and felt herself falling at speed towards the ground. She rolled once, the rough tarmac surface tearing at her face and body, and for a second felt too shaken to move. In the distance she could see the lights of the car speed away around the corner and she realised she was sitting in the puddle, her bike further ahead in the middle of the road.

'Are you okay?'

Nick looked up at a cyclist who had crouched down beside her. His friend had run out into the road and recovered her bike and soon she was surrounded by a group of five cyclists, all checking her and her bike over.

'We saw the whole thing. That moron came screaming out of a side street. Honestly, you wouldn't have seen him coming when you pulled out.'

'I've got the whole thing on camera,' said an older man.

Nick smiled weakly, she had a helmet cam as well, but given that she had been clipped from behind the chances were that the footage would only show her rapidly approaching the tarmac and then cloudy skies above. Suddenly the idea of her head lying on one of London's highways filled her stomach and she threw up.

'That's just the fear. I threw up as well when I got hit,' said a younger man. 'Come on, let's get you off the road.' Two of the cyclists had been directing traffic around her but now they all moved to the safety of the pavement.

'I've never come off my bike before. Oh God, is my bike okay?' Nick and the others looked over to where two of the cyclists were fiddling with it.

One of the girls smiled at her. 'The frame looks good, but the car drove over the wheel, so that's buggered. How far from home are you?'

Nick looked around. She was about two miles away, but she wasn't going to tell them that. She knew if she did they would try to help her get back and right now she just wanted to be on her own. Her elbow was killing her although she didn't think it was broken, the same was true for her hip and knee.

'About half a mile. I'll walk home and run a bath.'

'Would you like me to walk back with you?' asked one of the men. He had an eager smile and he'd spent the last five minutes asking if he could help. 'It won't be a bother.'

The third time he asked, one of the girls caught Nick's small frown and slapped him on the leg.

'Leave the poor girl alone. Hasn't she suffered enough?'

Nick smiled at her gratefully, then the girl gave Nick her number. 'I'm Max. We cycle out every Saturday. Join us if you want. More the merrier. I'll forward you the footage of the crash as well so you can report the driver.'

As she waved goodbye, she watched as they grouped up and continued their ride out of London, all rear lights blinking red, reflective strips on the spokes of the wheels and bright neon lycra suits. They looked like a shoal of fish, flashing through the dark waters of a stormy sea.

Leaning on her bike she began to limp home. She wondered if she should have been friendlier to the guy that kept offering to walk her back. Was this why her dates always fizzled out, because she was too stand-offish? As she slowly walked along the pavement, she considered it but no – she had seen the initial look of surprise as she'd stood and looked him in the eyes. She'd been on too many dates were men professed to not care about her height, as though it was an actual issue, but then by the second week were complaining that she was too masculine. Or too focussed on work. It was incredible. If the man was late for a date it was because something important had cropped up at work. The implication being that they were special and vital, that work couldn't manage without them. If Nick did the same thing the same man would feel slighted that he wasn't the most important thing in her life. The double standard always floored her. She was getting to the point where she despaired of ever meeting anyone worth the effort. Who knew a tall, good-looking, financially successful woman could be so off-putting? She wanted to curse her height, all through school she had been a beanpole, much like Paddy, but Paddy had never been short of dates or friends. It was lazy to blame outward appearances for her current situation, it was simply a personality thing. Nick had cultivated this quiet, private persona and now she had somehow become shut in by it.

After two pairs of cyclists stopped to ask if she was all right, she began to feel, if not better, at least a small outreach part of a community that had her back. She had never been one for team sports, but this sense of camaraderie helped distract her from the pain in her body. Nothing, however, could help her feelings of stupidity and embarrassment. Was she over the limit? Had her morning wine contributed to the accident? Nick stopped in a moment of horrible self-realisation. She *was* a sad, lonely, stereotype. A single female, drunk on a Saturday morning with nothing in her life beyond her work. There wasn't even anyone she could phone up to come over and commiserate with.

Eventually, she made it back to her apartment. She had made a small detour to her local bike shop and handed it over for repairs. Declining an offer of cake and coffee she continued to limp home. She thanked her lucky stars that the concierge was occupied, and opted for the lift rather than the stairs – she didn't think she could recount the story a fourth time. Once in her flat she stripped out of her clothes, slowly and painfully. Naked, she walked to the bathroom, if her neighbours in the block opposite caught a glimpse of her right now she couldn't give a damn. In the mirror she sucked her teeth as she looked at the grazes and the bruises already beginning to show.

After her bath she put on her dressing gown, sod getting dressed. This weekend was already over as far as she was concerned. Making a cup of hot chocolate, she put some macaroni cheese in the microwave and hit play on *The Princess Bride*, a family favourite. Right now she would trade everything she had achieved to have someone by her side doing everything for her, helping her with the plasters as she sat on the sofa and nursed her bruises.

So far, being twenty-seven was not that impressive.

Chapter 6

A week later Nick was typing away at work. Her staff had all been really sweet about her injuries and she had been touched to find flowers and chocolates on her desk on Tuesday. As suspected, nothing beyond her bike was broken, and whilst her bruising was spectacular, she had stopped limping and had even started running again by Wednesday. Max had been as good as her word and had sent Nick footage of the accident. It made for grim watching but Nick was tempted to join them on their next ride out. Maybe she would try to be friendlier to that guy. She could have misjudged him.

Her phone buzzed and she saw that it was Cressida from *Financial Focus*. After the last article, Nick had suggested that the magazine write a feature about companies that also had charitable endeavours. She wanted the whole business community to see the benefits to themselves as well as the recipients if they engaged more in outreach programmes. It was a longshot but worth a try.

Nick wasn't one for small talk and liked to get things done quickly so that she could move on. Efficiency in all things was the way to get ahead. Tapping the loudspeaker on the phone she placed the phone on the desk and carried on typing.

'Morning, Cressida. Is this about the article?'

'Sort of. Can you take me off loudspeaker?'

Nick stopped typing and looked at her phone in surprise and picked up the handset.

'All right. I'm all ears, what's up?'

'I've heard a bit of a rumour.'

Nick's ears pricked up. Cressida didn't tend to share gossip or rumours – if she was now, this had to be something major.

'It's about De Foix Investments. The FCA is preparing for an investigation.'

Nick had always considered the term *blood running cold*, a silly piece of poetic licence but how else to describe the sense of utter dread that now grabbed her? An investigation by the Financial Conduct Authority could mean the kiss of death to a business. Sure, they were supposed to be confidential before they gave their judgement, but in the City? Not a hope. By the start of a lunch hour, a nudge could have become a rumour, and by the end of the day all of Canary Wharf would treat it as gospel.

The FCA policed the financial world and were at the heart of every recent trading scandal. They had the power to temporarily suspend trading privileges, revoke trading licences, and prepare cases for criminal prosecutions resulting in fines and prison terms.

'Nick, are you still there?'

'Sorry yes. I. Sorry, that caught me off guard. I wonder where the hell that rumour came from?'

'Ugh. You know. Everyone likes a good gossip, especially against someone who's doing well. Obviously, there's nothing in it. It's not like they actually start investigations without evidence.'

Cressida's simple words started to calm Nick down. Her entire career had been squeaky clean, it wasn't in her nature to play fast and loose with interpretations of the law. As far as she was concerned if you needed to bend or break the law then you weren't up to the mark.

'No, that's true. Still, it's enough to make you feel queasy. Thanks for the heads-up...'

Nick's voice trailed off as she watched two strangers walk towards the reception desk at the front of the office. The two men were both in their fifties and looked like they could do with a few more meals, a good tailor and some basic love in their lives. If she couldn't already tell who they were, the reaction of Jimmy on the reception desk said it all. He almost recoiled as they introduced themselves, then looked over to her office with a worried expression. Nick recovered quickly – she couldn't let Cressida know that there was truth to the rumour. She might be a friend, but she was also the editor of the most popular financial magazine in the City.

'Anyway, I'd better get back to work. Thanks again. Bye.'

Certainly, it was more abrupt than she wished but she needed to get out to reception as fast as possible. Opening her door she walked out to the middle of the office space where the two men had stopped. They were about to speak to the workforce and Nick hurried to cut them off.

'Gentlemen, welcome. Would you like to come through to my office? Tea, coffee?'

She smiled as much for their benefit as for the staff – even the hint of an investigation was likely to spook the horses. Nick knew she was innocent of any malfeasance. A quick chat should clear things up and scotch any further rumours.

'Nick Byrne?'

Nick smiled and nodded, she didn't like his tone and wondered how bad this was about to get.

'My name is Paul Clements, and this is my colleague Benjamin Gervase.'

Benjamin smiled and she revised her opinion about him not having enough love in his life. The way his eyes gleamed right now told her that he was doing what he loved the most. Watching people sweat. That said, he remained silent as his colleague continued.

'We are from the FCA. Following a recent discovery we are investigating De Foix Investments for irregular practices.'

There was a sudden hubbub of noise as the staff broke out into shouts of protest. Nick smiled weakly; so much for trying to keep things low key. Still, it was nice to have the support of her workforce.

'I have worked for Nick for over a year and if you find so much as a trace of irregularity you can feed me to the hippos.'

Normally, Gyeong's overly dramatic statements made Nick laugh but right now she was struggling to keep it together. She knew they would find no evidence of wrongdoing but even their arrival could create damage. As she quickly glanced around the room she wondered which of her staff would resign in the next few months. In a set-up as small as hers, scandal had a habit of smearing everyone's reputations, she wouldn't blame anyone for wanting to steer clear of that. Clearing her throat, she returned her attention to Mr Clements.

'Surely you don't investigate every rumour that snakes around the City? Why have you chosen to visit me?'

'As you say, we don't investigate rumour we investigate solid tip-offs.'

For a second Nick was genuinely baffled. She had done nothing wrong so how could there be a tip-off strong enough for the FCA to investigate? In the silence Mr Clements continued to talk as Mr Gervase continued to smile.

'All staff must stop working as of now. We will be running a full digital and paper investigation of all transactions for the past twelve months. I have here the details of the scope of our investigations. Should we find evidence of the allegations we will then proceed to court.'

For a nanosecond Nick felt weak, everything that she had built up in the past ten years was being attacked. The suggestion of impropriety made her feel ill but the idea that these two men and their team would now be rifling through her accounts and transactions made her feel violated. She took a deep breath; she had never once run from a fight.

'Ayesha and Milo work on the charitable side of the business, they aren't involved in any deals. Presumably, they can carry on working?'

Finally, Mr Gervase spoke. 'No, we are investigating every aspect of the business. If we find dirt in one corner who knows what else it will have infected?'

Nick wished he'd kept his mouth shut. Clearly he wasn't here to play nice.

'How long will this take?'

'A few weeks, a few months. It depends on what we find.'

'Nothing. You will find nothing.' Nick was beginning to lose her rag. 'Look, this is ridiculous. What are my staff supposed to do? What am I supposed to tell my clients?'

'That is not our concern. We are here simply to ensure that justice is done,' replied Mr Clements.

'And what about justice for me? This could ruin my business.'

'Then just tell your clients you have decided to take a holiday.'

Mr Clements tilted his head and turned to his colleague. 'She could say she was unwell and taking a leave of absence?' The two men grinned at each other, then turned back to Nick, both with the same vulpine expression. She looked at them in disbelief.

'Holiday? Illness? I may as well tell them all I'm being investigated by the FCA.'

'Yes. We usually find the truth can be difficult for people being investigated of fraud.'

Nick ground her teeth and shoved her hands in her pockets. That stapler was within chucking distance and she was currently entertaining a pleasant vision of stapling his tie to his forehead.

'This is nothing to smile about,' admonished Mr Gervase.

–

The next few hours were indeed nothing to smile about. Nick had promised the staff full pay during the length of the investigation on the condition that no one spoke about it. They were going to run with the nonsense that Nick had taken a leave of absence due to family matters. It stank but it was better than nothing. Nick had negotiated that for the next few days the staff could tie up loose ends or delay projects so long as no financial transactions took place. She herself would pursue the outstanding issues so long as no money changed hands.

The next step was to call her clients and let them know that she was taking a short rest. She recommended a small company that she trusted and had already explained her predicament to them. Some of her clients decided to move to the small company, others preferred to wait until Nick returned. Every phone call made her feel weaker and weaker. Finally, in dread, she called her main client.

'Ari, I'm in trouble.'

As Nick poured out the whole sorry mess Ari listened, only jumping in when she didn't fully understand something.

'And they have the power to do this? Just pull the rug straight out from under you?'

'Yes. And it makes sense. If someone is embezzling their clients then you need to stop them instantly, before they can steal any more or destroy any evidence.'

'But you haven't done anything wrong!'

'But everyone says that. Too much trust in the financial institutions is what caused the last banking crisis. Nowadays they pounce at the first sniff of two twigs being rubbed together.'

'But what smoke is there? What evidence have they seen? For God's sake, it was you that warned the City of Harrington's problems.'

'You know what we say in the industry. Past performance is not a predictor of future gain. Looks like I'm being treated as a perfect example of that maxim. Anyway, we have a few decisions to make. I can't touch the Hiverton funds. I have been recommending my smaller clients move temporarily to Long Acre Investments or wait until I return. But Hiverton is too large an account for Long Acre to handle. I recommend simply pausing everything, although we might take a financial hit if the market does something and I can't move money around.'

'That's not important right now. You are.'

Nick kissed her teeth. How like Ari to say that money wasn't important. Nick knew she meant well but money was the lifeblood of the estate, without it everything would fall apart. She hated suggesting that the account lie dormant but what else could she do?

'Have you called George?' asked Ari.

'Are you mad?'

'Why not? Don't you trust him?'

'Of course I trust him. It's not that.'

'What is it then?'

Nick paused and looked at the ceiling. In the silence Ari carried on. 'Don't tell me it's because you're embarrassed.'

For the first time all day Nick lost her temper.

'Embarrassed? Are you insane? Of course I'm not embarrassed. I'm *mortified*. I have somehow failed to protect my business, my staff and my clients. I have revealed myself to be open to attack. Embarrassment is for when you break wind in a lift. I've just defecated all over the floor!'

'There's no need to be vulgar.'

'Vulgar!' Nick shouted down the phone. What the hell was Ari doing chiding her for impropriety? Her world was falling apart, and Ari had decided to get prudish. 'Look, I've got too much to do. I'll call you later when I think of a suggestion.'

Hanging up she headed into the kitchen and made a cup of tea. Her hands were shaking, and she was aware that even she may have drunk too much coffee today.

Taking a few deep breaths she began to wash and dry the cups on the sideboard and wiped down the surfaces. She emptied the contents of the fridge into the bin and switched it off. In the silence she leant her head against the window, the cool glass helping her focus as she watched the lights from the other office blocks and cars below – London was so pretty in the dark. She wasn't sure how long she had watched the lights moving but her phone startled her and as she pulled back from the window she could see a red patch on her forehead reflected back at her.

'Hello?'

'Nicoletta? It's George Flint-Hyssop.'

Nick pursed her lips. When she next saw Ari she was going to kill her.

'Ari has explained everything, or as such as she understood. Tell me what's happened.'

George listened in silence as Nick went through the whole debacle.

'Okay. This is bad. They don't act this decisively unless they are confident of success. That said they have been known to overreact. When we were investigated—'

Nick cut him off. The thought that George had gone through this was astonishing. 'You were investigated?'

'Oh yes, welcome to the club. The trick now is damage limitation. All the big players have been investigated at some time or another. You're smaller than their normal targets for an investigation of this size, which is a worry, but we can sort this out.'

Nick realised how much she liked the word 'we'. George continued.

'With your permission, I'll take over the Hiverton account until you are able to take charge of it. Who's handling your smaller accounts?'

George muttered approvingly as Nick mentioned the small firm.

'Good choice. If you want I can liaise with Simon at Long Acre in the morning, offer help if he's uncertain with the direction you were going with any of the accounts.'

Nick let out a huge sigh of relief, her clients were so important to her. They trusted her with their hard-earnt money and she had been fretting that her change in circumstances would impact on their financial health. She had every faith in Simon and Long Acre, they were sure and steady, but they didn't have the flair or acumen that she or George had. Growth might be down until she was back in charge, but with George's subtle guidance, no one should lose any money.

'Now,' he continued, 'which lawyers have you instructed?'

'I don't need a lawyer. I'm innocent.'

'You might be innocent, but you are also stupid if you think you can get through this without legal representation. I'll get someone to call you in a minute. Right, I think that's it for now. You probably have a thousand questions or will have over the next few days. Call me each and every time. The City needs more people like you. Now go home and find something else to do. The next few weeks will drive you insane if you don't have a project. I learnt Latin ballroom dancing.'

As he hung up Nick chuckled. The very idea of George in lycra was ridiculous. The man was always impeccably dressed in a pinstripe suit with a pocket fob watch and umbrella, all he was missing was the top hat. The idea of him in sequins made Nick snort in the silence of the kitchen and with a small sigh she turned out the lights and headed home.

Chapter 7

Slamming her apartment door behind her Nick leant against the wall and slid down until her feet were splayed out in front of her. She had done as much as she could preparing the clients and the charity – on Monday she would close down the office for a month but now it was the weekend, and her time was her own. She looked at her newly repaired bike – maybe tomorrow she would go out for a ride. In the past week she hadn't been for a single run and her body was crying out for some exercise.

All day and all night this week she had pored over her business's paperwork trying to find an irregularity. So far she had gone back nine months and found nothing untoward, she only had another three or so months to go. Although Nick had been trading for years she knew that she herself had never made a single transaction that could be misconstrued. It was only following the expansion of her business that she took on other traders to work for her. The irregularity had to be in there somewhere, although not for one minute did Nick think it would have been a deliberate act. Still, if she couldn't find it she couldn't fight her corner. It was this flailing around in the dark that was killing her.

She tried a few games of online bridge but ended up apologising to her usual partners as she made error after error, and eventually she stopped playing altogether. The more she thought about it the more she decided a bike ride was a good idea. Get out of the city, exhaust the body, try and get a decent night's sleep.

Pulling herself upright she started to wander around the flat, laying out her cycle gear for the morning and preparing a small backpack for the journey. She threw in a handful of energy bars, a repair kit and a spare battery for her phone. She liked to cycle as light as possible, but the portable battery was essential. The idea of being without a phone was an anathema to her. Clem and Paddy both lived in parts of the country where they were regularly out of signal. Nick wondered how they could bear it, to be out of touch with the rest of the world.

Opening her laptop she began to scour the news columns until she had a list of interesting trends and ideas to keep an eye on. She then sent it across to George and Simon – she had to be incredibly careful that she wasn't instructing anyone to do anything, just drawing their attention to certain aspects. Whether or not they acted on her information was entirely up to them. To be certain that she couldn't be accused of leading anyone she kept the information vague. For example, she highlighted a weather report that suggested an early monsoon in a particular Asian region. If that monsoon turned out to be as severe as predicted then the grain crop would be damaged causing an issue on the futures market for animal feed. That was the easy play, though – there would be other knock-on effects, and this was where Nick usually dabbled, guessing what those knock-on aspects would be. There were the micro reactions. Was there another crop that the farmers would turn to? Would there be a demand in labour to harvest the crop early, would that move in labour cause a shortfall elsewhere?

And then there were the macro reactions, if that futures market were knocked off course, which stock funds would have their pension portfolios affected? Which countries were gambling on that money becoming available and without it how would they pivot?

Each and every action had a reaction, the trick was determining what that would be. All Nick could do was send the two men a message linking to a weather report.

Of course it might come to nothing, 95 per cent of the time, the status quo would prevail, and sometimes the biggest impacts would come out of the blue. But a smart girl played the margins and always stayed ahead of the crowd. Even if she couldn't trade.

No doubt George had already spotted the same stuff that she had done, but he was doing her a favour by carrying the Hiverton portfolio and she wanted to show him that she hadn't given up.

She couldn't give up. How could she? If she couldn't do this, what could she do?

Yawning, she saw it was long past midnight and decided to turn in. There was nothing else she could do today except sleep.

Chapter 8

Four hours later Nick was on the road, cycling out of the city. The sun had just risen, and the streets were empty. The weather forecast had suggested perfect cycling conditions and as Nick had woken up from a fitful sleep she decided not to waste any time and had headed off. It felt liberating, just her and her bike tearing up the tarmac. Mile after mile her body eased back into the old familiar exercise. As her limbs stretched out Nick began to stop thinking about her business and global economies, instead she simply watched the traffic and the countryside. A few hours later she stopped to discover that she had pretty much zoned everything out and had got into the fugue state she loved on long-distance rides. It was only when she saw the signpost for Cambridge that she realised how far she had come.

It was lunch time and she had already travelled eighty miles. She could either turn round now and head back to the empty flat, with the hired furnishing and the silence, or she could ride on to Norfolk and Ari. Smiling ruefully she realised that whatever else happened she was going to have to find somewhere else to live; the apartment didn't feel like home, it hadn't when she had moved in and she hadn't managed to do anything to make it feel welcoming. It was just an impressive shell which she rattled around inside.

Swinging her leg up over her bike she headed towards Hiverton. The roads were wonderfully flat, and Nick knew she was making great time, but she was a little concerned that her saddle was becoming sore, and she was worried about developing a blister. She checked her phone and saw she had another thirty miles to go so decided to see if she could have a lift. Wanting to surprise Ari, she rang Seb and explained where she was.

'You loon. You've honestly cycled all that way?'

'It's only just over a hundred miles. And I did set off at five this morning.'

'Only a hundred miles, she says. You're a machine! Stay where you are. I'll be with you shortly. Ari is going to be so excited.'

Hanging up, Nick smiled to herself. 'Loon' – that's what families were for. Who else got to call Nick Byrne a loon?

She rode another two miles to the pub that they had agreed to meet at and ordered an orange juice and lemonade. She had to admit her legs were quite wobbly, adrenaline only got you so far. She'd have to catch the train home.

Families were enjoying the midday sunshine and children were running around the beer garden as their parents warned them to stay away from the river's bank. Others were paddling in the gentle flow of water, giggling and splashing each other. Nick stretched her limbs and sat gently on the bench. She closed her eyes and let the warmth of the sunshine dapple across her eyelids as the happy sounds drifted around her.

Chapter 9

'Hello, sleepy.'

Nick opened her eyes against the warm sun and blinked up at her brother-in-law.

'Hello, Seb. Fancy meeting you here.'

After a quick hug Seb placed Nick's bike in the back of the car and they headed home to Hiverton.

'Ari and the boys might not be back but they won't be long,' said Seb as they pulled out of the pub car park. 'They're over at my folks' playing in the swimming pool.'

'I didn't know your folks had a pool,' said Nick with a small hint of envy. How fabulous to have access to a free pool.

'They built it as an unashamed grandchildren lure. They also spotted faster than we did that the boys might be scared of water and drowning, following the river incident. So they had it built the second Ari said *I do*.'

'And has it worked?' Nick often thought about that dreadful day and wondered if it had left any scars. Children were so strange; the oddest things could echo through their adult life. For some, nearly drowning might have created a life-long phobia, in another they might barely remember it.

'Like a dream. Even Hector loves it. He's so chubby he floats more than swims, but I reckon in a few months' time he'll be giving his big brothers a run for their money.'

'I can imagine. If he's anything like us lot it will be his all-consuming passion to catch up with his siblings.'

'Well, it won't be long now before someone is trying to catch up with him.'

Nick turned in her seat and looked at Seb in astonishment.

'What? Is Ari pregnant again?'

Seb's face fell in horror as he tried to keep his eyes on the road.

'Oh God, I'm a bigmouth. I forgot she decided to delay announcing until things were more settled for you. Hellfire, can you act surprised when she tells you?'

'Wally. That's brilliant.' Nick suddenly remembered Paddy's news. 'I wonder whose will turn up first, Paddy's or Ari's?'

'Paddy's pregnant?' said Seb in surprise and Nick groaned dramatically.

'Oh God, she hasn't announced it yet either. We're bloody idiots, the pair of us. You can't tell Ari!'

'What do you mean I can't tell Ari! Have you *ever* tried to keep a secret from your sister?'

Laughing, the two of them drove on and Nick sent Paddy a quick text saying she had let the cat out of the bag and that Seb knew but not Ari. Five minutes later a text pinged back saying Paddy had just told Ari and guess what? Ari was pregnant as well! And what are you doing talking to Seb, is he in London?

After a quick phone call, where Paddy called Nick an idiot for cycling so far, she told her she loved her and invited her to spend a few weeks in Cornwall with her.

As she hung up, Seb looked at her speculatively.

'How are you holding up? A few weeks with one of your sisters might be a good idea?'

'Not really. I love all my sisters but after a few days they drive me mad, and I want to escape. Plus…' she sighed and trailed off, looking out the window.

They drove on in silence for a bit and Nick appreciated that Seb didn't pry. He was a good reader of people and happy to sit back and watch rather than push an issue. She tried to collect her thoughts.

Eventually, she continued, 'I'm embarrassed that I let them all down. My job is to take care of the finances. A thing I enjoy doing and find easy, and yet suddenly I have screwed up monumentally and I have no idea how. And if I can't fix it I run the risk of tarnishing the family's reputation. Even Clem managed to avoid doing that.'

'So, you'll stay with your sisters when you don't need them?' asked Seb carefully.

'Harsh.'

'I just think you're beating yourself up. You know none of them feels you've done anything wrong or let them down. They've all been desperate to swoop down to London and form a protective ring around you. Ari's phone has been ringing constantly from the other two. Aster is currently out of touch.'

Nick looked out at the passing countryside determined not to cry. She was supposed to be the calm, efficient one. The one that didn't need saving, the one with the solutions. Currently she was at risk of utterly ruining the entire Hiverton reputation.

'The thing is, if they find me guilty and prevent me from trading, what do I do? Who am I?'

'You're not just your job, Nick.'

'I don't think you get it. I love my job. I'm really good at it but it's more than that it makes me happy. It's my hobby and my favourite pastime too. I've been doing this since I was sixteen. I don't know what I am without it. I built this business from the ground up. I have helped so many people. I—'

'And none of that changes if you can't trade anymore.'

Nick looked at him in horror, he had totally missed how important this was.

'What do you mean? Everything changes.'

'Only externally. You'll still be a fiercely clever businesswoman. You'll still be someone that cares deeply. You aren't your job.'

She tried to collect herself. He didn't understand, for her there was no difference between internal and external. She *was* her job. Deciding that this conversation wasn't helping she changed the subject. Seb was a good sort, but he had other things in his life.

'So, what names for the new baby – is it a boy or a girl?'

Taking his lead from Nick, Seb spent the rest of the drive home filling her in on the children's adventures. From the way he talked about the three boys it was clear to Nick that he loved his two stepsons as much as his own child and Nick couldn't help but love him a bit more for that as well.

'Hello! How about that for timing?' As the car pulled off the main road and into the Hiverton drive they could see a Volvo estate heading towards the house. Once again Nick drank in the beauty of Hiverton Manor, an historic Tudor building spanning the centuries. Its warm red-brick walls, flint facades and multiple chimneys offered the assurance of strength and continuity.

As Seb pulled up behind Ari, she had already got out of the car and was unloading the children and their bags.

Hopping out of the car, Nick watched as he jogged over to Ari, giving her a quick kiss and opening the boot.

Almost shyly Nick got out of the car; she felt reluctant to intrude upon such a happy little scene of domestic life.

'Nick-knack!' Any hope of quietly approaching her sister was dashed as Will spotted her first, followed by Leo who in his rush to get to her first bowled over little Hector, who promptly burst into tears.

'Letta!' Ari shouted out their mother's pet name for Nick and came running over to hug her as Seb scooped up Hector.

Hugging Ari back she laughed, 'You haven't called me Letta in ages. What's up?'

'I don't know. I guess Mum's been on my mind a lot recently.'

'Is it because you're wondering how she coped with so many children?'

Ari looked at Nick suspiciously and then at Seb.

'You beast! It was meant to be a surprise!'

Laughing, Seb confessed.

'Do you know when I was speaking to Paddy just now she told me you had told Seb she was pregnant, and I wondered when the hell you had met him. Now it all becomes clear.'

'What's clear is that none of us can keep a secret for toffee,' said Nick with a smile.

In a caravan of bags and boys the three adults headed into the house, where the dogs came running out. Eventually Seb told the sisters to leg it and he would settle everyone down.

'Come on then,' said Ari. 'How long are you staying? Where are your bags?'

When Nick explained she had started cycling on a whim and had to be back in London for Monday, Ari rolled her eyes and told her to commute.

'No, I want to be nearby in case I get called in for anything. Besides which I'd go mad up here with nothing to do except look at trees.'

The girls settled down on one of the patios overlooking a walled flower garden.

'There is more to the countryside than looking at trees, you know. Plus the children would love it and so would I.'

Nick looked across at her big sister and raised an eyebrow.

'The children would be bored of me after five minutes and you'd keep trying to fix my problems and get upset when none of your ideas worked.'

'I promise not to interfere.' Ari crossed her heart, but Nick just laughed.

'Like that's going to happen. This is a battle you can't fight. Hell. It's even a battle that I don't know how to fight, and I'm supposed to be the smart one when it comes to corporate finance.'

Seeing that Ari was concentrating Nick knew her sister was still wrestling with the problem, trying to find a solution.

'Look, Ari, so far you have been brilliant. You have agreed to let George take over the finances, which has put my mind greatly at rest. You have agreed that the charitable section should continue, and that Paddy will keep an eye on that. This has also reassured me tremendously. All I can hope now is that the investigation draws a blank and I can return to work. In the meantime, I will continue to look through my old records to see if

I can see what caused alarm bells. After that I will just twiddle my fingers, going gently mad. In the meantime, I'm bloody famished and you haven't even offered me a drink!'

Chapter 10

In the morning over breakfast, Nick watched in poorly disguised horror as her nephews tried with varying levels of success to eat their breakfast without making a mess. The twins would laugh uproariously every time Hector threw his toasted soldiers on the floor and the dogs would bound up ready to grab any morsels.

Everyone seemed happy, but dear God, the mess, and the noise. Why couldn't they just enjoy their food in silence? And another baby was on the way; Nick loved her nephews, but she wondered if she could postpone visits for a few years. When precisely did children start to get clean and quiet?

A cat jumped up on the table causing Hector to reach out for it, his egg-coated hands knocking Nick's orange juice into her porridge.

'Oh dear,' sighed Ari, 'it's not usually this bad. I think they are just a bit over-excited. Seb, I told you it's not a good idea to have the animals in the kitchen when we're eating.'

'When you're right, you're right,' agreed Seb getting up and shooing the dogs and cats outdoors.

Ari watched him indulgently as he got rid of the animals and then came back in.

'Sorry about that, Nick. I thought it might be nice to have everyone together. Rose-coloured specs, I'm afraid.'

He leant forward and wiped the egg yolk off Hector's face and carried on. 'Why don't you girls finish your coffee on the terrace? I'll sort this lot out. Then what about a walk and after lunch I'll drive you back to the city?'

–

As they settled down on the outdoor patio seats, Nick looked around at the gardens and decided that Ari had a decent life if you liked that sort of thing.

'He's like Dad, isn't he?'

Ari looked at Nick in surprise. 'Impoverished Irish orphan?'

'Kind and loving. Doting husband, wonderful father.'

'I see what you mean and yes you're right. When I think how badly I screwed up with Greg I count my blessings every day that I met Seb.'

Nick nodded; the two men couldn't have been more different. Seb wasn't threatened by her intelligence; in fact, he regularly boasted to the boys about how smart their mummy was.

'Yes, Mum and Dad would have approved of him as well. Although I think Clem's Rory would have been Dad's favourite. You know – what with the Celtic vibe and both being musicians.'

'Yep. I think you're probably right,' said Ari thoughtfully, 'although Hal is quite the party animal and I think Dad would have liked him for that.'

'But maybe not for his daughter?' said Nick pointedly. Their father had always been very protective over Paddy's ability to fall for every wounded animal or sob story.

'True,' laughed Ari. 'It's sad, isn't it? We know so much about Mum's family; I mean, my God, we know them all the way back to the Middle Ages, but we don't even know who Dad's folks were. Oodles of generations on one side. None on the other.'

Both girls paused, thinking of the disparity in their knowledge of their parents' backgrounds.

'I think that's part of Clem's insecurities. She always felt so stupid at school and Dad was the one person who convinced her that everything was going to be okay.'

'I wish I had realised she was dyslexic,' said Ari sadly.

'It wasn't your place, Ari. It was Mum and Dad's and you know back then dyslexia was generally ignored at school. And it's not like Clem has suffered.'

'Well, she's successful but that's not the same thing, is it? She's still massively insecure.'

'She's doing better with Rory, isn't she?'

'She is. It helps that he doesn't pay any attention to her dramas.'

Nicked laughed softly, remembering her and Clem's last conversation about Clem's community enterprise. As with everything, it had had to be scaled back until the investigation was over. She had so wanted to get this up and running for Clem but once more she felt she was letting her family down. Thinking about Clem and their father an idea began to form.

'There must be records in Ireland of foster placements, birth records and the like,' said Nick thoughtfully. 'We have his birth certificate. That should be enough to make a good start?'

'What do you have in mind?' asked Ari curiously.

'I've time on my hands. Why don't I spend it trying to find out a bit more about who we are? After all, we are all half Irish, and we don't know a single thing about the place or any family we may have. What if Dad had brothers and sisters?'

'It might not be a very pleasant story, Letta?' Ari was worried that her little sister was rushing into something that might uncover further misery. 'You don't give your child up unless there are serious problems in your life. Who knows what our grandmother was going through? Is that something that you really want to delve into?'

'You're getting more and more like Mum every day,' said Nick fondly. 'I like hearing Letta again. But I promise you, I won't fall apart if I discover something unpleasant. I mean, it's bound to be unpleasant – as you say, no one gives up their baby easily. Or if they do, then maybe they aren't a particularly nice person. Either way, it will give me something to do. And I'd like to do it for all of us. I'd love Aster to have some new memories.'

'Memories?' asked Ari curiously.

'Well, not memories as such but she had the shortest amount of time with them. I'd love for us all to know a bit more about him and his life before Mum.'

'True, and with so many more additions to Clan Hiverton it would be nice to tell the little ones more about their other grandfather. Tony is lovely,' said Ari referring to Seb's father. 'And we treat him as Leo and Will's actual grandfather.'

'I should think so,' said Nick quickly. Lord Flint-Hyssop was a lovely man. Nigel, however, who was Greg's father and therefore the boys' biological grandfather, had first disowned them, and then tried to blackmail Ari and sue for custody when he discovered they would inherit Hiverton one day.

'But I do miss being able to tell them more about my father.' Ari picked up her cup and sipped it carefully. 'Do you know I think this is an excellent idea.' She leant across and squeezed Nick's hand. Then the two sisters watched as Seb played catch on the lawn with the boys.

-

By the time Seb dropped Nick back in London she had a hundred irons in the fire. She'd already started researching various genealogical centres and discovered a place in Cork that was a centre of excellence for family research. As well as distant family research the centre specialised in more recent records and was known for helping adoptive and foster children in recent history. Ballinfeen Hotel had once been a convent that had taken in orphans and foster children. When the convent was converted into a hotel, the centre had emerged as a sideline, paying for the accommodation to be first class. According to his birth certificate, their father came from Cork, so there was a chance they may have records.

Nick fired up her laptops and started to research the matter in earnest and then got on the phone to the hotel. By the end of the call she was confident that this was the best place to start her hunt for her father's history. With a room booked for the following night, she arranged a flight for the afternoon. Tomorrow morning she would tie off any loose ends in the office and head out. She dropped a text to Daisy to get her to give her a call but there was no reply. Reminding herself that it was a Sunday after all she dropped a quick text to Gyeong asking if she was free to talk. A minute later the phone rang. During the past week Gyeong had been in touch daily, suggesting ways in which Nick could get around the system and making suggestions for defence. She had also offered to help Nick look through the old paperwork. Nick was grateful for her support but there was genuinely nothing to be done until the FCA made a ruling.

'Hi, boss. What's up?'

Nick liked how Gyeong always went straight to the heart of an issue. In so many ways she was her right hand and indispensable.

'Nothing much but I'm off to Ireland tomorrow for a few days. I can't get hold of Daisy – can you let her know that I might not see her tomorrow? I'll text you the hotel's address in case anything comes up.'

'Okay.' Gyeong sounded disappointed, but what else could Nick ask her to do? Gyeong was on furlough and she didn't want to get any of her staff in trouble if they were seen to be working for the business. Only Daisy had a dispensation to help Nick until Monday, as De Foix Investments put all its operations on ice. After tomorrow, everything would be dormant until she was found innocent. Whenever that would be.

Hanging up Nick started to pack a suitcase then began to research the sorts of information that she would need for a proper genealogical investigation. For the first time in a week she had something else to think about and it felt good.

Chapter 11

The following morning Nick headed into work. She wasn't used to coming in so late and found the rush-hour crowds annoying. *If work was that important to you, get up earlier and don't waste time standing around in large crowds of people.* Then it struck her that maybe some of these people didn't actually consider work that important. She shrugged her shoulders and joined the queue for the lift.

Stepping into the office she was pleased to see that Daisy was already in ahead of her. She still hadn't replied to her text but now Nick would be able to explain her visit to Ireland directly.

Daisy was standing by her desk. A large wicker box tied with a bow sat on top of the desk and in her hand she held a white envelope. She appeared to be crying.

Nick stopped dead, was she resigning? She couldn't blame Daisy although she'd be sorry to lose her.

'What's wrong?'

The assistant held the letter out to Nick. She wasn't actually crying but it was clear from her red-rimmed eyes she had only just stopped.

'I'm sorry. I'm just so sorry.'

Nick took the letter but didn't open it.

'Is this your resignation? If it is, don't be upset, you've been fabulous. I couldn't have done any of this without you.'

Now Daisy started to cry in earnest which honestly annoyed Nick – crying just got in the way, but she tried not to let her exasperation show.

'I will write you the very best reference, if my word is worth anything after this.' Nick tried to make light of the situation and was alarmed when Daisy let out a small wail.

'No, stop,' she sobbed, wiping her face, 'you're making it worse. It's not my resignation letter. I'm so sorry. And I got you a present. I thought you might need something to fill the time.'

Now she started crying again in earnest. She gave Nick a quick hug, then almost ran out of the office, leaving Nick standing in silence again. She looked at the envelope in her hand; the address was handwritten and there was no postmark so someone had clearly dropped it off in person. It was already open so Daisy must had read the contents. Nick pulled out the letter and started to read. As she made her way to the bottom of the letter her cheeks flushed in embarrassment. She was being evicted. The owners of the office space said that they were terminating the lease immediately. Poor Daisy must have been mortified, seeing as how she had found these offices for Nick in the first place.

How dare they? And how did they know she was being investigated? It was still supposed to be undisclosed. Nick was tempted to call them out and threaten them with legal action but all that would achieve would be to draw attention to her current predicament.

Daisy had pinned a little note to the letter saying she would come in tomorrow and arrange for the staff to come in and collect any personal belongings.

Nick realised her hands were shaking as the letter fluttered in front of her. No wonder her assistant had been crying, she felt like bawling her head off as well. She scanned the letter again – *in a manner unbecoming*, the nerve of it; Lehman Brothers had offices running right up until the minute they collapsed half the world's currencies. It was all part of the old boys' network. She had seen it for years but here it was up front and sneering at her. The first step out of line and the City elite were going to eviscerate her.

Nick sat down at the table and wondered what the hell to do. Finding new office space would be easy enough, but what could she do about the fact that people were clearly talking about her and waiting to attack her. But why? This felt personal.

She wanted to know exactly why she was being evicted. It wasn't for higher rent, there were two other office suites on this floor that were vacant, so they'd be mad to get rid of a paying tenant. And she certainly didn't believe the *manner unbecoming* twaddle. For some reason they wanted to hurt their tenant badly enough that they were prepared to take a financial hit. Exactly whose toes had she trodden on?

The box barked.

Chapter 12

For a second Nick did nothing but look at the package in astonishment and then slowly she stood up and very gently unwrapped the ribbon and lifted back the flaps. As she let in the light a small bundle of fur sprang up against the side of the box and Nick stepped back in sudden surprise.

She stepped forward again and looked into the box at a small dog staring back at her. Picking her up Nick was surprised by how small she was, she seemed little bigger than a cat. Her coat was black and brown, and her long flappy ears were feathery brown. Her long tan face end in a cute black button nose. The two of them looked at each other, then Nick let out a sigh of exasperation. What the hell was Daisy thinking?

Stroking the little dog on the head she was surprised when it licked her hand and wagged its tail. Its nose felt a little dry and she wondered if it was thirsty. Walking through to the kitchen she filled a bowl of water and put both down on the floor and returned to the box to see if there were any clues. Beside the box was a plastic bag with some food and paperwork and a card from Daisy saying the dog was a present. According to the paperwork, she was a pedigree miniature dachshund, and her kennel name was Brightwater Miss Gableforth, which made Nick roll her eyes, what sort of a name was that to give a dog. Reading on, she discovered that Miss Gableforth was a year old, fully vaccinated and microchipped.

She returned to the kitchen where the little dog had finished drinking and was now wandering around the floor seeing what else there was to explore.

'Well, I can't keep you,' she said to the inquisitive little dog, 'so let's stick with Miss Gableforth, shall we? I hope for your sake that your new owners call you something better.'

Nick rang Daisy but again her phone went straight to voicemail. Leaving a quick message asking her to call her she watched the dog play with a balled-up piece of paper that must have got stuck behind the bin.

Her phone buzzed – was it Daisy? No, just the alarm reminding her that she needed to leave the office to prepare for her flight.

Nick swore. She rang Daisy again but there was still no reply. What the hell was she supposed to do? It was a lovely gift but also possibly the most stupid thing she had ever been given. She had never had a pet in her life, nor had she felt the lack of one. How was she supposed to get on a flight to Ireland with a dog?

She looked at her phone and dialled again. 'I have another problem.'

She pictured Ari sitting at her big, lovely leather-topped desk in her study, rolling her eyes to heaven, but Ari had dogs, she might know what to do. Nick outlined the problem.

'But that's insane? Who the hell gives an animal as a pet? What the hell was Daisy *thinking*?'

'I agree but now she isn't answering her bloody phone and I have this little dog charging around the office when I'm supposed to be getting on a plane.'

'All right, tell you what. Come up here and leave her with me.'

Nick thought about it. That seemed like a good idea – the dog was currently trying to get behind a bookcase and Nick jumped up and ran over to pick her up. She instantly wagged her tail and bumped her little face against Nick's. Her coat was incredibly silky; Nick sat down and tickled her tummy as she rolled around on her lap.

'If I have to drive to yours I'll need to hire a car and I'll miss the flight.'

'I could drive down and meet you at the airport, but I'll need to rearrange a few things first,' said Ari.

Nick placed Miss Gableforth on the floor where she ran over to a notepad that someone had dropped under their desk and started to play with it.

'No, don't worry. Maybe I can keep her with me, until I can figure out what to do?'

'You mean, cancel the trip to Ireland?'

Nick paused. She hadn't meant that, although now she thought about it how the hell could she take a dog with her to Ireland?

'I suppose she can't go on the plane, can she?'

'No!' said Ari in alarm. 'Honestly, let me take care of her for you.'

Nick was now sitting on the floor playing a gentle game of tug of war with the dog and the notepad. Nick hoped there was nothing important written on it because the pad was beginning to look like confetti. She stood up and walked towards the now-empty water bowl. With each step the little dog jumped and pounced on her feet as Nick stepped carefully, laughing as she did so trying not to squish her.

'What's the dog doing?' asked Ari as she listened to her sister laugh.

'Attacking my feet!'

'Wait until she discovers laces, Dragon loved to play with them,' grinned Ari.

'How about a ferry?' said Nick suddenly. 'I can hire a car and take her on a ferry, can't I?'

'You can, but are you sure?' said Ari doubtfully. 'Honestly, this is why you shouldn't give animals as presents to people that don't know what to do with them.'

'You're not wrong,' said Nick in exasperation. 'But the fact is I have her now and need to sort things out.'

'Very well,' said Ari, 'but don't forget to call ahead to the hotel and see if she will be a problem. And if you find a dog too much to cope with, I'll have her.'

Nick hung up and after a few minutes research on the internet and a call to the hotel, she changed her bookings. The little dog wriggled on her lap and tried to explore her sleeve. Gently she re-arranged the animal, absently scratching her head and continued searching. Minutes later she was looking at ferry timetables and car hire and before she realised what she was doing she had somehow decided to take the dog with her to Ireland.

She rang Daisy again, but this time was surprised with the relief she felt when her assistant once again failed to answer.

'Okay, little one. Back in your bed.'

As she picked up the dog she noticed that her feathery ears were mostly brown but were tipped black on both sides. Her tail, which hadn't stopped wagging yet, also ended in a black patch.

Popping her back in the wicker box, she tucked the blanket around the dog, she placed the box on the kitchen floor and added a small bowl of the dog food that Daisy had provided.

'Now, I won't be long. I'm just going to find something to carry you in.' She wasn't sure why she was talking to the dog; it was not like she understood her but it felt rude otherwise. She also needed to think of a name beyond Miss Gableforth, but it felt presumptuous to give the small animal a name. She wasn't even keeping her. For now though she was her responsibility.

Nick hurried down to the central plaza that served as a shopping mall for the various office blocks in Canary Wharf. She had seen plenty of women carrying dogs about in handbags so that was what she was going to do. It seemed daft, but it presented a temporary solution for now. As she rode down on the lift she booked the night-ferry crossing from Pembroke in Wales over to Rosslare and arranged car hire on either side. It would take her five hours to drive from here to Pembroke, so she had plenty of time. The ferry crossing was only four hours but she booked a cabin so that the dog had space to run around. It would then be a three-hour drive to the hotel, and she should arrive just in time for breakfast.

As she stepped out onto the concourse she had her first pangs of doubt. Just because she could do this, did that mean that she should? She was the least impulsive person she knew but suddenly she wanted very much to keep the dog with her. After a long, shitty week it was the best thing that had happened to her. Ever since she had discussed it with Ari she had felt re-energised. Researching the family tree and now looking after her new charge, were going to get her through this. But she was still feeling anxious and that knot in her stomach was tightening.

She tried to think what was wrong with her plan and wondered if it wasn't simply that she had left a dog alone in a box in the kitchen. Picking up her pace, she headed towards a leather goods shop. They always had a sumptuous display of handbags and suitcases in their window. Before now, Nick hadn't paid them much attention, but they would probably have something perfect. She headed into the shop trying not to think of the dog all alone. What if she got out of the box? The kitchen door was open, she might escape into the office. What if she chewed on the electric cables?

Nick quickly glanced around the showroom, there was a shiny display of bright pink and yellow handbags. Some looked like they might be big enough, but she wasn't sure she could bring herself to be seen in public with an orange handbag with a gold chain handle.

'Can I help you with anything?'

An assistant had peeled away from behind the counter and had come over to assist Nick. The way she was looking at her suggested she was ready to assist her out of the shop. All Nick had to do was casually display her gold credit card or mention her title or the fact that Holly McDonald was her twin and this assistant would be her new best friend. Instead, she smiled politely saying, 'No thanks' and continued to glance around the room.

She was still worried about Miss Gableforth. What if someone came in and she escaped out the door? But no one else was due in the office today. Nick relaxed for half a second and suddenly wondered if the cleaners would come in early if they knew the tenants were moving out. Would they see the box and throw it out? Would they squash it?

Nick yelped and the assistant returned.

'Maybe you're looking for a present? The giftshop across the way do a nice range?'

The assistant clearly wanted rid of this strange, inexpensively dressed woman who made noises to herself. Nick turned to her and this time decided to speed up the process. She had to get back to the office before something dreadful happened.

'I need a handbag. A large one, it needs a solid wide base.'

'Do you have a budget in mind?'

'No, but this is rather urgent so just point out what you have. Please.'

The assistant steered Nick to a range of large tote bags.

'No, it can't be open at the top like that, and I need it to be wider at the bottom.' If the dog was going to travel in the bag she needed space to move around.

The assistant pulled down a large overnight travel bag that Nick instantly assessed as suitable.

'Of course, this is the larger version of this design. We do have a smaller—' she paused '—more reasonably priced version if you would prefer to look at that?'

Nick scowled at her. 'This is the bag that I want.' Pulling her wallet out of her pocket she handed her card to the woman and was unsurprised to see an instantaneous change in attitude as she read *Lady N. de Foix* on the Coutts Silk charge card.

Was there anything else madam was interested in today? A new line in gloves, a matching wallet, an espresso whilst she browsed?

Nick dismissed all suggestions as thoughts of the dog's impending doom filled her head.

'No, as I said I am in a hurry. Please just charge the card.'

Nick followed the assistant to the till where another assistant was now praising Nick on her excellent taste. She just wanted to get out of here and back to Miss Gableforth. All this flattery was annoying her, she had a dog to rescue from one of the many ways she had now envisaged her dying.

'That will be £1,250.'

For a second Nick wondered if there was another customer in the shop.

'How much?'

'It's £1,250.' The shop assistant smiled nervously. She was so close to making her target for the week.

'I'm only buying the one overnight bag,' said Nick incredulously.

'Maybe you'd like to see the smaller version?' Even that would get her into the week's sales targets.

Nick shook her head in disbelief – she knew designer bags were expensive, but this was beyond the pale. If it hadn't been so urgent she'd have walked out the shop bagless and laughing. As it was she tapped her pin into the machine.

'What are you doing now?' asked Nick as the assistant whipped the bag away.

'This is the display model. Jody is just getting your own bag which we will gift-wrap and bag up for you.'

'Oh for God's sake, you're going to put my bag in a bag?' said Nick at the end of her tether. 'That's ridiculous. I just need it now. No gift-wrap, no bag, no flourishes and no membership treats. Please. I am in a hurry.'

Nick was all but snapping now. As the first assistant began to explain her ninety-day warranty and aftercare regime, the second assistant handed her the bag. Grabbing it Nick ran for the door. She could hear the assistant imploring her to store it in its cloth pouch when not in use. Why store it in a cloth pouch? Just how precious were these people about a sodding handbag – although at over a grand Nick thought they probably weren't precious enough. Nick wondered if the world had gone mad.

Tapping the button for the lift, she hopped about as she willed the lift to move quicker. Eventually, she gave up and ran up the ten flights to her floor. Puffing, she dashed back to her office and turned the key in the lock, relieved to see the room wasn't full of removal men throwing stuff whilst stomping on boxes. She dumped the bag on the table and ran into the kitchen. The box was where she had left it. It had not somehow caught fire nor had it become wet and soggy from the water thereby leaving the little animal cold and shivering.

Nick bobbed down and gently opened the flaps and watched as the dog's little chest rose and fell as she dreamt of chasing notebooks or rabbits.

Gingerly, she lifted her out and sat down on the kitchen floor recovering her breath. As the dog woke up she opened her eyes and looked at Nick. Her whole body began to wag her tail and Nick was suddenly aware of a sense of warmth in her chest. A second later she realised the dog had peed on her.

'Well, that's a first,' she muttered to herself as she put her on the floor and nipped back to her office, where she always kept a change of clothes for any eventuality. Admittedly she hadn't foreseen being weed on as a possibility but at least she was prepared. Heading back into the kitchen a distinctly unpleasant aroma indicated that all of the dog's body systems were functioning properly. Screwing up her nose, Nick cleaned the mess and then sprayed the area with disinfectant. As she did so she started laughing. Miss

Gableforth had just perfectly summed up what Nick felt about her landlords. Clever dog.

Grinning, she gathered her few possessions into her backpack, then took a towel from the bathroom, lined the bottom of her new bag and settled the dog into it. Taking one last look around the office she was satisfied that she was happy to leave the place for good. She and her new friend headed back to her apartment, ready for their adventures together to begin.

Chapter 13

Nick drove off the ferry and onto the land of her father. The crossing had been abysmal, so the fact that it was solid ground was enough for her to feel a sense of gratitude, as well as an affinity for her father's birthplace.

The drive to Pembroke had been surprisingly enjoyable. She had picked up a student hitch-hiking back to Wales – the girl had been standing in the rain on the forecourt of a garage, with a backpack by her legs. As Nick had filled the tank of her hire car, she watched the girl refuse the offer of a couple of lifts, despite the rain. The girl was clearly fussy, and so she should be, thought Nick. She was all for men being responsible for their actions, and felt that women should not be afraid for their safety wherever they walked, or whatever they wore – but still, the world was cruel and unfair.

As she watched she had a brainwave: the two women could help each other out. She would get her safely to Wales and in return the student could take care of the dog. She put the proposal to the hitch-hiker, whose name was Zara; who immediately agreed, and the five-hour drive passed in no time. They stopped regularly to let Miss Gableforth out and avoided all accidents, Nick had discovered that she was already pretty well house trained, the accident in the office had been a one off. The little dog thought the whole thing was a massive adventure and would keep tripping over her feet or ears as she tried to sniff all the new smells. Having dropped Zara off, she drove on to the ferry, grabbed a bite of food from the restaurant, then headed to her cabin. The boat was already swaying in the port and she had had a feeling that the crossing was going to be a rough one.

Now as she drove down the ramps and clanked onto the floodlit docks, she decided to watch out for another hitch-hiker and found a girl with a sign for Cork. Exactly where she was going.

Carrie had blown all her savings to go to a gig in England. The craic apparently had been on! It took a while for Nick to get used to the girl's strong accent as she chatted away about the acts she had seen and the mates she had made and how her friends back at school would be fierce jealous. When Nick realised Carrie was still at school she nearly freaked.

'What did your folks say?'

'Sure I told them I was going off on a Geography trip with the school.' And she laughed her head off, waking the little dog. Nick just carried on driving in silence, she didn't want to judge, plus if she was honest she envied the girl her freedom.

'So where are you heading to yerself?'

Once Nick had worked out the sentence she told the girl about Ballinfeen Hotel.

'Is that the fancy place on the island? Mam says they should get an Oscar for how well they fleece people.'

And then she laughed again and apologised. 'I'm sure it's lovely and all that. Plus they do have an awesome reputation for family research or so Mr Houlihan said, he's our History teacher. We went there once for a school field trip. I think they were trying to reach out to local schools.' She paused reflectively. 'Although the way I heard it, they stopped doing it after our visit, so I'm told. It's a dead boring place but you might like it yourself. There's the big old hotel that was once a convent, then there's the family history buildings, a total yawn fest if you ask me, and then a few other houses and then nothing except for the island itself. We nipped out for a bit of a swim but there was some awful shouting when we snuck back in and accidently started dripping on the microfiche. Mary Mac had said she would pack the towels, but you know Mary, she forgot, she's some gowl, so the three of us couldn't get our hair dry for love nor money.'

Carrie chatted on, entertaining Nick with tales of how Mary Mac screwed things up and how the world was out to spoil Carrie's life.

'You know,' she said with the sudden passion of a seventeen-year-old, 'you have to take what you want in life. Don't hurt other people, obviously, but if you see what you want, don't let anyone say no.'

By the time they reached Cork, the sun had fully risen, and Carrie hopped out at a layby and pointed Nick in the right direction for Ballinfeen.

'Thanks a mill for the lift now, girl, sound out! Take care of that wee dog now. She's adorable. And change her name, that one's ridiculous.'

Nick pulled out her wallet and took out a business card.

'If you ever find yourself in London and at a loss, give me a call and I'll give you a job. It's hard work and I don't accept slackers. Not interested in laziness or excuses, but if you work hard, you get paid well with plenty of time off to go and do your own thing. Whatever mad thing that will be, Carrie.'

The girl took the card in surprise.

'I can just see me standing in the middle of the stock market shouting, "Buy! Buy! Sell! Sell!"'

'As it happens so can I,' said Nick sardonically, already wondering about her rash decision. 'But that's not exactly what we do – you'd probably think it's terribly boring. But anyway. Keep the card. Even if you don't want a job, but you need a hand, just shout.'

As she pulled away into the traffic she watched in her rear-view mirror in amusement. Carrie was already pulling a school blazer out from her bag and slipping a skirt on over her trousers, before removing them and stuffing them in her bag. The lights turned green, and Nick pulled away grinning at the encounter.

Half an hour later, she took a turning for the coast and as the road bent around a corner she could suddenly see miles of coastline. The shoreline was white with small waves and out to sea the dark water looked grey under the cloud-filled sky, but she didn't think she had seen a more beautiful view. Maybe in sunshine this place would look like a picture postcard. Now it looked like the backdrop to a sweeping historical drama. The shoreline was craggy with fingers of land jutting out into the ocean and the road wove back and forth off into the distance; no doubt her destination was tucked behind one of these inlets. Finally, Nick took a left turn and ahead of her she could see Ballinfeen Island. The road crossed the water towards the island which stood in the shelter of one of the fingers of land.

According to the brochure it wasn't strictly an island anymore. The road had been built in the seventies for the nuns. The Church felt that at their age they shouldn't be having to row to shore if the tide caught them out.

Eventually, it was time itself that caught them out, and when the last nun retired to a mainland convent and there were no new nuns to the order, the Church sold the little island off.

The tide was in and the hotel was only accessible via the causeway. Across the water Nick could see the road rose up onto the island and a large house was built on the top looking out over the water. As she had approached the island she could see that it was a decent size with several properties on it. At the far end, high above the water's edge, stood a small whitewashed cottage. She wondered what the Wi-Fi was like.

Nick drove slowly over the causeway. The sensation of travelling across water was wonderful and she wanted to take it all in. She wanted to stop and show Miss Gable-forth, but she suspected she wouldn't care and as there were no passing spaces, and the causeway was only one vehicle wide, she might annoy traffic in all directions. As it was she could see both ends easily enough and no one was coming but still she decided to drive on. She was aware that Carrie would have stopped and shouted at anyone that told her to move.

Parking her car in the hotel car park, she grabbed her suitcase and the dog's bag and struggled into the foyer. The wind and rain pulled at her hair and tugged at her open coat, making her wet. She was looking forward to checking in and having a quick stretch and a shower. However, as soon as she entered the hotel foyer she saw she had been pipped to the post by a coach party. Grumbling to herself, she was grateful when a porter offered to store her luggage until she had a room. He also suggested she have a coffee whilst she wait but she was happy just to stand for a bit. Whispering into the bag she assured Miss Gableforth that they would be in their room presently.

Looking around, Nick could see no trace of the former convent, although she wasn't too sure what that would look like anyway. The large foyer was carpeted, with several sofas to one side surrounding a currently empty fireplace. Two giant, hairy-looking dogs lounged in front of it, dead to the world. The walls were hung with oil paintings of beautiful seascapes and there were also lots of coats of arms and family trees with swirly handwriting and red wax stamps. On the other side of the large room was the customary reception counter, currently swamped with the passengers from the coach. Nick smiled as she listened to the familiar rise and fall of Mandarin and braced herself for a wait.

No question was so worthless that it would be asked only once. Sometimes the same question would be asked twice by the same person, more likely everyone would ask the same question, over and over, only happy when the answer had been given to each and every one of them directly.

She put her head down and asked Miss Gableforth to hang on in there. This could take some time.

Chapter 14

Gabe drove his hire car up into the hotel driveway with relief. Despite it being early July, nothing about the weather indicated it was summertime. The ferry crossing had been horrific and all he wanted to do was to have a long bath. He'd seen a few poor souls leaning over the edge, but years racing yachts meant that he rarely suffered from seasickness. That said, it was widely acknowledged that the Irish Sea was one of the worst crossings and he was glad to put it behind him. Fingers crossed his flight home wouldn't also be cancelled. He wasn't sure he was up to a repeat performance.

He hurried from the car park to the hotel's reception – the storm hadn't lessened any, and the mercury was falling. He wished he hadn't agreed to come in the first place. But what could you do when your father was able to call in favours from your boss? Gabriel St Clair was part of the Harrington family. A financial institution who last year had fallen into partial ruin. Giles Harrington was the current patriarch and was as hard and as ruthless a businessman as you were likely to meet; he ran his family the same way. His first marriage had given him three children, Adam, Rebecca and Paul, each a chip off the old block. His second marriage to Sarah St Clair had resulted in two boys, Gabe and his twin Raphael. When he divorced their mother in their teens, they didn't really notice the loss. They saw him as much as they ever did, their mother had been well provided for financially and if anything seemed happier. And so life went on. The only change was that they took their mother's surname; even as teenagers, they wanted to distance themselves from their elder siblings. Their father had laughed and called them fools but Gabe still felt guilty from time to time that he had hurt his father. The third and current marriage had resulted in a little girl called Freya, who Gabe and Rafe doted on whenever they met up. A far more pleasing sibling than their older and meaner brothers and sisters, the twins would regularly offer to babysit or take her out for the day.

As the doorman opened the door Gabe was disappointed to see that a coach had arrived before him and he was at the back of a queue of frazzled-looking Chinese tourists. No doubt they had been on the same ferry as him. They were already divesting themselves of brightly coloured plastic rain macs and frilly umbrellas – perhaps donned to simply cross the car park – and were now generally causing havoc. Shaking off his own jacket, Gabe ran his fingers through his hair and realised that he probably looked like a scarecrow. His blond wavy hair was unruly at the best of times and he spent a fortune on keeping it in check. No one wanted a lawyer that looked like a surfer – they wanted thin and sharp-eyed, not a hale and hearty-looking bumpkin. He also laughed too much, he couldn't help himself, it was just how he was. However, a laid-back manner often meant that people underestimated him, and he was happy with that as well.

Looking around he could see a tall woman, about his own age, also waiting to check in. He had spotted her on the boat muttering to herself and had wondered if she was praying. There was a point when chairs had slid across the dining-room floor that he might have joined her.

Now her bag was clasped to her chest and she was still praying. Having nothing better to do than wait he decided to see what he could learn about her. It was a game he used to play with his mentor, to size up clients from only a few clues.

She was tall, slim and striking. So a model was a starting guess, but her clothes were distinctly ordinary. Smart brogues, black jeans, and a plain raincoat. She kept hitching up her trousers suggesting a recent rapid weight loss. Probably not a welcome loss or else she'd have replaced her clothes with new ones. Besides, she was already slim, and skinny wasn't healthy. So that was another cross against model.

Except for that bag. That was a large leather Mulberry hold-all, and he knew that couldn't be bought for under a grand. No wonder she had it clasped to her. So, she had money. No ring on her finger, no varnish on her nails. Chances are she bought it for herself. Doing what? Her profession was obviously well-paid but not focussed on appearance.

She turned before he realised he was staring at her and met his perusal with an arched eyebrow. Smiling, he nodded at her, and looked away quickly. So, she was confident as well. Lots of tall girls slumped, she didn't. She stood there looking around the room, gradually stepping forward as the queue diminished.

He recalibrated what he knew about her. Good-looking but probably single – although from her dismissive look just now, she wasn't in the market for a fling. She appeared confident, but her demeanour was nervous: the way she held the bag and kept muttering into it was odd.

She was certainly a puzzle and he still hadn't made up his mind about her as she got to the head of the queue and put her bag on the floor.

As he stepped forward in the queue he heard her chatting to the receptionist and grinned as he heard her strong East End accent. With her almost-black hair and bright blue eyes he had assumed she was Irish but now he knew she was as London as it got. Chances of the bag being genuine were receding. Just as he was about to pat himself on the back for having happily packed the woman into a box, his mentor's voice chided him. *Only a fool relies on statistical probability.* His other mantra was: *Judge a man by his words not his accent. Okay then*, thought Gabe, *think again, what do you know?* Working class, East End girl, confident, good-looking. He was happy with working class, as middle-class girls tended to ditch or blend their local accents. Bag fake or genuine?

He didn't feel like he had made much progress when four of the Chinese guests returned to the desk and swamped the concierge with rapid questions. Without their tour guide the concierge was at a loss as to what they were saying. Gabe wondered if he could try and help. He had a translation app on his phone that might be useful.

At that moment, the girl who had been the focus of his attention broke into Mandarin. The four now turned to her and attacked her with their questions and she smiled as she clearly asked them to slow down. Then she turned back to the concierge.

'I think they would like some extra towels in their rooms.'

She turned to the group and spoke again in Mandarin as the four all nodded.

'Yes. More towels, please. There may be more, but my Mandarin is not much beyond beginner level. They could also be asking for wildebeests.'

The concierge looked alarmed and then smiled.

'Tell them we're fresh out of wildebeest but I'll get extra towels to their rooms straight away if they can give me their room numbers.'

As the group left, they bowed to each other and the girl checked in. Gabe tilted his head. Proficient in Mandarin. That was a bit out of left field and raised the probability that the bag was genuine. She had dealt with both parties with manners and humour, and despite her saying she was a beginner she was pretty confident. Maybe she worked for a Chinese company? That would make sense.

As he continued to watch her she concluded her business, picked up her bag and headed off towards the staircase, once again muttering quietly. Good-looking, clever, weird. Well, whatever else she was, she was interesting.

He stepped forward towards the reception desk. 'Hello, Gabriel St Clair, I'm booked in for the next few days.' Gabe smiled at the man behind the desk, but he didn't get much further. The girl from a minute ago came running back in a complete state, any sense of her previous calm had completely disappeared.

'My bag! My bag has gone. This isn't my bag!' She waved the large Mulberry bag at the man. 'It's not mine! Where's mine?'

Well, that settled it, thought Gabe, the bag was genuine, no one would be this freaked out over losing a fake. Still at least he had a solution.

'Excuse me.'

The girl rounded on him, her expression wild.

'It's just that the Chinese party you were helping just now, one of the ladies had a terribly similar bag. Maybe—'

Her face lit up. 'The two bags got swapped over!' She turned quickly to the receptionist. 'Quick, call them. Please. I'll do the talking, what's their room number? Please hurry.'

The man recoiled under her urgency.

'I can't just give out the room number of other—'

'Yes. You can. Please. Quickly, what is it? I need my bag now.'

She was sounding panicky, and Gabe wondered about her recent weight loss. Could there be medicine in her bag that she needed? That might explain her desperation.

Suddenly, there was a call from the other side of the foyer and one of the two couples from earlier came hurrying back. They were walking in a curious manner as though they wanted to run but didn't want to jostle the bag. They held it out in front of them like it contained dynamite.

When the Chinese lady saw the second bag, she called out rapidly and the younger woman dashed across the foyer where the older woman offered her bag reverentially to her. She looked inside and Gabe looked on in astonishment as a tiny little brown nose poked out, followed by a long snout, two dark eyes and big floppy ears. A dog in a handbag. Well, he hadn't pegged her as the sort of woman that carried a pet dog in a bag. Looking at the little animal, Gabe decided it was a dachshund.

'Oh my God. I thought I was going to die.'

Gabe looked at her and was concerned, her voice was shaky, and all her previous reserve seemed to have disappeared.

'Can I get you a coffee?' he asked with a smile. Turning to the concierge he asked if they were serving breakfast yet and suggested a drink before breakfast. 'Come on. Why don't we go and settle down and recover from that awful crossing and then you can introduce me to your friend? I'm Gabe St Clair, by the way.'

Chapter 15

Nick looked at the stranger who had just introduced himself. She should decline and head to her room, but the idea of a drink sounded just what she needed. Her heart was beating ten to the dozen and she needed to calm down. Besides, he had a lovely smile and his shaggy blond hair and slightly crooked nose put her at ease. As they walked into the lounge, he guided her towards some armchairs by a roaring fire, Nick looked at the flames and thought how wonderful it would be to escape all her problems. Leave her past behind and re-invent herself in this cosy hotel, with a handsome stranger, and a little dog. Could there be anything less like her? Before she could change her mind she smiled at Gabe.

'I'm Letta. And thank you for being so kind. I feel a fool, but the dog is new and honestly, I'm out of my depth.'

As she looked in the bag she seemed eager to escape but she was uncertain if that was a good thing.

'I don't think I've met a Letta before, is it Polish?'

Nick laughed, why not? But then decided that was probably taking her re-invention too far. Better that she stayed close to who she was, just a version without the current tarnish.

'No, it's just a nickname my mother had for me. Do you have dogs? Do you know what to do with one?'

And then she explained how she came to be in possession of an animal that she had no idea how to take care of.

'It was a going-away present from work but honestly I think it was a really bad idea.' She picked the little dog up and put her on her lap. 'Not that I think *you* are a bad idea,' she said to the dog, 'I just think me having you is not great.'

Gabe smiled at the dog and then asked if he could hold her for a bit. He found himself laughing and twisting his head away, as the dog proceeded to lick his face and try to scramble over his shoulder.

'What's her name?'

'According to the paperwork it's Brightwater Miss Gableforth, but that's a dreadful mouthful and she doesn't seem to respond to it anyway. I've been trying variations, but they don't seem to be sticking either.'

Gabe paused. What a mad thing to give as a present, especially to someone that didn't seem to have any idea about animals. 'Maybe you should rehome her?'

Nick tilted her head. She had no idea what all the new terminology was regarding pet care. She was completely out of her depth.

'What does rehoming involve? Is that like litter training?'

'No, I meant, like, give it back or give it to a shelter.'

The girl glared at him. 'Put her into care?'

What a strange way to look at it, thought Gabe, but he shrugged his shoulders. 'Yes, I suppose that's one way to put it, but she's a cutie, she'll be rehomed immediately. And to someone that wants her and knows how to take care of her.'

Nick stood up and took the little dog from him and sat back down again stroking her as she promptly fell asleep.

'This little dog is family now,' said Nick fiercely. She hadn't been sure what to do with it, but the minute Gabe had suggested returning her she knew that she had passed that point. 'She is my responsibility and I'm not letting her go.'

'Well, in that case why not call her Ohana?'

Nick shrugged blankly. Was O'Hana some sort of Irish name?

'Have you not watched *Lilo and Stitch*? It means "family" and as Lilo says, *Family sticks together.*'

That sounded like a quote to Nick but she hadn't seen the film. However, it sounded suitable.

'Ohana it is then, although I don't know the movie. Is it some foreign arthouse thing? I'm afraid I don't go to the cinema much.'

Gabe winced and then gave Nick a guilty grin. 'I should say yes, shouldn't I? Pretend that I'm terribly cultured but actually *Lilo and Stitch* is a Disney movie. It's my little sister's favourite.'

Nick laughed as he explained how he and his brother would fight over the chance to babysit their half-sister. Sighing, Nick sipped her coffee and looked at the flames reflectively. What the hell did she know about taking on a pet? When she had opened the box and seen the dog for the first time she had been horrified and then had instantly fallen head over heels in love. When Gabe had suggested getting rid of her just then, Nick's feelings had solidified. She hadn't asked for this dog, but no one asked for the hand they were dealt; now she and the dog were stuck with each other. She was worried that Ohana may have got the poorer end of the bargain.

'The only thing is, I've never had a pet before. I don't know how to feed her, or take her for walks, or anything. So far she sleeps, and lives in a bag. That can't be right?'

'Not quite,' he laughed, and Nick liked the sound of it. 'But maybe later you could ask at reception for the closest pet supplier.'

Nick nodded her head. 'Good call, but I think for now I'm going to unpack and let this little one stretch her legs.'

Gabe stood as Nick got up and she smiled at the small courtesy. Letta and Ohana against the world. With her keys in hand she walked up the main staircase and headed off in search of her room. The girl at the desk had explained but it sounded a bit of a warren. The hotel had been built as a fortified manor house, before it had been a convent, and Nick wondered if the twists and turns in the corridors meant that the builders also feared attack from within. She could imagine running down these passage-ways and then leaning around a corner shooting as she went. She wondered if the nuns did the same in their day. Finally, she arrived at a heavy oak door. She turned the key and was pleasantly surprised by how modern her room was. Certainly, the beams running across the ceiling showed its age but there were wall-to-wall carpets and a state-of-the-art bathroom. There was a large flatscreen TV on the wall and looking out the window let her gaze out over the stormy Irish Sea.

Removing Ohana, she put her down on the bathroom floor and knelt down, smiling as she watched her skitter across the tiles, then pause, then carry on running. She pulled out two little plates from her bag's side pocket and emptied a portion of dog food into one and water into the other. Ohana walked across to the water bowl and then happily wolfed down her food. When she was full, she padded across what was left of the food and went off to examine the waste bin.

Laughing, Nick cleaned the plates and then filled up the water again and then sat back down on the tiles watching Ohana chase her tail, drink some water and sit on the plate. Incredibly as she sat there, her head nodded, and she fell asleep.

Alarmed, Nick poked the small dog who looked up blearily and fell back asleep. Moving Ohana to the main room, she placed her on a towel and looked at her fondly. Dogs were messier than she had anticipated but she was sure that the chaos would soon die down.

She plugged her laptop in but didn't fire it up and continued to hang up her clothes and lay out her toiletries. The whole time she kept checking on the dog, but Ohana was sound asleep. Nick realised that for the first time in weeks she hadn't thought about the case once. Instead she was looking forward to breakfast and beginning her research.

Chapter 16

The large dining room was mostly empty; a couple were staring at each other lovingly over their toast and an older woman was seated at another table reading a book. At the far end she saw that a collection of tables had been reserved – clearly for the coach party. Nick was determined to sit as far away from them as possible in case she got dragged into being an honorary interpreter. A movement caught her eye – at the other end of the room Gabe had risen from his table. Smiling, Nick walked over to say good morning before she even realised what she was doing.

She had plans for the day and chatting to random strangers were not part of them. Even ones that looked so pleased to see her.

'Hello, again. Would you like to join me?'

Now Nick was stuck. Having walked over she could hardly say no, besides which he seemed to know about dogs, she could quiz him for more information.

'Thank you. Isn't this place amazing? I've got incredible views over the sea.'

Gabe rolled his eyes dramatically and gave a deep sigh.

'I, on the other hand, appear to have drawn the short straw. I'm in the new wing with our mutual friends,' he said inclining his head over to the long table. 'They are incredibly noisy. They keep visiting each other's rooms, back and forth, back and forth. I may need ear plugs!

Now look, change of topic. I hope you don't mind but I searched online for nearby pet suppliers. There are a few within thirty miles that will probably have all you need for Ohana.'

Nick looked at him in surprise — that was a helpful thing to do, but did he think she was incapable of doing her own research? Thinking about it, all he knew about her was that she was someone who carried a dog in a bag, didn't have a clue how to deal with it, and freaked out when she lost her bag. Maybe his first impressions of her weren't of the cool, calm businesswoman she usually was.

'That's so kind of you.' She broke off her conversation as the waitress came over with some toast and a pot of coffee.

'Oh, what a little dote!'

The waitress had arrived just as Ohana had woken up and popped her little head out of Nick's bag. Nick was once more flustered. On the phone the hotel had said the dog would be fine, but she wasn't convinced.

'I am so sorry. She was a last-minute present and I didn't know what to do with her. I couldn't leave her behind.'

'Of course you couldn't,' said the waitress in a shocked voice. 'And don't you worry none, Mum loves dogs, wait 'til I tell her about this little pet.'

With that, she took their breakfast order and headed back to the kitchen.

'Don't look worried,' said Gabe reassuringly as Nick looked after the dog. 'It's not like you've unleashed a pack of wolves. The most damage that little one can do is lick you to death.'

The noise in the room increased as the coach party arrived, and Gabe gave a mock groan and slumped down in his chair.

'Save me. If they come over here please tell them I'm a terribly light sleeper. Where did you learn Mandarin by the way – was it Mandarin?'

Nick watched as the party arrived and settled down. She enjoyed watching how people moved in large groups. The lady with the matching overnight bag saw Nick and gave a little wave before sitting down. Nick waved back and returned her attention to Gabe.

'Yes, I know some Cantonese and Korean as well, but my Mandarin is better. A lot of my work is based in Asia so I figured I may as well learn the languages.'

'Just like that?' laughed Gabe.

Ohana was now wriggling around in her arms, looking for escape, smelling all the new shampoo scents in Nick's hair, and tickling her bare neck.

'I've got a good ear for languages. On my street were lots of families from Kenya and India, plus several Jamaicans. Then in school there were lots of Vietnamese, Poles and Lithuanians. The English language was very much an also-ran where I grew up.'

'Sounds like fun?'

'It was, actually. For all the talk of urban deprivation we had a good time of it.'

A woman had been helping to settle the coach party but now she peeled away and came over to join them.

'Oh sweet Mary. Roisin said you had a wee dachshund. She's a sweetheart. May I hold her now?' The woman stuck her hand out, whether for the dog or a handshake, Nick was uncertain. 'I'm Mairead Devaney by the way, this is my place.'

The woman was in her sixties and was dressed in a smart tweed set with a double row of pearls, and smart leather shoes, laced on the side, with a small heel. Every inch the country house proprietor. Nick smiled and passed Ohana across.

'Roisin said she was an unexpected gift. Honestly, what a thing to do. You must have been at your wits' end?'

Nick tried to reply but the woman carried on.

'We have dogs ourselves, but they're wolfhounds. This little one could probably sleep curled up in their collars. You can get sorted in Clonty's Pet supplies, up there in Cork.'

Nick nodded at Gabe; it was one of the names on his list. She was about to say as much when Roisin re-appeared with their breakfasts.

'Tell you what,' continued Mrs Devaney, 'why don't you eat your breakfast in peace and I'll take Ohana here for a little play in the office?'

Nick was worried; she had gone from being concerned that she had broken house rules to now imposing on this lovely lady's time. Mairead could see that Nick was about to protest and cut her off.

'Sure it's no bother. You'd be doing me a favour and I'll go further. I'll sort out this little one when you drive over to Clonty's. There's a big storm coming in this evening and it'll be high tide. You don't want to be driving then. The causeway can be a bit tricky in a big storm. We're advising all our guests to be back by mid-afternoon, or they may need to find somewhere else to sleep.'

Nick thanked her for the offer of entertaining Ohana, but now she was worried about the storm warning. As she watched Ohana leave with Mrs Devaney, she gave an embarrassed chuckle.

'I've only been with that little scamp twenty-four hours but I'm already missing her when she's not with me.'

'Not surprised, as they say around here, she's a proper dote, so she is.' Dropping the atrocious accent he continued, 'That storm sounds exciting, doesn't it?'

Exciting wasn't the word Nick would have used. She was comfortable analysing risk variables and she had decided that a drive to Cork was far beyond her risk parameter for this situation. There were too many things not in her favour. She didn't drive much at the best of times. She didn't know her way around this area. The storm could come in early. She already thought the weather was pretty dreadful – no one else did, though, which suggested that the storm was going to be truly beyond her comfort zone. However, she did need to get things for Ohana; if she left straight after breakfast and dashed straight back it should be all right.

'Can I tag along?' said Gabe.

Nick looked up from her food in surprise. She hadn't thought of asking for help but having someone with her would be reassuring.

'I mean, if I'm not imposing?'

Nick smiled and felt some of the tension leave her shoulders.

'You would be most welcome. In fact, I was just wondering if it was a good idea. I'm not much of a driver.'

'Tell you what then. Why don't I drive, and you can be my trusty navigator?'

'You're on.' And she leant across to shake his hand. It felt like the right thing to do, two partners in crime about to go on an adventure together but as his hand wrapped around hers in a firm grip, she felt a sense of solidity and rightness that caught her on the hop. He let go of her hand and raised an eyebrow, and then laughed.

'Come on then, Letta. Eat up and let's go exploring. My day seems to be getting better already.'

Nick knew she should feel uncomfortable about that handshake – it was clear that it had caught Gabe off guard as well – but instead, it seemed to cement something between the pair of them, and they both started chatting about the various adventures they had been on. Gabe almost won with his tales of mud slides in Nicaragua on a motorbike but had to concede to Nick's tale of shopping in Camden on Christmas Eve.

As she finished her breakfast she wondered about how relaxed she felt for the first time in weeks. Gabe's easy company was a tonic, and he was great to just chat to. Almost reluctantly she finished her breakfast but was now looking forward to the drive. Gabe checked his watch.

'What time shall we head off?'

Having agreed to meet up in half an hour, Nick went to the main desk and found that Mrs Devaney was more than happy to have Ohana for the day.

Chapter 17

Gabe ended the call to his half-brother and sighed in frustration. Honestly, Adam was repellent. Gabe had tried to remind him again that Harrington's troubles were down to Harringtons themselves. That De Foix Investments were not to blame, and that in fact, it was George Flint-Hyssop that had tipped off the City to the family's predicament.

'And how easy do you think it is to take down Sir George?' demanded Adam. 'De Foix Investments is a much easier target and will remind the City that we are still a force to be reckoned with.'

'Honestly, Adam. My advice to you is: that won't wash. If she's guilty, the FCA will prove it.'

'Exactly, and as whistle-blowers we will remarket ourselves as reformed sinners. Holier than thou. The safest place to invest your money. It's a great angle.'

'If she's guilty,' said Gabe trying to remind Adam that all this was pure speculation. He had no idea why Adam was so convinced of her guilt.

'Of course she is. That's why we need you to keep an eye on her.'

'Well, so far I haven't even seen her. Yesterday's flight was cancelled so maybe she isn't here at all.'

'Ask reception?'

'Very subtle. This is not some huge faceless hotel. If I asked reception they'd tell her in a second.'

'Well, give them some money not to.' Adam's voice was exasperated, and Gabe could picture him rolling his eyes. As far as his brother was concerned there wasn't a problem that couldn't be solved by throwing more money at it.

'People don't work like that, Adam.'

'They do for the right price.'

'Look, leave it to me but I think you're barking up the wrong tree. If she is here to do some sort of business deal I'd expect her to be staying in Cork city. This place is very isolated.'

'Gabe, I have to say, I'm disappointed. Where's your sense of family duty? You know what this did to the old man. For the love you owe him, can you please get a grip and find out what she is up to.'

'How many more times? Don't try to blackmail me like this. You know I'll do anything for our father, but I am not some pet lawyer, you have your own guys for that.'

'Well, we can hardly send them, can we? You are there in a strictly unofficial capacity. Find her and find out what she's up to.'

With that he ended the phone call. Gabe glared at the phone and then sighed. His half-brother was an arse. Fancy trying to blackmail him with talk of family and love. Love winning out was not the Harrington way, duty before dishonour was more their thing. What really stank was that he didn't know if Adam was working off his own initiative or if their father had asked but was doing it through his eldest son for a layer of deniability. Gabe was fairly certain his father wouldn't throw his children to the wolves, but he wasn't 100 per cent sure.

Well, he would oblige his father and brother, and keep an eye out for Miss de Foix, but in the meantime, he and Letta were off on an adventure.

Walking down to the main foyer, Gabe stopped for a minute to watch Letta who was currently on her hands and knees, laughing with Mrs Devaney. Ohana was scrambling over the two enormous wolfhounds. The shaggy beasts were sprawled in front of the empty hearth sniffing Ohana in amusement as she walked across their heads and fell down their noses, onto their legs.

As Letta's hair kept falling forward she would tuck it behind her ear but as it wasn't quite long enough it would fall forward again, causing her to fidget constantly. Pulling his phone out he grabbed a few quick shots and then came and joined them.

'Well, it looks as though Ohana will be in good hands,' he said lightly.

Letta turned quickly and smiled up at Gabe. 'Aren't they fabulous? Look at them – they don't seem to mind at all. In fact, Mairead says that they are cousins, Ohana is a hound, just like them.'

'Here, look, I took some photos. I thought you might like them.' Letta flicked through them and gave Gabe her number and he pinged them across.

Mairead Devaney shook her head at the simplicity of modern technology and got up from her knees. She was somewhat slower than Letta, but her smile was just as bright. 'They don't mind at all.' She brushed down her front and continued, 'Now look, reports are that this storm is going to be a big one, so you'd better be getting yourselves back sooner rather than later. If you get caught out and the waves are breaking over the causeway we'll put you up on the mainland.'

'Does that happen a lot?' said Letta curiously.

'Once or twice a year. More often in winter but the occasional summer storm can catch us on the hop as well.'

Letta looked at Gabe in alarm. 'Do you think this is a good idea?'

'Absolutely.' He sat down opposite Nick and watched as Mairead returned to the office with Ohana. 'What's the worst that can happen?'

'We could be swept out to sea?' she laughed nervously.

'Nonsense. I shall be like Canute and tell the tide to turn back.'

'You know the point of that story was that Canute wasn't capable of turning back the tide.'

'Fair point and correct. I shall be Moses then, and part the Atlantic Ocean.'

'Moses it is then,' laughed Letta and slapped her hand decisively on the coffee table. Just as she did so, the wind caught a door in some unseen corridor and slammed shut, making both of them jump.

'Do you normally have a soundtrack to your life?' asked Gabe.

'It's an East End thing,' she nodded, playing along. 'We all have one; you can barely make it through the day without hearing the drums going off.'

Letta laughed and then banged out the closing drum-line to *EastEnders* on the tabletop. Gabe joined in miming a drummer finishing his set on the top hat.

'I never realised you were all so afflicted,' grinned Gabe.

'It is a nightmare,' said Letta. 'At least once a week, some owner is shouting at you to get out of their pub. Even if you are just in the fruit and veg shop.'

'You have fruit and veg shops? I thought it was all pie and mash?'

'One fruit and veg shop per every ten pie and mash. It's the law, plus we need to think of the children.'

'Ah yes,' he put on a fake David Attenborough voice, 'and here we see a typical "EastEnder" discussing the single most important aspect of their lives, *the faamly*.' Gabe said *faamly* in proper *EastEnders* fashion making Letta snort, which made him laugh loudly.

'Well, *faamly*, as you say, is terribly important. Given that we are all actually related to the Kray twins and we all love our mums, it is vital that we don't get confused.'

'Is it true that you all have to have *Mum* tattooed on you?'

'At birth,' agreed Letta.

'And what about *Dad*?'

'No, silly. We don't acknowledge our father until he is either released from prison, returns from Spain, or following a TV show, we discover that our auntie's boyfriend is actually our father. Or brother. It depends. There's an annual lottery where we are awarded the next storyline in our lives.'

'Do you get told in advance?'

'As if. If we knew, there would be no need for the drums.'

Gabe tipped his head at how well Letta had played out the conversation. He couldn't remember when he had enjoyed just hanging out with a girl. Certainly, he knew lots of fast-witted, clever girls but something about Letta just seemed calmer.

She didn't seem to be putting on an act or trying to impress anyone, and that gave off a very relaxed vibe. He was glad he had offered to drive, spending time in her company would be no chore at all. He had already spoken to Mrs Devaney and she had explained the route. Just in case Letta's skills weren't up to scratch it was always good to be prepared. Not that he would tell her that. There was no need to let her know he didn't have 100 per cent trust in her, he just found that in his line of work it was better to cover all eventualities.

–

As they headed outside, Nick rolled her eyes at Gabe as he opened the door of the car for her. She was enjoying the banter with Gabe and looking forward to the day ahead.

'Thank you. I had completely forgotten my arms had fallen off.'

Gabe got into the car and shrugged his shoulders, smiling. 'Didn't you hear the drum roll when you lost your arms? Besides which, it's just how I was brought up. If I failed to open the door, it would say more about me than it would about you. Incidentally, I'm fine with you getting the door for me as well.'

'Would we ever get anywhere if we spent all day running around the car, opening the door for each other?'

'Let's take turns? Now then navigator, which way?'

Nick nodded, pleased with how Gabe had responded. Sometimes men could get so huffy. She too had been in a household where good manners were required, but she had noticed that too often, those good manners masked a belief that women were somehow inferior. So far her instincts about Gabe were spot on, he was one of the good guys.

Pulling the roadmap out of the bag that Mairead gave her, she gave it a quick glance them smiled at Gabe and looked ahead.

'Turn left after the causeway, then take the second right for good views, or the third right for a quicker drive.'

'Shall we take the third right then? We won't see anything in this rain, plus there's no point in dawdling, is there?' Nick agreed and Gabe quickly glanced over at the map on her lap. 'Did you get all that from the map?'

Nick looked at it again and it did seem to tally with what she had just said.

'No, I spoke to Mairead and checked it out on Google Earth as well.'

'Proper Girl Guide then, "Be prepared".'

'Girl Guide? Not likely.'

'D of E then? Good at map reading.'

Nick looked at him blankly.

'Duke of Edinburgh?'

'Ah yes, posh kids club.' Nick regularly saw references to Duke of Edinburgh on the CVs that came across her desk. Basically, it was a scheme that got teenagers to improve fitness, community involvement and skills. In all honesty it sounded excellent, but it tended to be offered in private schools rather than state ones.

Gabe frowned briefly and appeared to be about to say something. Instead, he smiled reflectively as he started up the engine.

Chapter 18

As they drove across the causeway, Nick looked at the beach in surprise.

'Tides always catch me out. This was all water when I arrived, now it's covered with dog walkers and children playing. It's very rugged though, isn't it?'

'I like it. Reminds me of Cornwall,' said Gabe fondly.

'I was thinking that!' exclaimed Nick. 'My sister lives in Cornwall and it looks identical.'

'Does she live on an island?'

Nick smiled; she could imagine Paddy as a princess in a castle on an island. 'Not at all but she does live by the sea.'

Gabe paused, distracted by a roundabout, then continued talking. 'So, what do you do?'

Nick scowled. *Talk about a pertinent question.* She really wanted to get away from questions about her life right now. She was finally beginning to relax and was enjoying the sensation of having run away from her problems.

'Sorry, I forgot Ohana was a leaving present, wasn't she? Okay then, what's next for you?'

Nick thought about it. Ohana wasn't exactly a leaving present unless Daisy was actually going to resign but the whole thing was too messy to try and explain. Besides which, she was having fun and didn't want to spoil it.

'I'm here to do some family research. Dad was from around these parts so I thought I would have a look at the family tree. See if I can discover anything. What about you?'

'Family business as well, as it happens. My father has asked me to check in on a competitor. Or rather my brother did on his behalf. It's not very edifying, is it? Running around snooping after a total stranger. But how do you say no to family?'

'I think sometimes people forget how important family is. I'd do anything for mine.' Nick thought about how she and her sisters were all working for the same goal, using their own particular talents. They had always pulled together; the inheritance had just given them more things to do. The goal was still the same. Family first. 'So, are you all in the family firm? That must be nice?'

Gabe frowned and shook his head.

'Not a bit of it. I'm a barrister and Rafe, my brother, is a property developer.'

Gabe had expected Nick to be interested – even hopefully a little impressed; he was proud of his brother's accomplishments – instead, she scowled and looked out the window. Given that she had just left her job, maybe it had been under tricky circumstances. He wanted to clarify that Rafe wasn't the same brother as Paul but looking at her face he didn't think now was the time to try and explain the Harrington dynasty. Deciding that discretion was the better part of valour he changed the subject and tasked her with tuning in to a local radio station.

'I don't like the look of those clouds.'

Nick looked up at the sky. *How did people do that? Know what different clouds meant.* So far as she knew if they were dark it was going to rain, and those were very dark clouds.

'Thug clouds.'

Gabe laughed making Nick smile. She liked his laugh, it was easy and it made his face glow. She liked the way a dimple on one cheek showed when he smiled but the dimple on the other appeared only when he laughed. Which he was doing now.

'Loitering with intent.'

Heading to Cork they made up silly charges for various weather phenomena. Hail got GBH, rainbows were clearly conmen, wind obviously was charged with gross indecency. Then Gabe entertained Nick with tales of his grandmother who said that children who broke wind at the dinner table would be forced to eat all their sprouts. 'Which always made the situation worse!'

'Oh my God, I always wanted a granny but not one that made you eat brussels sprouts!'

'She had far worse punishments that that, she used to pinch us. Hard enough to leave a bruise and if we complained she made our father spank us.'

'Bloody hell. That's child abuse.'

'No. Just "eccentric" behaviour. We used to hate visiting her, but happily when he divorced Mum, we weren't as welcome anymore.'

'Did you still get to see your dad? Or did he kick you all out?'

'After all that investment in our education? Not a chance. As I said from time to time he still calls in the odd favour. Honestly, it's like being in *The Godfather*.'

'Do you mind? What if you had wanted to do something else?'

'Like be a train driver?'

'You wanted to be a train driver?'

'Doesn't every five-year-old?'

'No.'

'Well, what did you want to be when you were five?'

'I wanted to not be a twin.'

'Oh, well now, that I can understand. Are you identical?'

'No, but Paddy wished we were so she would copy everything I did and wore.'

'Oh, that's tough, I'm a twin as well. We're identical but Mum encouraged us to dress differently and always allowed us to choose our own hairstyles.'

Nick started laughing. She loved finding out people were twins as it was an immediate shorthand to a familiar upbringing. No matter what walk of life you came from or how dissimilar you seemed, the minute you mentioned you were a twin, the other party immediately understood you.

'We both used to have really long wavy hair; mine was almost black, hers was red. If I put it in a ponytail she begged Mum for the same, if I undid a plait, Paddy would copy me immediately. It drove me insane.'

'So what did you do?' asked Gabe, despite paying attention to the traffic. They were heading towards the edge of the city and the roads were filling up.

'Who says I did anything?'

'Well, you strike me as the sort of person that sees a problem and fixes it.'

'Is that how you see me?' asked Nick, relieved. 'I thought after my appalling dog-in-lost-bag routine, you might think I was a total airhead?'

'It *was* a convincing performance,' nodded Nick. He kept his eyes on the road, but she could see he was smiling, teasing her. 'Although, prior to that, I thought you were actually away with the fairies.'

'What?' She wondered what on earth she had done to give anyone that impression of herself. It seemed an alien concept.

'Well, you kept talking to yourself.'

'But I was talking to Ohana,' Nick protested.

'Yes, because naturally when you see someone anxiously muttering to themselves, you instantly assume they are in fact talking to a dog in a bag.'

'Oh God, I wonder if anyone else thought I was deranged?'

Gabe paused and appeared to think about it.

'How long had you been chatting to Ohana?'

'Since London.'

'Well then, I imagine that only a few thousand people saw you, and assumed that you had been at the sherry. Frankly, in London, you probably blended in.'

'Probably as credible as talking to the fairies here then.' Nick paused and groaned. 'God, I must have looked totally unhinged.'

'Sorry. I shouldn't wind you up. I doubt anyone even noticed. I just like people watching. But we've become diverted. Tell me how you stopped your sister copying your hairstyle.'

Nick explained how she got her mother's fabric scissors and hacked at her own hair until it lay in strands around her feet. Paddy had instantly copied her.

'And then she cried for about a week because it turns out she loved her long hair a lot more than looking like her twin.'

'And has your hair been short ever since?'

'Pretty much, although I fancy a change. I'm trying to grow it out but it's driving me wild. Any minute now I may take the razor to it.'

Gabe grinned at the idea of taking home a skinhead to meet his grandmother and then realised he quite liked the idea of taking Letta anywhere.

'Rapunzel or Sinéad O'Connor. You're an all-or-nothing sort of girl, aren't you?'

'I'm a woman who knows what she wants.'

'Very well – and what is it you want right now?'

'Dog food. And lots of it.'

Laughing, the two continued to drive into Cork and headed straight for Clonty's where it turned out that Mrs Devaney had rung ahead, and they were waiting with lots of suggestions suitable for dachshunds.

Chapter 19

As well as bits and pieces for Ohana, Gabe had treated himself to a new pair of boots and Nick had purchased some walking boots and a proper raincoat. They had made plans to explore the area together and Gabe had suggested some suitable outdoor clothes. The drive home was less than an hour so they walked around the city, promising that they would return when it wasn't actually tipping it down. The weather was becoming wild, and both were aware that they had a potentially tricky crossing ahead of them. In the end they decided to skip lunch and head back. Nick felt that had she suggested eating out Gabe would have been all for it, but the thought of waves crashing over the causeway was making her nervous.

As they drove home they laughed and swapped stories of their childhoods. Nick marvelled at the difference in their backgrounds. For all that, though, she noticed Gabe never mentioned his father or his older half-siblings. How odd to have family that you didn't want to talk about. Still, they chatted about all and everything and fell into a relaxed banter until they approached Ballinfeen. Gabe pulled the car to one side as the pair of them looked at the sea, Nick worrying that they had left it too late to get back onto the island.

The tide was already halfway up the shore and the waves were crashing along the base of the causeway. The road sat a good two metres above the beach but now the occasional spray from a large wave slapped onto its surface.

Nick bit her lip. 'Do you think it's safe?' She didn't want to sound nervous, but she was completely out of her comfort zone.

'Absolutely fine, but I can see why Mrs Devaney said to be back before high tide. Ready?'

Nick appreciated Gabe's matter-of-fact tone and calmed down. After all, a bit of spray wouldn't hurt anyone. Gabe was driving slowly, conscious of shingle and seaweed on the road already. Ahead the island rose up offering warmth and safety if they could just get to it. As they watched the island a huge plume of white water rose up on one side of it and Nick gasped in wonder.

'That was amazing!' Turning to Gabe she was surprised to see concern on his face. 'It's okay, the wave was over there.'

'Waves don't stop, Letta, until they get to the shore. Hang on, this might be bumpy.'

Gabe started to drive quickly – he would happily drive on a punctured tyre, but he didn't want to be stuck on the causeway when that wave reached them.

'Ugh!' cried Nick in alarm as rain and wind blew in the window. 'Put the windows back up!'

'If we get pushed into the sea, the electrics will fail. You'll need to swim out of the window.'

'What! Should I undo my belt now?' Nick couldn't keep the fear out of her voice as Gabe sped towards the island, and the wave raced towards them.

'No, it's coming in sideways. Keep your belt on until we hit the water.'

Nick watched as the white plume moved towards them, crashing on rocks as it made landfall. Ahead of the white plume surged a lump of water, a beast of a wave heading towards them.

'Fuck!' The wave broke over the end of the causeway ahead of them. Gabe drove the car to the side of the road nearest the wave and stopped. 'Hang on.'

Nick looked at him in horror and he grabbed her hand smiling. 'It will be fine. Worst thing that will happen will be that we get a bit wet. Actually, look at it. I don't think it will be that bad.'

The two of them watched as the white spray hit the road, as the wave rolled towards the shore, the foam getting closer.

'It's only the spray, not the wave itself. In fact, windows up!'

A second later they were engulfed. A giant bucket's worth of water landed on the roof of the car and for a second all Nick could see was water and then just like that, the road was clear ahead of her.

Apologising for her small scream she turned to Gabe who was soaked but grinning back at her.

'I didn't get the window up in time!' he gasped, laughing at her.

'You look like you've been for a swim.'

'I think I drank some of it too. Come on, let's not wait for the next one.'

The car started first time and Gabe carefully drove back through the debris that the wave had left on the road. For a moment Gabe had thought it would be touch and go. He knew the water had the power to shift the car which was why he had driven to one side of the road. He had planned on still being on the road after the wave had passed them by. Now he felt exhilarated, and he grabbed Letta's hand and gave it a quick squeeze. She had been brilliant.

The pair of them dashed into the hotel as the wind and rain pulled at their clothes, dropping bags everywhere and laughing as they did so. A team of staff laden with towels met them, having seen their drive across the causeway.

'That was a rogue wave and a half. You handled it well,' said one of the porters with a nod of satisfaction. 'Mind you, you look like you went for a bit of a swim.'

Gabe explained how at the last second he realised the wave wasn't big enough to push them off the causeway, so he tried to get his window back up in time.

'There's not many would have thought to drop the window in the first place.'

'It's the first thing they teach you in D of E,' giggled Nick weakly and was cheered when Gabe replied with the *EastEnders* drum roll. The staff watched the pair of them and scratched their heads. The English were a mad lot.

Mrs Devaney joined the crowd with Ohana in her arms, who instantly struggled to join Nick, much to her joy. That tiny little bundle that she had only known a few days was desperate to be with her.

'That's a strong bond you forged already. Clearly you're doing something right.'

Nick tried to play it cool and aloof, but she couldn't help but beam as Ohana tried to lick her face.

'Now you don't want to let her do that,' said Mairead sternly and Nick agreed. Her new little friend was adorable but had awful hygiene.

'Ohana, no. And stop struggling. I need to manage you and the bags.'

Gabe, who had been watching the little reunion with a smile, offered to help but Nick took one look at him and shook her head. 'You need to go and change.'

Gabe wiped his face again, his wet hair dripping in his eyes. 'Agreed. Tell you what, join me for dinner?'

'It's a date,' laughed Nick and followed the porter as he carried her shopping up to her room. *Look at me*, she thought, *I'm one of those women who makes dates with wildly handsome strangers and carries her toy dog around with her. When the hell did that happen?*

--

After the porter left, Nick made up Ohana's dog basket and put some of the new chew toys in there as well. Then she set down some food and water in the bathroom and watched Ohana explore for a bit. Half an hour later Nick discovered that dogs were an excellent source of distraction and she stopped playing with her and fired up her laptop. It came as a shock to realise that she hadn't gone online in the past forty-eight hours. Nick struggled to remember if that had ever happened before.

Making herself a coffee, she settled down and began to run through the markets. After that she read a few blogs and tweets, keeping an eye on trends. A little anomaly would catch her eye and she'd follow that thread seeing what was going on there. Often it led to nothing, sometimes though it yielded interesting results. Making notes, she sent off a quick email to Ari with some suggestions to invest in some places and take money from others. There wasn't much going on, but it was good to keep an eye on things.

Having got everything in order she headed down for dinner, with Ohana asleep in her crate, and spent the next hour laughing with Gabe as they recounted their day. However, by the end she was furious to find herself yawning, then disappointed to see Gabe was yawning as well. Was she so boring? Did he think she was bored of him?

'Oh dear. This sea air is a killer, isn't it?'

'At least you've only had to deal with sea air. I think I still have sand in my hair.'

Nick liked the way he ran his fingers through his mop of hair. It was tousled and longer than she thought a barrister could really get away with but maybe he used the length to play out his boyish charm? Blinking, she realised she may have been staring at him too long and she blushed. God knows she didn't want him to think she was mooning over him.

'Early night for me, I think,' she said in a brisk tone.

'I don't think you'll get much sleep,' said Gabe as a sudden gust of wind howled past the hotel. 'Looks like we're in for quite a night.'

Nick agreed and then left quickly, feeling suddenly awkward. She hadn't worked out a way of leaving Gabe that didn't seem abrupt. The problem was, she thought, that she didn't actually want to leave him. He was such great company that she hated saying goodbye. No doubt he was already wondering what he could do to shake her off.

Chapter 20

The curtains billowed lazily in the breeze and Nick listened to the roar of the sea from outside. She had gone to sleep with the window open and the sea air had allowed her to sleep like the dead. At some point in the night the storm had become too violent, and she had closed the windows, but it looked like they might have a draught.

Ohana had been whimpering in the night and Nick was worried about disturbing the other guests. She scooped the little dog up and placed her on the bed by her feet and watched in amusement as Ohana fell straight back into a slumber.

Don't think you're sleeping on my bed when we get home.

Nick threw back the curtains and laughed at what she saw. Grabbing her phone off the bedside table, she took a quick photo and pinged a text to Paddy. Almost immediately a text came back.

Is that seaweed?

Yes!!!!

> OMG. I thought you were on the second floor?

> I AM.

> Wow. Wild night!

Wild night indeed. Nick signed off saying she was off to breakfast in a bit. If Paddy was texting rather than picking up the phone it meant that she didn't want to disturb Eleanor.

It was funny: growing up Nick desperately didn't want to be a twin and had done everything to disassociate herself from Paddy. Now in her twenties with Paddy's attention focussed on Hal and Elly, Nick suddenly felt the separation like a constant sad tug.

Her phone pinged again.

> Love you. Chat later.

Smiling, Nick put the phone back and headed to the shower. Ohana was asleep on the bed so Nick let her sleep, last night had been wild. The wind had screamed all around the castle, her windows had whistled, and she had jumped out of bed several times, convinced that the latches had come loose. There had been a huge crash at one point, and for a second Nick had thought the house was falling down. Eventually she and Ohana stopped shaking and fell asleep at about four in the morning, when it seemed that the force of the storm had passed through.

Having showered, she put food and water down in the bathroom for Ohana and woke her up. The little dog stretched out her long body and then gave a huge yawn, her little tongue curling back in her mouth. Nick put her on the floor and laughed as she instantly started running around the room and then dashed straight towards her food. Happy that Ohana was occupied, she got dressed and looked out the window again. The sea was still a cauldron of big white waves and the dark skies promised more rain. A large white gull tried to fly through the wind and Nick hoped that it would quickly get to dry land. Her shoulders felt sore just looking at that bird sweeping up and down against the black clouds.

Ohana attacked her foot and she realised with a start that she had been standing at the window watching the waves for too long. She had arranged to join Gabe for breakfast at eight and it was already ten past.

She threw on her clothes, popped Ohana on her lead and hurried downstairs. Walking through the foyer she saw a lot of people milling around the front door but didn't stop to see what was going on, too busy looking forward to seeing Gabe. The breakfast room was already full, and she scanned the room for him. It didn't take long as he stood up as she walked in and headed over.

'Good morning, Letta the Bold!'

Nick grinned. Gabe must have been watching the entrance waiting for her to come down. He reminded them of their shared adventure yesterday on the causeway. She clicked her heels together and offered him a quick bow.

'And a good morning to you, Gabriel the Brave.' Laughing, she pulled her chair out and sat down. 'So tell me, did you sleep better with a coachload of tourists or with a raging storm?'

Gabe poured Nick a coffee and grinned. 'My night was full of drama. A tree fell in the courtyard and smashed my window. Three a.m. and I was covered in wet leaves. I've never had so many adventures before. I blame you.'

Nick stared at him in alarm. He seemed remarkably chipper about something that would have terrified her.

'Are you serious? I mean about the tree?'

'God's honest. I imagine that's what the brouhaha in the hall is about. Trying to make the tree safe and secure the damaged rooms.'

'You seem so calm?'

'Always got to look on the upside. I got an upgrade into their family suite. It's huge and well away from my noisy neighbours. Unless you and Ohana decide to start howling.'

'We don't howl. But my God, the wind did last night.'

'Yes. I know.'

Nick groaned, of course he knew. Still, it was nice that he was in the main house now, she thought, although she wasn't prepared to investigate too deeply why she thought that. A holiday romance was the last thing on her mind; yet there was something about Gabe that felt so natural.

Just then, Mairead Devaney entered the room and clapped her hands together attracting the attention of all the guests.

'As you are all aware we had quite a storm last night.' She paused for a few chuckles and then carried on. 'Unfortunately, it has caused some issues. Some of you have already been inconvenienced by finding a tree in your bedrooms. However, the bigger concern is the causeway. It was damaged by the waves and is not currently safe to drive on.'

The room erupted as people called out, some getting to their feet. Nick and Gabe exchanged glances and waited for the guests to settle down.

'Highway engineers will be along at low tide to assess the damage, that will be around lunchtime. Can I ask that you all come back here at 1 p.m. so that we can update you? The main issue is that at the moment the seas are too rough to land a boat and at low tide you won't be able to drive off, but you may be able to walk off. Obviously, we know the issue is your cars but don't worry, we are dealing with this. In the meantime, please try and enjoy your breakfast and if anyone has an urgent need to be off the island, please come to reception now.'

Mrs Devaney left the room and Nick wanted to see if she could help, although at the moment she knew that she was as likely to get in the way.

'Bloody hell, trapped on an island. The adventure continues,' said Nick, who loved reading crime novels. 'Who do you think the first victim will be?'

Gabe choked on his coffee and laughing, began to look around the room.

'Him. The guy that wears his slippers into the dining room. Something very off about him.'

Nick loved the fact that Gabe instantly got the direction she was going in and the two of them spent a silly few minutes deciding who the murderer was and what the motive would be. They only stopped when Roisin came over to take their order.

'All go this morning, so it is. I've got a date this evening with Patrick and if I can't get off this fecking island there'll be ructions. I've been waiting for him to ask for months and now this. What if I can't make it and he doesn't ask me again?'

'He will if he's worth it,' said Gabe reassuringly. 'He's probably shy and has been building up the courage to ask you out.'

'As if. Patrick Donlan is the finest around. He has girls tripping over him.'

'Well, it might do him some good to be stood up then,' said Nick tartly. 'Like Gabe says, if he's into you he'll ask again, or better yet why don't you ask him? Just call him up and reschedule?'

Roisin rolled her eyes. 'So, the thing ye don't understand is that if I don't go on this date tonight he won't realise we're supposed to be together. He'll go out with someone else and that could be that. He finds his soulmate and it's not me!'

'Well, then you weren't supposed to be together,' said Gabe. 'I think it'll be fine.'

'Aye, it's all right for ye two. You've already found each other. All that laughing together and talking on about being adventurers and every time one of ye thinks the other isn't looking ye keep staring at each other. That's what I want. I want Patrick to look at me the way you look at Letta. Anyways, what can I get you?'

As Roisin left with their order the pair of them stared awkwardly at the tablecloth. Gabe tried to break the ice.

'Teenagers.'

'What do they know?'

'Exactly.'

The silence fell again. Nick didn't know what to do with it – it was like a large, misshapen lump that had landed on the table in front of them and kept swallowing anything she thought to say. The idea that Gabe was indeed staring at her flooded her with little giggles. She had been attracted to him almost immediately, he was clever and fast-witted but more importantly he made her laugh. She had laughed more this trip than in the past year but now she didn't know how to proceed. At that moment Ohana started to get restless and Nick thanked every saint she could think of as the dog peered around.

'Here, give me her lead,' said Gabe, 'I'll take her outside for a quick leg stretch. Call me when food arrives.'

Nick tried to protest but Gabe waved her off, telling her to enjoy her coffee. She had his number already. Gabe thought ahead and took charge of things, he was very much a kindred spirit.

When he returned to the table he was full of cheer.

'I just checked with Mrs Devaney and all the hotel's guests are currently here in the dining room. Which means that the person my father wanted me to keep an eye on isn't here and I can now officially play hooky. So, can I help you today with your research? Or entertain Ohana, or both? Maybe at lunch we can take a stroll around the island and inspect the damage. That's if the rain stops?'

Gabe was positively bouncy; it was clear that he had been reluctant to follow his father's wishes and Nick couldn't blame him. Sometimes working for the family was tough.

'That sounds like a plan. Help me with the research until you get bored then maybe play with Ohana and come and get me for the walk?'

With the plan made they agreed to meet over at the records office at nine.

Chapter 21

Grinning, Nick headed back to her room. Today was going to be a good one. As she gathered her laptop and notebook, her phone rang and she smiled as Paddy's face filled the screen.

'Hello, you! What's Ireland like? Have you found out anything about Dad yet?'

'Not a thing, but my trip so far has been eventful.'

'Eventful?' said Paddy intrigued. 'Clem eventful or Ari eventful?'

'Clem eventful.'

Nick smiled as she heard Paddy exclaim loudly and watched as she settled down into a sofa. 'I need all the details right now! Quick, before Elly wakes.'

And so Nick told Paddy all about the little dog and horrible crossing.

'—and Gabe says Ohana means "family", so I thought that sounded like the perfect name.'

Paddy had been listening as attentively to what her sister wasn't saying as to what she was. And for the first time in weeks she hadn't mentioned the investigations once. Nor did she seem particularly focussed on the reason for her trip to Ireland: to find out more about their father. If anything she sounded a bit scatty.

'And Gabe is?'

'Oh, he's another guest staying here. In fact, he's helping me with the research as the causeway is broken and we're all stuck on the island. It's a huge adventure,' she said happily.

'An adventure? You're stranded on an island with a stranger called Gabe and a dog called Ohana?'

'I know. Mad, isn't it?' Nick rarely spoke freely and the only person she did that with was her twin but now she was positively chatty. 'I don't know. I just feel reckless. And Gabe is a great person, he's got a great sense of humour and he's really—'

—

'—fascinating. I know it sounds daft. I've only just met her after all, but there's just something about her.'

Gabe laughed self-consciously down the phone as he heard his brother snort.

'You're supposed to be there to work. Not fall for some dog-toting airhead.'

'She is *not* an airhead. Did I mention she speaks Mandarin? She was just out of sorts when she arrived.'

'And you had to ride in and rescue her?'

'No, I—' Gabe broke off. There was no point in trying to hide anything from his brother. 'Anyway, I can't snoop on Nick Byrne because she's not here. Plus you know I thought this was a fool's mission. Anyone that smart is unlikely to leave herself vulnerable just because she has left the city. In the meantime, I will entertain myself as I see fit.'

'And does that entertaining involve a certain Letta?' Gabe chuckled sheepishly and Rafe continued. 'Honestly, I'm just teasing. Have fun. In a way I'm glad you didn't meet Nick Byrne. I'm fed up with our brothers yanking our chains. If they were stupid enough to screw up the bank that's on them.'

'So you don't think they were innocent either?'

'Seems unlikely, wouldn't you say? Knowing them as we do. Pretty convenient to have some traders to blame. I mean, clearly those traders were guilty but really, how independently were they working, do you think?'

'I know. We've been over this a thousand times. Father says he knew nothing about it. And I believe him.'

'So what about Byrne?' asked Gabe. 'Do you think she's innocent?'

'Oh, she's probably as bad as them. I'm sick of all of them. People who make money with no care for those they trample on.' Rafe sounded tired and Gabe was concerned, his brother wasn't usually so judgemental.

'Rough day?'

'Sorry, yes. Problems with the property.'

He and Gabe had bought a large dilapidated mansion in the Cotswolds. The main building had burnt in a fire and they were living in the east wing and renovating the west wing. The goal was to sell both halves when all the work was done. They were hoping that there would be enough profit for Gabe to start up his own firm and for Rafe to do the same. Both brothers wanted to be their own bosses and were working hard towards that goal.

At the moment, Gabe was working for a corporate law firm with strong ties to the Harrington business. He was using his salary to support the build, while Rafe had invested all his savings. This was their biggest project to date and Gabe was feeling the stress of it all. He wanted to set up his own firm but right now he and his brother couldn't risk the drop in income.

'Tell me about the house. What's wrong?'

Gabe listened as Rafe let out a deep sigh. He could picture his twin pulling at his hair in frustration.

'We've lost our site quantity surveyor – he's ill – and now lots of things are going awry. I'm trying to keep an eye on it, but my actual job is currently up in Northumberland and I'm a bit stretched.'

Gabe tried to think of a way to cheer his brother up. All he could do was reassure him that he knew he was working flat out.

After they'd hung up Gabe sighed. The house build was hopefully going to make them enough money but at the moment all he could do was pay the bills. Which meant doing his half-siblings' bidding: if they told him to jump he had better have a spring in his step.

Shaking his head, he decided to focus on the day ahead. At least that was something to look forward to. Who knew family research could hold so much appeal? Checking himself in the mirror he grinned and then headed off to the archives. A date with a girl in the stacks. He smiled, hoping he wasn't making a nuisance of himself, he wondered how he could make himself useful to her, without coming across as over eager.

Chapter 22

Gabe left the hotel foyer and crossed the courtyard into a large single-storey brick building. It had clearly been constructed in the seventies and owed all its charms to that decade. When the convent had been renovated into a hotel the architects had done all they could to improve it by surrounding it with high hedges, so that no one outside would have to look at it, and those inside would hopefully be too preoccupied to have noticed the loss of any view. Inside it was basically a large reading room with long desks with microfiche readers set up, and rows of shelves lined with bound newspapers lying spine down. There was a smaller section for books, but the majority of the shelves were lined with box files.

There was a reception desk but there was no one at it. Gabe wandered in and heard voices as he passed the vacant tables. Apart from the voices coming from the shelves the room seemed empty. As he got closer he could hear Letta's voice murmuring softly, then pausing to listen to the reply. He walked down a corridor flanked by tall shelves and saw an open door at the end. Walking through, he found himself in a large room of map drawers and filing cabinets.

'Hello, Gabe,' said Letta with a smile, 'isn't this place incredible? Talk about off the grid.'

'One day we'll get it all digitised but we're starting with the oldest stuff first to avoid further wear,' Mrs Devaney said, shrugging her shoulders apologetically. 'In the meantime, if you are after recent records then you have to use the CD-ROMs and fiches. You also have access to the online national database, which speeds it up a bit, but not much as you are looking through modern records and lots of that is restricted.'

She held up a birth certificate and looked at it. From her brief glance it was clear to Gabe that she had already examined it.

'You've your father's mother on here and his place and date of birth. Given that he was a local, so to speak, you may get lucky. He may have been one of the children that passed through the convent. If so, you might find some clues in their records.' She turned to Gabe. 'Come on then, make yourself useful.'

Heading towards one of the shelving units she pulled off a large ledger and handed it to Gabe, grinning as he sagged under the unexpected weight of it.

'You've got the place to yourselves today so you can set up anywhere.' She grabbed a second book and headed back to the main room. Letta followed carrying a collection of small microfiche boxes. She shooed him in front of her, laughing at the look on his face when Mrs Devaney handed him a ledger.

'Reckon she could have you in an arm wrestle.'

Gabe wanted to protest but he wasn't convinced she couldn't, so he made a joke about Weetabix that made Nick laughed. Cheered, he followed the two ladies into the reading room where Mrs Devaney was setting up a microfiche and laying out some more books.

'You may as well have the whole table. Don't forget to stop for lunch. No eating or drinking in here mind. And don't worry about Ohana, she's having a whale of a time annoying her cousins.'

Gabe remembered the tedium of poring over old ledgers and court cases as a law student, trying to find kernels of information. This was no different, although this time he was looking for a single name, Michael John Byrne. As he studied the records he wished that Letta's father had been called Algernon or Caruthers or anything equally unusual. From time to time they would stumble across a Michael Byrne or a John Byrne, born in the right year but in the wrong county, or in the right county but in the wrong year. On each occasion, Letta wrote them down in her notebook with the source they had found them in and then they returned to the hunt.

Eventually, Gabe's stomach rumbles became so loud that Letta looked up in alarm.

'Was that you!'

'I was going to blame Ohana, but I don't think that will wash.' He grinned apologetically and looked at his watch. 'It's half one, shall we stop for lunch?'

Letta looked back at the screen, slowly scrolling the dials and moving the text on the microfiche projector forward.

'Hang on.' She paused, read something and looked over her shoulder to the archives. He could see from her expression that she was on to something and was debating how much she needed to eat.

'No, you go on. I think I have something.'

He left, promising to take Ohana for a walk. Letta was already heading off into the back archive. It had been a long time since he had been that focussed on a piece of work and he envied her her dedication. The way the tedium of the research could suddenly spark into joy, as a lead finally revealed itself. As a boy he'd loved puzzles and it was something that had stayed with him as an adult. It was what made him so good at his job.

In truth, he felt he would have been a better investigator or researcher than a barrister, but his father had had other ideas. His mother would have supported him whatever he chose but he felt he had a duty to his father. Looking back he knew his father had manipulated both boys. Every time he wanted them to do something he would make some oblique or often blatant comment about the pain they had caused by taking their mother's name. One silence, one brief pause and Gabriel and Raphael would both instantly comply with what he wanted. By the time they realised his game, they were already on the path to their new futures.

And as much as Gabe enjoyed his job, nothing, as they say, sparked joy. Saving millions of pounds for corporations was fairly dull. There was the satisfaction of a job well done, a puzzle unknotted, an opponent thwarted. But over the past twenty-four hours he had suddenly remembered the silly in life. He also found himself wanting to brag and show off. Quite frankly Letta had turned him back into a teenager.

Whistling, he retrieved Ohana and took her for a walk around the island.

Chapter 23

Willie was out beachcombing. Last night's storm had been fierce and there was bound to be a few interesting things thrown up in the tideline. A tall man with a small, silly dog was walking towards him. The dog had tiny legs and looked little a millipede as it ran along. Willie ducked his head down again. He wasn't in the mood to talk to tourists who were after their roots, thrown up in the storm and adrift on the tides. All this travelling away meant the next generation didn't know who they were and floundered. At eighty years of age, he'd seen enough of humanity to know that if you didn't hang tight this world would wash you away.

'Found anything?'

The Englishman had walked over and was now turning over piles of seaweed with the toes of his deck shoes.

'Just some driftwood.' He looked back at the sand.

'What sort of thing do you look for?'

'Peace and quiet mostly.'

The Englishman laughed and then apologised. 'I shall leave you to it then, but if I find anything, I'll give you a shout.'

Willie cursed under his breath; it wasn't the stranger's fault that he had had a bad night worrying about the damage the storm was wreaking on his garden. Nor was it his fault that his knee had swollen up to the size of a turnip.

'Ah sure, don't mind me. I was going to stop for a coffee if you'd care to join me. I can show you some of my finds? I might even have a dog biscuit for the small one?'

Willie liked to have a treat for Mrs Devaney's hounds, and they made a point of running out to his cottage on a daily basis. As the two men walked up from the shore, Willie looked up at his cottage roof – from the sea, it was a long old climb up to the front door but at least it meant that when the waves crashed they didn't do so on his house. Still, last night hadn't been without issues.

'Oh, what's happened here?'

Willie looked at the collapsed wall of the old pigsty in bemusement. Any idiot could see what had happened here.

'Wall fell down.'

'In last night's storms?'

Well, when else? thought Willie. Did this man think he'd grown his runner beans under the collapsed bricks? Willie grunted. Small talk just made people sound foolish and he was already regretting the offer of a coffee. He was walking to the front door when he realised that the stranger hadn't followed but had instead let the dog off its lead and was beginning to move the bricks off the beans.

'I thought I'd stack them on the other side of the shed?' the man said as he glanced over at Willie.

Willie looked at him in amazement. He had rolled his sleeves up and was working diligently, carefully picking up bricks and moving them over to the lee of the old pigsty. He held one of the bricks up to Willie.

'Not much mortar on these, is there? Makes it easier in a way.'

Willie was still dumbfounded. 'How's that?'

'Well, if they were properly mortared they'd have come down in a large lump and been harder to move.'

'If they'd been properly bonded they wouldn't have come down at all. I'll bring out a coffee.'

Gabe watched as the grumpy old sod walked into the cottage, and laughed to himself. Maybe when he got to be that old he'd say what he thought as well, instead of always being polite. Pulling his jumper up over his head, he hung it over an upright shovel and got to work. The wind was still strong, and the clouds threatened rain, but he quickly built up a sweat moving the bricks. This cottage was the last on the island before it dropped away on the cliffs. Gabe couldn't imagine it had more than four rooms, but it was a pretty little building and mostly well maintained. The old pigsty had become dilapidated and now, after a big blow, it had collapsed.

'There you go.'

Will looked into a mug of pale brown liquid and wondered if he would be able to drink that without pulling a face. Instead, he smiled and said thank you and pointed to the bamboo canes.

'You start repairing the runner beans and I'll keep moving the bricks. Should be done in the hour.'

Having finally run out of steam, Ohana curled up under a rhubarb leaf and Gabe took a quick photo.

'Will you forget what she looks like if you don't take a picture?' the old man asked.

'She's not mine, she belongs to a friend who's doing some family research. I thought she'd like the image.'

'Right enough. So it's not yerself trying to find your family?'

Gabe laughed and said he knew exactly where his family was and where they had come from.

'That's a comfort. Knowing your roots are in place. Here, have a look at what happens when you aren't properly anchored.'

Willie brought out a box with the coffees and now both men stopped to look at the bits of flotsam that had ended up on the shore. A necklace of pearls, a Lego octopus, an old tank shell.

'No rhyme or reason, just washed up on the shore like the children.'

Gabe's ears pricked up. 'Children get washed up on the shore?'

'They may as well. No, I mean the children that used to come here. Babes taken from their mothers, little more than girls themselves. Children handed over by couples that didn't have the pennies to feed a tenth child. Babes left in the middle of the night. Each and every one of them severed from their roots. I was caretaker for the nuns back then. You hear some wicked stories, but the nuns here were a kind lot and did their best by their little charges. As did I. We all did, really. God had sent them to us, and we did the best we could.'

By now the two men had finished clearing the vegetable patch.

'Will the beans recover?'

Willie looked at them with a shrug.

'Maybe. Although the yield may not be quite what it should be. Having a wall land on you can certainly slow you down. Come on now indoors I'll show you some more of the flotsam.'

Inside the cottage the rooms were tired and worn. The small kitchen looked like an original fifties arrangement: there was a cooker with an overhead grill and a small freestanding fridge but no washing machine, a shallow metal sink, some cupboards and a table. An open door revealed a bathtub and probably the only loo in the house. To the right of the front door a fireplace was laid with tinder and logs and off the sitting room, Gabe guessed there would be a bedroom behind the door.

'It's not much but it's mine.'

Gabe looked around and smiled. 'It would do me. Although I think I'd want someone to share it with.' Unexpectedly, the thought of Letta staring at the microfiche, absentmindedly answering him, came to mind.

'I can see that from your face. Truth be told, I do miss my wife, but the good Lord saw fit to take her to Himself some years ago and now I just share this place with my memories and photos.'

He pointed to a wall in the sitting room that was completely covered in photos of children laughing, some gurning at the camera. There were also pictures of nuns at work, hanging out laundry, digging in an allotment and the occasional photograph of the old man himself smiling out from his youth.

'Your wife was the photographer then?'

'Yes. Always behind the lens. I've only the one photo of her and that's of us on our wedding day.' He glanced over to his bedroom door and Gabe was certain that that photo sat on the old man's bedside table. Giving the man his privacy he looked along the photos – his wife had had a good eye for catching a mood. These people seemed alive in a way that photographs rarely captured. Looking at the images, he could imagine them turning to him and asking him to pass a peg or lend a hand. What a strange community it must have been on this island of nuns and children. He looked at their faces: what must it have been like to not know your parents or why you had been abandoned? Were they lonely, angry, sad, unwanted or was it a Blyton-like paradise, free of parental interference? Certainly, the children in these photos seemed happy. As he was musing that it likely fell between both camps – different for each child – a familiar face smiled out at him.

'Who's that?'

Gabe pointed to a boy who was standing in a group of children, his arms draped around two of them. The tallest in the bunch, he looked to be about sixteen or seventeen. The boy was wearing the standard brown nylon slacks of the seventies and a tight-fitting orange T-shirt. He had dark curly hair, and even in the photo you could see his eyes were a bright blue; if his hair had been just a touch longer Gabe would swear that he was looking at Letta.

'Let me look now.' The old man shuffled slowly, making his way past the chair as Gabe stepped aside. 'Ah young Mikey Tiger. Lovely lad. Came to us as a boy rather than a baby and left the day he turned seventeen.'

'A boy? How old would he have been?'

'Around five, I'd say. Always rough at that age.'

Gabe tried to understand what that must have been like. He had memories of ski trips with his family from the age of five, his nanny taking the boys out during the day as they learnt how to ski. In summer there were long flights to hot places where people would spend all day running around entertaining him and his brother. In the evening they would join their parents as everyone would tell them how beautiful their mother was and how lucky they were to have such an important father.

The idea of suddenly having all that taken away was hard to comprehend. The misery those children must have endured. Still, he was here to track down Letta's father and despite the uncanny resemblance, the name was wrong.

'Unusual surname?'

'Ah, well now, Tiger was just his nickname, so it was. I think I knew it once, well, I did, of course. But time clears away so much stuff.'

'Could it have been Byrne?'

'Ah that's it, right enough. That's it now. That boy was as fierce as the poem, so the nickname stuck.'

The man paused and nodded.

'Do you know him then?'

'I think my friend might. I think that's her father,' said Gabe excitedly. 'Do you think I can bring her here?'

'Go on then. I'll put the kettle on. Does she prefer tea or coffee?'

Gabe considered Letta's reaction to the coffee and picked tea. Promising that he would be back presently Gabe headed off along the overgrown driveway and returned to the hotel. Dropping Ohana back at the desk with Roisin he hurried over to Letta.

–

The door swung open, and Gabriel dashed into the room.

'I've found him!'

Nick looked up confused. Gabe had been gone for well over an hour and now he had returned missing his jumper and sweaty with bits of mud on his face and hands.

'What?'

'Your father. I think I've found him. Or rather a photo of him. Come on.'

Nick followed Gabe as he led her along an old path past the building and across the island. As they walked Gabe explained that Willie had worked as a caretaker when the nuns used to take in children and now was retired helping out at the hotel as and when.

'He has a wall covered in photos of the children and one face jumped out at me. God, Letta, it practically shouted at me. And when I asked, Willie said the lad's name was Mikey "Tiger" Byrne and the picture was from the seventies. It all fits, doesn't it?'

Gabe was talking ten to the dozen, but Nick was quiet; she wouldn't get her hopes up only to have them dashed. Better to watch and wait.

As they got to a small whitewashed cottage, Nick wondered if the tin roof was terribly noisy in the rain. Gabe's jumper was hanging on a shovel and there was a vegetable patch looking somewhat the worse for wear. She wondered if Gabe had helped or hindered.

The door swung open, and an old man invited them in. He was wearing a shirt and tie, and his hair was slicked back. Nick could smell soap and a small cut on his chin suggested he had just shaved. Inviting her to sit down, he poured her a cup of tea and talked about the weather.

'Now then, miss, before I let you look at the photos just know that if it isn't your da, you're not to fret. It can be a long struggle, patching up an old tear, sometimes the threads aren't always willing to be found.'

Nick wondered at his insightfulness but then he had probably witnessed decades of people coming onto this island trying to find their family. Not all would have been successful.

'Fair enough, let's have a look.' She stood up and followed him into a small sitting room where he pointed to a wall that was covered in photos spanning the decades, all the faces staring out at her. All these unloved, unwanted or desperately missed children. Had their mothers given up on them or had they been torn out of their mother's arms? Were they orphans with no family to take them in? She took a step back from the wave of pain that radiated from the wall.

'Come on, lass, sit down. It can be a lot to take in sometimes.'

Nick shook her head. She had come here to try and find out more about her father, to do something positive for her sisters. She couldn't buckle now that the reality was starting to hit home. 'Sorry, that caught me off guard, but I know these children loved whoever was taking the photos. Look at those smiles. At least they had some sort of happiness here.'

Willie smiled at her softly.

'Oh, that they did. We all did our best by the children. There was some as came to work here that blamed the children for their situation, but Sister Bernard would have none of that. They were soon given their marching orders. That's not to say that the children were perfect, they were divils at times, but we did what we could.'

Nick had remained standing and was running her eyes over the photos. This was a fool's errand – how would she possibly spot her father amongst all these little faces. Her eyes snagged on something and she looked closely at a teenager smiling directly into the camera. If it wasn't just that he reminded her of Ari or Aster, it was simply that he looked like her dad. The girls had some photos of their parents when they had first met in college. This picture could have only been taken a year earlier. Smiling at her across the years and beyond the grave was her own beloved father.

Chapter 24

'Dad.' Nick's fingers gently touched his face. Without asking permission she removed the picture from the wall and looked at him closely. He looked so young and so happy.

'Come on, now. Sit down and let me tell you about Mikey Tiger. I take it he's passed over?'

'How did you know?'

'If he was still with you today you wouldn't be so hungry for a simple image of him. Come on now.'

Nick allowed herself to be guided to the sofa and was aware that Gabe hadn't taken his eyes off her.

'Are you okay?' he asked as the old man went to brew another pot of tea.

'Yes. It's a bit of a shock. I didn't expect to be so successful. To find someone that actually remembers him. As children he told us he had been stolen by pirates and lived on an island full of penguins. He had so many tales that I did wonder if they had in part been based on this place, but I couldn't let myself hope. And of course when he talked about penguins we thought he meant the birds.'

Willie came back in and Gabe jumped up, took the tea tray from him and began to pour three dark-looking cups of tea. Willie's tea was as strong as his coffee was weak and Gabe wondered if his teeth were turning brown with every sip.

'Your father came to us as a boy of maybe four or five, rather than a bairn. I don't know why, the Sisters probably kept records, but it was tough for children at that age. People want to adopt babies. Who wanted a child that cried for his mammy all day and all night?

'Occasionally Mikey would leave and try to settle into a new family, but it never worked out. He was too loyal to his mam and wouldn't settle in the new house, however much they tried to make him feel at home. After a while it wasn't his mam that he called for, but the nuns and the island which was becoming more a home to him than the one of his birth.

'The last time I remember he was about twelve, and what we thought were a nice couple came and took him away. A week later he came walking back along the causeway – he'd hitched and walked all the way from Mallow. When asked about it, he simply said that the man tried to touch him and that no other children should go there.'

Willie shook his head sorrowfully. Nick went very still and was grateful when she felt Gabe hold her hand. She squeezed his fingers and asked Willie to continue.

'A day later the man and his wife arrived with the Garda, claiming that your father had attacked him with a cast iron skillet. Sure enough the man had a black eye and a cut on his forehead. Sister Bernard called me in as a witness – I was one of the few men on the island. And she told the Garda what Mikey had alleged. Oh, there was war. The man was fearful angry, accusing Mikey of being a liar, but it was his Christian duty to give the boy another chance. His wife just sat there, the colour of lard. Sister Bernard then told the Garda that if he didn't escort the couple home immediately she would take her own skillet and finish off Mikey's handiwork!'

'What did the policeman, the Garda, do then?' asked Nick. She hadn't let go of Gabe's hand and felt his strength holding her up.

'Well, now. For all the problems that Ireland has had and the reputation we've gained for shaming mothers and abusing children, the fact is that most of us cared for those children as if they were our own. The Garda warned the couple that if he ever heard of them trying to adopt or foster a child anywhere then he would charge them himself. Having first taken more than a skillet to them.'

'Good,' said Nick fervently. 'So what happened to Dad after that?'

'Well, after that he refused point blank to go anywhere. He was a lovely boy and whilst he could be wild and would sometimes lead raids on the vegetable plots, he was kind at heart and great with the little ones. Eventually the nuns agreed that he should just stay on with them until he was old enough to leave. There were a couple of children like him that never got fostered, and they helped around the convent. Some left as soon as they were able to, others stayed on and became the caretaker.'

He gave a small laugh. 'There have been children on this island for many decades. I reckon I'll be the last of them but it's lovely to meet them when they return, or their children do.'

He passed Nick a biscuit, which she dunked into her tea and ate thoughtfully.

'So he had a happyish childhood?'

'It wouldn't have been perfect, and he missed his mother when he was little but yes, this was a kind enough place.'

'Can I take a photo of this?' said Nick, holding out the image. She wanted to take it with her, but these were Willie's memories and the relatives of the other children in the photo may one day come calling. She took a copy using her phone and leaving the old man in peace, she and Gabe headed back to the archives.

'How are you doing?' asked Gabe. He hadn't let go of her hand and she found that she didn't mind.

'Okay, I think. It's quite a lot to take in. I was looking for my grandmother, but I didn't expect to discover so much about Dad instead.'

'It must be a shock but at least you are much closer to finding out who his mother was. If he came here then the records should still be here as well.'

As they walked back into the archives a young man was seated behind the desk. Gabe explained that the Michael Byrne they were looking for was actually once a resident on the island. After a quick phone conversation the man put down the receiver.

'Mrs Devaney apologises she can't come over as they are in the middle of sorting out solutions for the causeway. However, she did say I could break out the convent records. Given that you are a relative, your father has passed and as he wasn't adopted we have no legal issues with privacy and confidentiality.'

It sounded like a speech that he had had to make many times. Adoption records were strictly embargoed – in fact, family research was in some ways a lot easier once everyone was dead. Searching the recent past was a minefield of privacy issues.

'Come with me.' Grabbing a set of keys he beckoned them to follow him, and they headed to the back of the building. When they got to the microfiche store they turned left instead of right, and the research assistant unlocked the door.

'When you are finished let me know and I'll lock up. You can take copies of anything you find but I'll need to ensure you've only taken stuff directly relating to your da.'

Nodding in agreement, Nick and Gabe headed over to the shelves and pulled out the boxes up to five years after his birth. It didn't take long looking through the ledgers before Nick found an entry that read: *March 18th, Michael Byrne, aged five. Mother Mary Margaret Byrne.*

And that was it. On the next shelf, Gabe found boxes with children's names on them. Looking inside he could see that each box contained the details of a child's time on the island. Closing it quickly he began to scour the shelf until he found Michael Byrne and he brought it back to the table where Nick was still going through the convent records.

'Letta, look. I think the nuns kept the details for each child.'

Lifting the lid, Nick pulled out annual education report cards: *easily distracted, unwilling to apply himself.* She laughed; she could be reading Clem's report cards. Then there were details of many unsuccessful placements, each shorter than the last.

Finally at the bottom, the nuns had kept some of his work, poems and drawings. If nothing else told her this was her father as a teenager, the artwork did. Even as a young student his style and talent were undeniable. At the bottom were a few photos of him. As a child he'd glared at the camera but as he'd grown older the glare had been replaced with a laugh and Nick was glad that her father had learnt some happiness.

'I wonder why he left so abruptly?'

'A seventeen-year-old boy on an island full of nuns?' asked Gabe. 'I bet he couldn't wait to go and explore.'

In spite of the solemnity of Nick's findings her stomach gurgled. Gabe pointed out that she hadn't stopped for lunch and it was now closer to dinner.

'Why don't you put this away for the day? It will still be here in the morning and now you have a new name to search for: Mary Margaret Byrne.'

Overcome with tiredness, Nick nodded. Locking up the room they headed back over to the hotel.

Up in her room she had a quick shower to revive herself and then set up a group chat on her phone and shared the photos she had taken so far with her sisters. The next hour was a flurry of texts as the girls asked questions and offered advice. Eventually, with her stomach still rumbling, she popped Ohana in her crate and headed down to dinner.

Chapter 25

'How are you doing?' asked Gabe as she sat down to join him. She wasn't surprised that he asked but she was fine. Her sisters had asked the same but if anything today had been a great success and she wished people wouldn't keep asking how she was.

'I'm fine. Let's talk about something else, though,' said Nick quickly, 'this must be a bit boring for you.'

Gabe looked at her carefully, then smiled and changed the subject. 'Guess what I found in my room?' he asked, his eyebrows wiggling.

Nick sat back and pretended to guess. 'Another tree?'

'That would be impressive. No, I have a family collection of DVDs and one of them is *Lilo and Stitch*. After dinner do you fancy joining me, and you can see what inspired Ohana's name?'

Nick was delighted. She had had a great day in Gabe's company and hadn't wanted it to end. Besides which, she didn't want to go back to her own rooms and think about what she had discovered about her father. A movie night sounded like an excellent idea and was a better option than dwelling over the revelations of her father's upbringing.

'It's a date!' she said and then blushed. 'I mean, it's not. A date, that is. I mean. Ugh.' She threw her napkin on the table in disgust at her own awkwardness.

Gabe shrugged his shoulders. 'I'm cool if you want to call it a date. Maybe Ohana can act as chaperone?'

'Movie night it is then.'

–

When Roisin came over to see what they wanted for pudding, Gabe asked if there was any popcorn in the hotel and maybe some milkshakes? He had seen how awkwardly Letta had reacted to his suggestion and he was determined not to make her feel uncomfortable. Tonight was just going to be a fun, no-pressure sort of evening. He wasn't against one-night stands or short flings but there was something about Letta that seemed worth going slowly for. Plus, what if he made a move and she rebuffed him? Better to go slowly and make sure that she was as into him as he was into her. It would be really embarrassing for him to discover she just viewed him as a friendly companion.

As they headed into his rooms Gabe suddenly felt nervous. This all seemed too fast – not that he had any intentions of doing anything, it was just the expectation of a couple entering a hotel room together. He shook his head – he was overthinking this, his brother would be laughing at him right now, he was acting like a schoolboy on a first date.

Letta had already crossed the room and was looking out the window.

'Nice view.'

Gabe laughed. It was pitch black outside and you couldn't see a thing.

'It looks out towards the headland. It is quite dramatic when you can see it.'

'I think my rooms must be on the other side of the building, I can only see sea. Plus I seem to be up a thousand flights of stairs. You appear to have nabbed an easy-access room.'

'Family suite, remember.'

In fact, Gabe had been impressed with his upgrade. There were two separate bedrooms, a living area with a small area for preparing baby meals, and a generous bathroom. Plus a library full of board games, DVDs and books.

Letta was now looking through the collection.

'No PlayStation or Xbox? Very traditional.'

'Do you play?' said Gabe, mildly surprised.

'Everything and anything. I love games. An ex used to have a PlayStation and after a while I realised I was staying with him just so I could play *Assassin's Creed*.'

'Let me guess. You bought your own and broke his heart?'

'Honestly, I don't think he even missed me.'

Gabe highly doubted that but talk of ex-boyfriends seemed to draw attention to their current situation. He cleared his throat.

'Look, I realised earlier it might seem that asking you up here to watch a film might make you think I'm trying to make a move on you. I'm not. I just thought it would be a fun way to end quite an emotional day. But nothing else.' Christ, was he blushing?

'So, basically what you're saying is my virtue will remain intact?'

At that moment, there was a knock on the door for room service and both Gabe and Nick broke into relaxed laughter. Ohana barked noisily.

The kitchen had sent up a tray of movie night snacks as well as some dog biscuits.

'Tell you what, before the film do you fancy trying any of the board games?'

'Are you prepared for a drubbing?' asked Letta with a glint in her eye. As a twin Gabe knew all about being competitive and immediately responded to the challenge. He figured she was also competitive, so this should be fun. If he started to win too much he'd pull back a bit. A total whitewash would be rude.

–

Two hours later he looked at the chessboard in disbelief. So far she had won at Cathedral, won at cards, won at Sorry and won at backgammon. Now however, she appeared to be losing at chess by making a very stupid move.

'Are you letting me win?'

Letta looked at him innocently.

'You are! You games witch.' Laughing he laid his King on its side, conceding the game. 'Well, you did warn me about a drubbing. Tomorrow night will be a rematch and you had better watch out.'

Jumping up, Letta headed over to the microwave and put the popcorn in. 'Time to watch the movie?'

Ohana was fast asleep again. Gabe made himself comfortable in the armchair leaving Letta and Ohana the sofa. Gabe loved *Lilo and Stitch* and was grateful to his little half-sister as it meant he could watch as much Disney as possible. In fact, he and Rafe often fought over whose turn it was to babysit and sometimes the brothers would both go over together.

He was so engrossed in the film that it took a while for him to notice that Letta was crying. It was the part of the film where the two sisters had just had their disastrous meeting with the social worker; they hadn't even met Stitch yet or explained what the word Ohana meant and yet Letta was beginning to cry in earnest and trying to hide the fact. Gabe was devastated, what had he done to upset her? Surely it wasn't the film? He hit pause and gave Letta a second to rapidly scrub her face with her sleeve.

'Is everything okay?'

Letta looked red, blotchy and cross with herself.

'Hayfever?' she paused and looked at him to see if he bought it. When he continued to look concerned she tried again, 'Oh honestly, aren't I an idiot crying at a movie?' She laughed but it was more of a hiccup.

'It does get better. But maybe another day?' He checked his watch and saw with surprise that it was already midnight.

'Look, stay here tonight. Sleep in the children's room. Go on, splash your face and I'll bring you in a hot chocolate.'

Picking up Ohana he gently moved her to the second bedroom and turned down the covers and went back to make a hot chocolate. By the time Letta came out of the bathroom he could see she had been crying again and was alarmed that such a silly film could have upset her so much. Still Nani, Lilo's big sister, had just lost her job in the movie and Gabe remembered with a dawning horror that Letta also had job worries. They must be more severe than he had realised. On top of all she had discovered today about her father, she was probably overwhelmed.

'Are you sure about this?' She sounded exhausted. 'Ohana and I can find our own way back to our rooms?'

'Don't be daft. Here's your cocoa, now go to bed. And don't snore. And don't blame the dog if you do.'

With a weak smile, Letta took the drink and closed her bedroom door behind her. Wondering what he could do tomorrow to make it up to her, Gabe switched everything off and headed into his own bedroom and went to sleep.

—

Gabe opened his eyes into the dark. Something had woken him up and he lay in his bed straining to hear what it was. Remembering Letta was next door, he grabbed his dressing gown and very quietly opened his bedroom door. In the dark of the living room, the television was playing *Lilo and Stitch* so quietly that Gabe could hardly hear it. What he could hear was Letta's muffled sobs as she cried into a cushion. From where he stood he could see her shoulders shuddering as she took great gulps of air before she stifled her wail with the cushion. Gabe had never seen genuine grief, but he knew he was watching a human being utterly broken down by their misery.

Trying not to alarm her he walked into the living room, picked up the remote control and switched the television off. Letta continued crying. He pulled her to her feet and walked her into his bedroom. She hadn't let go of the cushion and was still crying into it, huge shuddering wracks of tears as her body convulsed out of control. Tucking her into bed, he went to her bedroom, grabbed a spare duvet and then came back to his room and lay down on the bed on top of her duvet beside her. He pulled the second duvet over him, then drew her towards him and hugged her gently, stroking her hair until gradually she stopped shaking. Exhausted from her crying jag she quickly fell asleep. Gabe lay in the dark, his arms wrapped around her spooning her body and wondered what could have happened to her to make her so wretched.

Not once had she given any indication of the level of grief she was carrying. He thought about every moment he had spent with her and could only see a fast and lively wit. A competitive and intelligent way of acting with a soft spot for dogs and Chinese tourists. Really, there was no hint of the darkness that was currently troubling her. Even with the discoveries about her father's childhood this seemed much deeper and more present.

He hugged her again. Hugs always fixed Freya's problems, but he imagined fixing grown-up pains wasn't so easy. So far Gabe's life had been relatively charmed – his parents' divorce had barely had any impact, his relationships had always fizzled out as he realised he and whoever he was dating weren't really going anywhere. His greatest angst in life was working for the family but he and Rafe had plans to change that. Probably the only tragedies he had encountered had been when family pets died. Whatever had broken Letta's heart was all-encompassing, and yet every day she got up and smiled at the world.

At around six, he felt her begin to stir so he left and went into the spare room. When he heard the bathroom door close he got up and put the kettle on, poured a glass of water and dug out two painkillers. He then hid the *Lilo and Stitch* DVD. He didn't know why a little film about family loyalty and sisterhood could have hurt Letta so much, but he didn't want to remind her of it. He also knew beyond a shadow of a doubt that she would not want to talk about last night. He was opening the curtains when the bathroom door opened, and he glanced over his shoulder.

'Cup of tea on the table. Plus some aspirin and water. The sun has come out, so it looks like a good day to explore the island if you're up for it?'

Letta was still standing by the bathroom door. She was clearly trying to decide what to do next: explain, apologise or run. Instead, he watched as she took a deep breath and headed for the tea. *That's my girl*, thought Gabe.

'A walk sounds good. After breakfast?'

'Then more research?'

'I might take a break from that today.'

'A walk it is then, and after lunch you have to let me try and beat you at these games.'

She smiled weakly, although from the way she winced he guessed she had a cracking headache.

'But maybe no more films?'

'Absolutely. Disney is dead to me.' Gabe paused to see if Letta was going to say anything more, but she just sipped her tea. Clearly, for now, that was as much as either of them was going to say on the matter. Putting the cup down she stood up decisively.

'Right, Ohana and I are heading back to our rooms to shower and get changed. See you at breakfast.' And with that she scooped up the dog from the floor where she had been playing with one of Gabe's shoes and left.

Chapter 26

Nick stood under the cold water of her shower trying to get a grip. She had started to cry again as she remembered the scene where Lilo explained to her dreadful, little alien pet what Ohana meant. As she had watched that little cartoon family trying to cling together, Nick was reminded of how often Aria and Clem would be interviewed by concerned social workers all trying to convince them that their sisters would be better off in care. She, Paddy and Aster would sit quietly, answering all their questions, saying how happy they were at school and showing the adults their homework and tidy bedrooms.

Get a grip, she muttered to herself. The tears had taken her by complete surprise. She had spent weeks trying to save her business but she hadn't stopped to think how she felt about it. She realised that not only was she hurting deeply but she missed her family dreadfully. She was so driven to make a success of her business and steer the Hiverton Estate into a position of stability and growth that she hadn't noticed how lonely she had become. She didn't mind being alone – in fact, growing up in a house of seven people she valued her space – but for the first time she realised she had become lonely. Now, as she faced losing her business, she realised she had nothing to fill her days. It wasn't simply that she was dreading the empty days – she could fill them easily enough, that wasn't an issue

– but what would it mean to no longer be a trader? No longer able to play amongst the stock markets and help people with their financial lives. She lived it and loved it, without it what would she be?

Which was when Ohana barked.

Switching off the shower she apologised to her little friend. She quickly got dressed, then decided to take Ohana out for a quick walk before breakfast. Ohana didn't need much but Nick would benefit from the fresh air. Looking in the mirror her face still seemed puffy, her eyes bloodshot, so she slapped on a load of make-up and headed out, sunglasses at the ready in case she met anyone.

She was looking forward to spending more time with Gabe. Despite totally embarrassing herself last night he was clearly happy to pretend nothing had happened and she was grateful to him for that. A day of walks and games sounded just the ticket. Besides which, she was certain that spending the day reading about young mothers being forced to abandon their babies would set her off again. The thought that her father had grown up abandoned and unwanted… She took a deep breath as tears began to form. No, definitely no research today.

Looking at her phone she saw a text from Gabe. Did she want a full fry-up? She laughed and texted back, *100 per cent*. Pleased that he had ordered for her she headed down to breakfast chatting to Ohana about the day ahead.

As she got to the table Gabe stood up and kissed her on the cheek then sat down again. Nick took her place, slowly trying to process just how much she had liked him kissing her. She could still feel his hand on the top of her arm, and decided she liked it very much indeed.

'About last night…' she began.

Gabe stopped buttering his toast and looked at her. 'It's okay, you'd had a rough day.'

'No, it was more than that.' Nick suddenly wanted to share. She wanted to see more of Gabe but to do that she was going to have to open up.

'My parents died when I was fourteen.'

'Christ.' Gabe put his toast down. 'I knew your father had died but I didn't realise—'

Nick held up a hand. 'How could you? I know I haven't talked about my family much but it's just my way to keep my personal life as private as I can. If that makes me seem cold…'

Gabe looked at her in surprise. 'Cold? Not in the slightest; reserved at most but honestly some people give you the life story of their entire family tree before—' he laughed '—well, before breakfast.'

She drank her coffee and smiled at him. She did consider herself reserved and was pleased that he saw her the same way.

'The thing is, after my parents died we had no relatives to take us in, so my elder sister had to fight to keep us. We regularly had visits from the social workers nosing into everything we did, attacking the slightest sign of neglect or suffering. If there's one term I can't bear to hear even today it's "failing to thrive". Our parents had just died, for God's sake.'

Gabe looked at her and put his hand on the table. It seemed instinctive and she reached out and held it.

'And how old was your sister?'

'Eighteen.'

Gabe recoiled in shock and Nick missed the warmth of his hand.

'Eighteen. Dear God. So it was just like the film last night – sisters trying to fight to stay together against the social workers.'

'Pretty much,' laughed Nick weakly. 'I know it was just a cartoon, but it was so on the money that I freaked. And on top of what I learnt about Dad, well, I lost it.'

Gabe leant over and squeezed her hand again before pouring a second cup of coffee.

'Of course you did. Quite frankly, if it had been me, I'd be crying still.'

She smiled. She didn't want to tell him about the investigation, that really was too raw, but once she was exonerated she would tell him about that as well. She liked the idea of having someone to share things with beyond her sisters.

'That's a nice smile. Is the picture of me crying so funny?' he asked with a grin.

'I've never met such a happy person, it's impossible to think of you sad.' In fact, Gabe's smile, whenever she saw it, was becoming a highlight of her day.

Chapter 27

She was about to reply when Mrs Devaney called for everyone's attention. The causeway had been deemed safe enough for cars to cross, and almost-normal service would resume. Repairs would be ongoing but for now if people wanted to leave by car they could. The Chinese guests would have to walk across or be ferried in several carloads and collected by a second coach on the other side. Everyone clapped and cheered, although Nick had enjoyed the almost enforced isolation with Gabe. She wondered if it would have been so much fun if he hadn't been here on the island as well.

'Well then,' said Gabe. 'Shall we make plans? I propose today we explore the hills, tomorrow some more family research. Then a cycle ride – I'll let you win. After that there's a marathon that I was thinking of signing up for in York, we could make a weekend of it?'

By now Nick was properly laughing. It sounded too easy and wonderful. It felt reckless and spontaneous but what the hell.

'Yes to all that.'

Now Gabe was laughing as well. And then he stopped and smiled shyly at Nick.

'Good,' he said softly and then smiled again as his breakfast arrived and the two began to make plans for the day's walk.

—

Half an hour later Gabe knocked on Nick's door. She had changed into a pair of shorts, with a T-shirt and a jacket. She was wearing trainers but had her new walking boots and socks in a bag.

'You look nice,' said Nick as she opened the door. 'Letta the Bold. Ready to take on the world.' She waved him in and smiled as he kissed her on the cheek. This was something she could get used to.

'Am I dressed okay? Hill walking isn't something I've ever done before.'

'You're perfect and we'll have Ohana with us so it's not like we'll be doing anything too tricky.'

'Tricky? Who mentioned tricky?' Nick looked at him in mock alarm.

'Well, we survived a tidal wave, an avalanche will be nothing to us.'

Nick laughed and then looked worried, trying to work out if he was joking. Was Ireland known for avalanches? Maybe he meant landslides. After all the rain could he mean mudslides. Her mind raced through all the possibilities – then Gabe burst out laughing. She stopped and realised he had been pulling her leg. Laughing at herself she threw a cushion at him.

'You should have seen your face! I promise you there will be no avalanches. Today is going to be perfect. I can feel it in my bones.'

Nick smiled. She felt the same but first she needed to arrange her return crossing. 'I'm just going to confirm my booking for the ferry, and then we can go.'

'It's a shame that you can't fly back with me. It's going to be very dull without you.'

Nick felt herself blush. 'Well, I'll call you the minute I get back to London.'

'I could meet you at the ferry terminal?'

'And then we'd both drive back to London from Wales in two separate cars?' Nick hated to be pragmatic in the face of such a romantic gesture, but romantic gestures only went so far.

'Fair point, I—'

'Hello, yes, I'd like to confirm my booking for tomorrow.' Nick mouthed an apology to Gabe for cutting him off and then reached over for her diary and pen.

Stepping away, he started to tidy up her morning teacup and pot for housekeeping. It was much easier for them if everything was on one tray. Looking away from Gabe, Nick carried on chatting on the phone.

'Yes, the ten o'clock sailing. One car, one cabin. Yes, oh sorry, yes my name is Nicoletta Byrne.'

Behind her a cup crashed onto the metal tray and startled, Nick turned round to see Gabe with his back to her on the floor trying to pick up the broken pieces of pottery. The voice on the other end of the line tried again and Nick found her attention torn between the two.

'Sorry about that. Small accident at our end.' She watched as Gabe stood, wondering if he had cut himself. His face looked ashen and if she didn't know better she thought he was about to cry.

'Hang on a minute,' she said to the person at the other end of the phone. 'Gabe, is everything okay?'

Gabe looked at her blankly and then seemed to shake himself.

'I'm fine. Let me go and let reception know. Carry on with your call.'

Nick watched as he left the room and then glanced over at the broken cup, had he broken something else as well? He had looked devastated.

'Hello?'

Apologising, Nick put the incident out of her mind and continued to check the details for the crossing. Once confirmed she checked the weather forecast and saw with relief that it should be a calm crossing. Whilst she waited for Gabe to return she looked up some of the stock markets until her activity monitor beeped on her watch and she realised she had been sitting still for over an hour.

Surprised that Gabe hadn't returned she headed down to reception to see if they knew what had happened to him. The desk was busy as guests were leaving and new guests arriving now that the causeway was stabilised. Roisin saw Nick and waved an envelope at her. Nick came around to the side of the counter.

'Gabe asked me to hand you this. Said to say he's sorry.'

Roisin handed Nick the envelope and returned to her queue of guests. Walking through to the lounge, Nick sat down and opened the letter.

> Dear Letta. Sorry, family emergency. Had to go home. Gabe.

Nick turned the page over but that was it. Ten words. Puzzled she dialled his number, but it went straight to voicemail. Instead of leaving a message she sent a quick text.

> Hope all is okay? Let me know if I can help in any way. I'll be home the day after tomorrow and will have time on my hands if you need anything. I've had a lovely weekend because of you. See you shortly. The next round is on me.

Friendly, helpful, concerned. Hopefully not needy. The last thing she wanted was to sound clingy, but she was suddenly aware of how much she was already missing his company. They had discussed going to the theatre next week as well as going out for a drink to celebrate their seven-day anniversary of the Battle of the Causeway. Now he had disappeared.

Feeling deflated, she headed back to her room where Ohana was still asleep and began to write up her notes. The day's exploration of the hills no longer seemed as appealing on her own, so she decided to catch up on the family research instead.

–

Two hours later she called Ari.

'I've hit a dead end.'

'How so?'

'Dad's mother is called Mary Margaret Byrne and may well be still alive.'

There was a pause at the other end of the phone.

'I see… popular name and likely that she is still alive.'

'Exactly. There are so many Mary Margarets or Margaret Marys over here that I'd have as much success as looking on Facebook as searching the records.'

'Okay. Well, you won't be the only person who has hit this blank wall. What do the people in the research centre say?'

Nick thought back to her earlier conversation with Mairead.

'She says to hire a local private investigator and let them take over the search.'

'Well then, what's the issue?'

Indeed. There was no issue, it was the sensible course of action.

'I don't know. I'm feeling guilty about leaving. Like I haven't finished my task.'

There was a pause before Ari continued. 'That doesn't sound like you? You've found the name of Dad's mother. You've found out loads of information about Dad. In fact, you have easily hit your targets and accomplished more than we could hope for. Unless—' she paused again thinking '—is there another reason why you are leaving early? Has it been too draining? Honestly, Nick, you have so much on your plate right now. Are you okay?'

Nick hurried to reassure her sister – the last thing she had meant to do was worry her.

'Honestly, I'm fine. It just seems to have ended abruptly.'

'And there's nothing else making you want to leave.'

That was the nub of it. Nick knew it was time to go but she also knew that one of the reasons she was eager to leave was that she wanted to see Gabe again and that was making her feel guilty that she was in some way betraying her father.

Ari continued. 'Truly, Nick, you've achieved loads. Come home or stay on and have a proper holiday. Either way, you've gone as far as you can for now.'

Listening to the wisdom of her sister, she called the ferry company and arranged for a night crossing that evening. The sooner she was back in London the sooner she'd be able to help Gabe if needed and honestly, the appeal of the castle had suddenly dissipated.

Something new was beginning to grow and she wanted to investigate it. Smiling, she headed home.

Chapter 28

The damp weather affecting Ireland seemed to have disappeared and London was looking down the barrel of a July heatwave. The tabloids were already reaching for SCORCHER! and pictures of girls in bikinis in city parks. She had dropped off her luggage and Ohana's new purchases, then driven back to the car hire company. They had offered to drop her off at her apartment, but she didn't want to risk them hearing Ohana in her travel bag. She was fairly certain that was against the terms and conditions of her hire contract. She was already living on the edge; she didn't want to push her luck. Smiling to herself she set off. Breaking rules made her come out in a cold sweat, but it also added a tiny bit of danger. Letta the Bold indeed.

She checked her phone for the umpteenth time but there was still no reply from Gabe. She had forced herself not to message him again until he replied but it was hard. Usually, she was a good judge of people and every instinct had told her he was genuine. Maybe he was just freaked out by her crying fit. She couldn't blame him, but he had seemed fine the following day. Frowning, she just couldn't work out what had caused him to change his mind about her and then she chided herself. It almost certainly had nothing to do with her. Maybe someone had died, and he had his hands full. He didn't need some holiday romance pestering him right now.

As she crossed the road the heat of the tarmac rose up and smacked her in the face. The familiar oily smells of the city in summer reminded her of Clem walking into the kitchen with tar on her bare feet and getting it all over the lino. Their mother had been furious and had made Clem scrub it all off. God, the fuss she made!

Was this summer going to get that hot? Leaving the pavement, Nick decided to cut across the park. Scooping Ohàna out of her bag, she put her lead on and started a few small exercises, patting her every time she returned to Nick's 'heel'. For the umpteenth time she did wonder why she had to be so tall and Ohana so small – but this was proving to be a great work out for her glutes and calves.

As they walked along, she smiled as people stopped and pointed at the little dog, its long body whipping and bouncing away. A few dog walkers asked if she was happy for their dog to say hello, and when she agreed Ohana started jumping and playing like a little flea.

An older woman with a pug stopped to say hello. Ohana and the pug appeared to be instant best friends.

'Sociable little one you've got there,' said the woman. She was wearing a long cheesecloth dress and a pair of heavy leather sandals. Her long white hair was unbraided and a pair of sunglasses were pushed back, holding it off her face. Nick wondered if that's what her grandmother looked like. She had found that since she had possibly discovered her father's mother she was determined to track her down. She shook her head and focussed.

'Yes, I've only just got her. I'm a bit of a beginner and would love any tips. The books and websites only go so far.'

The older lady nodded agreeably.

'The most important issue you have right now is the heat. Keep her hydrated and don't let her walk on the pavements. They'll be too hot for her little paws.'

Nick looked at the woman in alarm – she hadn't even considered the heat might hurt Ohana's paws.

'This grass is okay though, isn't it?'

'It is, but after a few more days of this weather I tend to only walk Bubbles here in the early mornings and evenings and not for long. He doesn't breathe so well so I keep his walks short and sweet. Better a bored dog than a dead one.'

'What if it's already too hot in the morning?'

Nick was thinking back to last year's heatwave. How did a city dog cope then?

'Then we don't go out at all. I'd advise the same for your little one. Everything is a bit tougher for a small dog, but just keep her hydrated and cool and you'll be fine. And you might want some toys for her to chew. If she can't get out she might build up a lot of energy and develop bad habits.'

Thanking her for her advice, Nick got to the other side of the park and hailed a taxi to take her the rest of the way home. Best she get Ohana indoors immediately, neither a stuffy bag nor scorching pavements seemed a good choice. Entering her flat she put the mail by the kettle and opened the windows. She would switch on the aircon later if needed but the smart design of this building meant it managed the heat pretty well. She knew some flats had dreadful heating problems and she was once again grateful for this one.

Settling Ohana down, she ran a shower and enjoyed the tepid water. At one point she looked through the glass door. Ohana was leaning up against it, her tail wagging, making her body flip from side to side with her long ears waving.

'You won't like it in here, silly.'

She opened the door and Ohana quickly jumped in, skidded around the tray and then jumped out again. Nicked turned the water off and followed Ohana with a towel mopping down the little wet footprints that now covered half the flat. *Well, at least they're clean*, thought Nick, as Ohana promptly peed on the blue silk rug.

'Oh, you monster!' groaned Nick. As she cleaned up she wondered if a furnished apartment was a good idea with a dog. In fact, was she even allowed a pet? She would need to check her rental agreement.

Swapping her towel for a pair of shorts and a racer back T-shirt, she let her hair dry naturally. The idea of the hair dryer in this heat made her feel sweaty. She flicked open her laptop and remembered her mail. It was so unusual to get actual letters and she wondered what it was about. Then, after adding some ice to a pint of water, she settled down at her desk and opened the letter.

A few seconds later she started swearing. Normally, she didn't believe there was any need to swear – there were enough words in the English language to properly express your feelings without resorting to expletives. Now she cursed like a navvy.

The letter was from her property agent informing her that she had violated her contract by having a dog on the premises and that she was being ordered to vacate the apartment within forty-eight hours. She was flabbergasted. How did they know? She had had Ohana less than a week and the little dog hadn't even spent a night in the flat yet. In fact, no one even knew she had a dog except for Gyeong, whom she'd told whilst trying to track

Daisy down. This seemed ridiculous: why would Gyeong tell anyone and how could they evict her without even discussing it? What evidence did they have?

She got up, drank her water and grabbed her trainers before she realised she couldn't run this out – Ohana would be left alone, and she had no idea if that were acceptable with a dog. Watching Ohana yawn, she picked her up and moved her into the dog crate that she bought in Ireland. She put down some water and some toys and closed the latch. Ohana didn't so much as flinch. Quickly, Nick grabbed her trainers and hoped to God that this was one of Ohana's long naps. Closing the door softly she began jogging straight away to the lifts and then once she was out of the main entrance she remembered the heat. Like any sensible person she avoided running in full heat but what choice did she have? She needed to think this out. Heading towards the river in search of a slight breeze she began to consider her upcoming eviction.

People said things came in threes. Well, she was being investigated, she'd been kicked out of her offices and now she was facing eviction. Was there a connection? She knew she was losing the offices because of the investigation, but now she was losing her home as well. It just seemed like a horrible coincidence, but she realised that she needed to sit down and look at her contracts. Backtracking she headed for home, already dripping sweat – but now she knew what she needed to do, her mind was clearer, and she had a plan. She didn't believe in coincidences; it was time to wake up and see what was going on.

After another shower and an espresso, she pulled out both property contracts and started to look through them. As expected, she was in violation, but the speed of enforcement was surprising. The office space had a clause about 'disrepute' – she could fight it and probably win but her heart wasn't in it, not with the ongoing FCA investigation as well. She read through the residential contract and the terms were clear about no pets, but Nick knew of several pets already in the flats; maybe they had acquired a dispensation prior to moving in?

However, she couldn't find a link between the two contracts. She paused, turned both contracts over and started scanning each document from the back pages forward, ploughing through all the small print. As she got to the front pages she still had nothing. She made another cup of coffee. Ohana was still snuffling, gently curled up towards a fluffy rabbit. Gabriel said that Ohana was bred to chase down rabbit holes which astounded Nick but for now she was ready to take him at his word. She looked at her phone again but still nothing from him.

Sitting down again, she pulled up the company details online and within a second she had the connection. There was no point in being annoyed in the time wasted looking through the individual contracts, research was never a waste. She had learnt that both evictions were legitimate but now she also had the connection. Both firms were owned by the same parent company and that parent company was a subsidiary of Harrington Holdings.

Nick threw her pen on to the desk and watched as it skittered across the top and fell to the floor. Of course it was Harrington's. Sodding bloody Harrington's! How had they known?

Now they had a fight on their hands. Five minutes ago she was prepared to walk away from the contracts but now she wanted them to know that she wasn't going to make it easy for them.

Adding some food to Ohana's bowl, she turned the radio on, pulled the blinds and headed out the door. Ohana was safe, had food and water, was cool and had the voices of Radio 4 for company. Nick felt bad leaving her, but she had business to attend to and heads were going to roll.

Chapter 29

Nick had left the apartment in a hurry but now she slowed down. The last thing she wanted to do was arrive at the offices of Harrington Holdings hot and sweaty. The afternoon heat was banking up and any hope of a breeze had slumped under the humidity. Whilst she had been in Ireland battling storms and waves, this heatwave had been building and she wondered if a storm was gathering here as well. This was typical of a London summer – it was always all or nothing, heatwaves and flash floods, or plain old drizzle. What was wrong with a nice steady run of warm sunny days with a refreshing breeze? She slowed down again. She could feel herself itching to get to Harrington's. There wasn't much she could do, but she just wanted to look them in the eye and let them know that she knew, and that she would take them to arbitration.

After one draining tube ride and a ten-minute walk amongst the taxi and bus fumes of central London, Nick walked into the main reception. Quickly taking a photo of all the businesses shown on the reception board, she headed to the lifts and rode up to the third floor of Harrington Holdings, owner of Meridian Properties and Golden Homes. Nick walked up to the reception desk with a polite smile and a confident demeanour and the woman behind the desk issued an appropriately reciprocal smile. Polite, professional, and in charge.

'Good afternoon. I'd like to have a quick word with Giles Harrington.'

Some of the energy that had driven Nick to these offices began to fizzle out. What on earth was she doing? He might not even be here. Storming over here like some wound-up petitioner was not smart.

'Do you have an appointment?'

Nick was torn, should she announce who she was and have her say. She knew the minute that she revealed she was Lady Nicoletta de Foix the receptionist would see if he was in the building. Even if she didn't know who Nick was, the title alone would pull strings. It always did and she regularly used it around the City when she needed an advantage. But was this smart? The better course of action was to go home and cool down. Don't get personal, don't get involved. Christ, she was acting like Clem. Deciding to be smart she smiled again at the receptionist.

'No, I'm sorry I don't. Let me go back to my offices and I'll ring up to arrange one.'

Both women smiled at each other again, happy that neither was going to have to start any sort of conflict. A door to a large glass-fronted meeting space opened and the receptionist's eyes flicked quickly from the door to Nick.

'That's a good idea. Thank you.' Her response was a little too hurried – Nick realised that she didn't want her to see who was behind the door. Suddenly, neither did Nick. Having decided to leave quietly she was concerned that it might be too late as the door opened fully and two men walked out. The older man was well known to her from his photo; here in front of her was Giles Harrington. His hair was thick and wavy and swept back off a patrician brow. It was more grey than black but nothing about him made you think of a retired pensioner. This man was like a raptor, ready to tear flesh.

Standing beside him was clearly his son. The man was taller than his father and impeccably dressed. His dark hair was swept back off his face and he radiated power and arrogance. He had taken one look at Nick – standing in an outfit that cost less than £100 from head to toe, wearing no jewellery – and had dismissed her. His father was not so lazy in his assumptions, though. You didn't get to be the head of a bank as once powerful as Harrington's by making lazy assumptions. Nick wondered idly if the over-extension of the bank was the son's fault. Either way it wasn't her problem. The way that Giles Harrington was looking at her, though, was. Just as she prepared to head out of the building his face lit up in surprise, as he finally worked out where he recognised her from.

'Lady Nicoletta. What a pleasant surprise.' He even sounded sincere. *Damn*, thought Nick, *do they learn this stuff in school, this easy sense of charm and entitlement?*

'What can we do for you? Are you having a spot of trouble with your leases?'

Well, that confirmed it. He did know she was renting his properties and he was playing with her. Now she was here she was just going to have to try and brazen it out, but she realised that the energy that had brought her here had fizzled out. Nick wasn't one for showdowns and dramatic revelations. She just liked to sit quietly in the background and get on with her job. It was losing her offices and her home, whilst waiting on an FCA investigation, that had pushed her over the edge into recklessness.

She was about to speak when the man standing beside her interrupted. He had already done a double take when his father had announced her. Now he was staring at her malevolently. Maybe he hadn't gone to the same charm school his father had after all, or maybe it was just a thing that you were born with.

'This,' he said looking at her derisively, 'is Nick de Foix?' Nick wondered idly if a man that sneered that much had to shave the insides of his nostrils.

Harrington senior tutted.

'Where are my manners. Lady Nicoletta, allow me to present my son. Adam Harrington. Adam, this is Lady Nicoletta de Foix, and quite the little thorn in our side, eh?' He looked at her with a warm smile. His raised eyebrow suggested that she had done nothing more harmful than serve champagne at room temperature. Nick inclined her head slightly; if they were going for pretend civility she could play along and then get the hell out of there.

'Lady Nicoletta has a bit of a problem at the moment,' he said to his son. 'Something about having a pet and bringing disrepute to the freeholders.' He looked back at Nick questioningly. As though he wasn't already 100 per cent certain of the facts and he wanted her to confirm. As a courtesy. Of course. 'Quite the infringements of your leases, aren't they? And we know how important it is to you to uphold the letter of the law. I mean, I know how much it means to you, so we are just trying to help you maintain your admirably high standards.'

Adam smirked at her. Giles didn't need to smirk, his words said enough.

'Have you come here to plead your case? Or threaten us? I must admit I'm surprised you're here at all. Still, desperation is an uncomfortable bedfellow. Maybe we can find some way to help out an old friend such as yourself.'

Giles turned away from her and leant back into the meeting room muttering a few words.

'My other son is in charge of the properties portfolio. Maybe you can have a word with him. Plead your case. Don't worry, I'll put in a good word for you.'

Just before Nick could tell him where he could shove his good word the door opened, and Gabe joined the other two men. Nick stared at him in horror. She could feel her hands shaking and she quickly shoved them in her pocket as she tried to regroup. He looked different in a suit but standing there next to his brother and father the family resemblance was unmistakable. They were an exceptionally good-looking bunch of unscrupulous bastards.

'Lady Nicoletta, allow me to introduce another of my sons,' he chuckled indulgently, the paternalistic bonhomie in full flow.

Before he continued his son stepped forward and stared at Nick in surprise.

'Letta?'

Nick turned on her heel and headed towards the stairs as fast as she could. The lift doors opened just as she got there and was about to step in when Gabe grabbed her arm and pulled her back.

'Letta, I—'

'Fuck off! How could you? How could you spy on me like that? Was it all a joke to you? I thought—' She broke off determined not to reveal the depth of her feelings. Yanking her arm out of his grasp she jumped into the lift as the doors slid closed and leant against the wall of the empty lift.

If she could just get out of this building she would find somewhere to catch her breath – there were bound to be security cameras in the lobby, and no one was going to see her cry. Realising there may well be a camera in the lift as well she took a deep breath then forced herself to laugh a bit and study her fingernails. It was all she could do to hold it together, this betrayal hurt more than anything. The evictions, the investigation, none of that wounded like this searing pain in her heart. What had been building between her and Gabe had felt wonderful and genuine, now it made her want to throw up.

As the lift came to a rest at the ground floor she smoothed her hair, tucking it behind her ears. She pulled out her phone, casually swiping through the apps. If her fingers shook a little she hoped the camera wouldn't pick it up.

The lift doors slid open, and Nick walked into the lobby, straight into Gabe coming in through the main doors.

Chapter 30

Nick took a step back and tried to work out what had just happened. How could he possibly have got outside before her – and then the penny dropped. The man upstairs must have been Rafe. Gabe's identical twin.

'You utter bastard. Are you all in this together? Did you arrange for your twin to evict me? Did you tell your father about Ohana? How *could* you?' So much for not making a scene, she was now shouting at him. 'All that talk about how important family is. God, I'm a mug. You made it clear from the start how important it is. Christ.'

Pushing past him she stumbled out into the bright sunlight. The afternoon was just tipping over into the first stream of early rush-hour traffic – everywhere was noise and confusion and for the first time ever Nick looked at the City with hatred.

'Letta, wait.' Gabe had caught up with her again. 'What are you talking about? Why would we evict you?'

'Why? Because you are sick. This is some sort of pathetic revenge. Because a year ago I happened to notice that your family bank was over-extended. Which again is not my fault but yours.'

Nick was puffing with rage. She had run out of things to say. She had a million words but every one of them dried up as she looked at him, her heart breaking.

He ran his hands through his hair and continued to frown.

'Look, I don't understand what you're talking about. I didn't even know you were being evicted. That has nothing to do with us.'

'You own the sodding property I live in and the office that I rent. It has everything to do with you.'

'We run thousands of properties in the city, it's one of our businesses. I'm sure it's a coincidence.'

'Rubbish! Your father just said as much.'

For the second time she ran out of steam. Just looking at him was reminding her of how much fun they had had in Ireland. A commuter walked past her, shoving her out of his way. As she stumbled, Gabe put his hand on her arm to steady her and called after the commuter to watch where he was going. He turned back to Nick and realised he was standing too close to her. Stepping back he guided the pair of them to the lee of the building.

'Look. Can we talk about this? Let's go and sit down and thrash this out.' He stopped and looked at her, his face unusually grave. 'And can I just say how incredibly good it is to see you again. I can't tell you how much I have missed you and how wretched I've been.'

The brutal honesty completely disarmed Nick and she nodded mutely as he flagged a taxi down. It was foolish but she was desperate to hear him out. That somehow this was all a terrible dream.

'Let's go somewhere where none of this lot will pry.' He glanced back over his shoulder towards the office block then as the taxi pulled up he opened the door and she climbed in. As she watched him take charge she wondered if she was still being duped – was this some elaborate plan?

'It really is great to see you. Where's Ohana?' He felt his pocket and pulled out his phone. Looking at the screen, he paused and then muttered, 'Hang on, this might shed some light.'

Having read the text on the screen he passed it to Nick.

> Where are you? Table is booked. Just seen your girl Letta. Hell of a mess. Turns out we've been renting her some property. Father has known all about it and for some reason chose now to evict her. You might want to call her after all. Our family stinks.

Nick read through the text and then handed it back to Gabe who quickly typed something and handed it back to her.

> Met Letta outside. We're going for a drink. Make my apologies. Don't mention Letta.

Nick looked up and saw that Gabriel was watching her closely.

'Hit send if you are okay with what I've typed.'

Nick liked the level of trust that he was trying to establish but still felt at a loss. He worked for Harrington's. He *was* a Harrington, for heaven's sake. He went to Ireland to spy on her didn't he? Hadn't his brother's company just evicted her?

The phone buzzed in her hand and she saw the message before she had time to return it to Gabe.

> Dur. Will say you've met a girl. Tell her I'm sorry.

She handed the phone back to Gabe and leant back against the seat looking out the window. The brothers seemed so genuine, but they were Harringtons. She needed more information.

'One drink only. I don't want to leave Ohana too long. No doubt your father has the RSPCA on speed dial. First thing's first, how did Rafe know to call me Letta?'

Gabe sighed. 'That, at least, is easy, because I haven't stopped talking about you since I first met you. Rafe and I chat every day. So naturally when I discovered you were Nick de Foix, I told him that as well.'

'Okay,' muttered Nick. It made sense – she shared everything with Paddy after all. 'It was quite a shock when I saw him. I thought he was you. I might owe him an apology for swearing at him.'

'He's heard worse and to be honest, I think obliquely we both deserve it anyway.'

The taxi pulled to the side of the road and they both got out. Nick had chosen a large pub, its only really claim to fame was a large riverside patio. While Nick went and found a table, Gabe got the drinks in.

He sat down and handed her her wine. 'No Argentinian, I'm afraid, but they claim the South African is decent?'

Nick sipped her glass and disagreed, but it was better than nothing and she needed some fortification. Her stomach was churning, and she wanted to wind the clock back to when she thought Gabe was one of the good guys.

Gabe took a drink of wine and winced and then cleared his throat.

'Full disclosure then. My name is Gabriel St Clair, Giles Harrington is my father. After the divorce my brother and I took our mother's name in solidarity with her. That said, we both work for our father. The law company I work for has Harrington's on retainer. And Rafe runs the property arm.' He took a smaller sip. 'God, this really is nasty wine. Anyway. Adam is one of my half-brothers and works for the financial wing of the business and is Father's right-hand man, followed by my other two half-siblings, Paul and Rebecca. On the record, they are not the most impressive examples of human beings. But they are family.' He shrugged and reached for his glass before withdrawing his hand.

'A week ago I got a phone call saying that the architect of our family's fall from grace – that's you, by the way – was heading over to Ireland and could I check, as Adam had heard a rumour that you were doing a spot of insider trading.'

He took a gulp of wine. 'If you remember, I said it wasn't something I wanted to do but I thought if Nick de Foix was guilty of insider trading, then that wasn't on.'

Nick had listened to everything he said so far and could see how it had all come to pass from his side, but it still hurt to hear that someone was fabricating claims of insider trading against her. She sipped her wine and then paused looking around, until she caught the eye of a server.

'Excuse me. This is revolting. What wine have you got that's decent?'

The server smiled at her sympathetically and suggested a lager.

Gabe continued as they waited for a change in drinks.

'So there I was waiting to spy on some hard-nosed London whizz kid when I saw you talking into your overnight bag, and I was fascinated. And when you introduced yourself as Letta, I completely failed to spot who you were.'

The drinks arrived with a small apology and she asked if they were finished with their wines. With a laugh both Nick and Gabe agreed, and Gabe took a sip of his beer.

'God, that's so much better. So. My total apologies but I honestly never knew who you were. When I heard you booking your return crossing you used your full name and I wanted to howl. Honestly, I was having such a good time with you. I thought we had a real connection and suddenly I find myself in the middle of a Shakespearean tragedy.'

'So you legged it?' asked Nick sourly.

'Guilty as charged. And yes, I knew that made me a coward, but I needed to regroup. I didn't want to spend another second with you in case you said something that might implicate you in whatever my brother was accusing you of.'

'But I wasn't doing anything. I was there for family research.'

'I know but honestly – I thought for a minute you must have known who I was and had given me a false name deliberately.'

'What? Why would you think that?'

'My mind was a mess. I had met this amazing, wonderful, gorgeous girl who suddenly was not who she was meant to be.'

'And who was that?'

'My ideal partner.'

He paused and drank, waiting for a silent Nick to respond. A loud party boat made its way down the Thames towards Tower Bridge. A champagne cork popped, and cheers rose up and drifted across the river on the warm air.

'You hardly know me,' said Nick quietly. Everything she had hoped for was coming true but now she knew he was a Harrington what was the point?

'So what?' tutted Gabe. 'When you know something, you just do. I had been looking forward to seeing if she felt the same way that I did. I thought that maybe we had something.'

He looked hopefully at her. Confused, Nick looked at her watch, in a pretence to stall for time and suddenly remembered Ohana.

'Hell. I have to go.'

Gabriel's face fell slightly and then returned to a polite smile. In a light tone of voice, he said, 'Of course. Can we meet again tomorrow? I can let you know about the evictions, maybe I can get them delayed?'

God, those bloody evictions. It was either the Harrington family hounding her out of her home or the FCA hounding her into court. She wanted to escape all of it and just spend time with Gabe. She was about to say so when she realised that he didn't know about her investigation. Overwhelmed with disappointment she saw that she couldn't have the life she wanted. Not right now.

'Leave it. I have other places I can go.' She didn't want to draw attention to herself right now. She'd been mad to storm down to the Harrington offices – although the FCA must be nearly finished with their investigation into her she needed to keep her head down. Storming in and arguing about leasehold violations had not been smart. That said, she did want to see him again very much, but she didn't want to make another stupid mistake.

'Tell you what. When I have my new address I'll text it over, but I'll be pretty busy over the next few days with the move.'

'Can I help? I'm a dab hand with cardboard boxes and parcel tape?'

Well, he was persistent; she'd give him that. But was that evidence of sincerity or just another opportunity to spy on her? Declining his offer, she pushed back her chair and walked out of the pub. She refused to look back at him as she walked away and only when she got in the taxi did she turn around – wondering what she might be driving away from.

Chapter 31

The following morning, Nick woke up and tiptoed to the shower. If she could just avoid waking Ohana she could have her morning shower without feeling guilty. She hated seeing Ohana in the crate and as soon as Nick was clean and dressed she could let Ohana run free. She had read lots on this subject and everyone seemed to agree that a dog crate provided security and stability for a dog in a new environment, but Nick just saw a cage.

Yesterday she had called Ari and checked that the Hiverton London townhouse was empty. Sometimes it was used by friends, family and employees who were after a break in the city. Ari never charged and felt it was a nice way to make use of the property. Happily, no one was booked in for a few weeks and Nick asked for it to be blocked out whilst she found somewhere new to live.

'I'm coming up and bringing the boys! They'll love Ohana.'

'They'll terrify her!'

'She'll adore them. Children and dogs go together like strawberries and cream.'

Nick wasn't convinced, her nephews were noisy messy beasts. Just as she thought that, Ohana walked across the food plate and then fell asleep on one of Nick's trainers that she had chewed earlier.

'Okay. You might have a point.'

Hanging up, she had cleared up the mess and placed her trainers up on a shelf along with a chewed pair of sandals. For the rest of the evening she finished packing, not that it took long at all. The apartment was fully furnished and she herself hadn't much in the way of possessions. Her bike, a pile of books, her clothes, a photo album and framed pictures of the family. A mug that her nephews had painted, or rather Ari had painted, and they'd splodged their little handprints on too. She double-wrapped that in a few jumpers, if it was too precious to actually drink out of, it was certainly too precious to simply bubble-wrap. She wrapped up her parents' small carriage clock in a winter coat and realised she was done. She had always travelled light and looking at the small pile, she realised that Ohana had more stuff than she did.

Now, as she ate breakfast, she sat on the floor letting Ohana run over her legs as she played with the toy rabbit. She was shaking it quite vigorously and Nick wondered if Gabe had a point. She stirred the berries in the yogurt and wondered what the hell to do about Gabe. Even if he was sincere, the fact that he was a Harrington was a massive problem. Imagine family lunches. She shuddered as she tried to remember what Gabriel had told her about his family. There were three siblings from the first marriage, who Gabe didn't really get on with. Well, she had met one of them and could see Gabe's point. Then he and his twin came from a second marriage, and finally there was a little sister from the third and current marriage. Nick wondered about Gabriel and Raphael's mother. She was clearly an independent sort, to have gone back to her maiden name rather than continue to trade on the illustrious Harrington name, and her sons followed suit which meant the bond between the three of them must be very strong. Nick wondered if the extended family ever met altogether – probably only for hatches, matches and dispatches.

'Right,' declared Nick to Ohana, 'no point sitting here doing nothing. Let's have a quick walk before the day heats up and then we'll hire a car and move.'

–

Happy to have a plan in place she swung into action and a few hours later she was settled into Foix Place. It was a bit of a fag carrying everything in herself but who else was there? It was too much stuff for a taxi ride, and she couldn't quite imagine a taxi driver helping her carry it all in. There wasn't enough to warrant a removal company and she simply didn't have the sort of friends or acquaintances she could call on for some quick help. Fantasies about a bunch of friends all piling round and chipping in – whilst she cooked a big pan of pasta sauce and passed around the beers – came and went. It was a nice idea but as she thought about it the noise and the mess of her daydream began to alarm her and she shook her head with a groan. The simple fact was that she wasn't a party animal or an extrovert or someone that fed off the energy of lots of friends and she was genuinely happy with that. At the moment her loneliness was a symptom of her current upheavals, not because she was alone.

Now she was seated on one of the kitchen stools at Foix Place overlooking a simple green garden. The sisters had decided that if they were going to keep the townhouse the garden had better be pared back for ease of maintenance and now it was a simple mix of lawn and topiary. Elegant or sterile – it could go either way – Nick described it as efficient. Foix's was valued at several million and Nick liked knowing that she had a tangible asset that she could dispose of in a heartbeat if the family finances became dire. As ever, she was reminded of Ruacoddy, their Scottish Castle, a constant financial drain that would be slow to sell and would barely make half what this townhouse was worth, despite it being vastly larger. Clem had made good on her promise and stopped the decline of the castle. She had very grudgingly hosted twice-yearly house parties where ludicrously wealthy overseas guest came for the Scottish experience. Clem had decided to play to her audience and wore the mantle of Lady Clementine to perfection. When they weren't around, the textiles line was busily growing from strength to strength and adding a strong income stream to the family coffers.

The kitchen was stocked with basic food staples and the freezer had a small selection of ready meals. The idea was that people could stay free of charge but to leave the place cleaner and tidier than they found it, replace any store cupboard items and make sure that the next person wasn't hungry if they arrived late at night. By the back door was a tub with a note on it in Ari's handwriting saying *Please feed the birds*. Always happy to do as her sister asked, Nick opened the back door and smiled as Ohana rushed out, running in a thousand circles, tripping over her ears in delight.

Nick filled up the bird feeder then poured herself some iced water. Brushing off a few small leaves, she sat down on the patio sofa, then closed her eyes to enjoy the warmth and relative silence of Kensington. Nowhere in London was truly quiet but this background hum of birdsong and distant traffic was a calming one. It wasn't the peace she had felt in Ireland, but it felt good nonetheless. It also felt good to have a place where she could get Ohana properly housetrained. God knows she hadn't had much routine yet but at least now they could settle here for a bit whilst she looked for somewhere new. A butterfly danced into the garden, flying just out of reach of Ohana's excited yaps and leaps. It would be a while before any birds came into the garden if they had to put up with an overly excited dog. Clicking her tongue and calling Ohana's name the dog came bouncing over and Nick rewarded her with a tummy rub.

For a while Nick and Ohana just dozed in the shade of the canopy until Nick had had enough of the inactivity and headed indoors and fired up her laptop. She would go for a quick run this evening when Ohana was asleep. In the meantime, she had fallen behind on the financial news and markets and meant to plug herself back in. She needed to be ready for when the FCA said she could start trading again.

Chapter 32

Two days later, Nick felt that her world was gradually getting back under control. She had found some basic offices for her and the team and whilst there was no fancy view or executive kitchen, it was warm, dry and convenient. Based in Stepney it was neither the City or Canary Wharf and she knew the staff would feel a bit out of place, but for now it was all that was needed. She'd find a better location once she was up and running again and screw Harrington's.

She hadn't called Gabe. Everything seemed so fragile at the moment – she wasn't certain she could cope if he had betrayed her after all and was simply pretending to like her to spy for his family. However, she missed his lazy smile and his funny face. She missed the way he jumped up when she entered a room and looked delighted to see her. And she missed their conversations and games; he had been a friend, and she had hoped something more.

She had also got back into a routine of early morning runs before Ohana woke. The heat was already too much for her but at least she had the garden to play in. Kicking off her trainers, Nick closed the front door behind her and went to see if Ohana was awake yet – today's run had been longer than usual, and Nick felt a bit guilty as Ohana sprung up and started wagging her tail. Clearly, she'd woken some time ago. As she opened the dog crate her phone began to ring. She was expecting it to be from the researcher she had hired to track down her grandmother. However, as she picked up her phone she saw it was from the solicitors she had hired to help her with the FCA investigation.

'Nick, I have some bad news.' Gareth Glebe was a reserved man at the best of times. If something was bad it was more likely to be awful.

'Is the report delayed?' That was all she needed, she just wanted to get back to work. The longer she was out of the workspace the more likely it was that rumours would start.

'No, not delayed. They have submitted their findings and they have informed us that they have enough evidence to proceed with a case against De Foix Investments.'

'That's impossible.' Nick stood up and started pacing. 'We haven't done anything wrong. I went back through the records and it's squeaky clean. As expected.'

'The matter under investigation happened eighteen months ago.'

Nick stopped and looked at the phone. 'But I was a one-woman show back then?' Nick hadn't bothered looking that far back. Any irregularity that the FCA had heard of would have been committed by one of her staff and it was their trades that she had focussed on.

'Nevertheless, that is the focus of their investigation. Which, of course, means that the source of liability becomes that much tighter.'

'You mean me.'

'Yes. I'm afraid so.'

Nick took a deep breath.

'Okay, well, if anything, this makes it easier because I know I haven't done anything. For a while I have to admit I was worried that someone I had employed had made a mistake or worse yet had acted knowingly. But this is easier.'

'Except they wouldn't be proceeding with a trial if they weren't confident of their evidence.'

'Let me get a pen.' Nick walked back to the study and sat down. 'Exactly what do they think they've found?'

'They say they have seen proof that you used a client's funds in order to purchase stock for yourself.'

'Rubbish!' Mixing funding pots was a cardinal no-no in the financial world. Since the Wild West days in the eighties boom, no one was allowed to use money that was not their own for financial gain without being explicit about it.

Nick had read and studied the financial markets of the eighties and was in awe and horror of the ease with which an individual could bring down a bank, but she had learnt her trade in the tightly regulated markets and wouldn't dream of being so reckless. Besides which, having grown up with barely a pot to pee in, she knew the value of every penny that someone gave to her to trade on their behalf. She would never play fast and loose with their trust.

'Can you send over the "evidence" that they've found? This won't take long to dismiss. I don't know what they've found as there isn't anything.'

There was a pause at the other end.

'What?' asked Nick. She was aware she had snapped but she was annoyed; this was ridiculous.

'Obviously, they sent us the evidence that they are going to use to proceed, and the issue is that it looks viable.'

'I don't understand.'

'We have seen the records and they show you clearly used client funds for your own transactions.'

'But—'

'We are your solicitors, and we will of course continue to represent you, but I have to inform you, the evidence is pretty conclusive. Unless you can find an explanation for these transactions, our advice to you will be to plead guilty.'

Nick reeled.

'But – no, that's rubbish. Send everything over. I feel like I'm punching in the dark. I haven't done anything wrong so let's not be running around with "guilty" suggestions. Hold your nerve and wait until I've had a look.'

'Of course. As I said, we are here for you and will work in whichever way you instruct us.'

He paused but Nick had the feeling he hadn't finished speaking.

'Gareth, is there more? Of course there's more. When is there ever not more? Spit it out.'

'The story has been leaked to the press. I would say deliberately. The FCA don't post their news bulletin until lunchtime. Someone already has the story.'

The FCA lunchtime press release was a dry old stick full of yawn-worthy articles, God knows, she read it every day to see if anything interesting was happening. News of her investigation was certainly going to cause a stir, but she had hoped she had a few hours to get ahead of the announcement and maybe even find the error in the evidence before it went public.

'Is anyone interested in the story?'

'We've already had ten calls this morning. Your new location will obviously buy you some time. But expect the odd reporter to track you down by tomorrow.'

'Fine. Although by tomorrow this will be a non-story. Email the stuff over and I'll get back to you with an initial comment within the hour.'

Hanging up, Nick walked through to put the kettle on. She was tempted to take Ohana out for a quick stroll, but she knew it wouldn't help. Until she saw the files and read through the nature of the accusation she wouldn't be able to settle. The FCA weren't fools, if they had found something they would be thorough in making sure it was credible. What the hell had they found? When was it from? Was it possible that she had made a mistake? It seemed so unlikely, but she had to accept every possibility. Was it during the early months of taking over the Hiverton accounts – had she screwed up then? Or maybe when Ari and the boys had fallen in the river? That had terrified her, had she slipped up somewhen in the following days?

The was a knock at the front door, and she was grateful for a reprieve from her frantic thoughts.

A young man in a pair of trainers and a hoody stood on the doorstep.

'Nick Byrne?'

Nick paused. Had the solicitors chosen to courier the files over instead of email? She nodded, looking for his satchel.

'Care to comment on today's allegations that you stole your client's money to feather your own luxurious nest?'

Chapter 33

Nick stared at him in horror as she realised that someone on the street was holding their phone up, either taking a photo or filming the whole thing. Without saying a word she slammed the door shut. Running upstairs she looked out of the bedroom window and could see the two young men talking to each other and laughing. They didn't seem to be in a hurry to go anywhere.

How the hell did they find her here? A picture of her at the front door of Foix Place destroyed all sense of privacy that she had always tried to maintain for the family. Certainly, she liked the publicity for the estate's positive enterprises but no one in their right mind could view this as a positive development. Deeply embarrassed she called Ari – as head of the family she needed to know what was going on. It was even possible that the press would be making its way to Hiverton as well.

'Morning, Ariana. I have bad news, but I am on it. Just thought you needed to know.'

'Hang on.' Nick listened as Ari called to Seb to take care of Hector and then returned to the call, every bit the efficient Countess of Hiverton. 'Carry on.'

'The FCA have concluded their initial investigations and have apparently found enough evidence against me to proceed to trial.'

'Nonsense. One of your staff must have screwed up.'

'I wish, but no, it relates to a period of time when I was a solo trader. Look, that's not the issue right now. The files are being sent over to me and I will have a look at what they've found. Pretty certain that once I see what I am accused of it will be quickly resolved. But that's not the problem. Someone has tipped off the press; I have two blokes outside my door.'

As she spoke there was another knock on the door. She walked through to the front room only to find a photographer leaning against the railings, taking photos of the interior. Three more reporters were standing around the front door.

'Bloody hell! Ari, I've got a small crowd of reporters hanging around the street and taking photos through the window.'

She pulled the curtains closed, ignoring the shouts of the photographer for any comment and hurried through to the other downstairs window and pulled the curtains shut there as well.

'Close the curtains.'

'On it.'

'*All* the curtains. A neighbour was telling me how paparazzi were using drones these days to get photos.'

'That's illegal!'

'Yes, but better they don't get the shots in the first place than sue them later.'

'Fair point,' said Nick as she started to walk around the house closing curtains and switching on lights in the middle of a heatwave. She wiped her hands on her trousers, she was suddenly shaking and sweating. All these people were hounding her, and she couldn't stop them. She took a deep breath making sure her voice was calm and steady before she spoke again.

'This was the main reason I called you. The reporter made a comment about my having a title and a luxurious nest. I'm guessing they are going for a fat-cats angle. Given that you're my sister and my main client I thought they may come after you as well and I'd hate for them to bother the children. Now you've mentioned drones I wonder what the hell you can do to stop them. I don't know how to help you.'

Ari laughed darkly. 'If anyone sends a drone up into our airspace Seb will just take his shotgun to it. But thank you for the warning, I'll alert the staff. Now back to you. What can I do?'

'Nothing, I need to look through the evidence and take it from there.'

'What do the solicitors say?'

'They suggest I plead guilty.'

'Absolutely not!'

'No, I agree, but as yet, I don't know what I'm being accused of.' The door banged again, and Nick flinched – today was going to be a nightmare if the press pack kept this up. 'I've got to go, the email should have arrived by now, keep your phone nearby. I'll let you know what the problem is as soon as I know.'

Heading to the back of the house she picked up Ohana and hugged her and breathed in her scent as she waited for her nerves to calm down. A panic attack would help no one and she needed to batten down the hatches.

As promised a collection of files were sitting waiting for her to read in her inbox. Rather than open her solicitor's letter she went straight to the attachments to have a look. She would be able to understand the data far quicker than her solicitor, even though they were experts in the field and employed financial experts as well. But this was her data, this would be like looking inside her own mind.

–

Half an hour later she had a splitting headache. No matter how many ways she interrogated the files or which accounts and trades she looked at they all showed the same thing. A solid week where Nick seemed to be using her client's money to buy shares for her own company. Some days any profit she made was shared between herself and her client, other days in that week she kept all the profit herself. It was an utter mess.

None of this made any sense. It was insane. As things stood though the FCA had more than enough to accuse her and strip her of her licence to trade. Hell, there was enough here to send her to jail.

A loud knock on the front door jolted her back to reality. Furiously trying to deal with what she had just seen she grabbed a bucket from the kitchen and ran to the upstairs bathroom. Having filled the bucket with water she headed to the landing above the main entrance and peeked out of the curtains. The press pack seemed to have grown, it was intolerable. Nick felt like a fox run to ground – the minute she moved, they would tear her apart. Very slowly she slid open the window above the doorway and took a gleeful delight in tipping the freezing cold water over the reporter.

As the man yelped in protest, she smiled and slid the window down just in time to hear his outraged shout.

'Letta!'

Chapter 34

Nick froze – that was Gabe's voice. She had just thrown a bucket of icy water over Gabriel in front of all the journalists and now he must be standing there dripping wet whilst they all took photos of him.

All this was going through her mind as she sprinted downstairs. Opening the front door ajar she stood behind the door unseen, then closed it again as he hurried indoors. Outside the clamour of the press pack rose, shouts and questions barracked her, and she slammed the door shut on their baying voices.

She turned to Gabe. Her aim had been excellent – he had been drenched and was now dripping on the carpet. Surprisingly, he was grinning.

'That is an ideal if unorthodox way to greet your guests in a heatwave! Would you mind if I took my top off though and maybe you have a towel?'

Nick watched as he took his top off and couldn't help but be distracted by a well-honed torso.

'If you don't mind?'

With a start, she blushed and then dashed back upstairs. As she returned she found Ohana trying to lick Gabe's face whilst he held the dog in his arms. Just watching the semi-naked man and the dog for a tiny second cleared all Nick's thoughts of trials and accusations.

'Here you go,' she said clearing her throat. 'There's always some spare clothes in the wardrobe,' she said as she held out a towel and a polo shirt. 'I think this is Seb's, my brother-in-law.'

Gabe towelled his hair dry and then struggled into the pale blue top.

Nick watched as the fabric strained across his chest, ending just above his hips, the sleeves tight across his biceps. He smiled again.

'Is Seb a girl?'

Oh God, groaned Nick. First she'd thrown water over him and then she'd given him Ari's top to wear. Trying to apologise Gabe waved her off.

'How about a drink instead and you can explain what half of Fleet Street are doing outside.'

'Those bastards,' snapped Nick. 'You didn't tell them who you were, did you? Or let them take a photo?'

'God, no. Never talk to the press. Family mantra, I'm afraid. They may have got a picture but I'm a very low bit player in the family and I never make it to the social events, so they probably don't have a clue who I am. So, what's going on?'

Despite the heat, Nick liked to talk over problems with a coffee so switched on the kettle and began to grind the beans. She briefly considered the wisdom of talking to Gabe and then realised it didn't matter even if he did say anything to his family. It was now a matter of public record. She began to recount the FCA investigation. As soon as she had mentioned FCA Gabe's face had winced and as she continued his expression became more and more serious.

'So you see, I'm completely innocent, but in my eyes only.'

'And mine.'

'What?'

'Look, Letta, I haven't known you long but in that short time I know you wouldn't do that. It's just not you. So what now?'

Nick exhaled loudly. 'That's just it. I have no idea. I was going through my diaries. I keep a handwritten ledger every day of what I have done. My diaries for that week confirm I was trading in those companies. All those trades were done on behalf of the Hiverton Estate. No one else, according to my notes, was involved or benefitted from it. But that's not what the digital records show – they show I used a client's funds and pocketed the profits. Now, that's tantamount to stealing and they'll throw the bloody book at me.'

'But you did make these trades?'

'Yes. But I didn't mix the funding sources to do so.'

'And yet the digital records show that you did.'

Nick's shoulders sagged. 'Yes.'

'And your handwritten notes only confirm the trade, but don't clear you of misusing funds.'

'No.' Now Nick's voice was tired and flat. She sipped at her drink. 'My solicitor advised me to plead guilty, which now I understand. I won't, but that means a court case, and I dread the idea of dragging the family name through the courts. I can't stand the idea that I am about to utterly destroy our reputation.'

She sobbed once and then caught her breath. Ohana was scratching at the back door and Nick was grateful for the excuse to do something and recover herself. She picked the dog up and gave her some food.

'Let me represent you,' said Gabe suddenly. 'I know you're innocent.'

'What!'

'I know my way around financial law.'

'You don't think your father might have an opinion on that? Besides, I have a team.'

The pair fell silent. Nick was overwhelmed by his offer, and then she became angry with herself for wondering if he had an ulterior motive. She had to stop thinking like this.

'Fair enough,' said Gabe sadly. 'I probably feel too much like the enemy after the evictions.'

'Yes. No. Honestly, I don't think you knew about that and I am incredibly grateful that you have offered to represent me, but it just wouldn't work. I mean, I know Harrington's aren't involved in this, but I still think it would cause some sort of conflict of interest.'

In the hallway the letterbox clattered, and a voice shouted through, 'Have you any comment on defrauding your investors, Lady Nicks-it-all?'

'Oh, for fuck's sake. Lady Nicks-it-all? That's going to sodding stick, isn't it?' she wailed. If she had one of Seb's shooting rifles with her right now she wasn't sure she would trust herself with it.

'Hold on.' Gabe picked up his phone and called someone.

'Yes, can you send a pair over to Foix Place. Two will be fine. Basic stuff, just ensure no one comes to the door. PDQ please. Thanks.'

Hanging up, he turned back to Nick. 'I can't keep this out of the paper, but I can make sure those vultures get as little as possible. We often have to hire security for our clients, at least I can do this for you.'

'And in the meantime, I have to hide in here?' she snarled, sick at the idea of making it to the papers. 'Sorry, that was bloody ungracious of me. Thank you. In fact, I should start getting my butt into gear.' Her phone rang and she saw it was Ari. 'Hold on, I have to take this.'

Gabe nodded and got up to make the pair of them a fresh cup of coffee. Nick watched as Ohana ran back into the kitchen and followed after him. She briefly smiled at the sight of the pale blue polo top stretched across his shoulders and then steeling herself she spoke to her sister.

'Ari, it's a sodding mess—' and she proceeded to explain what they were up against. Ari suggested that she was going to send over a security team, but Nick explained that Gabe had already set that up.

'Is this the Gabe that Paddy mentioned, from Ireland?'

'Yes. Long story. But probably not right now.'

'Okay. Look, I've got in touch with Davinia.' Davinia Joy was the estate's publicist. She mostly handled Clem and occasionally Paddy and was worth her weight in gold.

'Can she help?'

'I don't know – she's created miracles out of less. Remember when Clem was in Florence with Otto? If she can gloss over that she may be able to do something here. At the very least she can keep abreast of the story and let us know what we are going to wake up to. I've rung the girls – expect calls, and I sent Aster a text, so God knows what to expect from her. In the meantime, wait until it's dark then come up here and stay with us.'

'I don't have a car.'

'Hire one and get it delivered.'

'That would rather tip off the paps, wouldn't it? They don't deliver cars in the dead of night.'

'But I don't want you there on your own.'

'I'll be okay, I have Ohana. Look, I agree, I don't want to be here either. When I have a solution I'll let you know.

In the meantime, I need to get back to the accounts and start again and see what the hell has happened. And I am so sorry for all this.'

Ringing off, with Ari's admonishment that she wasn't to blame still ringing in her ears, she sipped on the fresh coffee that Gabe handed her.

'I have an idea.'

Nick raised an eyebrow.

'I couldn't help but overhear and I have a suggestion. Why don't you lay low at my place? The house Raffy and I are working on. No, hear me out. One wing is properly inhabitable. Neither of us live there full time so you would have the place to yourself. Ohana would have bags of space to run around. We have great Wi-Fi so you could continue your work, and no one would suspect for an instant that you were staying at a Harrington property. The only other people there are the builders working on the other wing. You'd even be doing us a favour if you were able to keep an eye on works?'

Gabe took a breath as he finished rushing through his proposal and Nick stared at him, trying to find a flaw in the plan.

'I get that it's a bit rushed. And you probably still haven't decided if you can trust me. But I won't be there, I spend most of my time in London, for my sins, and no one will know you are there. Stay as long as you like. If it helps I can promise to not visit at all. I just feel that my brother and I owe you a roof over your head having turfed you out of your own.'

The more he talked the more the idea appealed. She had been tempted to go and stay with one of the girls but her feeling of shame would simply be magnified every time she looked at one of her sisters. Plus, none of them were short on opinions and whilst Paddy would be the easiest to stay with and the least likely to tell her what to do, her twin was tired and pregnant and didn't need another burden right now.

'It will be better for Ohana as well if she can get outside without worrying about photographers?'

Grimacing, Nick saw that Ohana had had an accident by the back door and was whining softly.

'At least she had the right idea,' said Gabe. 'She's as smart as her mistress, I reckon.'

'I don't feel like the smartest person right now.' Nick hurried over and picked up Ohana giving her a quick cuddle and reassuring her that it wasn't her fault.

'Quite frankly, after all you've been going through I'm impressed you can string a sentence together.'

'Which makes me wonder if saying yes to your offer is an act of genius or stupidity.'

'Genius. There's a car up there that will be at your disposal – it's only an old Golf, if that's good enough for your ladyship? Is Letta the Bold ready to sally forth into a new adventure?'

He grinned at her and whilst she felt an urge to say 'yes' she choked it down and counselled caution.

'Thank you, but I'll manage here just fine.'

She tried not to be bothered as his face fell.

'Now, I need to get back to the paperwork and I need to start calling my clients, which frankly is not a task I am looking forward to. I want to let them know personally before the press start creating a stink.'

Retrieving his top from the tumble dryer, she handed back his shirt and threw the polo shirt in the laundry pile. As she walked him to the front door she tossed him a bobble hat and a scarf from under the stairs.

'To disguise you.'

'In this heat I'll probably pass out after ten yards. Still, it's a good idea.'

Just as Nick was about to open the door she stopped and looked at him.

'Why did you come over, by the way. I don't think you said?'

Gabe rolled his eyes. 'No, I didn't, did I? It was to let you know that we have issued a full refund of your deposit without inspection. A small way to apologise. Rafe also wants you to know we will supply excellent references.'

'And how did you get my address?'

'You gave the concierge your forwarding address.'

'Do you think that's where the reporters got my address from then? Only I didn't tell anyone.'

'I doubt it, our staff are very discreet, most likely that a stringer got lucky this morning. Took a gamble that you would have moved into the family townhouse and then told everyone else?'

Nick nodded but that didn't seem likely. Still, for now it wasn't high on her list of things to sort out.

'Can I try one last time to convince you to come to the Cotswolds?'

Nick shook her head and opened the door as Gabe gave her a worried look then dashed out past two security men at the front of the house. She wanted to stay and watch him until he was completely out of sight, but the press pack had surged forward, and she slammed the door again.

Chapter 35

It had been a horrible day. After Gabe had left, Nick returned to the kitchen to find Ohana curled up in the polo shirt fast asleep. On the counter was his business card on which he'd scribbled a note to call him at any time. For a while she had thought there was something between them but ever since he had discovered who she was he had backed off, and now he knew she was being charged with financial misconduct his tone seemed to be more helpful than hopeful.

She had rung her solicitors back to tell them about her handwritten diaries, but their response had been predictably cautious. It was, after all, unlikely that she would have made a handwritten note saying she had done something illegal. Nick groaned – the evidence that proved she was innocent could also be used against her, showing the lengths she had gone to to cover her tracks.

'But what about the bank statements? If they won't take my word for it, what about them? They show which account I was using that day.'

'That certainly is a better piece of evidence and the diary can be used to show your extreme diligence. But the facts are that your own computer records show a different story. The opposition will argue that you moved the money around at an earlier date to cover your tracks. Leave it with us. We'll run a forensic analysis of your bank accounts. I have no doubt the FCA are doing the same right now. I certainly feel happier with a plea of "not guilty" now, but the evidence is still damning.'

As they hung up Nick rolled her eyes. Well, at least her solicitor felt happier. Then she chided herself for being sarcastic – that was hardly going to help.

Dismissing any of her own hopes, she started to call her clients. Ari had been in touch to say Davinia and her solicitors had issued a press release. It simply stated that she fully supported the FCA and looked forward to working with them to clear her name of all false accusations. The standard response of everyone facing an investigation.

No sooner had she hung up than her phone rang again. She was tempted to ignore it until she saw it was Paddy.

'I've made your room up. When are you coming?'

Nick laughed, genuinely happy for the first time all day. 'I'm not but thank you.'

'You have to. Ari told me you're being prosecuted and that you have the press outside your door. You can't stay on your own.'

'I can, and I am.'

'Nicoletta!' barked Paddy. 'This is not one of those I-can-do-this-by-myself moments. If you won't come down I'm coming up. Hal can have Elly.'

Nick was shocked; the idea of Paddy being parted from her child for any length of time was unheard of.

'Absolutely not. Besides which Hal wouldn't let you travel all that way with the pregnancy you've been having. And neither will I.'

'Then come down here! Nick, how do you think I'm going to cope knowing you're trying to do this all by yourself with the enemy banging on the door? It's impossible.'

Nick paused, uncertain what to say.

'Does that silence mean you're coming?' asked Paddy hopefully.

'No, it doesn't, but look – if it puts your mind at rest, I have had the offer of a private retreat where the press won't follow me. I just don't know if it's a good idea?'

'Of course it is,' said Paddy incredulously. 'Get out of London. The place is a cesspit and owes you nothing. The City should be on its hands and knees thanking you, not hounding you.'

Nick smiled; Paddy could be just as passionate as Clem when riled. The difference was that most things riled Clem, only family could upset Paddy's equilibrium. Then God help anyone in her way.

'So what's the problem?'

'It's Gabe's place.'

'Gorgeous Gabe from Ireland. He got back in touch. Oh my God,' yelled Paddy, 'this is far more exciting. Tell me everything.'

Nick took a deep breath, she needed to confide in someone.

'There's quite a lot to tell.' And she gradually explained the rather messy situation both she and Gabe were now in.

'Right,' said Paddy, 'that *is* a mess. Okay. How do you feel about him?'

'Confused. I really thought something was starting in Ireland, we were making plans. He's funny and really quick-witted and I love being in his company. But since he found out who I was and now knows I'm being invest-igated for financial misconduct, he's treating me like I'm a liability.'

'He's offering you his home as a refuge. That doesn't sound like he sees you as a liability at all.'

'But that's because he's a genuinely nice person. And I do believe he likes me, but I think if he thought about me romantically then that's been blown out the window.'

'I don't get it?' said Paddy, confused.

'He's a barrister. He can't be seen to be hanging out with felons.'

'Oh, Nick, don't be dumb. You're not a felon and I bet he doesn't think of you like that at all. Why else would he offer you his home?'

'Because he feels guilty. He said as much; he and his brother feel bad for evicting me.'

Nick listened, waiting for Paddy to reassure her that he was clearly mad for her and that she was being an insecure idiot.

Instead, Paddy sighed. 'It's a bloody mess, right enough. And a Harrington to boot. What are the chances?'

'Pretty high, seeing as he was actually in Cork to spy on me!'

'Oh Nick, what are you going to do? Please come and stay.'

Nick hung up promising her sister she would sleep on it. Taking a moment she curled up on the sofa and played with Ohana – at least with her there were no complications. The little dog adored her and right now that felt pretty remarkable.

Chapter 36

Finally, when she could put it off no longer, she called George and Simon and then started to call her clients. Everyone sounded supportive on the phone, but she wondered how many, if any, would return to her when her name was cleared.

Absentmindedly she sipped at her coffee again then got up and poured it down the sink. The press pack had left an hour ago and the security detail, Jeremy and Charles, said they would be back at eight the next morning, just in case. Charles handed her his card and said if she had any trouble in the night to call and they would be over. When she asked if she should have Jeremy's card as well Charles just laughed.

'He'd sleep through an earthquake. Just call me and I'll nudge him. We can be with you in ten minutes so don't hesitate.'

Thanking them, Nick wondered what it was like working with your partner. Would you get fed up with each other or would it bring you closer together?

Muttering to the dog she picked up the phone. 'Ohana, it's time to be bold.'

Gabe answered on the first ring. 'Is everything okay?'

Just that simple concern almost undid her but Ohana seemed to sense her indecision and gave a quick bark of support.

'Is that Ohana – have the reporters come back? I'll call the security team.'

Nick would have been happy to just listen to him talk but was quick to stop him.

'No, everything is fine. I've just decided to take up your offer of accommodation, just for a week or two. And I have to pay rent.'

'You don't but whatever you want. I'll be over shortly.'

That caught Nick on the hop. 'I thought you'd need to hire a larger car?'

'Did it when I left earlier today.'

'How on earth did you know I'd change my mind?'

'Because this is the right thing to do, but I know you don't like to rush things. I figured you'd get to this conclusion sooner or later. Now, start packing I'll be over in a jiffy.'

–

Three hours later they were heading into the Cotswolds. Ohana sat on Nick's lap and Gabriel spent most of the drive chatting about the house he and his brother were renovating.

Parscombe Court was built in the early 1800s. It was a huge, imposing building in the Palladian style – tall windows and columns nestled between the warm Cotswold stone. At first it had simply been a very wide house in the shape of a rectangle, but subsequent generations had added two wings at either end, forming a capital letter I. However, a fire in the 1940s had gutted the main body of the house. Unable to repair the extensive damage, the owners had pulled the centre down, leaving the two wings standing in woeful isolation. Trekking the two hundred metres between each wing in the wind and the rain was miserable so the family retreated into one wing, leaving the other to deteriorate. For a couple of years it sat in probate after the last resident died and then the beneficiaries of the will took one look at the properties and walked away in horror. A few years later they decided to sell it when Rafe approached them and asked if they were interested in getting rid of it.

Now the brothers had all their hopes pinned on it being their ticket to an independent business and launching their careers.

As Gabe chatted on, Nick sat watching the passing countryside. She had taken a leap of faith that this was the right thing to do, and she was feeling unsure and vulnerable. But as Gabe filled the silence with his easygoing charm she felt that everything might just work out.

The car turned off the main road as the sun was gradually sinking. Two imposing buildings stood out against the evening sun – they looked wrong without the central building joining them – and Nick thought privately that for all the size and grandeur they weren't a patch on Hiverton.

Gabe showed Nick around the building she would be staying in and then the one they were renovating. Hers was only marginally more habitable than the building site. In fact, the way the renovations were coming along Nick could see that soon the building site was going to be a very desirable property. Her building, on the other hand, was the poster boy for shabby chic. Worn rugs, bare floorboards, buckets in the attic, and an oven from the Ark. Two bedrooms were made up with two decent beds, and a sitting room had some sofas and a table – it looked like the brothers had raided Ikea for some quick furnishings.

'We sold everything else to raise funds, although the good stuff had gone decades ago. Probably to cover the death duties.'

Nick and Gabe walked around the echoey rooms. 'Once the other property is sold we'll have enough to bring this one up to spec and hopefully at the end of it enough money, experience and reputation to shake free of the family altogether.'

Ohana had raced around the house, then out the back door to do her business before running round until she exhausted herself.

The air between them was uncomfortable and Nick wasn't sure what to say. She wanted to be back to how things were on the island but since then his family and her investigation seemed to have come between them.

Rummaging around in the kitchen, Gabe put some jacket potatoes in the oven and when they were almost done, put some beans in a pan and opened a bottle of red. The evening passed quickly, as they debated whether the grated cheese went on the potato or the beans and generally talked about nothing at all.

Gabe grinned at Nick with a challenging look, then waved a packet of cards at her. 'Time for me to redress the balance, I think.'

She smirked and stretched her knuckles out in front of her. 'Come on then.'

–

Half an hour later he challenged her to a best of three, laughing as she shuffled the cards again.

'So, Gabe, when you sell this place for oodles of cash, what will you do?'

Gabe talked as he dealt the next hand. 'Probably leave my current chambers. Maybe leave the profession altogether. I've lost the sense of enjoyment I used to have in work. I think I need something new in my life.'

He looked at her with a raised eyebrow. Confused, Nick changed the subject. 'What about Rafe?'

Gabe leant back and looked at his hand. If he was disappointed that Nick had changed the subject, he didn't show it. 'Well now, he *does* know what he wants. He will set up his own property development company. I think he really chafes at working so closely in the family business. I'm only on a retainer, but Raffy has plans and I want to help him with those. I may even join the business with him.'

Nick looked up from the cards she had been studying in surprise.

'You'd give up all that training? Your professional life?'

'It's only a job, Letta. It's not who I am.'

Nick played the wrong card and Gabe pounced, winning the next few sequences until she lost the hand entirely.

'That's your fault distracting me with revolutionary talk. "Only a job".'

'I need every tool at my disposal if I'm going to beat you,' chuckled Gabe. 'Watch out for seditious rumours about a work/life balance coming your way soon.'

'Work/life balance sounds like fighting talk to me. My work *is* my life,' declared Nick.

Gabe stopped dealing and looked up at her thoughtfully. 'I'd be happy to add a little turbulence?'

Was he flirting with her? She was certain he was, but how to respond, she always preferred the direct approach but at the moment she didn't feel she could commit to anything.

'I think I have all the turbulence I need in my life right now,' she said in a cautious tone. 'But when the court case is settled—' she paused and smiled hesitantly '—yes, I'd like that.'

'Right, well, on that note… I have an early start so I'm going to turn in.'

Nick was gutted; she would have played cards until dawn with him. Should she have been more eager? Now she was so disappointed it was ridiculous.

'But you're winning.'

Gabe paused and leant on the back of the kitchen chair. The curls in his fringe framed his eyes as he smiled warmly at her. Nick felt her heart glow as the two of them looked at each other, neither looking away.

'I always retire when I'm ahead. Good night, Letta.' And with a small bow he left the room.

Chapter 37

Nick blinked and tried to work out where she was. Sunlight filled the room, and she could hear cows outside. In the past fortnight she seemed to have been constantly waking up in other beds. Not one of them felt like home, not even her clean and well-ordered apartment in London.

'Come on, Ohana. Let's explore.'

As she headed into the kitchen she saw Gabe had set everything up for her for a morning brew. A mug and some sugar and coffee had been placed by the kettle. Propped up against it was a note, written in a strong confident hand.

Call me if you need anything. X

Nick looked at that 'X' and wondered if he signed all his notes that way. Was it just a flourish or a kiss? Did he still like her? God, this was so frustrating, she felt like a sodding teenager, reading too much into every little message. Looking around she saw there was also a sprig of lilac in a jug of water. That wasn't there last night, and Gabe must have cut it for her this morning before he left at five. Nick smelt the blossom and was surprised by how sweet it was.

Making her coffee she slipped her feet into a pair of trainers and stepped out the back door. It was a Saturday morning, and she couldn't hear anything beyond the birdsong. Checking her phone she saw it was seven o'clock. Was the whole world asleep?

'Just you and me then, old girl. Lead on.'

Ohana wagged her tail and darted off through the long grass between the two buildings. To one side ran the old patio but this middle section where the burnt-out house once stood was now a wild meadow. Various flowers were growing up through the grass, not that she could name any of them. They didn't smell as sweet as the flowers Gabe had cut, but she picked them anyway until she had enough for a few bunches.

'Let's make the place look a bit more welcoming, shall we?'

Ohana barked in agreement and they headed back indoors.

'Where shall we put these then? A bunch in the sitting room, you say? I agree.'

Nick had found several beer bottles and was now using them as flower vases. From the sitting room she wandered along the dusty marbled corridor and wondered what it would look like when it was renovated. The rooms were huge, and Nick imagined they would be hell to heat. The tall ceilings wouldn't help either. Each room once boasted intricate mouldings on the ceilings; in some rooms these had fallen to the floor and been swept to one side. Halfway along was the marble staircase that led to the next floor. Based on Clem and Ari's homes she knew that there would be other staircases and continued along the corridor. Finally, she found a discreet wooden staircase tucked away in an antique kitchen. She had thought the one at the front of the house was pretty decrepit, but this one belonged in a museum. No doubt when the old owners had decided to bring the kitchen into the twentieth century they simply picked a different room and started again.

'It's a bit gloomy back here, isn't it? I think I like sunshine with my coffee as well.'

As she continued to wander around the late-Georgian manor house she had a sense of rooms built just for the sheer scale and number. Given that this hadn't even been the main house it felt utterly wasteful. These rooms with their bold painted walls and cobwebbed corners again seemed too grand for the servants. What were they for? Rooms just to hang paintings? Maybe a family member kept to a suite of several rooms – a little aristocratic commune.

'I wonder how many mad old aunts they kept up here? Maybe Will and Leo are already working out where to store me? What do you say?'

Ohana barked.

'I agree. Talking to oneself is clearly a problem but I am talking to you. Although if you are going to be impertinent I shall start talking to the birds instead.'

Ohana spotted a mouse and raced off down the corridor barking as Nick shuddered. Gabe hadn't mentioned the extra house guests.

Ohana came bounding back, her tail wagging.

'Good girl. Yes, you are. Now, just make sure our guests stay well out of our way and I'm sure we will all get along together.'

She walked past her bedroom and then Gabe's, and couldn't resist peering in. Like hers the bed had been made, the duvet turned down and the window left slightly ajar. Nick placed some flowers on his bedside table.

Ohana sat down and tilted her head, her ears flopping to the side.

'Well, obviously, I'll replace them when he next comes down. Who knows, he might find time to get back during the week?'

Ohana tilted her head the other way.

'And you can stop that as well. I know there's nothing in it, but I can dream.'

Finally, she put some flowers in the bathroom. The floor was laid with horrible black-and-white chequered lino. A large window with clear glass looked over to the other building and Nick wondered if the previous owners had enjoyed flashing the other house. There was no shower which was disappointing, and the bath was so big that by the time the water warmed up enough it barely filled five inches.

'Cold baths are good for me anyway!'

She had already stood on the loo and pulled on the overhead cistern to make sure it was secure. Who could forget the time that Mr Shankles had flushed the loo and pulled the cistern down on top of him and knocked himself out? All the adults from the street spent the next week telling the children to stop laughing. Looking back she could see that it hadn't been funny at all, but as children it slipped into local legend. Along with the time the men in the street had to bump start a neighbour's car and pushed it straight into a letterbox.

'Come on, old girl. No point standing around here laughing at other people's bad luck – I have enough of my own to laugh at. Honestly, Ohana, you're a bad influence on me.'

Ohana wagged her tail in agreement, and they continued to walk around the shell of the house, their voices echoing as they put the world to rights.

–

Several days passed and Nick found herself settling into a routine. At first she had been reluctant to give her sisters her address but in the end Ari told her if she didn't tell her, then Ari would call Aster to track down Nick's IP address. At that point Nick gave in – Aster loved playing with computers and would pinpoint Nick's new location within a few hours. She knew her sisters were intrigued that she was staying at Gabe's place, but they wisely chose not to comment.

Once again she had turned down all their invitations to stay, often quite forcefully, until they had finally stopped asking. Although every night Paddy would send a text asking what she would like for breakfast and Nick would fall asleep with a smile on her face.

Training Ohana was coming along in leaps and bounds and she was impressed with how smart her little companion was. The floors of Parscombe Court were as yet uncarpeted which helped with Ohana's accidents, but they were now few and far between. Once a day, she would put Ohana in her crate and having made sure she had everything she needed, took the bike out and explored the countryside. First and last thing, they would explore the parklands that the house sat amongst, avoiding the cows that ambled freely across the fields. They were huge shaggy brutes with long horns and made Nick think of Clem up in Scotland. An electric fence kept them away from the properties, but she was still a little concerned.

She had eventually tracked down the farmer to ask if they were dangerous – he laughed and told her they were a docile rare breed. Sensing her interest, he invited her over to the farm where she learnt more about the cattle industry than she had ever thought possible. Buying some of the farm produce, she and Ohana drove home and enjoyed scrambled eggs, some home-made cheese and home-cured bacon for lunch.

There was also a supermarket, some ten miles away, and a pretty market town, where everyone fussed over Ohana and had no issue with striking up a conversation. In fact, Nick had spoken to more strangers in the past week than in the past year in London. She wondered if that's what country folk did, lure the city person into a false sense of security then take her out and burn her? Making a note to herself to stop reading crime and horror books for a bit, she tried to carry on with her old life.

The Wi-Fi at the house was excellent so she could track the markets, but the inability to take part frustrated her. She still played cards online with her friends but was finding it harder and harder to stay awake into the early hours.

July drifted into August and the weather had for once played fair. Rather than raining, it had settled into a warm front without the horrors of the earlier heatwave. The Cotswolds in late summer were a very pretty place and there seemed to be as many caravans and coaches as there were cars winding down the small roads. One time she had found all the traffic standing still whilst a tractor and a caravan had come to a stand-off. Knowing that that wasn't going to be easily resolved she turned around and found another lane to explore.

Parking her bike against the kitchen wall, she left her helmet on and strode across to the other wing of the house where she was currently expending most of her energies.

'Morning, Letta,' shouted Callum from the joists above her head. 'John's at the far end.'

Nick thanked him and then began to make her way through the shell of the house. Callum was one of the electricians currently finishing the cables for the first fix. Once the walls were finished and all the paper and paint done, he would come around again, running the second fix, basically putting on the switches and boxes. For now, though, this house was still in its first stage of renovations. It was at least watertight with a repaired roof and restored windows.

'Morning, John. How's it all going today?'

When they had driven down, Gabe had explained how Rafe was struggling to manage the project remotely. They had hired a quantity surveyor who was also working as the project manager, but he had become ill and was no longer able to work. At this short notice Rafe couldn't find anyone he trusted to take on the job. A quantity surveyor and project manager basically kept all the plates spinning, making sure the supplies arrived on time. They also interpreted the architect's plans and kept all the tradesmen in order. There was no point in hiring a plasterer if the joists were still being cut.

'Sounds like a giant Gant plan,' said Nick.

'That's exactly what it is, and it all knocks onto each other with huge cost implications. Last week no one had remembered to cancel the digger for the patio drainage. Where he was supposed to be digging is currently full of tiles for the kitchen and bathrooms that arrived too early and are sitting outside under tarpaulins.'

'So what happened?'

'The builders sent the digger back to base and we had to foot the bill. And of course we'll have to pay again when we are actually ready for him.'

'Seems high-handed on behalf of the builders?'

Gabe shook his head quickly. 'Not a bit of it. It's a huge build and they can only do so much. John Barlow is the lead foreman and according to Raffy, worth his weight in Carrera marble, but there's only so much he can keep an eye on whilst trying to do his own job.'

Now, a week later, Nick had a much better understanding of the issues involved and had taken to the logistics like a duck to water.

It was a fine balance between just-in-time delivery, who you knew, and good luck. Nick wasn't fond of relying on luck but knew to have safeguards and contingencies in place for when the tides turned. She believed in two maxims: 'you have to be in it to win it', and 'I work damn hard to be this lucky'.

Other issues she could be more proactive on. John had explained that a shortage of lime for the interior plaster-work was causing a knock-on delay. She rang around all the building merchants, but rather than see who had any left she asked who had placed large orders. She then went after them, checking if anyone had a surplus. Returning to John, she got him to break down everything that they had in volume that wasn't needed for a while. John pointed to the interior tiles.

'We're a month away from needing those. And even if we can't get them again there's always other tiles.'

Calling Rafe to explain what she had in mind, Rafe then checked with John and gave her the go-ahead. After that, Nick calculated a small financial hit and exchanged the tiles for the plaster and John was able to get the team back to work. Since then Nick had looked through the bill of quants – basically a shopping list for everything the project needed – and checked deliveries, locked prices and shopped around to confirm if there were any deals to be made.

It wasn't all plain sailing, though. On the first day she had been subjected to some gentle hazing by the builders. She had gone around checking to see what stage they were at and if they had any pressing needs. In her desire to get things right, she had wasted nearly a full day looking for tartan paint, a specialised bucket to catch sparks from the angle grinder and a left-handed hammer. By the time she told the workmen she had been unsuccessful they all rolled around laughing. Apparently, it was customary to prank any new apprentice and whilst she smiled gamely at them she was tempted to swing one of those mythical left-handed hammers in their general direction. She'd wasted an entire day and muttered darkly to John about it.

'I haven't learnt a bloody thing.'

'Well, I think you've learnt a fair bit about builders?'

Nick muttered some more and spent most of the evening reading the project manager's notes. The following day she made her own mistakes ordering forty boxes of screws rather than a single box of 40mm screws, but she only made a mistake the once and she kept running things past John until she started to find her feet.

–

By the end of the week, some of the site workers were shouting out to her, asking questions that she didn't have a clue how to answer. It was good to be part of the team, but her skill set was incredibly narrow. She didn't know one end of an RSJ from the other, but she knew how much it cost, who had them in stock and how quickly they could get them on site. The previous quantity surveyor had left excellent records and Nick was able to quickly fit into his shoes. It was a steep learning curve, but she was pleased to have a distraction from the investigations.

Communications with Gabe were limited and awkward. He had sent her some pictures of Ohana on the island. She sent back pictures of the little dog playing with the cattle. Every time she wanted to write more she found she had nothing to say. Until she knew how he felt about her she didn't want to make a fool of herself. As far as she knew, he was doing her a favour because he thought he owed her. At the same time she guessed she had read too much into their time together. She thought there had been a connection, but he seemed to view her more as a sister. And a problematic one at that.

In fact, over the past week, she had spent lots of time talking to Rafe. Despite their awkward first meeting when she had sworn at him mistaking him for his brother, she and Rafe were working well together over the phone and he was trusting her judgement calls. He had his brother's sense of humour but whenever she talked to him she felt none of the tension that she did with Gabe. By the same token she didn't feel she could confide in Rafe the way she had with Gabe. She didn't know how things stood with Gabe. Since their heart-to-heart the night he had driven her up, he had been as good as his word and backed off. Now she was worrying that she had completely misread him – as if her life wasn't messy enough.

Chapter 38

Nick rolled out of bed and fired up her laptop. Scrolling through and deleting the customary junk mail, she wondered again how these spammers got her email address. Really, did anyone ever fall for these things? How many did they have to send out before they caught the eye of some unwary victim? Obviously, it was worth the spammers' efforts, but Nick wished the technology were implemented to track these criminals down. The financial markets were regulated and one day the online world would be as well. And how many innocent people would get caught up in those regulations? wondered Nick.

There was no reply from her solicitors which she supposed could be interpreted as good news, but the waiting chafed. No matter how much she was enjoying being helpful to the building team, their surveyor would soon return to work and then she would be back to staring at the wallpaper. About to close the laptop, she hit refresh and a new email popped up from the investigator she had hired to find her grandmother. The email had a collection of attachments, so Nick picked up the laptop and headed down to the kitchen. She poured herself a cup of coffee, then she read the email.

Mary Margaret Byrne of Ballyfeard was almost certainly the mother of Michael Byrne. She had had the baby when she was sixteen. Nick's investigator had hired a local agent to go to the town and start asking questions. Missing fathers and unexpected babies were something of a taboo subject in public but behind closed doors, sure, everyone had a theory. The strongest theory for Mary's partner was the son of a local well-to-do family. Mary and the boy had walked the same way to school and were said to be friendly. No one claimed fatherhood of Michael, but Mary's family hadn't thrown her out, and there was always money for the baby. Then, after about five years, the boy and his family moved away. Soon after that Michael was sent to Ballinfeen Convent and soon after that, Mary travelled to England.

Nick paused and considered what she had read. Reading between the lines, the boy's family had been prepared to support the baby but when they moved away they stopped. Why would they do that? Then Mary's family decided not to take care of Michael any longer? Why? Surely after five years they had grown attached to the child? And what of Mary? She was twenty-one by that stage, hadn't she developed a bond with her child? Had she come to England to get a job to support herself and Michael but if so, why leave him behind for adoption? Had Michael's father moved to England? Had she followed him and left the child behind?

It was all too easy for Nick to picture Michael standing on the causeway waiting for his mammy to return. Did he scour each car, did he keep watch out of the shoreside windows? How long had he watched and waited? She knew that he had run away from every placement. Clearly he had never stopped waiting for her.

Nick stood up and put her running shoes on. She was furious with a woman she had never met, and it was clouding her judgement. It was a Saturday, so the other house was empty, and she decided to run sprints between the two properties, the quickest way to tire herself out. As she ran back and forth the cattle watched her from beyond the electric fence. Having assessed her behaviour as peculiar but not threatening, they returned to chewing the grass and dreaming of a light breeze to keep the flies away.

Puffed out, Nick returned to the kitchen where Ohana was now awake and let her out. She instantly bounded out to say good morning to the cattle who all sniffed a good morning to her. Having done her own business Ohana ran back in and Nick cleaned bits of grass off her, fed her and returned to the email.

Mary had arrived in England and then seemed to spend a few years moving around. Eventually she had settled in Birmingham and worked as a cleaner at a private residence for a couple of decades. She had retired a few years back and still lived in Birmingham. She had never married, had no further children and had never been arrested. She also had no clear political allegiances and to all intents and purposes had led a quiet and uneventful life.

Nick checked the roads; it would take her two hours to drive up there. It was a Saturday; she had an address, and she could be there before ten. Aware that the last time she had done something on the spur-of-the-moment, it had gone horribly wrong as Giles Harrington had pretty much laughed in her face. She decided to have a shower and think it through. Eventually, she called Paddy.

'So, what should I do?' said Nick.

'Go up there immediately and ask her what the hell was she thinking!'

'You don't think this is a mistake then?'

'Not at all. How could she? How could she abandon her five-year-old son. Jesus, Nick, I can't imagine doing that to Eleanor and she's not yet one. I couldn't have left her after three minutes. Tell you what. Give me a few hours and I'll come up with you and we'll go and confront her together.'

Nick stared down the phone in bemusement. Paddy was the most mild-mannered of the girls – everything was about conciliation, kindness, turning the other cheek and generally soothing the water. But when it came to someone she loved or God forbid a child, she was vicious. It was a trait that had really blossomed after the birth of Eleanor. Nick realised that having her shouting at some stranger might not be for the best.

'Tell you what. I'll go up today and report back. I'll let the others know as well that I've found her.'

'Better if you hadn't,' said Paddy darkly.

Hanging up, disturbed by her sister's level of venom, Nick slipped into a pair of sandals and packed for Ohana, and then the pair of them jumped into Gabe's old Golf and headed north.

As she drove along the motorway her phone rang and she saw with pleasure that it was Clem.

'Morning! What can I do for you?' she smiled. She and Clem weren't great ones for chatting on the phone and generally only talked shop, preferring face-to-face chats for daily life stuff.

'Nothing, actually. I was just calling to see how you're doing. You've been through a lot recently and I know you don't like change.'

Nick smiled ruefully, a touchy-feely call from Clem. Her life must look dreadful to her sisters.

'I don't mind change, it's the chaos I dislike.'

Nick smiled as Clem laughed down the line. 'It's the chaos that makes life great!'

'Hmm,' snorted Nick.

'Well, tell me are you still able to go for a morning run followed by a shower and a spinach omelette, then brush your teeth, then wear the outfit third from the left?'

Now it was Nick's turn to laugh. 'Are you taking the mickey out of me?'

'A little bit. Tell me I'm wrong?'

'Very well. This morning I went for a run—'

'Ha! See!'

'I ate last night's ratatouille for breakfast.'

'Very edgy.'

'I picked some flowers for the bedrooms.'

'Flowers?!'

'And now I'm driving up the motorway to see if I can find Dad's mum.'

'You're what!'

Nick was happy to have surprised Clem and went on to explain the email she had just received. Now she was off granny hunting.

'Just like that?' mocked Clem. 'No research, no studying the area, no follow-up investigations. No calls to your sisters to discuss the next steps. You just got in your car and went?'

Nick laughed nervously. The way Clem described it, it did sound mad. What was she doing?

'Do you think this is a mistake? Should I have consulted you all first? I did run it past Paddy, but she wanted to come up and lamp her, so I said no.' Nick was beginning to look for exits off the motorway – maybe she should go home, this impulsivity sat uneasily with her.

'Are you mad? Sound like an excellent thing to do. Like going to Ireland in the first place. All of Dad's stuff you found. That was incredible. Trust your gut, Nick, let the chaos in.'

'God, that sounds like a dreadful idea. But do you think this is okay? Only now I'm starting to doubt myself. What happens when I find her? What happens if I don't? What if she doesn't want to see me?'

'Lots of questions there, hen. You'll only get answers by going there. I think it's brilliant. Do you know, for the first time since all this crap landed on your shoulders I feel something good may come of it.'

'Bloody hell, Clem. I might be about to lose my business!'

'Aye. But you won't. And look at what you are gaining. Chaos, creativity, conflict. Bring it on!'

Nick was now openly laughing as she listened to her sister – she could stir up the dogs of war with that speech. Beside her Ohana started barking and Nick had to quieten her.

'Look. I have to calm Ohana down. I'll let you know how it goes and thanks for the chat. You're a tonic!'

With a final cry of 'Chaos!' from Clem, Nick ended the call and shushed the now thoroughly excited dog. Despite Clem's reassurances, Nick was somewhat apprehensive, she was driving into a situation she hadn't studied or planned for.

–

After a relatively easy drive she pulled up on a terraced street and switched the engine off. All the houses faced directly onto the street without even the small front garden that she had grown up with. Otherwise it had a similar vibe, and she was certain that somewhere along the street, someone had clocked her arrival and was already taking notes for the Neighbourhood Watch. Locking the car, she and Ohana walked a little way down past the binbags that lined the pavement and knocked on an ugly white uPVC door. It was nine thirty, hopefully Mary was at home but up and about. Nick had already demonised her into some freewheeling baby-abandoning goodtime girl. The house would smell of fags, booze and regrets.

The door swung open and a woman in her late sixties looked out. She held her door wide open with a questioning expression. Her hair was cut in a neat bob, mostly grey. She was wearing jeans and a Levellers T-shirt. Whilst she was shorter than Nick she was tall enough. Nick was momentarily surprised not to see tattoos, nicotine-stained fingers or morning tremors. This woman looked sharp and alert, although the T-shirt suggested a certain level of feistiness that the private investigator hadn't picked up.

Nick realised she was staring and hadn't spoken yet, but she was looking at her one and only grandparent for the very first time. She wasn't sure how to proceed.

The older lady looked at her, puzzled. 'Hello? Do I know you?'

Nick cleared her throat. 'No. We haven't met. Can I ask, are you Mary Margaret Byrne?'

Mary nodded slowly; her expression still puzzled.

'For the life of me, I am certain that we've met. You remind me of—' Her voice trailed away as an old memory crossed her mind and her expression became hostile. 'Who are you?'

Ohana was snuffling around her ankles investigating the exciting smells from the bin bags. In the distance Nick could hear the beeping of the binmen's lorry making its way along the terraces. Despite the outside world, time seemed to freeze, and Nick felt a buzzing in her ears.

'My name's Nicoletta Byrne. I'm your granddaughter.'

Chapter 39

Gabriel called through to his secretary and asked if she had the information he had been looking for. Letta had told him not to look into the FCA investigation, but he couldn't help himself. He was certain she was innocent, and he wanted to help prove that. The fact that his father had chosen to hit Letta when she was at her weakest and evict her was a thorn that he couldn't excise. He knew the old man was ruthless, but this was simply spiteful, and he hated the fact that he was connected to any source of misery imposed on Letta.

At least now he understood the depth of her tears. He had looked up her bio online. There wasn't a lot, but the bare bones made for a rollercoaster read. Born into a large and happy family she had been orphaned at the age of fourteen and her eldest sister had fought through the courts to take legal guardianship of her little sisters. Ten years later they inherited the family title and estate and swept from poverty to the upper echelons of British society. Letta – he couldn't bring himself to think of her as Nick – had already built her own business, though; she was properly self-made. Being investigated and evicted must have reminded her of being orphaned and threatened with foster care.

The investigations on the island must have ripped straight through any plaster that she had applied to her grief and fears.

Elena buzzed him and told him the links were on his screen and he started to look through the social media photos that Elena had culled from various accounts. Apart from a LinkedIn account Letta had almost no social profile. She turned up in lots of photos standing beside her sisters, although Paddy had stopped posting after she stepped down from the modelling world and Clem's accounts were full of her fashion rather than herself. Ariana's account was scrubbed clean, presumably to protect the privacy of her children. The youngest sister Aster didn't even have a profile.

There wasn't much to go on and if Gabe was honest he was wasting time – he just liked looking at photos of Letta. She rarely smiled directly into a camera lens but in unguarded group shots he would spot her somewhere in the back of a crowd; he imagined that she was looking for the exit. He laughed as he looked at the next one – it was clearly an office Christmas party and Nick was actually standing in a doorway ready to leave. The foreground was dominated by a group of people laughing and chatting in front of the camera, champagne bottles were swinging, and poppers were streaming. In his desire to look at another picture of Letta he almost missed it. Staring closely at one of the girls, blowing on a party streamer, he recognised her face.

Pressing his intercom he asked his secretary to get HR on the line and waited. A minute later he was connected; he might not appreciate being a Harrington, but no one in his father's company would ever keep a Harrington on hold.

'Mr Harrington, it's Lydia Rodham here. What can I do for you?'

Lydia was exactly the right person to speak to, she was head of HR for all the Harrington subsidiaries.

'It's a bit sensitive, I'm trying to remember the name of Luke Rees's fiancée. I think she worked in Acquisitions.'

Luke Rees was one of the bankers that had been found guilty by the court during the collapse of the Bank of Harrington's. No evidence had been found against any of the Harrington family directly but some of their staff had been found to be behaving beyond the scope of the law. Luke was one of four men that had been found guilty and given a custodial sentence. They hadn't done much actual prison time, but their days were over in terms of being able to work in the financial sector ever again.

'That was Daisy Hall.'

'Thank you. And does she still work for us?'

'Hold on. No, she left about eighteen months ago. And we don't seem to have any details of where she went.'

Gabe looked out the window and wondered.

'Is there anything else I can do for you?'

'Do we have any notes on how she responded to Rees's trial?'

'Lots of sick days, a few reprimands from her line manager. Quite aggressive towards the company, her colleagues, couriers. Basically, it looks like she was a hot mess before she left.'

'Was she fired?'

'No, it looks like she just handed in her notice and disappeared.'

And turned up in a photo with Letta at a work Christmas do, thought Gabe. Thanking Lydia, he hung up and asked his secretary to find out when the photo was taken and what was going on in the image.

Why did a woman start working for the person who had been instrumental in sending her fiancé to jail? He could think of a few reasons but none of them were good.

Chapter 40

Mary stared at Nick and let out a small moan.

'Grainne, you look just like my Aunt Grainne. Holy Mary. I prayed that one day I might find Michael and now his daughter's found me.'

At this point Mary started to weep. Feeling awkward, Nick ushered her into her house and made her way to the back kitchen where she put the kettle on.

'You are Michael's girl, aren't you? You have such a look of the family? Does he know you're here?'

Nick searched for a tea caddy. In her desire to track her grandmother down she had completely failed to consider that she would have to tell her her son was dead. But she had abandoned him as a child, what did she care? Although looking at her now, sobbing and clutching a handkerchief to herself, Nick realised she was going to care a great deal. Mary had pulled a rosary out of her pocket and was moving the string of beads through her fingers. Nick felt a prickly wave of resentment, what right did this woman have to make her feel bad about what she was about to do? Waiting for the woman to stop crying, Nick poured out two teas and put a bowl of water on the floor for Ohana.

'Does he want to see me? Does he forgive me?'

Nick winced, this had to end now.

'I'm terribly sorry, Mrs Byrne. He's dead, he died over ten years ago.'

Mary's head hung forward and she made the sign of the cross. Nick watched in silence as Mary began to pray quietly under her breath.

Finally, she looked up, her eyes red and glistening but she had stopped crying.

'So. That was God's final punishment for letting him out of my sight. Very well.'

Her stillness was so profound that Nick wanted to somehow reassure her that her son was still alive and well, that the past twelve years of Nick's life had not been shrouded by grief. Instead, Mary sat in mute sorrow, visibly shrunken by the crushing weight of her new know-ledge. Her head dropped and her shoulders slumped, her whole body appeared to have sagged in on itself. Thirty years of hope had kept her inflated and now with that loss, she was a deflating shell. If Nick could not share the load maybe she could lighten it. She began to explain what her father had meant to her and what her childhood had been like. As she described her sisters and their children, Mary's face lit up.

'I have great-grandchildren?'

'You have three and another two are on the way. Paddy and Ari are on a race to start a dynasty, I think.'

When she had explained how it had been when her parents died Mary started apologising and twisting her rosary again.

'I should have been there for you. Your mother's parents sound wicked but why didn't Michael's adoptive parents help you?'

Nick looked at Mary in confusion.

'He wasn't adopted.'

'He was. He was adopted straight away by a couple of vets that had a practice in England. He was taken away almost as soon as my parents took Michael from me.'

'They took him from you?'

'Yes, Callum had got engaged to a new girl – one who presumably had learnt to keep her knees together – and her folks insisted that Callum had no more to do with any previous indiscretions. That's what Michael and I were. Indiscretions.'

Mary stirred her spoon in her cup as she cast her mind back forty years. 'So Callum's parents told mine that they would no longer send my folks any money for Michael's upkeep. Mum and Dad decided I would do better at finding a husband if I didn't have Michael and so they took him to an orphanage. Callum's parents had paid them a lump sum of hush money and they donated that to the convent.'

Nick sat and just stared at the woman sitting in front of her. How could her parents have been so cruel?

'When I found out that they had taken him, instead of going to school I hitched half the way across Ireland visiting every orphanage I could. Finally, my folks told me that he had already been adopted and had moved to England.'

'But he hadn't!' said Nick, shocked. 'I've seen his records. Why would your folks lie?'

'Ireland was a difficult place then, maybe they thought the nuns could offer my son a better future than I could? All I know was that I went upstairs, packed a suitcase and left home for England. And I've spent the last forty-odd years looking for him.'

Nick stared at the old woman in horror. She hadn't run away to England to get a job, or follow her boyfriend, she was desperately searching for her son. Who all that time had been standing on the causeway waiting for her to come and take him home.

'So who did adopt him? Why didn't they step in and help you when he died?'

'No one adopted him, Mary.' Nick leant across the table and held Mary's hand. 'He played up at every foster placement and adoption family. He kept returning to the island. He already had a mother that he loved, he didn't want another.'

Nick wished she had found different words. The grief on Mary's face as she castigated herself was too painful to look at.

'Did he hate me?'

Nick was still holding her grandmother's hand and she squeezed it again now, desperate to console the distressed older lady.

'No,' she said quickly, 'he said you were the prettiest woman in the world, but some fairies kidnapped him and took him to their fairy island where he grew up as a changeling and sailed the seven seas, riding whales and dolphins and generally having the time of his life. He never once said a bad word about his childhood other than it was better than many and he had all the family he needed now.'

Mary wiped at her eyes. 'I used to tell him fairy stories. Stories of the giant Finn McCool.'

'And the first salmon!' laughed Nick. 'He used to tell that to us as well. He clearly never forgot you. And you never gave up on him. Like you said, you spent all that time looking for him.'

'Mother of God, I made a nuisance of myself. I don't think there was a single vet that I didn't phone up and ask if they had adopted a little boy. At the end of a week I'd take all the money I had saved that week and would spend it making phone calls in the local area. When I had exhausted all the vets in the area I would move towns. Find another set of lodgings and another job and start the hunt again.'

Nick drank her tea and wondered about a twenty-one-year-old girl in a foreign country trying to find her child.

'Did you ever go home?'

'How could I? I swore to my parents that if I ever saw them again I'd kill them. And I meant it. No, England was good enough for me. God knows it has its faults, but hypocrisy and secrecy aren't amongst them. The English have never had any shame to begin with. Taking whatever they fancy and only handing it back when it's broken. The upper classes and the bankers eat the poor over here but at least they don't steal their babies.'

She took a sip of tea and getting up flicked the switch on the kettle.

'Right, tell me about yourself. What is it that you do?'

Nick looked at her grandmother's T-shirt and at some of the posters on the wall. Che Guevara's fist raised in salute. The suffragettes marching into battle. She took at deep sigh; she didn't steal babies but apart from that Nick didn't think Mary was about to look favourably on her granddaughter's life. She sighed: in for a penny, in for a pound.

'Well, the thing is, Mary, I work as a stockbroker and I actually have a title. I'm Lady Nicolette Byrne.'

Mary looked up from her teacup and tried to see if Nick was joking. When she saw she wasn't she slammed her hand on the table and roared with laughter.

'All these years! All these years I've hoped for a family reunion and when I finally get it I discover I'm surrounded by sharks and aristos!'

She pushed her chair back and grabbed a set of keys leaving Nick confused at the change of tone.

'Come on then, girl. It's a lovely day and the park is nearby. Let's go and walk your funny little dog and you can tell me more about your life.' Rubbing Ohana's ears she gave her a little bit of cheese and stood up again. 'So what do I call you. Am I supposed to curtsy?'

Nick's eyebrows shot up in alarm.

'Absolutely not. Not even to Ari and she's the countess. As for what to call me, how about Letta? I'm trying out something new at the moment.'

'Not Nick then?'

'No, I'm having some trouble at work at the moment. Actually, it's a lot worse than that, I'm under investigation and I wanted to hide for a bit. I'm finding I quite like Letta, it was my mother's name for me.'

'That's as good a reason as any. So tell me more about being on the run from the law. Maybe you're my kind of girl after all. A modern-day Robin Hood?'

As they headed out of the house Nick wondered exactly what sort of woman her grandmother was. Passing Gabe's car Nick looked concerned.

'Do I need a parking permit?'

'Theoretically. The council just imposed it one day. Without so much as a do-you-mind. I rallied a petition and we fought them to a standstill in the courts. Now only new residents have to apply, but the wardens don't come down here anyway. I saw to that as well.'

Nick dreaded to think. 'So which is your car?'

Mary laughed. 'As if I could afford to run a car, girl. The buses are good enough.'

Nick was confused. 'So why did you lead the action?'

'There's always someone trying to put the working classes in their place. A worker's toil is what makes this country grow and what thanks do they get? Resident permit parking, planning rejections and school holiday fines.'

'So I won't get a fine for parking there?'

'Stick with me and you'll never get a fine again. Now tell me all about your current investigation.'

As they walked around the park, Nick found herself relaxing. She explained her situation and Mary admitted that it was well out of her league, but she was impressed that Nick was so powerful as to be so pursued. Nick didn't see it in quite the same light but kept her opinions to herself. Mary also seemed prepared to accept that Ariana was doing a good job with her title and she approved of the charitable foundation the sisters had set up.

'You seem like a fine family. Michael would have been so proud of you all, I'm sure. I just wish he was around to see it.'

There was nothing to say to that and they walked for a bit in silence. Mary suggested the path leading down to the pond had some lovely views but Ohana went ballistic when she saw the ducks crossing in front of her and in the end Nick had to pick her up and distract her.

A woman with a pushchair tutted at them and Mary stopped and looked her up and down.

'My granddaughter, Lady de Foix, is simply training her dog. Maybe you need to mind your own business. I also note you have bread in your hands. This is contrary to the bylaws of Birmingham City Council; waterfowl are not to be fed bread in the council-run parks as it is bad for their digestions and encourages rats. Would you like me to call the park warden over?'

The woman huffed and muttered something to her toddler but put the bread away and quickly pushed the stroller back up the path.

'I think she'll have trouble when her little one starts calling people silly old cows, don't you?' said Mary to Nick with a huge grin on her face. 'Still, maybe if we walk over to the bandstand? Less to distract Ohana there.'

'Was that true about the bread?'

'Absolutely. The only way to beat people at their own game is to know their rules better than they do. There isn't a council by-law that I haven't studied and there's a fair few I've changed as well.'

At the top of a hill they sat down and looked out over the city.

'So, Letta, now what? Do you drive home? Do we exchange Christmas cards?'

Her voice sounded breezy, but Nick thought she heard a tremor. Over the past hour she had become rather attached to this woman. She had heard the phrase 'blood is thicker than water' but she had never experienced it with an apparent stranger. However, every now and then – from the way Mary spoke, to the turn of her head – Nick was reminded of her father or one of her sisters – it was there in the line of her jaw, a fleeting smile that made her think of Clem, a way of walking that brought Ari to mind.

'If you want? But I think my sisters would very much like to meet you. There's a lot of us, though, it could be overwhelming. Maybe you'd like to come and stay with me for a few days? Get to know us in stages? Plus I've got

Dad's things from the orphanage back where I'm staying, you might like to look at those. And we've Mum's diaries of when they met, so you get to hear about him through her eyes. I don't know, it really is up to you. I've rather intruded on your life…'

Nick trailed off; she was rushing but she suddenly wanted to fill in the gaps in Mary's life.

'And you think I want to waste another second of it? Ignore a family I've just discovered?'

'Well—' Nick took a deep breath, this was so out of character for her, she wondered if she was making a mistake. 'Why not drive back with me and stay for a few days and look through Dad's stuff? We can then work out from there how to meet the others.' As soon as she said the words out loud she knew it was going to be okay, there was no sense of dread as the words were vocalised, no regret, just a small kernel of hope.

Mary looked at her and nodded. 'You know, you really do look like Grainne when you ask a question you're not sure of the answer. So let me speak plainly. Nothing would give me greater pleasure, but just for a few days. I don't want to outstay my welcome.'

It hadn't taken Mary long to pack a suitcase and then they were back on the road. They stopped for a quick break on the motorway and whilst Mary went to the loos, Nick called Ari and told her what was happening.

'Okay. Who are you? And what have you down with my cautious level-headed sister?'

Nick winced, Ari wasn't wrong. Nick prided herself on being predictable and well-planned. This felt insane.

'I know, but I spoke to Clem and she thought it was a good idea.'

'You're taking Clem's advice? Dear God, have I woken up and it's opposites day?'

'No,' grinned Nick.

'No what?'

'You said it was opposites day, so I was making a joke, sorry. And yes, the world has gone mad. I woke up and decided to bag myself a grandmother.'

Nick wondered at the silence on the other end of the line. Ari must have a thousand questions. Probably the most pressing being if her sister had lost her mind?

'What's she like?'

'She seems lovely, but Christ, she's had a brutal life. Look, she's coming back now…'

'Okay, take care and let her know I can't wait to meet her.'

Nick hung up and saw Mary smiling at her.

'One of your sisters?'

'That was Ari, and she's dying to meet you.'

Mary smiled nervously. Suddenly everything was beginning to feel surreal, and she felt her life was about to take a massive change in direction.

Chapter 41

Later that evening, Mary joined Nick at the kitchen table and handed back Lily's diaries.

'Thank you for letting me read these. Seems like my son married a lovely girl. I'd have loved to have met her.'

'Mum was the best, but then I'm biased. It is wonderful to have her diaries, though, we get to see a side of her we never saw as her daughters.'

'And I got to meet my son. He seems to have been a lovely man.'

'The very kindest, and the funniest. He'd always get us laughing, even if we were in a mood. Especially, if we were in a mood. He and Mum were both musical, so they were always singing and playing on the piano. There was one time this lad called round to take Ari out and Dad sang Ari a love song as they walked off down the street. Ari was mortified but her date made sure he brought her back on the dot. Dad had a funny way of letting people know he meant business. It was always through humour, but no one ever messed him about.'

'It must have been tricky for him having five girls to worry about!'

'He said his greatest hardship in life was having to wait in line for the bathroom.'

Nick put some cheese on toast under the overhead grill of the antiquated cooker. Mary rummaged through the fridge pulling out bits for a late supper. There wasn't a lot and Nick made a note to go shopping.

'He would have been so proud of you all, from what you've told me. You are all so successful.'

Nick snorted inelegantly. 'I think I might be letting the side down somewhat at the moment.'

Mary looked across at her and Nick returned her stare. She might be her grandmother but what did this woman really know about her? If she was about to say something trite, Nick would just have to bite her tongue.

'Yes, I suppose you have, haven't you? In your eyes.'

Nick was flummoxed and Mary continued.

'You don't see yourself properly. You haven't taken time to view yourself as an individual.'

Nick was still at a loss. 'I don't follow. I'm totally independent?'

'Well, you are and you aren't,' she paused and put some pickle on the toast that Nick handed to her. 'But that's hardly surprising, is it? The five of you grew into adults knowing that you had to pull together as a family. And I don't mean knowing in some airy-fairy way. I mean if you didn't, you would have been physically separated. Taken into care.'

'You make it sound like us pulling together was a bad thing?' Nick chewed on her toast thoughtfully. She wasn't sure what Mary was driving at, but it was interesting to have an outsider's viewpoint. Sometimes a fresh pair of eyes could throw up a new angle.

'Not in the slightest, but it has made you all over-achievers, and that can be tough to handle when things go wrong.'

'I'm not sure you could describe us as over-achievers? The inheritance was utterly outside of our control, we didn't even know about it.'

Now Mary snorted. 'That has nothing to do with it. My son and your mother had a strong marriage and created a loving family that shaped all of you. Their deaths forged and tested you in a way that few have to cope with. And it made you who you are today. A fancy title and lots of money has nothing to do with that.' She poured her tea checking the colour and then continued. 'Ari fought to make the best of a bad marriage for the sake of her children and sisters.'

'But that was a mistake,' said Nick. That had had nothing to do with over-achieving. 'She should have kicked him to the kerb years before.'

'I don't disagree,' replied Mary sipping her tea, 'but all she knew was that she had to keep everyone together. I mean, from what you said, she gave up everything at eighteen to do that. When she took Greg on, no doubt she felt the same overwhelming desire to protect her marriage as well as her family.

'Then there's your twin, a girl that had a talent for modelling but no passion for it. But she rose close to the top simply in order to put food on the table. The same with Clem, fighting her way into the fashion industry, working in sweatshops just to put money in the family coffers. Then there's you, taking those pennies and turning them into pounds. And finally your baby sister Aster getting a double first from Cambridge. If that's not an over-achieving family I don't know what is.'

Nick shrugged. 'I've never looked at us that way. We just went to work and got on with it.'

'Indeed, and you've all done a bloody good job of it. But some of you now have other things to focus on beyond the day job.'

Nick had just started to eat her toast but now it felt like a heavy lump in her mouth. 'A husband or a child? Modern women don't think in those terms, Mary.'

'Rubbish. Modern women are still humans. And humans like love. They like company.'

'I like my job!'

'And what if you don't have it anymore?'

'Then I've failed.'

'Failed how? Failed who?' Mary challenged Nick as the two women snapped back and forth.

'If I go to jail. Christ, I can't even think about it.'

'So don't. You won't go to jail, unless you did do something wrong.'

'I would never!'

'You might have if you needed to protect the family?'

'Oh.' Nick stopped short. She and Mary had been going back and forth but suddenly she came to a halt. Would she break the law to protect the family? 'I'm not sure that I would ever do something illegal,' she said hesitantly.

'But you're only not sure. Not certain. Do you see how much your family means to you?' asked Mary.

'But that's a good thing,' protested Nick.

'Of course it is, it's incredible. And I am so proud to see my son's children pulling together like this. All I'm trying to say is that you need to start thinking about doing things that make *you* happy, not just that are good for the business or good for other people. Take some time to think about what makes you smile.'

'Work makes me smile!'

'And if you can't work?'

'We're going around in circles!'

'Yes, we are, and I suspect it's time for bed. Come on, child, leave those dishes and go to bed, I'll tidy up.'

Bemused, Nick said that she would go for a ride first. Mary had given her a lot to think about and she wanted to stretch her legs.

–

An hour later she cycled back to the house, the full moon had made the ride enjoyable and spooky at the same time. As she cycled along the drive she listened as an owl called out in the woods. Propping her bike by the kitchen door she walked into the kitchen to see that Mary had indeed tidied up. Ohana was fast asleep in her bed and Nick tiptoed past, careful not to disturb her.

It all seemed so simplistic through Mary's eyes, but Nick didn't think she properly understood the severity of Nick's plight. Like Seb, Mary seemed to think Nick would manage just fine if her trading licence was revoked. But they didn't know how that made her feel. How she wanted to retch every time she thought of the shame it would bring, and how much she would miss doing what she had loved doing for a decade. Maybe Gabe was right, maybe she needed to think the impossible and start to consider a new five-year plan.

Thinking of Gabe she sent him a quick text explaining that she tracked down her grandmother.

> I'm afraid I invited her to stay with me for a bit. Is this a problem?

A second later the phone buzzed as if he had been waiting to hear from her.

> Wow! That's incredible news. Of course it's not a problem. There are some old beds on the top floor if Rafe or I need to stay over. Please tell your grandmother to feel at home. As much as is possible in that place. X

> Thank you.

She paused typing. She didn't want to keep the conversation going but didn't want it to end either. Instead she attached a photo of Ohana in the kitchen sink with a tower of soap suds on her head. Nick didn't know what the dog had rolled in, but she had never smelt anything quite so rank.

> That's fabulous! Can't wait to see you again. X

> Agreed. Good night. X

Nick looked at her message. She rolled her eyes at 'agreed' and then laughed at the 'X'. Talk about mixed messages. She tried again.

> It really will be lovely to see you again.
> Sleep tight.

Happier with her second attempt, she smiled as he returned a picture of a pack of playing cards.

She typed another reply.

> You're on. Now I have to go to sleep!

> ♥

Nick looked at the little heart on the screen and wondered what to make of that. Smiling, she fell asleep.

Chapter 42

Two days had stretched into five and neither woman felt the strain of it. The second day, Nick had driven Mary into the local town. Mary wanted to go to church and pray for Michael.

'They're not one of those guitar-playing types, are they?'

Nick then had to explain that she didn't go to church and wouldn't know. Mary frowned but was slightly mollified to hear that Ari and Paddy did, although mostly just high days and holidays. Nick had to grudgingly accept that she also went to church on those days but made it clear to Mary that she didn't actually believe.

Nick felt Mary looking at her as though she was a particularly recalcitrant piece of local legislation, but she held her ground and told Mary to call her when she wanted a lift home.

—

Four hours later Mary walked down the driveway and straight into the bath. Mary's long walks became a feature of her stay, she would head out with Ohana for a small stroll whilst Nick worked across in the renovation. Then in the afternoon she would head out for several hours. Each time Nick saw her grandmother change. She looked like a person decompressing. At the beginning she would return with a blotchy face and red swollen eyes, but soon she started smiling and laughing more regularly.

Her grandmother was clearly walking her way out of decades of grief. Nick commented on it now as they sat beside the stone steps leading down to the once-formal gardens. The women had taken to eating their supper outside as the warm air made this a magical time of day. Now in the dusk, they looked over a meadow, as a barn owl glided in the distance looking for any little mice, bold enough to be out and about.

'Where will you walk tomorrow?'

'I don't know where I walked today.' Mary paused and ate some of her salad. 'But I think I'll start by turning left at the large oak rather than right. See where that takes me.'

Both women fell silent as they watched the barn owl make another swoop.

'You enjoy walking then?'

A silence fell, only punctured by a bird calling in the distance. Nick wondered if she had somehow offended or overstepped the mark, when Mary replied.

'I find that walking has changed this past week. I hadn't realised but before, whenever and wherever I walked, I was always looking for Michael. I didn't know I was doing it until this week when I stopped. I know where he is now. And I know through my prayers, that he can hear me and know the truth of his childhood. Now when I head out, I'm just walking, not searching. I feel a lightness in me.'

Silence fell again. Nick was glad that Mary was healing like this – she had no truck with her father being in heaven watching over them, as much as she wanted that comfort, but she wouldn't deny Mary's belief in it. Everyone had to find their own truth to navigate their journey through life.

'Okay, I'm turning in. Rafe is coming down in a few days for a site inspection and I want to make sure everything is on track.'

Picking up her plate and empty glass she headed back into the house, leaving Mary to watch the owl.

–

Something woke Nick. She had been dreaming of a great storm, the wind howling around the building, with the dead rising from the graveyard. Now she was staring out in the dark, uncertain if she was still dreaming. She listened, ears straining in the silence and then heard a bang from downstairs. That wasn't a dream. She couldn't hear Ohana, but would Ohana bark if there were burglars? What if they had hurt the little dog? Grabbing her dressing gown, she quietly opened her bedroom door and crept along the passageway towards the top of the stairs. The corridor was suddenly full of light and Mary stood at the other end of the hallway in a pair of pyjamas holding a hammer.

'Can you hear that?' she whispered.

'Why are you whispering?' whispered Nick terrified.

'I don't want to alert the burglars.'

'Do you think they won't notice the light?' Nick was shaking. In London she always locked her doors, took care when she walked at night and always carried a can of mace. Here in the countryside she had let her guard down. Now Mary had alerted a whole gang of thieves to their presence.

'Good point. Bugger.'

The two women looked at each other as they heard the sound of a chair leg being dragged along a downstairs floor.

'They're not very quiet thieves?'

'Maybe they think the place is empty? Bang on the radiator there with your hammer, see if they react.'

The metallic noise clanged through the otherwise silent house and there was a sudden commotion downstairs.

'Bloody hell? How many are there?'

At that moment, a terrified moan called out through the night and Nick seriously considered having a heart attack. She had never even entertained the idea of ghosts and yet here she was in the middle of the night, in an ancient house, listening to the blood-curdling moan of a—

'Cows. Bloody hell, Letta, I think the cows have got into the house.'

Mary rushed downstairs with Nick following sheepishly behind. When she reached the hallway she was horrified to see large shapes moving in the shadows. Flicking on the light switch Mary revealed the full horror.

From where she was standing she could see three cows ambling along the hallway. They seemed to have come from the kitchen and from the sound of it there were more in there. From their direction of travel they were heading into the sitting room, and by the sounds of it some were already in there. One of the wooden kitchen chairs was in the hallway and a large groove was etched through the rather worn wallpaper.

'Oh Monty!' sighed Mary, admonishing one of the long-horned cows. 'What have you done?'

From Monty's other horn hung a tea-towel. He swung his head in a slow, confused manner, in Mary's direction.

'I know, I know. Let's get you out of here, shall we?' Mary put her hammer down on the staircase and looked up at Letta.

'Right. We don't want to spook them, not in an enclosed space. Let's stop any more from coming in and then carefully herd out the rest. We'll use the patio door in the sitting room, so we won't need to turn them around.'

Mary stepped into the corridor, then carefully passing Monty she headed into the kitchen.

'Mary. Wait!' hissed Nick alarmed. 'You can't leave these cows to wander amok.'

'Tell you what then, I'll go this way, see how they're getting in and stop them. You go that way and open the patio doors. Try not to alarm them as you squeeze past.'

Nick looked to her right as another cow, with its long shaggy coat, wide horns and heavy feet ambled into the sitting room and decided to follow Mary instead.

'Good choice. Now, mind where you stand, the girls aren't house-trained.'

Indeed, Nick could hardly miss the smell of the occasional steaming brown lump. Her heart sank with the thought of cleaning it all up and she gingerly made her way down the corridor after Mary. The kitchen was a mess: pots and pans were on the floor, the table had been shoved to one side and one of the chairs was now only good for firewood.

At the far end, the door stood open to the night, and a cow peered in.

'Angus!' shooed Mary. 'Away with you. The others will be out soon enough.'

Scolded, the cow stepped back apologetically as Mary closed the door.

'Have you actually named all the cows?'

'No, I just give them names as I go along. I know a few by sight and if I stayed longer I'd know the lot, but it seems rude not to give them a name. Now come on, let's go and sort out the others.'

As they walked back along the hall, Nick winced at the mess. A few months ago she would have freaked out at the chaos, now it seemed like a daily occurrence.

'You seem very at ease with them? I have to admit I find them a bit unnerving out in their field. Indoors, they are – well, they're really quite big, aren't they?' said Nick nervously.

'My folks had a farm, and I grew up looking after the animals. Turns out some skills never leave you.' She walked into the sitting room and stopped in the doorway. 'Oh dear. That's quite a sight.'

The two women stood side by side and looked at the eight Highland cattle that had now finished their wandering and were lying down between the sofa and the chairs. As unfurnished as the house was there was actually just about enough room for them all, but the side table's days were over, and there was a waste basket poking out from under one of the cows. Worst of all, Nick's laptop lay broken on the floor, a hoof print in the middle of it.

'Bollocks!' Nick was about to dash in to retrieve it when Mary grabbed her arm.

'Shh. Nice and easy. These ladies won't mean to hurt you, but do not startle them. We can fix and replace a laptop; we can't replace you. Now, let me think.'

Nick looked at her laptop in despair as one of the cows waggled her ears apologetically at her. 'It's okay, Molly, not your fault.'

'That's the spirit,' beamed Mary as she got her phone out and started to dial.

'Mr Ferguson? Sorry to call you so early. It's Mary Byrne over at Parscombe's. I'm afraid the electric fence has failed, and we have your girls milling around the place. I've got eight penned up safely in the sitting room. Yes. Sitting room. The others are milling around outside. I'm just worried because the end of our drive doesn't have a cattle grid, they'll walk straight out onto the road. Okay. Yes, I'll put the kettle on.' Hanging up she smiled at Nick, 'If we still have a kettle.'

'Are we just going to leave them there?'

'Yep, safest place for them.'

'But my laptop?'

'I could try and fetch it for you?'

Nick looked at the size of Mary against the cattle and shook her head. They were in a strange place and no doubt spooked. As Mary said, there was no point in agitating them.

'No, leave it, fingers crossed, it will be fine. I'll retrieve the hard drive later.'

When the women returned to the kitchen, the kettle was happily working and before it had even reached the boil, the farmer had arrived with a few drovers. In the early dawn light the men began to herd the cows back down the lawn and into the meadow below.

'Right then,' said Mr Ferguson. 'Here's where the fence failed. Bloody bad luck. I'll get that fixed this morning and get one of the men to stay here until I do. Now, let's go and get your squatters.'

As they trudged back to the house, Nick prayed that the cows hadn't done any more damage. Granted, this house hadn't been modernised yet but still she felt like a caretaker and she was currently failing in her duty.

'They're through here.' As the men walked into the room they gave a low chuckle.

'Sorry, Letta, I shouldn't laugh.'

'Ah it's okay, it looks like one of my sister's more ridiculous photo shoots. Mary thought they could leave via the patio doors?'

A plan of action was soon agreed and two of the men stood outside ready to guide the cows out. Mr Ferguson then made his way carefully through the now-sleeping cows and gently opened the patio doors. The next part of the plan was that Mary and Letta would close the sitting-room door and Mr Ferguson and his farmhands would coax the cows out and home. It was going to be a slow and careful process. However, as the doors opened, the cows smelt the fresh grass in the morning air, a hint of dew for their parched mouths, and they sprang up. Or as much as a tonne of weight can spring anywhere. In a hullabaloo of moos, they banged into each other and the furniture in a rush to break free. Grabbing Letta, Mary dragged her out of the room and quickly closed the door behind then. There was a thud on the door and generally a lot of lowing and then silence.

Mary cautiously opened the door and peered in the room. One cow was left, standing in the patio doors, reluctant to leave.

'Come on now, Cecily. Out you go.' Mary clapped her hands, and Cecily swung her huge head to look around at Mary reproachfully, then with dainty, careful steps she headed towards the open door where Mr Ferguson was calling her through. She sniffed the air, paused to empty her bowels all over Nick's now-shattered laptop, then stepped out into the dawn.

'Is everything okay?' whispered Nick from the hallway.

Mary looked at the rather crumpled room and the steaming pile of dung. 'The cows are okay. The room less so and I'm afraid I think your laptop is past recovery.'

Nick joined Mary and looked at her laptop in horror.

'Yeah, that's dead.' She looked around at the scene of devastation and then shrugged her shoulders. 'Cup of tea?'

–

A couple of hours later she and Mary had cleaned and scrubbed down the house. Rugs were drying out on the patio and some of the builders had helped carry out the broken furniture. Letta showed them the pictures on her phone and pretty soon they were circling around social media. A new laptop had been ordered and Pat, Mr Ferguson's wife, had driven over with a load of food including two evening meals.

'I don't reckon you fancy cooking after the day you've had.' Letta invited her to stay and join them, but she waved them away saying she had to sort out her children and left them to it.

The following morning Rafe and Gabe were due to come over and now Nick would have to explain why they were down a sideboard and an armchair. Hopefully, any lingering smells would have gone by then. Laughing at their adventures, the two women turned in and Nick wondered how things would be with Gabe.

Chapter 43

Nick woke to a foul smell and wondered if the cattle had got in again. Gabe and Rafe were arriving this afternoon ahead of this weekend's viewing and they wanted to get everything prepared.

As she wandered into the kitchen Mary was baking and apologised for the smell, promising it would be gone in an hour or so. Whatever she was cooking Letta didn't want to eat, the smell was noxious.

The builders had arrived early as everyone wanted to make sure they were ahead of schedule when the brothers arrived. Out of the window she could see Jordan walking across and they obviously had some questions before they got going. She had backed her computer up to the cloud but trying to open the spreadsheets on her phone was a pain. Surprisingly, though, her world hadn't actually fallen apart. Two months ago she would have gone insane if she had lost her laptop, now it was a nuisance but no more than that. Still, it did make it harder for her to help with the building quants. She leant out of the large sash window and called out to Jordan.

'Morning. I'll be with you in a minute. I just need to open a few more windows.'

Jordan looked at her blankly as though pretending there was nothing to smell, and Nick felt the need to justify herself.

'Mary's been making sage butter and apparently when you roast sage it can be quite smelly.'

'Yeah, that's not sage butter,' smirked the young builder, grinning from ear to ear. 'That's weed.'

'Why would Mary eat weeds?'

'Not weeds, weed. Hash, ganga, cannabis. Marijuana Mary, hey?'

At that moment Mary breezed into the kitchen. Nick turned and stared at her grandmother.

'Mary, Jordan says that smell isn't sage?'

Mary took in Letta's horrified expression and Jordan's smile as he leant in through the window, and knew the game was up.

'It's medicinal.'

'It's what?'

'Medicinal. Oh, I don't know,' said Mary in an exasperated fashion. Why was she being forced to justify herself. 'I have arthritis and it helps with the pain. I don't like to smoke it, so I turn it into butter and eat it.'

'But it's illegal.'

'Well, I don't make the laws.'

'No, but you are supposed to abide by them!' Nick was furious. Mary knew that she was currently under investigation. What the hell was she thinking? This wasn't even her house. Now she was turning the house into a drug den.

'Rafe and Gabe will be here this afternoon for a site visit. You know they have buyers coming this weekend. What if this place still smells? For God's sake, Mary, get rid of it now!'

Slamming out of the kitchen, she stormed across to the other house. Had she overreacted? She didn't want to abuse the guys' hospitality and she certainly didn't want any more investigations. She understood that people did use cannabis and that it probably wasn't the end of the world, but right now it just seemed like one problem too many. Playing at building renovations was an enjoyable interlude but she missed her day job and wanted to be trading again.

Her phone pinged an alert. Her heart raced as she saw a text from Gabe. They had got into the habit of sending each other little brain teasers or photos. She tapped a quick reply.

> Yolks are yellow!

She smiled when he sent back a laughing Road Runner meme.

The phone pinged again. Did he ever work? she wondered. This time it was a link to a cycling event in Cornwall. It was for next spring and she liked the idea that he was planning that far ahead.

> Looks good! Got to get back to work, my landlord is down later and he's very fussy.

She laughed out loud as the next text was simply a picture of a raspberry. Pocketing her phone, she carried on assembling the furniture.

All day long, deliveries arrived for the set dressing. Rafe wanted a few areas to be made up to suggest what life would be like once the house was fully renovated. He had ordered an outside set of table and chairs with parasols and a patio heater. An oak pergola was festooned with fairy lights. There was also a set of outdoor cane chairs and loungers and a large firepit. As each item arrived, Letta had it assembled and placed in various locations on the large stone patio running between the two properties.

She kept the table closest to the house on the principle that if you were bringing meals from the kitchen you wouldn't want to be walking too far. Plus the shelter of the house helped with any breezes. In summer, a breeze might be welcome but in spring and autumn, a breeze was likely to be less pleasant. She placed the firepit and seats closer to the sweeping stone steps in the middle of the patio. The view was excellent and was perfect for just lounging around, maybe playing games with a friend. Popping back to her house, Nick was relieved that she could no longer smell anything.

'I wanted to say sorry for losing my rag earlier. That wasn't the best way to handle things.'

Mary smiled apologetically for pretending it was sage.

'It is quite stinky, isn't it? And I hadn't thought it through. I've spent my whole life not having to think of other people and I rather forgot my manners.'

Nick nodded glad to have cleared the air, she hated drama.

'Now I'm heading into town,' Mary continued. 'I'm going to cook tonight for the four of us. Jordan's giving me a lift – can I get you anything?'

Nick shook her head. 'There's no need, I already suggested to Rafe that I could cook but he said we'd just order some pizzas or something.'

Mary pulled a face. 'I don't eat pizza. Besides, I want to say "thank you" properly. Their generosity has meant I have had time to spend with my granddaughter and get to learn about my family. Going Dutch on some pizzas doesn't really work for me as a way to say thank you.'

Knowing that Mary was determined on this point, Nick decided to let it go and returned to the building site. She watched as a little while later, Mary drove past with Jordan. Drum and bass was pounding out of the window and Mary was waving her arms in time to the beat. As grandmothers went, Mary didn't seem to fit the mould. Leo and Will were going to think she was excellent.

A few hours later the horn beeped, and Mary waved as she drove past. Startled, Nick looked up from her Allen key and was astonished that the time had flown past. Gabe would be here soon, and she had wanted to have everything set up for him and Rafe when they arrived.

–

After a successful site visit, the brothers were impressed with the progress and felt comfortable that the property was ready for prospective buyers. This way any current purchaser would have the option of detailing their own finishes. Mary and Letta sat down at the table as Rafe and Gabriel insisted on carrying the food out to them.

'Mary, this smells delicious, and I can't even believe that the house was full of cow dung yesterday,' remarked Gabe. 'I'm so sorry you had to cope with that.'

Everyone laughed as Mary started to serve up.

'Well, I'm just sorry that I've kicked you out of your bed.'

Despite the size of the house the boys had only set up two bedrooms, which Letta and Mary were now occupying. Despite the women's protests Rafe had opted for the sofa and Gabe had a camping mattress.

'Trust me. We've slept in worse places.'

'Agreed. Plus the company more than makes up for it.'

As they ate, they chatted about everything and nothing and studiously ignored Nick's upcoming trial and previous entanglement with the Harrington family.

–

Mary thanked Rafe as he topped up her glass and the pair of them watched as Letta and Gabe headed down the stone steps. His laugh drifted up to them and Letta pretended to recoil then punched him playfully on the arm as they carried on their stroll.

'Do you think it's serious?' asked Mary, watching them closely.

Rafe studied his brother. 'I can't speak for Letta, but Gabe is head over heels about her. When he met her in Ireland he couldn't stop telling me about her.' Rafe chuckled. 'Actually, he hasn't stopped talking about her since. The problem is that he's worried about our family's involvement in her current predicament. Evicting her when she was under an FCA investigation has made him feel dreadful.'

'About her feelings for him?' said Mary in surprise. 'I think they're clear?'

'No, I think he's worried that she blames him for being a Harrington. I think he's so besotted with her that he can't conceive that she might feel the same way as he does.'

'If you ask me, I don't think she has even noticed how she feels. She has so much else on her plate that she hasn't had a chance to just switch off.'

'Letta doesn't seem the switch-off sort, though, does she? I mean, look how she's stepped in here to help us with supplies. And when she's not working, she's running or cycling.'

'She's exhausting.'

'Makes the rest of us look bad.'

'Lazy Buggers United, I say.'

Mary raised her glass and Rafe chinked it as they fondly watched Letta and Gabe follow Ohana down to the meadow.

Chapter 44

Gabe helped Letta over the electric fence and pointed as Ohana ran off and said hello to the cows.

'Mary names them all, you know. I think that one is Genevieve.'

'Any Nicolettas?'

'Did you just call me a cow?' Letta laughed and hit Gabe playfully on the arm. He recoiled and started to stammer an apology. He had been looking forward to seeing Letta all week and the first thing he did when they had some time on their own was insult her.

'No, I just meant long pretty names.'

'I know, silly. I was teasing you.'

The two walked on a bit, not sure what to say. Gabe liked this new Letta. Despite all that was facing her she seemed more relaxed.

'Do you know, I wanted to thank you for letting me stay here. I think it's been good for me.' A breeze caught a lock of her hair and swept it in front of her face. He wanted to reach out and remove it but was uncertain how she would respond.

'God, my hair is killing me.'

'I like it.'

Letta paused and looked up at him before she carried on walking. *Very smooth*, thought Gabe and moved quickly to catch up with her again.

'I'm glad we could help – you've been a godsend in getting the build back on track.' He paused and wondered if he should continue. 'You seem happier? I mean, not *happier*, maybe more relaxed.'

'What? With a court case looming and the risk of a jail term, you think I look more relaxed?' She laughed to take the sting out of her words, and he realised he could spend a lifetime listening to her laugh. He was about to try and explain himself, but she cut him off.

'But you're right. I do feel calmer. Mary is a bit of a wild card, but I've enjoyed her company and I think I've been helping her. It sounds dumb but helping people feels good. I mean genuinely good. Oh, I don't know, I sound like a hippy, but I think you know what I mean.'

'Stands to reason – the first thing you and your sisters did when you got all your money was set up a charity to help others. It's obviously something that means a lot to you.'

'It does. I love making money, too, there's a real thrill in being proved right and jumping ahead of the market. But recently I was spending more time making the money without seeing how it was being used. Now I'm helping again, and I can see a direct response to my actions.'

She tucked her hair behind her ear. 'I'm wittering but it's also been fun to spend time with people who aren't staff. I think I'd got stuck into a cul-de-sac.'

'Was it tough with Mary?'

'Beyond tough. She's had such a rough life. You know, she didn't abandon Dad, he was taken from her and then she was told he had been adopted and gone to England. She followed immediately and spent the rest of her life searching for him.'

'Christ. That's appalling.'

'I know. I'm just so glad I went to Ireland.'

'So am I.'

Gabe was used to calling Letta bold, now it was his turn.

'In fact, going to Ireland has been the best thing that has ever happened to me.'

'Gabe, I—'

'No, hear me out. I've been kicking myself for not telling you how I feel about you. Every day felt wrong, there always seemed a good reason to put it off. Not least that I was – scratch that – I am afraid of making a fool of myself.'

Letta stopped and smiled up at him. 'You feel foolish?'

'It's the side effect of being in love.'

'In love?'

'Foolish and unrequited?'

'No, just foolish.'

Letta walked on and then looked over her shoulder at Gabe who was frozen to the spot staring after her.

'Not unrequited?' He could hardly hope that Letta felt the same as him. Maybe she was just being nice? How could she possibly feel how he did? Since he had come home from Ireland he hadn't been able to stop thinking of her.

Now she stopped walking and turned to look at him properly.

'No, not unrequited.'

Gabe took a step forward. Emboldened, he tucked the hair that was blowing about in the breeze behind her ear.

'Letta, I…'

Letta smiled at him wistfully but shook her head. 'Gabe, it's not unrequited in the slightest. But honestly—'

She paused and stepped away from him – he hoped he sensed some reluctance in her movement.

'I can't focus on a new relationship right now; I need to clear my name. Until that's done I just can't think about my personal life. Not until my professional one is fixed.'

Gabe took a deep breath. She was worth the wait, plus what he had discovered back in London may speed up her acquittal. He realised he was grinning like an idiot, but he couldn't help himself.

'Okay then, I can wait.'

'You can?'

'Letta, I can wait a thousand years. I don't care how long this takes. When you are ready I will be with you.'

He wanted to step forward and kiss her to seal his declaration, but she had taken a deep breath and spun away, walking back towards the house. He paused, uncertain what to do. Had he come on too strong? She stopped and looked over her shoulder at him and gave him a huge smile that made his heart explode.

'Come on, slow coach. I've got to hurry up and clear my name. New goals and all that.' Grinning she turned back, and he punched the air laughing before he ran to catch up with her.

As they rejoined Rafe and Mary, the pair of them were smiling like children and were entertaining the party with tales of crashing waves and fallen trees. Mary produced a pack of cards, and under the fairy lights the night fell and the evening was punctuated with laughter and owl calls.

Chapter 45

'Letta!' John's voice echoed along the hallway to where she was discussing nails with some of the team. It had never really occurred to her that there was much to a nail, but since working with the carpenters and joiners, she had had her eyes opened. Though not with nails.

Calling out to the foreman she was surprised to see him jogging towards her.

'There's a dirty big Rolls-Royce coming down the drive – it's not the buyers, is it? I thought you said they were coming tomorrow.'

'They are. They were. Hell.' Nick scrambled up from her knees. She was wearing long shorts, steel-toed boots, a sleeveless T-shirt and a hard hat – it was not the look she would have chosen to greet a prospective buyer.

'Let me go and have a look and if it is them, call Raphael and Gabriel immediately.'

The brothers had left the place two days ago and since then Nick had been dancing on air. Gabe felt the same way she did and now she was desperate to get her life back in gear. She had been bugging her solicitor for updates on the case. The evidence didn't stack up. From one angle she was guilty as sin, on the other, nothing had happened. She wanted it tested and thrown out. In the meantime, she wanted to do all she could to make this house a success for Gabe and Rafe. Their project manager was coming back to work next week, and Nick wanted to hand over the property and focus on her own trial.

Running to the kitchen sink she washed her hands, then looked around for something to dry them on. Sighing, she wiped them on the back of her shorts. The kitchen might have a sink but that was it, the units wouldn't be going in for a while yet; it was too much to hope that there might actually be a hand towel.

Crossing her fingers that the owner of the Rolls-Royce was just a curious neighbour, Nick ran out the front door as a Korean couple stepped out of the car. Nick guessed they were in their mid-thirties and from the way they were looking at the house they were not passing through.

'Mr Lee and Mrs Chung. I am delighted to meet you.' Nick gave a respectful bow to the correct depth and was pleased to note their approval. The Lees may be the epitome of modern money, with almost limitless wealth, but that meant the traditions became more important. She most certainly would not comment on the fact they had arrived a day early. To do so would be to suggest error. But bloody hell. She didn't want to be responsible for screwing up this sales pitch – hell, she didn't even know how much money the boys were planning on selling it for. She turned to Jordan who had arrived by her side.

'Please fetch hats for our guests.' Quietly she continued, 'Tell Rafe to text me the house sale details.'

Returning to the couple she apologised for the delay but invited them to join her on a tour of the exterior.

'We are happy to wait, and the weather is lovely,' began Mr Lee Kwang-jin. 'Incidentally, I apologise for turning up early. We were in the area, so we thought, what the heck.'

'You are most welcome whenever you choose to call.'

By now John had returned with some hard hats and Nick asked him to start the tour of the interior. As they walked inside, the house had fallen silent. All the workers had stopped and were now somewhere out the back. John talked at length about the historical features that were being repaired and the architecture of the house. He also spoke at length about the craftsmen working on the project, where they had trained, the buildings they had worked on before, which included various palaces, castles, cathedrals, even the Houses of Parliament. Buying this house was not about the bricks and mortar but about British history and John was doing a fabulous pitch. Nick was surreptitiously trying to read Rafe's texts.

> 10 million.

> What finish?

> Whatever they want.

Nick was about to text again when she saw Mrs Chung Ki-soon glance over her shoulder at her and smile conspiratorially. Tucking her phone in her pocket, she grinned back and rejoined the conversation.

They walked into the large ballroom and Ki-soon clapped her hands excitedly. Nick was glad that she could see through the bare walls and the unfinished surfaces. She thought this room had wonderful impact and although it was a little impractical for the average family, Mr Lee and Mrs Chung were anything but average.

Ki-soon spoke quickly to Kwang-jin in Korean, Nick caught the word 'wannabe' and laughed loudly.

'Yes!' 'Wannabe' was a K-pop hit by the band Itzy – the video was set in a large ornate ballroom. It had multi-coloured painted walls in a chinoiserie style and rococo mouldings, proving the old adage that 'more can always be more'. Nick began to sing the words to 'Wannabe' and Kwang-jin and Ki-soon joined in, including the complicated shoulder dance and fast steps. John watched on in bemusement as Nick – who was normally so quiet and reserved – and Mr Lee laughed and danced along.

'You know K-pop!' said Ki-soon.

'I love K-pop! I worked in Korea for a short spell and really got into it.'

'Can you do Apink's hand dance?'

'Yes, but I don't think we'd be any good together.'

Ki-soon frowned prettily. 'I know I am too short.'

'Rubbish,' laughed Nick, 'I'm too tall.'

'What about SF9's pinwheel?' asked Kwang-jin. The pinwheel was an incredibly difficult dance and Nick told them how she and her fellow workers had tried once, and they nearly had to call out the emergency services to patch them up.

'The pinwheel is one of my husband's specialities,' said Ki-soon proudly. 'He and his friends are excellent at it. He even joined SF9 on stage once to do it.'

Nick was suitably impressed. Of course money could buy them anything, but even so, performing live with a K-pop band would be brilliant fun. 'You know, you could always invite Itzy over here to recreate their video in the ballroom?'

Ki-soon's eyes lit up and Nick wondered if she had just sealed the deal. Laughing, the three of them continued the tour and Nick could see they liked the property, even in its unfinished state.

By now they had wandered outside and were sitting at the patio tables and chairs that they had set up the other day. Nick was about to apologise for a lack of refreshments when she saw Mary walking towards her with a team of builders carrying trays of drinks and nibbles. In front of Mary, Ohana led the way.

As she arrived, Nick stood up and the Koreans followed suit.

'Hello, darling. I thought you and your guests might like a drink?' Mary was acting as if ordering builders to do her bidding was an everyday occurrence and fair play to them, the lads were laying out the dishes beautifully and pouring glasses of cucumber and lemon iced water for everyone. Nick could only applaud the speed with which Mary had rustled something up.

'Grandma, may I present Mr Lee and his wife Mrs Chung. Mr Lee, Mrs Chung, my grandmother.' Formality was going to be her friend here. 'Grandma, will you join us?'

'Will you forgive me?' Mary gave Letta and her guests a charming smile. 'Ohana needs her morning stroll and I think it's going to be too hot for her later on.'

Ki-soon and Ohana had been bonding over ear rubs but when she heard the dog's name she looked up in surprise.

'Did you know Ohana means "family" in some Pacific cultures?'

Nick nodded. 'That's why I named her; family is everything to me.'

'Are you both living here?'

'Just for a short while. We are spending some time together and then we will go and join my sisters. I just offered to help Rafe whilst I was between projects.'

As Kevin finished pouring the drinks he turned to Nick. 'Can I get you anything else, Lady Nicoletta?'

Nick smiled inwardly; *no weapon left unused, hey, Mary?* Smiling warmly she told him that would be fine, and they could get back to work now.

'I'm glad you aren't stopping them from working on our account. Industry must out,' observed Kwang-jin.

'Yes, for your own safety they stopped whilst we were in the house but soon the noise level will pick back up again.' Although Nick was prepared to bet that John wouldn't be using the drills or angle grinders until the potential buyers had left.

'May I ask,' said Ki-soon, 'he called you Lady Nicoletta. Is that a title?'

'It is, but these things don't really matter amongst friends. Please just call me Letta.'

Mary chipped in. 'And please just call me Mary.' Nick worked hard not to laugh as her grandmother – who had no title but was acting as though she was a duchess – continued. 'The only title we tend to pay attention to is that of Letta's eldest sister, she is the Countess Hiverton.' Mary paused, as though everyone would know immediately how important Ariana was. Naturally, the couple didn't have a clue, but they understood countess was a big deal, and nodded respectfully. Nick was certain that Kwang-jin was impressed. 'Anyway, if you will forgive me, we have taken up too much of your time.'

Standing to leave, everyone rose with her and only sat down again as she and Ohana headed for the trees.

'I like this house,' said Kwang-jin decisively, 'but it is missing a few things.'

'Such as?'

'A swimming pool.'

Nick nodded in agreement. That would be a lovely addition and easily arranged. She pointed to a patch of land in front of them. 'I think over there would be perfect and the views over the countryside would be incredible.'

'It would be too cold!' exclaimed Ki-soon, giving a mock shudder.

'It would be heated, naturally,' Nick tried to reassure her. She was determined to give the very best sales pitch she could.

'And in summer the paparazzi would send over helicopters and drones to spy on us.'

'After a few shotguns they soon tire.'

'I usually find that threatening to bankrupt the publishers puts paid to any intrusion,' said Kwang-jin and Nick gulped. This was some serious level of power being bandied about.

'But in winter it would rain,' protested Ki-soon. *Good grief, doesn't this woman want a pool?* thought Nick.

'That didn't bother us when we were in the Japanese national parks,' said Kwang-jin turning to Nick. 'We had the place closed to the public and we played in Shibu Onsen.'

Ki-soon laughed happily. 'That's right, it was snowing, and the monkeys were all at one end of the pool with snow on their heads as they submerged themselves in the hot water.'

'That sounds like a lovely memory,' said Nick, 'although I don't think there are too many monkeys in the Cotswolds, so I don't think you'd have to share the pool.'

'I still don't think I'd like to swim in the wind and the rain, though, no matter how warm the water.'

Nick thought it sounded lovely but then she wasn't buying the place.

'Build a second one then.' Nick thought quickly. On the other side of the house there was a small rise of ground with the same views. 'We'll excavate the land and put the pool into the side of the hill, then we can landscape over the top of it and all anyone will see is a wall of tinted glass. Warm and private and great views.'

'And how would we get to it? We'd still have to run out in the wind and rain.' She stood up and mimed herself trying to run in the wind whilst pulling a towel around her. Her high heels clattered on the stone, and her jewelled handbag swung on her elbow. Nick was working hard to imagine the towel. Kwang-jin laughed indulgently and Nick smiled – at this rate, she wasn't even going to build them a duck pond. Who would have thought convincing someone to have a swimming pool would be such hard work? Still, he clearly wanted one, so Nick continued.

'Naturally, we'd build an underground passageway. I was thinking we could tile it with mosaics, like a Roman villa?'

'And these swimming pools, they are in the asking price?'

'That would be additional.'

'And the asking price for this one?' asked Kwang-jin. 'We are looking at a few, it's hard to remember.' *Nice touch*, thought Nick, as he sought to remind her that she had competitors.

'I believe Raphael is looking at around £10 million.'

'Oh, that's a good price,' said Ki-soon excitedly and lapsed into a sudden silence as her husband frowned at her. Nick wondered about inviting her to play poker.

'It is a good price, as my wife says. But I would expect a helipad. Is there one?'

'No, but we could throw one of those in with the asking price.'

'How about over there behind those trees?' he said, pointing to a small copse beyond the wing of the house that she and Mary were currently living in.

'Ah, I'm afraid that area belongs to that property.'

'The £10 million doesn't buy that property?'

'No, that's for this half of the estate only.'

'Ten million is a lot of money for next-door neighbours.' He frowned; suddenly the asking price seemed more reasonable but not the bargain he thought he had been about to scoop up.

'You'd pay that in Kensington and you'd have a whole street of neighbours,' said Nick, determined to keep him on the hook. 'Still, I'm sure if you made an offer for the entire estate, Raphael would consider it?'

Nick wanted to move away from the negotiations. It wasn't her place to talk financials and she had no idea what plans the brothers had for the second house.

'So tell me,' she asked, changing the subject. 'Why the Cotswolds? Is it this property that interested you or the location?'

Kwang-jin laughed and leant over and touched his wife's knee. 'Ki-soon here is hoping to bump into Rupert Campbell-Black!'

Ki-soon swatted her husband's hand away and laughed loudly.

'Monster! Of course I'm not.' She winked at Nick. 'But wouldn't it be fabulous? I fell in love with the area when I was reading the books.'

Nick grinned back at her – who indeed could resist the fabled charms of the notorious womaniser.

'Snap. I have to confess; I would always pinch my sister's copy when she wasn't looking. Honestly, Jilly Cooper is wonderful.'

Laughing, the two women raised their glasses in a toast.

'To K–pop, the Cotswolds and Rupert Campbell-Black!'

Chapter 46

It was Monday and Nick found herself at a loose end. Rafe told her that the Lees were interested but as yet hadn't made an offer. Bernard Payne, the building's project manager, had arrived on site first thing and she had spent an hour with him handing back the reins. After that, her time was her own. Leaving Ohana with Mary she grabbed her bike and decided to exhaust herself with a big ride through the Cotswold hills. As she returned she was already making plans to head over to the Malverns tomorrow; that would be a much tougher day and she needed to check if Mary was happy to have Ohana for the entire day. As she cycled past the building site she heard a girl's laugh peel out of one of the open windows and she screeched to a halt. Dropping her bike on the verge she ran towards the house and into the ballroom.

'Aster!'

Aster had been crouched on the floor with a group of builders, where she was apparently demonstrating something with the plaster that they were using. Turning as she heard her name, she sprang up and ran over to her sister, giving her a big hug.

Neither girl was given to big displays of public affection, but they hadn't seen or spoken in ages and they clearly missed each other.

After a huge hug both stepped quickly back.

'Ugh, too much!'

'You're so needy!'

Laughing at each other, Nick asked Aster what she was doing with the builders. Jordan explained how Aster was demonstrating a way of using plaster to polish it and give it layers of colour.

'And what the hell do you know about plastering?' asked Nick incredulously.

'It's called Venetian stucco, actually. And I picked it up in Italy, I was working on a building site and it was an indoor job so I asked if I could do that.'

Nick had so many questions. 'Why were you working on a building site?'

'A girl's gotta eat.'

The ridiculousness of that statement – coming from a girl with a private bank account and a title – didn't pass by either of the sisters, but Nick decided to let it go. She would find out what Aster was really up to later. Or not. It didn't matter, what did matter was that Aster was here and had clearly flourished under the Italian sun.

'Look at you, you're nearly as tanned as I am.'

Nick and Aster used to delight in annoying their pale-skinned sisters by being able to tan without going red or freckly. Clem and Paddy, with their gorgeous red hair, didn't stand a hope of a tan without resorting to a tub of creosote. Ari felt that having dark hair it was hugely unfair that she also burnt at the first hint of sunshine. Nick and Aster tended to go walnut in a heartbeat and their father had joked that it was his pirate blood coming out.

Jumping up, Aster brushed the dust from her knees. She was wearing a pair of dungaree shorts in a dark blue linen, and a short-sleeved white blouse. The elegant casualness of it made her look very Italian.

'I like your hair up like that.'

Aster's hair swung from a high ponytail.

'Trying to make myself a bit taller, what do you think?'

'I think you'd need stilts.'

Unlike Clem, Aster had never been bothered by her lack of height, like Nick she liked blending into the background.

'Right, come on then, hugs and insults exchanged,' said Aster decisively. 'Let's get to work. We need to sort your mess out. Sorry it's taken me so long to get here, I was at sea and only got Ari's message yesterday. Why didn't you call me?'

Saying goodbye to the builders she strode out of the ballroom and shouted over her shoulder at Nick to hurry up. She smiled sheepishly at Jordan and ran to catch up with Aster. Nick could always rely on Ari, Clem gave her constant grief, Paddy was her rock, but Aster tended to be 'kill or cure'. She tended to provoke heart attacks or offer brilliant solutions. Nick wondered what she had come bearing this time.

As they walked towards the other wing, Nick saw Mary and Ohana approach and had a bad feeling. Aster was incredibly protective about her family. It was the one thing that the sisters could rely on – Aster would overreact to any perceived threat or insult. She had embraced Ottoline and the girls felt that she had met a kindred spirit in the older woman, but Nick wasn't sure how she would perceive Mary.

'Play nicely,' muttered Nick as she waved to Mary.

'I see you got a dog and a grandmother whilst I've been away. She's very small.'

Nick wasn't sure who she was referring to but now they were too close for her to ask. Plus she didn't like Aster's tone, it was bored and disinterested, sure signs of trouble ahead.

'Aster,' said Nick, 'this is Mary. Our grandmother.' Smiling at Mary she continued, 'And this is my youngest sister, Aster.'

Mary looked at the unsmiling girl and nodded her head.

'It's a strong family resemblance and you scowl like your great-grandmother.'

Aster decided to ignore the comparison. 'So, you're the woman that abandoned my father?'

Nick jumped in quickly ready to stop the building row in its tracks.

'Mary didn't abandon Dad, Aster. He was taken from her whilst she was at work. She spent the rest of her life looking for him.'

'She didn't find him though, did she?' Staring hard at Mary she ignored the pain in her eyes and turned to Nick. 'Come on, I've set up in the sitting room.' She began to walk towards the house, but Nick was furious.

'No. You can bloody well apologise to Mary.'

'For saying the truth?'

'For being rude.'

'Oh, and manners are more important than family, are they?'

'She *is* family.'

'In blood only.'

'It's all we've got!'

The two sisters were now roaring at each other and Ohana was cowering behind Mary's ankles.

'Enough, or I'll bang your heads together.' Both girls fell silent, startled by the expression that their father always used to break up a fight. 'Letta, you have had a while to get to know me, and you went to Ireland and saw where your father grew up. Aster has had none of that. Her reaction is hardly surprising given what you girls went through. She was only ten when she lost her parents. She's bound to be more sensitive than you are about it. Now take Ohana, you've scared her.' She then looked at Aster. 'This is a shock, I know. And it is for me as well. You may not like me or the situation and that is your right. I hope that we get to know each other but for now I'll keep out of your hair.'

Turning, she walked back off towards the woods.

'That was bloody rude of you.'

'So what?' Aster looked curiously after her grand-mother's retreating back then shrugged her shoulders. 'Right, tell me the dates you apparently tampered with your files.'

Nick narrowed her eyes – there was no point in continuing the discussion with Aster. She had clearly dismissed the issue of Mary for now and wanted to crack on with Nick's problem.

'First off, I'm having a shower, I'm sweaty after my ride plus I want to calm down.'

'Calm down?'

'Over how you treated Mary.'

Aster rolled her eyes. 'Are you still going on about that?'

'It was a minute ago and she's been my guest these past few weeks.'

Aster's eyes narrowed and her mouth dropped into a flat line. 'Are you choosing her over me?'

'Jesus, Aster. I'm not choosing anyone. And if I did it would always be you. But she is an old woman who has had a sodding hard life. She had her child stolen from her and when she was finally reunited with her family she discovered the child that she has been searching for all her life died over a decade ago. For once in your life, try to see it from the other side.'

With that, she headed off to have a shower, shouting out the dates in question back to her hostile little sister.

–

When Nick came back downstairs she found Aster tapping away at a laptop and scribbling on a notepad. A full cup of tea was to one side.

'Your tea's going cold.'

Aster looked up at her and blew her cheeks out. She was about to speak then, thinking better of it, returned to the screen.

'Would you like *me* to make you a cup of tea?'

Aster nodded and carried on typing.

Nick picked up the cup and walked into the kitchen where Mary was reading a book.

'Did I make it wrong?'

Nick sighed – how to explain her sister?

'Aster's really protective and cautious. She won't accept anything from anyone until she is completely happy about the exchange of obligations. It's a bit difficult to explain.'

Mary smiled. 'Not difficult at all. Incredibly old-fashioned – I mean positively medieval – but I know where she's coming from. It's a trust thing.'

'Yes! It is about trust. When you're in you're in, but until then…' Nick trailed off. 'If it helps, Ari was married to her first husband for three years; Aster never once accepted a thing from him.'

'He's the one that drowned?'

'Yes.'

'Well, let's hope she comes to accept me before I die.' Mary took a sip from her own tea. 'Tell me, your other sisters? Do you think they will react the same way?'

Nick was cross all over again at Aster.

'Absolutely not. Aster was always going to be the tricky one. Clem is likely to try and track your parents down and shout at their graves. Paddy will weep a lot and hug you until you can't bear it and Ari will find you something to do.'

Mary smiled. 'I look forward to meeting them. In the meantime, go and help your little sister and I'll cook dinner.'

Nick walked back into the sitting room where Aster was leaning back in her chair smiling at the screen. As Nick walked in she smiled up at her.

'You're in the clear.'

'Just like that?'

'Yes. I've just checked the back-ups and they show a different pattern of trading. Quite frankly, I don't know why you haven't already done this? Unless there's something more?'

'What?' Nick stepped forward to look at the screen. 'The back-ups are the problem. They prove I've allegedly been fiddling the system.'

'Yes, *those* back-ups do, but I also installed a redundant back-up. It goes to a non-writable file, more like just taking a picture of what happened each day. The critical thing is it can't be altered. I thought it would be good for you to have some sort of permanent record in case of a catastrophic failure of your database.'

Nick stared at Aster in astonishment. 'Why didn't you tell me about this?'

'I did. You asked me to run over your computer network and make sure it was stable and secure.'

'But you didn't mention a back-up of the back-up!'

'Of course I did. Maybe you misheard me? Anyway, that's not important right now, what is important is that it is a solid piece of evidence.' Aster smiled at Nick. 'Especially in light of the other back-up.'

'Are you sure? My solicitor felt my handwritten accounts from the time were borderline.'

'Understandable – you could have written a false account as an insurance plan, but these files show the actual transactions, how the money was moved, where the money came from and where it went. And each transaction is at odds with the "official" record that the FCA have. What I have here shows what actually happened on the day and can't have been tampered with. This totally exonerates you.'

Nick slumped down on the sofa in relief. 'Christ, you have no idea how good it is to hear that.' She fell silent – the news was almost too momentous to comprehend. She knew better than to celebrate just yet, she wouldn't do that until the FCA dismissed all charges but finally she had hope that that would happen. Realising that Aster hadn't said anything more she looked at her sister who was still working on the laptop.

'What are you doing? You've found the evidence, what more is there?'

Aster frowned at Nick. 'You're not normally stupid, what's wrong with you?'

'What? I'm innocent, you've found the evidence.'

Aster signed and stopped typing. 'Of course you are innocent. That has never been in doubt but the fact that this anomaly occurred is suspicious and now that I'm looking at the two files its really clear to me. This isn't a mistake. This was a deliberate act perpetrated over several weeks at least.' Aster paused and looked as angry as Nick had seen in a long time.

'Nicoletta, you've been framed.'

Chapter 47

Over dinner the three women sat and ate as Aster explained her findings.

'It's not random or accidental. I'm cross-referencing the two databases and I'm beginning to get a better idea of how and when it was done.'

'Have you any idea how whoever it was broke into the database?'

'That's the problem. It wasn't "broken" into, so to speak. It was done by someone with full access. Basically, one of your staff did this to you.'

'Aster—'

'No, Letta. I'm in no doubt. Without sounding melodramatic, this was an inside job.'

Nick blinked, uncertain what to say.

'The thing I don't understand,' continued Aster, 'is why you didn't see this sooner. Is it so inconceivable to you that someone could frame you?'

'Frankly, yes. And the idea that it's a member of staff that I'd hand-picked and have worked with for over a year is preposterous.'

'And yet the evidence is as clear as day. Wake up, Letta!'

'But why would anyone do that to me?'

'Well, given that you don't exactly make waves or throw your weight about I can only think of one name. The Harringtons. Which brings me to my main question.

What the hell are you doing here? In one of their properties?'

Nick was still trying to catch up with what Aster had said and shown. Someone had not only successfully framed her, but it was a member of staff. Worse still, Aster thought the Harringtons were behind it. Nick wanted to protest that the two events were unconnected but now she began to feel queasy. The connection was obvious.

'I'm helping out some of the Harringtons, but they aren't connected to the banking arm.'

'But they are part of the family?' asked Aster quickly.

'Yes. But it's not like it sounds. Look, it's complicated.'

Mary pushed her chair back. 'I think that's my cue to pour the wine.'

'I've put some rosé in the fridge,' said Aster. 'Grab one of those and let's go sit outside.'

As the women resettled on the outside sofa, Nick explained her two evictions and the subsequent discovery that the Harringtons had been involved. Gabe and Rafe had been mortified and offered her this place as a bolt hole whilst the story of her FCA investigation broke.

'Which I thought was incredibly kind,' said Nick defensively as she watched her sister's eyebrows become more and more alarmed.

'Have you become stupid?'

'What!' Nick snapped at Aster's blunt tone.

'You are evicted from your office and your home at the same time that the FCA launch an investigation into your accounts.'

'That's just Harrington's putting the boot in. Kick a girl when she's down.'

'And how exactly did Harrington's know you were being investigated? At that stage it was supposed to be hush hush.'

'It was, but the City still gossips.'

'And how did the lettings agency know you had a dog?'

'I guess maybe the concierge noticed?'

'You yourself said that the dog hadn't slept in the flat yet. So the concierge makes no sense. But apparently you spent a loved-up weekend with a Harrington in Ireland where he knew all about the dog.'

'Gabe wouldn't do that!'

'Oh, wake up, Nick. The events are all connected. Look at them. If you weren't sitting in the middle of all this you would have put it all together in seconds. You know you're innocent of anything the FCA are accusing you of – that alone should have made you alarmed, but now you have the evidence that you have been framed and you still haven't put two and two together. Everything that has happened to you has been down to the Harringtons. And here you are sitting in one of their houses helping them out whilst they try to put you in prison. Nicoletta, wake up!'

Nick stared at her sister dumbfounded. She could hear her words and knew the truth of them, but she also refused to believe that Gabe was implicated.

Mary cleared her throat. 'Aster, I can't speak for all the shenanigans of the banking sectors or what happened before with the Harringtons. And what you say makes sense, and even sounds about right. But I've watched Gabe with your sister. His feelings for her are sincere. If he's an actor he's the best I've ever seen. The same goes for his brother. They are doing all this—' she waved her arm around in the evening air to take in properties and the estate beyond '—to distance themselves from their family.'

'Sorry, Mary,' said Aster shortly, 'but when the chips are down families stick together.'

'Not always. Yours might but if I can remind you, mine threatened to throw me out when I was sixteen and pregnant and they only kept me when the boy's family offered to pay for the maintenance of the baby. When the money stopped, my mum and dad took my son to an orphanage whilst I was at work and I never saw him again. So, no, families don't always stick together.'

Nick was torn; she knew Mary was right but in a family as large and as powerful as the Harringtons surely they pulled together when needed? And yet she had felt certain that Gabe had told the truth when he said he loved her.

She had been running through her options as Mary and Aster spoke. Her brain seemed to have finally woken up. The horror of being investigated and evicted seemed to have clouded her judgement, allowing her to wallow in emotional angst. She finished her wine and put her glass down.

'We're leaving in the morning. Aster, you're right, I'm being an idiot. Personally, I don't think Gabe is conning me, but I can't stay here. Bernard Payne, their project manager, is back at work, so I'm not needed here.'

Aster sat still and watched her sister run through her plans.

'Mary, I'm sorry to cut your visit short. I'm heading to Norfolk – you are most welcome to join us, meet Ari and the boys.' She turned back to Aster. 'You'll come with me, won't you? See if you can figure out who planted the evidence?'

'Of course. But what if I can't find the culprit?'

'Doesn't matter,' said Nick. 'I've got enough circumstantial evidence. I went to Ireland and discovered Dad's childhood, I found our grandmother and I am going to find the evidence against Harrington's and absolutely destroy them.' She stood up. 'Good night, ladies, we leave first thing in the morning.'

Chapter 48

Nick hadn't slept a wink. For most of the night she stared at the ceiling and at 4 a.m. she got up and started to pack. 'Do you know what, Ohana, when this mess is sorted I am buying a house and it will be mine and I will sleep in it for ever and ever until the pillows wear out and the roof falls down.'

Ohana wagged her tail enthusiastically.

Nick nodded emphatically but her heart wasn't really in it. She felt sick with Aster's revelation that she had been framed. Even worse that Gabe may be implicated. She didn't believe that Gabe had told his father about her dog. She knew he had come to Ireland to check her out, but she completely believed him when he said he had no idea who she was. A second later she wondered if she was allowing her emotions to cloud her judgement again. She had fallen in love with Gabe and now there was a very real possibility that he had been playing her along. A minute later she would remember all the texts and conversations and was convinced of his sincerity all over again.

And so the night turned to dawn. Eventually she began to realise that it didn't matter one way or the other, they were never going to have a relationship. If Aster was correct – how could Nick doubt the evidence? – Gabe's family were trying to have her thrown into jail.

Nick sent a joint text to Rafe and Gabe telling them that Aster had returned to the UK, so the three women were returning to Norfolk. She kept the text light and brief but said nothing about the new evidence. Maybe Rafe had betrayed her? Maybe Gabe had said something to his twin who had passed it on. Nick groaned. There were too many 'maybes'. All she knew was that she had finally fallen in love with someone that she could never have.

It took less time for Aster and Mary to pack. Nick wanted to say goodbye to the builders, but she was worried that she might get emotional and they would alert the twins to a change in her behaviour. Her emotions were on the surface right now, and a kindly word from John might set her off. Feeling rude she left a note in the builders' kitchen and then drove away in Aster's rental.

Eventually, we all come back to Hiverton, thought Nick, smiling across at Aster.

'It does feel like coming home, doesn't it?'

During the previous evening, Nick had gathered the evidence Aster had found from the static database and sent it all over to her solicitor. Whilst they had been driving to Norfolk he had called her to say that he was putting in an emergency request to the FCA and to the judge to throw out the trial. He had sounded cautiously optimistic for a solicitor.

'The evidence that those figures have been manipulated is clear. Things might move very quickly now. The FCA don't like to waste time on a case that has no grounds. They'll probably want to pick over it, but my experts came to their conclusions pretty quickly.' Hanging up, he promised to let her know the minute he did.

Now the sun was high in the sky and shining down on the Hiverton estate as they drove down the main drive to the house.

'Ari says Seb has taken the boys swimming,' said Nick over her shoulder. Mary was seated in the back holding Ohana for reassurance. 'It will give you time to settle in.'

Meeting Letta had been wonderful, meeting Aster had been terrifying, now as they drove down a private road and the huge ancient house loomed up in front of her, Mary was petrified. Both girls talked about Ari in glowing terms, but she was the Countess Ariana Hiverton. How could someone so grand be her granddaughter? She laughed and Aster turned around and raised her eyebrow.

'I was just thinking that the granddaughter I am about to meet is very grand indeed.'

'Are you nervous?' asked Aster surprised.

'Of course she is,' Nick interrupted. 'After her meeting with you she's probably petrified.'

'Ridiculous,' snorted Aster and turned to face the house again.

Nick looked back at Mary and smiled sympathetically. As she turned again the front door opened, and Ari stepped out to meet them, waving her arms madly with a huge grin on her face. Her pregnancy wasn't showing yet, but Nick thought she looked as happy as she had ever seen her. She loved family reunions and she was about to meet her grandmother. As they all got out of the car, she ran forward giving Aster and Nick huge hugs and then turned to face Mary.

'What would you prefer?' Ari asked bluntly. 'Gran, Granny, Grandmama, Nan, Nanny?'

'Mary will do,' and Ari's face fell imperceptibly. 'It's just I never dreamed I would be someone's granny and now here I am with five granddaughters.'

'Of course, Mary,' said Ari. 'Whatever you feel comfortable with. We will do everything we can to make you feel welcome.'

Mary looked at Ari fondly and felt a surge of affection for the young woman who – like her sisters – looked so familiar. 'I suppose I like Granny the best?'

Ari beamed at her and then at her sisters. 'We have a grandparent! You are clever, Nick, finding her and bringing us together; and Aster, you are brilliant – fancy putting in a back-up for the back-up!'

Chattering, she ushered the three of them indoors and then told her sisters to put the kettle on whilst she showed their granny to her bedroom.

–

Half an hour later the three sisters were sitting out on the terrace drinking homemade lemonade.

'Do you think she's lost?' asked Nick.

'I told her we'd be sitting out the back and to join us when she's ready.'

'She's not a new cat,' laughed Aster.

'I think the analogy works quite well. These are new surroundings and new people. It is a lot to take in. She'll join us when she's ready.'

Nick hadn't heard back from her solicitor and was feeling anxious. With the good news on the horizon she just wanted it all settled. The past month had been horrendous, and she wanted it behind her as quickly as possible.

'What are you going to do when this is all over?' asked Ari.

Nick looked over and smiled at her sister, perceptive as ever.

'Do you know, I've been thinking about that. Obviously, I'm going to pick up the Hiverton account again, although George probably has it running better than I ever could.'

Her sisters both protested, and she laughed. 'No, no false modesty, George is a genius. I can learn a lot from him. But that aside, I'm going to be choosier about my other clients. Obviously, I'm going to lose some, but it will give me an opportunity to really focus on my core principles, helping start-up businesses with little or no social or financial clout.'

Both sisters nodded in agreement.

'I also want to build up the charity more. I'm not good at digging ditches in Africa, or helping families with legal aid, or delivering medical supplies but I am good at making money. And I'd like to focus on that. I also want to spend more time on a social life.'

Aster and Ari both laughed in mock horror at their workaholic sister's pronouncement.

'And what are you going to do about Gabe?' asked Ari.

The smile on Nick's face disappeared and instead she looked coldly at her big sister. That was a topic she wasn't prepared to discuss yet. She'd already had three texts from him today and had had to fob him off each time. 'Move on.'

'But—'

'I said, leave it. I don't want to talk about him.'

Nick could see that Ari wasn't prepared to do that and was relieved when Mary walked around the side of the house.

'Ariana, your home is a warren. However do you find anyone?'

'Wait till the boys come home. They are so noisy you always know where they are. It's when they go quiet you need to start running.'

As Ari poured Mary a glass of lemonade, Nick's phone beeped. Everyone looked at her expectantly as she read the text.

'Well,' she breathed out heavily. 'That's a step closer. The solicitors have just let me know. The case is going to be reviewed by Judge Percival Applethwaite in two days' time. The documents have been forwarded to the FCA as well. The end is almost in sight.' She took a sip of the sharp lemonade and turned to Aster. 'Do you think you'll be able to work out who planted the evidence in time? It would be great to be able to prove at the hearing that I've been set up.'

Aster nodded. 'I'll give it my best shot.'

'Do you know, I may even be able to help,' said Mary with a small smile.

The sisters all looked at her curiously. It was unclear in what way she could possibly lend assistance, but they were keen to hear what she had to say.

'I know Judge Percy Applethwaite, or at least I think I do. It's hard to imagine that there could be two of them.'

'How do you know the judge?' asked Aster intrigued. From all that she had heard about Mary's life she couldn't see where their paths had overlapped.

'Letta, do you remember me saying that for a long time I worked as a cleaner in a private residence?'

Nick nodded and Ari interrupted. 'Do you know, I love hearing you being called Letta again. Sorry, Mary, continue.'

Aster still hadn't decided if she approved of anyone else calling Nick by their mother's name for her but if Nick was okay with it she was prepared to delay her judgement. Besides, she wanted to hear what Mary had to say. The way the woman was sitting, Aster was certain that she had a tale to tell.

Mary took a sip of her drink and continued.

'Well now. I got the job when I bumped into a girl that I used to lodge with. She was a really good-looking girl and always well turned out. We got chatting and I discovered that she had found a good job and had bought a flat. Now, you can imagine I was very impressed. She was younger than I was – I was in my early thirties by then, and didn't have two pennies to rub together – and there's herself buying her own property. Anyways, she laughed and said it was a coincidence her bumping into me after all these years. Her boss was looking for a cleaner-cum-housemaid, she wanted a tidy Irish girl with no family. The sort that could be relied upon to work hard and keep herself to herself. At the time I was stacking shelves at night for a pittance so when Fiona or Philippa, I forget now, told me what the salary was I was all for it.'

She stopped and took another drink, emptying her glass. Aster leant forward and refilled it.

'So, I puts on my best clothes and take the bus over to the address that this girl gave me. The house was in the posh end of town that I never went to. Huge houses set back from the road with their own gravel driveways and a big brick wall at the front. This one even had some big trees at the front. Anyway, I knocks at the door like the timid little thing that I was and this smart girl in a maid's outfit escorts me into the house and asks me to wait in a study for her employer. I tell you, if it hadn't been for the fact that I hated stacking shelves so much I'd have turned tail. What right had I to be shown around a big grand house by a maid? I was about to get up and leave when this woman walks in. She must have been in her sixties and had the poshest voice I had ever heard, like the Queen, but with a hint of Brummie. She carried a little Pekinese dog and a cane; I tell you, looking at her I was so scared. It makes me laugh now to think how nervous I was on that first day, when it turned out that it was the turning point of my life.'

She stopped and looked out over the rose garden causing the sisters to look at each other and grin. Big pauses at all the dramatic bits. This was exactly how their dad used to tell a tale!

Chapter 49

'You were saying?' nudged Ari.

Mary took a deep breath but suddenly the house was filled with distant shouts and two little boys and two wet dogs came running around from the side of the property. Seb sauntered behind with Hector struggling to get free and join the rest of the pack. Leo and Will dived on Aster and Nick shouting excitedly and Ohana leapt onto Nick, as George and Harry bounded over.

'Seb! Help, we're under attack,' laughed Ari. 'Did you have a lovely time, boys?'

Turning to their mother they nodded enthusiastically and finally spotted the new face.

'Why are you crying? Did Harry eat your shoes? He's just teething, he didn't mean to hurt you?' Leo looked at the lady, his eyes full of concern. He didn't like seeing grown-ups cry but he was worried that Harry was in trouble again. Yesterday he had eaten one of Daddy's shoes and Daddy shouted a lot and then Mummy shouted that she had told him not to leave them there. Leo felt bad because it was him who had given Harry the shoe to play fetch with, even when Will told him not to. Now this old lady was crying, and he wondered if he was in trouble again.

'Bless you. But the pair of you are the absolute spit of my little boy at your age.'

'Oh, Granny,' said Ari jumping up and giving her a hug.

Both boys looked at the old woman again. They knew who their grandma was, she had a swimming pool. So who was this lady?

'Boys. This is my grandmother. My daddy's mummy, which makes her your great-grandmother.'

A great-grandmother sounded cool, but Hector was struggling to get all the words in order, making his big brothers laugh at him.

'How about you call me Gee-gee, instead of Great-Grandmother.'

'Like the horses?' ask Will curiously.

'Yes,' laughed Mary through her tears, 'why not?'

'Would you like to see our bedrooms? I have a picture of my favourite horse in there,' said Will, tugging at her skirt.

'I should like that very much, if that's okay with your mummy and daddy.' She looked at Ari and Seb who smiled.

Aster stood up. 'Come on, let me lead the way. If they play up I'll throw them to the crocodiles. Seb, why don't you get some fresh drinks for us all.'

Having put everything in place she and Mary followed the boys who were excitedly telling Mary about all the things in their bedrooms.

As the silence settled, Nick put Ohana back on the floor and glanced at Ari who was beginning to look tearful.

'I feel so sorry for her. I can't imagine what it must be like to lose your only child at that age.' Her eyes welled up and she wiped them with the palm of her hand. 'Stupid hormones.'

'I feel sorry for her too. And at least Aster seems to be thawing towards her.'

'Is Aster doing her whole "strangers bad" routine?' tutted Ari.

'And then some. Mary was so worried to meet you, Aster has been abysmal. In fact, she might not be thawing to Mary at all but making sure the boys are safe.'

Ari looked momentarily alarmed until Nick reassured her that Mary was absolutely lovely, and Aster was over-reacting – if that indeed was what she was doing.

'Like I said, I *think* she's thawing.'

'And how about you? How are you doing through all this? You're looking tired – the last time we spoke you sounded happy. Now you're about to be exonerated and you look exhausted.'

'I think it's all catching up with me.'

'And what about Gabe? You haven't mentioned him much recently. I thought that there might be something there?'

'So did I but he's a Harrington and Aster is convinced that they are behind all this.'

'But not him, surely?' pleaded Ari.

'I honestly don't think he's involved in any of this but what does that matter? It's his family. There's hardly any future for us when they are trying to frame me.'

'Oh God, Nick. What a horrible mess. Are you sure they're behind this?'

Nick shrugged her shoulders. 'I don't know but Aster is convinced, and honestly, the coincidences are huge. Plus, who else out there would hate me this much?'

Ari squeezed the slice of lemon over the ice at the bottom of the glass and fanned herself with the coaster. After everything that Nick had done for the family it seemed beyond cruel that someone would be pursuing her so relentlessly.

'Don't worry. We'll clear your name and let's hope that Aster is mistaken.'

'Aster is never mistaken,' called out a voice from the patio door. She and Mary walked out carrying a fresh pitcher of lemonade.

'I've convinced Seb to entertain the children for a few minutes so that Mary can finish her tale. Then you can explain why you think I am mistaken.'

'About Gabe,' said Nick in a flat voice.

Aster scowled but said nothing and Mary quickly returned to her story, settling down and trying to diffuse the tension between her granddaughters.

'Where was I? Ah yes… my life would change forever. Well, you see, Mrs Cherry needed a new housemaid and cleaner. Someone to help her run her establishment. The way she said "establishment" made me pause – it didn't sound right – so I asked her politely if she didn't mean her lovely home. Or was she talking about somewhere else? Well, she looked at me for a bit and then asked if Fiona of Philippa hadn't explained what her job was.

'Which is when I discovered that the establishment in question was where gentlemen would visit to find pleasure outside the marital bed.'

'No!' laughed Ari. Aster looked confused and Nick laughed at her. 'A brothel.'

Mary tutted. 'Yes, if you want to be so coarse but brothel always seems such a loaded word. What Mrs Cherry ran was a safe establishment for girls to make a lot of money. They could always say no, Mrs Cherry kept them healthy and when it was time to leave she would set them up with loans and business advice.'

'So did you ever—'

Ari cut Aster off. 'Aster, that's none of our business. Everyone makes the best of their own life and they don't need us prying into those choices.'

'Thank you, dear,' said Mary laughing, 'but no, my salary for cleaning and tending was enough. Sure, I never made enough to buy a house, but I could have bought a car if I wanted. And every year I would holiday abroad, and I built up a nest egg for Michael to give to him or his children. Although now looking around I'm not sure that you need it.'

Ari leant forward seeing the older woman's distress. 'We need our grandmother far more than we need her money.'

As Mary looked up Nick was nodding, and Aster was just watching her carefully.

'Anyway. That's what I did for the rest of my working life and I got to know all the regulars – politicians, bankers, nobs and even judges. Which is where my story starts. Judge Percival was also known to the girls as "Soots", because he had a thing for streaking his face in coal dust. Mrs Cherry always charged him more because I had to wash the sheets twice to get the marks out. If you like, before the ruling starts I could go and say hello. Remind him of the good old days.'

Nick and Ari stared at Mary in astonishment and Aster burst into laughter. 'Oh, I might like you after all.'

Mary smiled shyly. 'You see the thing I learnt working there was, that at the end of the day, for all their power and influence, men are easily led and quickly undone. The things I could tell you about some of the people I see on the television.'

'Go on,' said Aster, but Nick interrupted her.

'Not now, the children are returning.' The distant sound of hullabaloo was drawing closer. 'And thank you, Mary, for the offer but I want to win this because I'm innocent, not because some chap remembers he used to be called Sooty.'

Chapter 50

Aster and Nick hit the keyboards whilst Ari, Seb and the boys took Mary to a nearby wildlife park. The rest of the summer holidays lay out ahead of them and Ari was pleased that they had this opportunity to meet their great-grandmother before the family went abroad. As they wandered around the meerkat enclosures Ari was delighted to discover Mary had a keen interest in local government and planning law. The village of Tregiskey, down in Cornwall, was having a problem with its road. It was too narrow and too long and was the source of constant bottlenecks on sunny days and holidays. Only recently a tourist had nearly died when the ambulance couldn't make it down the hill due to the traffic jam. Eventually the coastguard had to be called and he had to be airlifted out and resuscitated twice on the way to the hospital. Over the years there had been regular calls for improvements to the road and plans submitted but nothing was ever approved.

Mary's eyes twinkled: this sounded like an issue she would love to tackle. Something about Mary's smile reminded Ari of Aster and she wondered what on earth she was about to unleash on the Cornish planning department.

Back at Hiverton, however, Aster was not smiling.

'I need more time to go through your employees and properly research them. So far I have nothing. Whoever hacked the database did it from various different log-ons. Which is a smart way to muddy the water. Do I assume they are all innocent, or is the hacker hiding amongst them? Did they at some stage log in from their own terminal? All I can say for certain is that it wasn't accessed remotely.'

Nick sighed. 'Well, it was unlikely you would find the answer right away, but we still have time. Hopefully, you will have a name before we present our case to the judge. Plus I won't be able to rehire any of the team until I know for certain who the mole is.'

'I wouldn't re-employ any of them, just to be safe.'

'You do you Aster. I couldn't function without Gyeong or Daisy or any of them.'

'That's rubbish and you know it.'

'Okay. I could function without them, but I don't want to. They are excellent at their jobs.'

'But you'll never truly trust them if I can't find your mole. For what it's worth those two are my prime suspects. Daisy gave you the dog, Gyeong knew you were heading to Ireland. Daisy set up the property contracts, Gyeong has a Master's in Computer Science.'

Nick looked at her in astonishment. 'Seriously, Aster, it's neither of them.'

Aster looked at her and shrugged. 'Best I crack on then. Cup of tea?'

Nick pushed away from the desk and headed off to make two teas. Aster was right, trust was going to be a huge problem if this wasn't fully resolved. But suggesting it was either of her best employees was ridiculous.

Just as the kettle boiled her phone rang. Putting down the teapot she looked at the screen and saw it was her legal team. Her stomach clenched.

'Nicoletta? It's Giles here. The judge has asked for us and the FCA to meet him tomorrow morning.'

'So soon?' Nick panicked, what had gone wrong?

'Yes. I can't say what he has in mind, but I feel optimistic. It's unusual for a judge to call in both parties before a trial and suggests that things are about to move dramatically.'

Nick explained to Giles how she was currently trying to uncover the mole which he encouraged her to pursue.

'Every bit of evidence in our arsenal will count in our favour.'

Arranging a time to meet in the morning, she hung up and headed back to Aster to let her know the development. Instead of looking happy, Aster just frowned and started to type faster.

'If the case is thrown out and we haven't uncovered the mole then you will always look guilty. Like you got off on a technicality. We need a confession or people will say there's no smoke without fire. You have to be exonerated beyond all doubt and the guilty party hung out to dry.'

Nick had just poured them both a cup of tea, suggesting that Aster should take a rest but now the tea lost all its flavour. She had been so excited that the end was in sight that she had failed to see that angle. Aster was right, of course. Someone had planted that evidence, but gossip mongers would still look at her and point fingers. Was it planted by herself to cover up a greater misdemeanour? Had she done it to avoid future inspections? She needed to find that mole and press charges against them. To save her reputation she would need to destroy theirs, and after what they had put her through it was a task she was looking forward to.

Chapter 51

Gabe drove along a leafy street and parked outside a smart row of houses. Checking the numbers he headed towards a blue door. According to his findings this was Daisy Hall's address. Daisy who had been engaged to Luke Rees at the time of the scandal and court case. Whether or not she still was he didn't know, but he wanted to find out why after leaving Harrington's she went straight to work for the woman who had allegedly been instrumental in putting her fiancé in jail.

He was worried about Letta. She had left Parscombe Court unexpectedly and whilst he understood her sister returning had caused a change in plans, she had stopped contacting him. He'd sent a few texts, but she'd barely replied. He had been closely following the court case and knew that the judge presiding over it had called Letta and the FCA to his chambers. What he didn't know was why Letta hadn't told him. After her declaration to him, he would have thought she would have shared this with him. Something had changed and he didn't know what. All he could do for now was try and clear her name. If the judge was seeing them tomorrow, Gabe needed to secure the evidence as quickly as possible.

He knocked on the door and smiled as it opened. Daisy looked dreadful. It was harsh but it was the only way he could describe her. In his memory and in all the photos she came across as a well-presented young woman. Now she was without make-up, her hair was unwashed, and her roots were showing. She was barefoot and wearing a pair of baggy joggers and T-shirt that had a red wine stain on the front.

'Hello, Daisy. Do you remember me? I'm Gabriel St Clair Harrington, I was hoping to have a few words.'

Daisy looked at him nervously and then looked over his shoulder to see if anyone had noticed him on her doorstep. Tucking her hair behind her ear she invited him in and showed him through to the kitchen.

'Give me a minute to freshen up. I wasn't expecting guests.'

As she disappeared, Gabe put the kettle on. The kitchen was a mess, but he found two cups and giving them a clean, proceeded to make two cups of coffee.

'Oh, thank you,' said Daisy, to Gabe. She seemed flustered. 'Do excuse the mess, we had a bit of a party last night.'

Gabe looked around the kitchen. Everything suggested days if not weeks of neglect, not a one-night party, but he laughed along with her. She was nervous and he wanted to try and put her at ease.

'So, what can I do for you?' Daisy sat down at the kitchen table and was fiddling with her newly brushed hair. 'Did your brother send you? If so, tell him I don't care. I'm not doing anything else.' She slammed her coffee cup down for emphasis. Then she apologised and started to cry.

Gabe stood up and found a roll of kitchen towels. He tore off a sheet so she could dab her eyes and with another he wiped up the coffee. He was clearly on the right track and his heart sank. What had his family done? He may as well cut straight to the chase.

'Daisy, why are you working at De Foix Investments?'

The young woman stopped wiping her face and looked at him warily.

'Don't you know?'

'No. Why don't you tell me?'

Now Daisy looked terrified. 'I can't. I promised I wouldn't.' She stood up from the table. 'I think you had better leave.'

Gabe remained where he was and sipped at his coffee. 'You're clearly not happy. Maybe I can help?' He returned to his drink whilst she made her mind up. Finally, in the silence she let out a small groan and sat down.

'Will I go to jail?'

Gabe's heart sank further. How bad was this going to be? He remembered Daisy only vaguely, but she had been a bright lively girl, in the middle of all the social functions whooping everyone into action. She and her fiancé had the fastest cars, the biggest houses, the best holidays, the loudest parties. Now she was wiping freshly applied mascara onto a kitchen towel, her nails were unmanicured and her hand was shaking.

'Daisy, I don't know. I don't know what you've done but I am a lawyer. If you tell me I can tell you how serious things are.'

'Only your brother said I would go to jail if I spoke to anyone.'

'Well, he's not a lawyer, so let's see. And you don't go to jail for *talking* about what you've done. You go to jail for what you have actually done.'

'So maybe I shouldn't say anything, like Adam says.'

'But that doesn't change the fact that whatever it is that you have done, you *have* done it. Wouldn't it be better to get it off your chest, before someone else discovers it? Come clean before you're found out.'

'I suppose it won't hurt to tell you. You are family.'

That worried Gabe and he cut her off before she could say anything else.

'Daisy, if you or my family have done something illegal I can't hide the fact, nor will I ignore it.'

She stood up again in alarm and Gabe cursed inwardly. He didn't want to frighten her off but equally he didn't want to lie to her. He drank some more coffee.

'Imagine how good it will feel to get this off your chest. You're clearly not happy with what you've done. I met Nicoletta Byrne; she thinks you are wonderful. I can't believe you two aren't friends.'

'We are! We were, she's wonderful.' Daisy broke off again and started to sob in earnest. Gabe stood up and guided her back to her seat and put the kettle back on again. When she had composed herself he put a fresh cup in front of her.

'Tell me all about it and start at the beginning.'

Daisy took a deep breath. 'In for a penny in for a pound,' she laughed self-consciously. 'That was Luke's maxim. He always went large. Which of course was his downfall and why he ended up in jail. I was devastated, my whole life fell apart. The parties, the invitations, the money; everything stopped. And yes, I know how shallow that makes me sound but honestly, that was who I was. I was losing control at work and eventually I was pulled to one side and told to pack my bags.'

Gabe winced but had read her personnel files, it was a reasonable if unsupportive action.

'I was livid, after all that Luke had done for Harrington's—'

'He brought the bank down!'

'He did nothing that Paul and Adam hadn't approved.'

Well, that confirmed Gabe's suspicions that his brothers' hands weren't clean. Daisy continued.

'Adam had said he would take care of Luke and I suppose I felt that included me. So when I was fired, I stormed over to his. I was screaming and shouting at him, calling him this and that and somehow through the meeting he convinced me that all my problems were down to Nick. That it had been all her fault, and I'm ashamed to say I totally bought into that. By the end of our chat Luke was nothing more than a maverick who had been unfairly caught out. One more deal and everything would have been fine, but she put a stop to that.'

Which is absolute bollocks, thought Gabe, but he knew that Daisy was aware of that.

'Anyway, me and Adam hatched a plan.'

Gabe thought that Daisy probably had nothing to do with hatching any plan whatsoever. She was a vulnerable person who had been easily manipulated. He listened as she explained how easy it had been to get a job working at De Foix. Adam Harrington built up a fake CV for her, and Nick welcomed her with open arms. At the time she was struggling with her workload and found Daisy's tireless efficiency just what she needed. Daisy arranged two properties at ridiculously reduced rates – Nick had been thrilled to get such great locations and relieved that the search had been taken off her hands as she tried to keep on top of her business.

In those first few weeks and months Daisy found it child's play to go in and alter the historic databases. When the time was right Adam would nudge the FCA to have a look and down would come De Foix and Nick Byrne with it.

Gabe was horrified. This was evidence deliberately planted to destroy Letta. He knew she thought it was a case of sloppy bookkeeping or maybe a genuine mistake. She had no idea she had been deliberately targeted.

'But why would you do that?'

'Because I hated her. Because she was to blame for the fact that my fiancé was in jail. Because all my friends had disappeared. I know, I know. Of course, she wasn't but that wasn't how I was thinking back then. I would go out for drinks every week with Adam and give him a progress report and it was lovely. Suddenly I was being wined and dined – we always went somewhere very exclusive, and I fell right back into the glamour and the lifestyle.'

'So what happened?'

'What do you think happened? I got to know Nick. She's lovely. She's kind, quiet, hard-working. She works into the night helping other people, she never seeks praise, she's just industriously beavering away in the background. And I fell for her.'

Gabe raised an eyebrow.

'No, not like that, but it was a bit like hero worship. I wanted to be like her, I wanted to turn my life around and start over.'

'So what happened then?'

'I told your brother that I wanted out.'

'And?'

'And he told me that if I backed out now he would tell the police he had uncovered evidence that I was prepared to blackmail Nick. *Psycho fiancée seeks revenge*, that was how he said the papers would run the story. He assured me the press would hear all about it.'

'What happened after that?' Gabe was listening to this tale of coercion and greed slowly play out and his heart broke. He was going to save Letta, but he knew now that she would never speak to him again once she realised what his family had done.

'Well, the wining and dining stopped for a start. But that was okay. The scales had finally fallen from my eyes and I knew I was up to my neck in it. I knew at some point Paul would pull on the noose and I didn't know what to do. When it all started to fall apart I panicked. I went to your brother and told him I was going to the police and he scared me so much with tales of prison that I slunk away. I was so ashamed of myself. But he did surprise me by doing something nice.'

'He did?' said Gabe in surprise.

'He bought a dachshund and told me to give it to Nick as a present. He thought it might make me feel a bit better and give her some company in the days ahead. That was kind, wasn't it?'

Gabe looked at Daisy incredulously. Had she really believed after everything he had done to Letta, that he would suddenly give her a present?

'He used the fact that she had a dog to evict her from her apartment that you had set up for her.'

'No!' Daisy wailed and started crying all over again. Gabe felt sorry for her, she had been stupid and initially spiteful but had been manipulated by someone with no soul or conscience.

She started hiccupping through her tears and blew her nose on the kitchen towel. Gabe went and got some loo roll and asked her where she kept her painkillers. Taking two she waved the packet at him.

'I should take the lot.'

'That would be the coward's way out. Nick needs you.'

'I know, I'm being dramatic, I just can't believe he would use a dog like that. I was clinging onto that one tiny act as something nice I had done.'

She took a deep breath. 'I don't want to go to jail.'

'I know. But it might be unavoidable.'

She fell quiet for a bit; her head hung down with her hair over her face. Gabe didn't know what she would do next and waited patiently. Eventually she sat back in the chair and looked straight at him, her eyes were red, and her skin was blotchy.

'Okay then. What do I do?'

Chapter 52

The following morning Gabe walked into his father's study. He knew this conversation would be the hardest of his life but there was nothing else he could do. He and Rafe had spoken last night and were in agreement. Gabe shouldn't speak to their father until it was too late for him to interfere.

'Hello, Gabriel. This is a pleasant surprise. What can I do for you?'

Always with the easy charm, thought Gabe. Old-school civility ran through his father's DNA. He wanted to believe that his father wasn't involved in Adam's scheme, but he had little hope. His father may have stepped down in public, but behind the scenes, Giles was still very much in charge.

'Oh dear, you do look serious. Sit down and get it off your chest. Drink?' He lifted a decanter and poured himself a whisky. Gabe shook his head. He didn't want a drink but thought it was probably just as well that his father had something to steady his nerves. The next few minutes were going to be brutal.

'I've been to visit Daisy Hall.'

His father looked at him blankly from behind his desk and raised an eyebrow.

'She used to be engaged to Luke Rees.' That caused a reaction in his father, but it was just a small nod to continue.

'She has confessed to planting evidence at De Foix Investments to make it look as though Nick Byrne was using client funds improperly.'

'Well, there's a turn-up for the books, eh?' His father chuckled to himself. 'And she's prepared to confess this, is she? What a silly girl.'

Gabe watched his father; he was certainly playing things coolly.

'There's more. She said she did it under the encouragement and insistence of Adam.'

'Adam who?'

'Harrington. Your son.'

Now Giles looked startled and offended. 'What sort of bloody rubbish is this? She had better not go round saying that sort of guff in public.'

'The thing is, she taped their conversations. I've heard them. He clearly instructed her in what to do and how to do it. She also attempted to come clean to De Foix and Adam then proceeded to blackmail and intimidate her.'

'We have to stop her.'

Gabe looked at his father in weary disappointment. There was no sense of denial, just an immediate rush to cover it up. Was he protecting his son or was he already aware of his actions?

'That's not going to happen, Father. She's going to make a full confession to the FCA.'

'For God's sake, why didn't you call me? What did you offer her not to do it?'

'I didn't offer her anything. I encouraged her.'

Giles shot up, his tumbler spilling over as papers fell to the ground. 'You did what!'

'It's the right thing to do. De Foix Investments need to have their name cleared.'

'It is being cleared, the FCA have evidence of tampered files, that will be enough to drop all charges. Her name will already be cleared. There's no need to drag Harrington's into this.'

'Sorry, Father, that won't cut it. You know how it is. If no one comes clean, there will always be suspicion that it was a cover-up. You know how the City likes to gossip. Besides which you can't keep on behaving like this. Either Adam did this without your knowledge and you're protecting him, or he did it with your approval in which case the buck stops with you. Either way you are condoning what he has done.'

Gabe winced at the disgust with which his father was looking at him.

'You're forcing me to choose between my children.'

'No, I'm not. You can do what you want but I'm going to do the right thing.'

A sly look passed over Giles's face as he tried to think of a new line of persuasion.

'Have you even met her, Nick Byrne? She's a dreadful person. Just a jumped-up shrew. No real talent, just traded on her family name and hires and fires people all the time. The City doesn't need her sort. She won't even thank you.'

'Hopefully, she won't even know I had anything to do with it. She despises us and rightly so. All I can do is make amends and hope that she is able to set her life back on track and that none of this crap you've thrown at her sticks. And for what it's worth, I have met her, and I think she's incredible.'

'You're a fool,' snapped Giles.

'I can live with that.'

Giles paused again. Badmouthing her clearly wasn't going to work – maybe he could trade on some family loyalty. He sat back down and shook his head sadly. Slowly he leant down and picked up the tumbler from the floor. Making sure Gabe could see his hand, he added a small tremor as he poured himself a fresh glass.

'But you are my sons, my family – how can I choose between you? I don't understand how easily you can choose an outsider over family?'

'Because I love her.'

Giles frowned and knocked back his drink, the tremor gone. When the hell had Gabe met Nick? Why hadn't he known about this? 'Then you're an even bigger fool. She won't want you after this.'

'Yes, I know, but it's not the point. I'm doing this because it's the right thing to do. Not to gain brownie points.'

This was getting him nowhere and Giles needed to act.

'Right then, give me forty-eight hours to get things in motion. Then tell this Daisy tramp to go blabbing to the FCA if she wants.'

Gabe stood up. 'I'm sorry, Father, the wheels are already in motion. I just came here as a courtesy to let you know what's about to happen. The judge already has Daisy's confession and is meeting with De Foix Investments and the FCA right now. The only thing you can do is call your lawyers and decide whether you accept responsibility for Adam's actions or not.'

As he went to leave the glass tumbler smashed on the wall by his head and he slammed the door behind him.

Chapter 53

Meanwhile, across town, Nick and her lawyer were sitting in Judge Applethwaite's private offices. Two representatives from the FCA were also present but neither party had spoken to each other.

The judge entered the room and Nick wiped her palms on her trousers. It was an informal gathering, and he was wearing a suit rather than his robes, but Nick still felt the weight of the British legal system enter the room. Having ensured that everyone was comfortable and offered them all drinks he cleared his throat.

'Now, this is a little irregular, but I don't believe in wasting taxpayer's money, or my time so let's get down to it. Mr Clements, I understand that the FCA has now had time to read through the additional evidence that De Foix Investments have put forward?'

'We have,' said the man who then stopped speaking, proving that he was not prepared to offer more than the very minimum.

'And?' asked the judge tersely.

'And having reviewed the documents we are reasonably confident that the files were tampered with over a sustained period of time in order to portray an alternative reflection of the reality which they were intended to represent.'

Really, thought Nick, it was either like pulling teeth with the FCA or verbal diarrhoea. No in between.

'And in light of this "alternative reflection" is it your intention to drop your prosecution?' asked the judge.

'It is,' said the man succinctly.

Nick sat stunned as her lawyer turned to shake her hand. It was over. Just like that, weeks of gut-wrenching fear were gone. The judge smiled at her kindly and finally Nick could relax enough to remember that he used to be called Sooty and smiled back, relief flooding her face. She felt her face prickle and really hoped she wasn't about to start crying in a room full of men. He was about to speak when Mr Clements spoke again.

'There is more.'

Nick's heart sank. Now everyone stared at the investigator who seemed reluctant to speak – in fact, the pause went on so long that the judge snapped at him to get on with it.

'The fact is, last night we received a confession from an individual owning up to the tampering of the files. She says she did so at the direction of a third party. We are happy that given this confession and the previous evidence, De Foix Investments are innocent of all charges and are in fact the victim of a crime themselves.'

Finally, he turned and looked at Nick directly.

'For which we are very sorry, and we shall now be pursuing charges based on this confession and the evidence you uncovered.'

Nick was stunned, the mole had voluntarily confessed. This meant she would be utterly above suspicion.

'Who was it? Who is the third party?'

Mr Clements seemed reluctant to speak. A man used to keeping a closed lid on all aspects of an investigation. That is until the judge poked him.

'For heaven's sake, you pursued this poor girl with false evidence and nearly dragged her through the courts. The least you can do is supply her with a name. Or need I remind you that she is now the victim and due all care and attention?'

The two FCA agents looked at each other and then nodded.

'The perpetrator is a Miss Daisy Hall.'

Nick gasped in disbelief; Aster had warned her, but it seemed impossible. She sat in stunned silence as Mr Clements continued.

'She alleges that she acted alone within De Foix Investments at the direction of Harrington Holdings. We have already issued charges against Miss Hall and will be inviting Harrington's in for an interview. It seems Miss Hall secretly recorded many of their conversations where they discussed how they planned to frame you. I imagine arrest warrants will follow the interview.'

Tears leaked out of Nick's eyes. How could Daisy have done this to her? In hindsight it seemed obvious, she had found her the properties that turned out to be Harrington properties, she gave her the dog. She simply hadn't seen the connection because Daisy was a friend and a trusted colleague. Christ, she had often referred to her as her right hand and had meant it.

'Excuse me, I—' Words failed her as she stood up. 'May I leave?' she asked the judge who nodded sadly. Turing to her lawyer, she asked him to tidy things up for her and walked out of the room and down to the lobby where her family were waiting.

Ari, Aster and Mary were all waiting in the downstairs reception area. The women had all travelled down to London the previous night. Mary was finding the constant change of scene invigorating and she was enjoying watching her granddaughters in action. They were a formidable team and she looked forward to meeting Clem and Paddy at some point. Ari had invited them both to come to Hiverton and had offered Mary a small cottage on the estate if she wanted it.

The idea that she would be able to see Leo and William on a regular basis had made her decision easy. She had a decent pension thanks to Mrs Cherry, as well as a decent nest egg. As much as she enjoyed the company of her neighbours in Birmingham, her property was rented, and the move would be straightforward. She had said yes immediately, and Ari was delighted. Now they sat and waited for Letta to come out. A door closed upstairs, and Letta came down towards them visibly crying. Aster and Ari ran forward hugging her but Mary remained where she was as she watched the three girls embrace each other until they broke free, all wiping their eyes. Eventually they walked over to her.

Aster looked murderous, Ari looked overjoyed, and Letta looked as though she had been hit by a train.

'What happened?'

'The FCA have withdrawn their investigation. Nick has been cleared of all charges,' said Ari, still holding Letta's hand.

Mary looked questioningly towards Aster.

'Turns out Harrington's were behind the entire thing and Nick's personal assistant – who was with her right from the start – has been working for Harrington's all along. I'm going to destroy them.'

'No, you're not, Aster,' said Letta, finally finding her voice. 'The law is going to do that.'

Mary looked at the three girls – they should be celebrating but she could see the cost of the betrayal on Letta's body. She knew what it was to have her reality shaken to the core, but the girl would rally, she had her family around her, and her business and reputation had been restored. To be sure this was a blow, but she would get over it.

'Right, girls, back to the house. Letta, I know this feels like a blow and I'm sure that's what you're focussing on, but you need to stop that right now. Life happens too fast to waste time on regrets and introspection. There's champagne at home and we are going to raise a glass to a successful outcome.'

—

Outside the building and across the road Gabe leant against a brick wall and waited. He was desperate for a final view of Letta. He was certain she would be exonerated, and he wanted to see her smiling. After all his family had done to her he couldn't bring himself to talk to her, but he hoped that the universe would permit him just to sit back and watch. All his hopes for a future with her had turned to ashes when he discovered the depths of his family's involvement. How she must hate him right now.

Across the road the doors opened, and four women walked down the steps laughing. He recognised Mary, and two of the other girls were clearly sisters, but he only had eyes for Letta. She was laughing but at the same time wiping tears from her face. He loathed the thought that people close to him had inflicted such pain on her, but he hoped now, that in some way, he had managed to atone for their betrayal. As he walked away he knew that he would never forget how beautiful she looked laughing and crying in the sunlight surrounded by her family.

Chapter 54

A fortnight later, life had begun to return to normal. Nick had moved into her new workspaces and would commute from Foix Place until she found somewhere new to live. As she settled back into the business Nick was aware that things were still unsettled. Work was going well but she was aware of a deep sense of unease within her and she couldn't put her finger on it. She had been delighted when all her staff wanted to come back and work for her. Gyeong pointed out that she hadn't hired any idiots, just one traitor. Nick had raised her eyebrow at that but then remembered that she preferred straight talking and honesty over sweet talking.

On the first day she found that her desk was covered in dog biscuits and she laughed with the staff, saying that next time she wanted champagne instead. Ohana came into work with her every day and had been generally considered the office mascot. In terms of team building and office downtime, Nick felt that all offices should have a pet. Far cheaper and more effective.

She had lost a few clients but mostly they were ones that she had been prepared to cut anyway, people that hadn't been with her from the start. George had managed the Hiverton accounts exceptionally well and she was in awe of some of his trades; the man was a genius. All in all, work was great.

There had been a small fly in the ointment at the beginning. The day after the FCA withdrew their case against her and pressed charges against Harrington's and Daisy instead, it was all over the newspapers. She'd got straight on the phone to Aster who had assured her it wasn't down to her. Just a slow week on Fleet Street and the chance of a bit of gossip. Happily, following a presidential gaffe and a royal baby she was knocked off the gossip columns. Before she hung up Aster pointed out that whilst it hadn't been her she was glad that the news had got out. Nick came out of it looking great and Harrington's entire empire was now being picked apart by regulators, whilst its founders were hiding behind their lawyers.

Which brought Nick back to Gabe. She found that everything brought her back to Gabe. She saw something funny in the street she wanted to share it with Gabe. She saw a trailer for a movie and wondered if Gabe would enjoy it. She played cards online and remembered how she had beat him, and then how he had won at the video game. She remembered that final walk around the house. Bats were swooping around in the warm dusk, the air smelt sweet, and she was falling in love. She had thought he was as well, something new seemed just over the horizon. And then it all fell apart. Now she wondered how was he coping with his family's disgrace? Nick still didn't know if he had any knowledge of what they had done, and it was eating her up.

She had misjudged Daisy, had she also misjudged Gabe? She swore under her breath. Gyeong was working at the desk opposite and looked over at her.

'Oh no boss, don't do it.'

'What?' said Nick defensively.

'You've been threatening for the past two weeks to talk to Daisy. No good will come of it. She fooled us all.'

'I just want to know.'

'She's right, Nick,' chimed in Tony. It wasn't a large office and there was no such thing as a private room or an executive kitchen. 'Let it go.'

Nick leant back in her chair and looked at the ceiling. 'No. I've waited as long as I can. It doesn't feel so raw now. I'm going to look her in the eye and see why the hell she did it.'

She pushed her chair back and stood up. Her staff watched her offering no further comment. Their boss was a smart woman, if she wanted to do this then she would. And maybe once she had, she would feel less restless.

-

Daisy lived not far from a tube station in Wimbledon and Nick soon found herself wandering down a leafy residential street. It was a nice area and seemed suited to the Daisy that she thought she knew, not the woman that had played her for a mug all this time. Knocking on the door she was aware of an anger building inside her and she swallowed it back down. Shouting, no matter how much of a relief, wasn't going to solve anything. The door opened a crack and Daisy peered out, when she saw Nick her head fell but she opened the door fully and stepped aside. Nick took it as an invitation although Daisy hadn't said a word yet and she walked into a pretty hallway.

Closing the door behind her Daisy walked towards the back of the house and sat down at the kitchen table, waving Nick to do the same. Nick sat and waited in silence until eventually Daisy started talking, her head bowed as she looked at the table.

'I won't cry. I can't,' said Daisy in an exhausted voice. 'All I've done for weeks is cry, I don't think I have any tears left. But I can say sorry, and I am. From the bottom of my heart I apologise for what I did to you.'

At that point she looked up and stared Nick straight in the face. 'I am so sorry.'

Nick had been expecting a justification, recriminations, a shouting match. She hadn't expected this abject misery.

'Daisy, the thing is… I don't understand why. I haven't seen your full confession; all I know is that you were working with Harrington's to plant evidence.' She sighed and uncurled her fists, entreating Daisy for an answer.

Getting up Daisy flicked on the kettle and began gathering things for a coffee. All the while she spoke and told Nick who she used to be engaged to and what had happened after the court case. How Adam had approached her. How she had been easily convinced to plant evidence.

'But then it all started to go wrong. I guess I also had time to think. I knew Luke had been in the wrong, I knew Adam was complicit. It was like slowly waking up out of a heavy fug, and when I looked around I realised I had sleepwalked into a very stupid position. And of course as I was coming to terms with my stupidity I was getting to know you. And it was blindingly obvious you weren't to blame for Harrington's downfall. You never crowed about it at work, you wouldn't have it discussed even. You never bragged or boasted about any of your success. You were just a bloody pleasure to work for and I realised that what I had down was terrible.'

'So why didn't you tell me?'

'I made a mistake.' She laughed weakly. 'Turns out I am very good at that. I went to Adam and explained that we had made a mistake; that you were innocent and that we should undo the wrongs. He told me if I did that he would call the police on me for planting evidence at yours and would make sure I was thrown in jail. I was terrified. And so I did nothing. I did nothing more to harm you but equally I didn't warn you. As the months passed I thought that Adam had heeded my words and had decided to move on. I began to relax but then the FCA investigation started, and he rang me to remind me to keep my mouth shut.'

Nick listened in dismay. She had wanted to hate Daisy for what she had done and now saw that she had been duped all along – not evil, just angry and then scared.

'What a mess.'

'I'm most ashamed about the dog. Adam told me to give that to you and I honestly thought he meant it as some sort of apology. Turns out it was simply an excuse to get you evicted from the flat.'

Nick smiled in relief. 'I did wonder about that. I felt that was such a cruel act and I wondered what I had done to make you hate me so much.'

'I don't hate you. Not at all. I'm just so bloody sorry for the weak, shallow person I was.'

'So what now?'

'Now I go to jail,' she said in a shaky voice. 'Unless my lawyer can get me off.'

'Will they be using a coercion defence?' asked Nick curiously. She had no desire to see Daisy in jail. She would happily see Adam crushed under the full weight of the Old Bailey, but not Daisy. Still, it was unlikely to happen, Daisy was the perfect scapegoat and Harrington's would have hundreds of lawyers protecting them.

'I hope you've got a good lawyer. You know you have an uphill struggle if you want Harrington's to share any of the blame.'

'Gabriel St Clair is my lawyer. He's already assembled a team to fight my case.'

Nick looked at her shocked. 'Gabriel St Clair. Giles Harrington's son?' She waited for Daisy to say no she meant someone else, but Daisy nodded her head.

'The very same. It was him after all that worked out I was the mole and got me to confess.'

'He what! You mean you didn't confess this voluntarily?'

Daisy closed her eyes and dropped her head. 'See, I told you I was weak. I couldn't bring myself to tell the truth and save you from an inquiry. Then Gabriel showed up on my doorstep and confronted me.'

Nick thought back to the last time she had seen him. He had told her he thought he might have a lead that could help her. No wonder he hadn't been prepared to tell Nick. Accusing Daisy would have been too much for Nick, she'd have never believed that her right-hand employee would have stabbed her in the back. Not without Daisy's own confession. Which also meant he was unaware of Aster's discovery, as far as he was concerned this was all that saved Nick.

'But his family? How can he defend you against them?'

'I asked him that and he just said it was the least he could do. He doesn't owe me anything so I didn't understand but I could hardly turn his offer down.'

Nick pushed her chair back. She didn't want to stay here any longer. This talk of Gabe had suddenly confused her, and she really didn't want to stay in Daisy's company any longer. She didn't hate her, and she thought in time, she might even be able to forgive her, but she couldn't stomach the other woman's cowardice and she needed to get some fresh air. Leaving Daisy staring into her cup she let herself out and started to walk home. It was a few miles but that was okay. She had a lot to think about.

Chapter 55

A day later and Nick didn't feel any more had been resolved. She had tried to thank Gabe but everything she wrote seemed lame. In the end she sent him a pathetically stilted text saying she had met Daisy and how grateful she was for his actions. His response came within seconds saying it was the least he could do and wished her well in the future.

She looked at the curt text and shrivelled inside.

She understood Daisy's actions, but Gabe's had completely confused her. What was he doing? He had saved her but in doing so had sacrificed his own family. It made no sense to her. Did he now hate her for the inadvertent role she had played in his family's downfall?

Her phone rang displaying an unknown number. It was Saturday morning, and she was in the garden with Ohana. She was tempted to let it ring off but deciding she could hang up just as easily she answered the phone.

'Letta? It's Rafe St Clair. How are you?'

Nick's stomach turned over. Did he also blame her for his father's downfall? Was he calling to berate her? In all her focus on Gabe how could she forget his twin, how they both must be suffering.

'Letta, are you still there?'

Nick pulled herself together. He didn't sound angry.

'Hello, yes, you just caught me unawares. Is everything all right?'

'Well, it's all a bit of a clusterfuck at Harrington's but that's not why I've called you. It's about Parscombe Court.'

Nick felt a spasm of relief. This she could deal with.

'Okay, what can I help you with.'

'The thing is you must have done one hell of a job on the Lees. They have offered £30 million for the entire estate!'

'Bloody hell.' Nick ran some quick calculations through her head – that should be enough to set the brothers up in their own practices immediately.

'I know. We are somewhat impressed. Anyway, the thing is they want us to include some of the items you suggested. I understand there are two swimming pools and a helipad we need to discuss and a *neon* baroque ballroom?'

Nick laughed. 'Oh dear, sorry about that.'

'Not to worry, the thing is they weren't very clear on the details and told me you knew what they wanted. So I wondered, could you come down today or tomorrow and you can walk me around the site and explain what was discussed?'

She paused, she was desperate to see Gabe again, if only to thank him to his face and say goodbye properly but she also knew she might spoil it. He wanted no more to do with the girl who was the cause of his family's dishonour. Granted, he hadn't sided with them, but she still knew that she would be a constant reminder and how could he live with that?

'It will just be me,' said Rafe, correctly interpreting her silence. 'Gabe's away this weekend.'

She wasn't sure if she felt happier or sadder about that but at least it made the decision easier.

'Of course. I'm cycling with friends tomorrow. What about later on today? Let me see about hiring a car.'

–

A few hours later, Nick was heading along the drive to Parscombe Court. Ohana sat beside her and as they drove past the cattle she let out a merry bark. As soon as the car stopped the little dog rushed over to say hello to her friends. Nick walked towards Rafe who had come outside to greet her. One look at Rafe's ruffled hair and Nick chided herself for a fool – the brothers were near identical, how could she look at Rafe's scruffy hair and easy smile and not think of Gabe.

'Hello, Letta. This really is very good of you, in light of everything some of my family put you through.'

'It's okay, I know you weren't involved and it's nice to come back and help on the project. Great news about the sale, by the way.'

As they got down to business, Nick's tension faded, and soon the pair of them were laughing at the shopping list that Nick had so blithely offered to Mrs Chung.

'An actual tunnel?'

'Well, maybe you can get away with an enclosed walkway, but you might check with them first?'

'And what's this about a K-pop music video? Are they serious?'

'Deadly, you don't joke about K-pop to Koreans, you never know if they're a fan or not. But that might be something for their designer to tackle rather than you. Again, run it past them?'

Nick was now completely relaxed and felt emboldened to ask Rafe about the past few weeks.

'And how are you doing? I am terribly sorry about what's happened.'

Rafe looked at her incredulously.

'You're sorry. What on earth for? None of this is your fault.'

Nick laughed bitterly. 'I know that. I just meant that it must be horrible in your family right now, and whilst I can't pretend to feel any remorse for your father or siblings, they are still your family.'

'Not anymore, they're not.'

'What?' Nick looked at him in astonishment. How did someone just turn their back on their family?

'I'm done with them. Obviously, I can't change the fact that they are blood, but to hell with them. They have behaved disgustingly. Not just to you but to everyone. It's all coming to light now. I still don't know how much my father was aware of Adam's schemes but for now he's choosing to support him, which is enough for me to walk away. Even if it weren't, Gabe chose you.'

Nick stopped walking and looked at him in surprise. They were in the lower meadow pacing out where she had suggested the outdoor pool could go.

'I don't follow.'

'You have a twin, don't you?' asked Rafe.

'Yes.'

'Well, when the chips are down whose side would you stand by, no matter how wrong they were?'

'Paddy's,' said Nick with an obvious shrug.

'Even if she were wrong?'

'She wouldn't be wrong.'

'See. Twin Thing.'

'But he hasn't chosen me?'

'No?' asked Rafe with a smile. 'He's fighting Daisy's case to expose the Harringtons' corruption.'

'I thought he was doing that for Daisy?'

'No, he's doing that for you. He's trying to make amends.'

'But he hasn't spoken to me in weeks. I thought he hated me?'

Rafe laughed and then cocked his head as the sound of a motor came along the drive. Nick heard a car door close and then some very excited barking from Ohana.

'Come on then. Let's see what he has to say for himself.'

They climbed the stone steps back up to the house as Gabe walked towards them carrying a very excited dog. How could she think Rafe and Gabe looked alike – Rafe was a shadow to Gabe. His energy shone out of him, that crooked nose and boisterous laugh filled the space around him.

'I thought you said he was away this weekend,' hissed Nick, desperate to get in her car and drive away at high speed. She couldn't bear to see him. Rafe was wrong, if he had chosen her as Rafe said, he would have called.

Rafe grinned at her. 'I might have lied about that.' Turning he called out to Gabe. 'Look who's here! Now I'm just heading off to the shops. Back in a bit and by then I expect you both to have sorted this out.'

And with that he got in the Golf and drove off leaving Gabe and Nick staring at each other.

–

'Hello, Letta,' said Gabe, his face blank. 'How are things?'

Nick swallowed her joy at seeing him and snapped at Ohana to stop licking his face. Looking at him she wondered if he had lost some weight. He looked tired, no doubt leading the prosecution against his family was draining him. She wanted to spare him that and would suggest he passed the case on to someone else.

Gabe put Ohana on the floor – bored, she ran back to lying in the grass with the cattle.

'Is Mary well?'

'Yes, thank you. She's staying with my sister in Norfolk for now. I think she may move down permanently but we are happy to be reunited with her.'

'That's good,' said Gabe formally. 'And you are here today to—?'

'Rafe called me to discuss where the swimming pools are to go. Congratulations on the sale, by the way.'

This was excruciating. Gabe was being polite, and his smile had disappeared – whatever Rafe may think, Gabe was clearly not pleased to see her.

'Thank you. Although we are in your debt again for that.'

'My debt? Not at all, plus you were doing me a favour in giving me somewhere to hide away from the press.'

'That were hounding you because of the actions of my brothers and father,' he replied stiffly.

'But not yours,' she said desperately. No matter how much he didn't want her in his life she wanted him to know that she didn't blame him.

'No. I—' He stopped and looked at her. 'Letta, I know you must despise me for everything my family has done to you, but I never knew anything about it. I would never have allowed them to utter so much as a bad word against you had I known what they were up to.'

Nick looked at him. This was exactly what she had feared and what she wanted to reassure him about. Maybe they would have a chance at friendship if she could convince him. It would be a weak shadow of what she really wanted, but even a casual acquaintance would mean he was in her life. Right now, as she looked at him, she knew even those small crumbs would be enough to make her day.

'Hate you? Why would I hate you? I'm just appalled that I have become a wedge between you and your father. I know how important family is and I hate the fact that unwittingly I have become a problem in yours.'

Now it was Gabe's turn to look confused and he laughed scornfully.

'Any division in my family was not down to you but down to them. I have severed all ties. I can't have anything to do with the people that tried to destroy the woman that I—' He stepped towards Letta, then stopped.

'But how can you turn your back on your family? I don't understand.'

'I haven't. Rafe and my mother are my family, as is Freya. But I can't have anything to do with anyone who tried to harm you.'

'I thought you hated me?'

'Idiot,' he laughed sadly. 'How can I hate you? I love you.'

Nick stopped and looked at him, her face thunder-struck.

'You love me?'

'Yes. Surely you knew that? You're all I've been able to think of since I left Ireland, you occupy my every waking thought. And I thought for a while that you might be growing fond of me too, until my family tried to put you in jail.'

'But that was your family,' protested Nick. 'Not you. I know I had a wobble that day at the property offices, but I've never doubted how I felt about you.'

'So do you think—' Gabe's voice caught, and he tried again. 'Does that mean you can forgive me?'

'Now who's being an idiot?' laughed Nick. 'There's nothing to forgive. I love you too. Call it a moment of mad spontaneity but when we raced the wave across the causeway, I think I fell in love with you then and there.'

'You love me?' Gabe stared at Nick in amazement as she nodded with a big grin on her face.

'And you don't care who my father is? Or what my brother tried to do to you?'

'Not in the slightest. We don't get to choose our family, we only get to choose who we love. I love my family and I love you.'

Gabe blinked. It was incredible that this beautiful brave clever girl loved him. What had he done to deserve so much from such an incredible person?

'Yes!' he roared, laughing. He tilted his head back and faced the sky punching his fists in the air. Then he ran towards Nick and picked her up, swinging her around. As the moment passed he slowly placed her back on the ground and she stood within his arms, smiling up at him.

'Yes,' she echoed, with a smile as bright as his.

Bending his head, he kissed her gently on the lips, afraid that this may still be a dream and that she would push him away in disgust. Instead, she stepped into his embrace and ran her fingers up through his hair. As he wrapped his arms around her back, a dog started barking and the cattle joined in the chorus with approving bellows.

But Letta the Bold and Gabriel the Brave carried on kissing until Rafe returned with champagne and the celebrations continued on into the night.

Epilogue

'Are you ready for this?'

Gabe looked over from the steering wheel as Letta glanced up from her laptop. He had offered to drive from London as Letta wanted to catch up on some work. She had told him she had no intention of working when she got to Cornwall, but she wanted to clear the decks first.

'Meeting the whole family, altogether,' replied Gabe with a smile. 'What can possibly go wrong?'

'Exactly. And they will love you as much as I do. Plus, this is the first time Mary will be meeting some of them so no one will even be looking at you.'

'Suits me.'

'I was joking. You and Mary are going to be the centre of attention. I'm not worried about you but I do hope Clem gives Mary an easy time. Last time I saw her she was pretty uptight.'

'She's the second sister, right? The one with a trigger finger?'

'Yep. Huge inferiority complex coupled with an enormous talent. Although I think Otto and Rory are proving to have a really good effect on her.'

'Will Otto be here? She's not family but you seem to talk about her as if she might be.'

'Don't know, she's been invited.' Letta looked back at her screen. 'Right, let me finish this off and then I can put it away for the whole weekend.'

Gabe flicked on the satnav so that Letta could concentrate on her work. The past two weeks had been a whirlwind. Three days after he told Letta he loved her and miraculously she had replied the same, he pretty much moved in with her in her townhouse. It seemed no time at all, but he knew beyond any shadow of doubt that he wanted to spend the rest of his life with her. She and Rafe got on like a house on fire and she had met Freya and Beth in the park. His father would no doubt have something to say about that – but as they weren't talking he'd have to explain to Freya why she couldn't see her brothers. Given how she had him wrapped around her little finger, Gabe thought that was unlikely to happen.

The roads had now funnelled down to the customary Cornish bottlenecks and Gabe was looking forward to the weekend. Apparently, this was a new family custom, all the family headed to Cornwall for a September weekend barbecue.

'Do you sail? Hal said the conditions are perfect for taking out the little dinghy. He's teaching Leo and Will.'

'Good plan,' said Gabe approvingly. 'You can never start too soon. Do you sail?'

Letta looked across at him with a raised eyebrow. She closed her laptop and placed it on the back seat.

'Yes. Growing up I spent all my time at gymkhanas or at the sailing club. Bunty and I would have the best time and in winter we'd spend Christmas in Aspen.'

Gabe rolled his eyes at her. 'So that's a no then?'

'Yes, that's a no.' Laughing she pointed to a large open gateway. 'In there. We'll park up and walk down to the beach.'

'Did I bother you? Asking about the sailing?' Their lives were so different, and he was always concerned that he might say something tactless or thoughtless.

Letta leant across and kissed him. 'How can it bother me? You asked a question. I don't have time to waste being offended with mock social outrage. So long as you weren't offended by me being sarcastic.'

Gabe laughed and kissed her back. 'Being offended that my gorgeous girlfriend has a smart mouth and an even faster brain? I'd be a bloody fool.'

Seeing that there was nowhere to park, Letta had told him to drive around to the front of the house.

'Come on, Ohana, time to wake up.'

Gabe watched as Letta opened Ohana's travelling crate and the dog stretched and yawned her way out, her tail already wagging. As she sorted Ohana out Gabe looked up at the beautiful country house, it was positioned to look down the valley and out over the sea.

'This place is incredible. Who lives here?'

Letta untangled Ohana's lead, and walked over to join him. 'No one. We rent it out for charity holidays, luxury retreats and film locations. And every now and then, us.'

Gabe took it in and figured it probably slept maybe sixteen or so people. 'You must lose quite a bit of income blocking out a September week?'

'True. But using it this way is priceless. Now look, everyone's already here, leave the bags. We can do that later. I want to see everyone.'

He loved this side of Letta; she was eager and enthu-siastic and clearly loved her family. She spent so much time telling him about them that he felt he knew them better than he knew her. But as she praised them she always revealed a little more of herself. She viewed herself as the least talented and also the quietest. This didn't bother her in the slightest. She almost hero-worshipped her eldest sister. She was extremely protective regarding her youngest sister, and generally steered any conversation away from her. Paddy was clearly her best friend and Gabe prayed to God that he and Paddy clicked. Finally, there was Clem, who according to Letta was the most talented in the family but the most likely to start a fight. When he had asked how he ensured that didn't happen she told him most seriously never to use her hand cream. Then laughed.

'Come on, slow coach!'

Ohana wagged her tailed as she and Letta stood waiting for him to the side of the driveway. Slung over her shoulder was a beach bag she had packed in London.

'You can change at the cottage. Come on, come on.'

Smiling he caught up with her, her enthusiasm was infectious, taking the bag from her so that she could hold Ohana's lead, they held hands and walked down the small lane.

–

As they approached the beach Gabe stopped in wonder. A pretty cottage stood on a large terrace just to the side of a small cove. The sea was gently lapping against the sand and out on the water a little sailboat was nipping about with screams of laughter drifting across the water. On shore a large barbecue was being tended by two men who were laughing about something. Several groups of people were sitting about, and a woman was playing in the sand with two toddlers.

As he and Letta appeared there was a shout from the side of the house and a short woman in a spectacular sarong came sprinting across and hugged Letta until laughing Letta had to peel her off.

'Hello, Clem, I'd like you to meet Gabe.'

And so the introductions continued. It was all a bit overwhelming trying to keep track of everyone, but he thought he had it.

As they had walked over to the woman in the sand she tried to get up, but her late pregnancy was slowing her down somewhat. Gabe was struck by how incredibly beautiful she was. Her long red hair and pale skin made her look like a pre-Raphaelite model and her cheek bones were remarkably pronounced and framed large violet eyes that looked so familiar to him.

Gabe stepped forward helping her up. 'Hello, you must be Paddy?'

'Ha! Well observed.' Paddy smiled at Letta. 'Did you tell him I was fat, lanky and ginger?'

'She said you were the most beautiful woman in the world. And after Letta, I think I agree.'

Paddy and Letta both laughed. 'You'll do. Come on, let me get you a drink and show you where to change. Nick seems to have forgotten.'

'That's not fair! I – well, yes, okay, guilty as charged. Sorry, Gabe, I got carried away.'

Paddy smiled. 'I like you getting carried away over something other than a spreadsheet or a race. Come on, Gabe, tell me how you have managed to bewitch my sister. Nick, keep an eye on these two.'

366

Gabe watched as Letta kicked off her shoes and knelt down with the toddlers and instantly started to build a moat and canal for the castle. As they walked towards the cottage, he lent Paddy his arm – this section was stony and he didn't want her to stumble.

'So tell me,' he said as they slowly navigated across the loose stones. 'Letta has filled me in on most of you but I don't really know much about Aster. What's her story?'

Paddy laughed. 'Oh dear, has she been brusque? Aster is fearless but also the youngest so we tend to over protect her. She's not great with strangers but she will come round.'

—

An hour later, Gabe was taking a moment to pause and watch the family as they played and chatted together.

Hal had been talking to an older couple who Letta had said were Otto and Louis. Given their French connection he could hear as much French as English – apparently Hal's stepmother was French and she and Hal's father now lived over there and Hal ran the estate over here.

Rory had taken charge of the barbecue and was enjoying the central role whilst not having to interact too much. Given how often people came over to talk to him it was clear that he was well loved. He was going for a sail with Hal in a minute and had found Seb to be remarkably good company.

He had gone to school with boys like this, centuries of family growing up in the same estates bred a certain level of confidence and easy charm. His own family might have more wealth on his father's side, but the lineage of these men swept back generations. His mother's family swept back centuries as well but they were Italian, and the English boarding school always viewed foreigners with polite patronage.

He was just ready to go and rejoin Letta when he saw Mary walking over to him and he smiled. He wasn't the only newcomer today.

'How are you doing, Mary?'

'I'm grand, and all the better for seeing yourself.'

A gull swept overhead but decided that Rory was keeping too close a watch on the grill and drifted across to the larger beach where there would be more unprotected chips and pasties.

'So what do you make of them?' asked Mary with a smile. 'My family.'

Gabe swept his eyes over the gathering. He had been to so many large family functions before but none of them were like this. There was no waiting staff walking around with trays of drinks or canapés, mostly everyone was barefoot. The children and adults were playing together. Lots of the adults were in and out of the water covered in sand. Admittedly Otto was on the terrace telling Rory what to do but Louis was down on the beach playing cricket with Clem, Aster, Will, Leo and Ohana.

It was as relaxed and as happy an occasion as he had ever witnessed. Ariana and Letta were sat in the shade, no doubt putting the world to rights and he hadn't wanted to intrude. Letta was just shining with happiness surrounded by her sisters.

'I think, Mary, that as families go, you may have the most marvellous one.'

'And are you missing your own?' she asked kindly.

He wasn't surprised by her blunt concern, but it touched him nonetheless.

'I still have my family. My mother and brother will never be divided from me. As for my family and half-siblings, we shall see. You can't choose your family, but I love Rafe and Mama and that is enough for me.'

Ariana and Letta had now walked over to join them, and Gabe felt guilty, he should have moved quicker, Ariana looked ready to deliver at any minute.

'Hello, you two,' said Ari, 'are you discussing us lot?'

'We are, actually.'

'Do we pass?' asked Letta, her eyes shining but he also sensed a hesitancy in her question.

'A strong B+, I'd say,' said Gabe and then laughed as Letta hit him. He threw his arms up in protest and then hugged her to him. 'You're perfect, what can I say?'

Letta smiled up at him. 'Do you know, you're pretty perfect as well. Welcome to the family.'

A letter from Liz

Writing this book through the pandemic has been a blessing. It has given me somewhere to escape, but also to dwell on what is important in life. I think it's no surprise that this story focussed heavily on how important family is. Work is important and it was essential that at the end of the story Nicoletta is still the high-powered City trader she was at the beginning. However, I wanted her to have more in her life and I hope with Ohana and Gabe by her side she has found the balance that she needed.

I too am grateful for all that my friends and family give me. I am less grateful for the treats that my animals give me, but I wouldn't be without them. The animals, not the treats.

As ever I am particularly grateful to Alexandra who read through the first draft and to Simon Warsop for helping me to navigate the financial waters.

I am also grateful to my cousin, Carrie. I'm half Irish myself but it's been a long time since I went back, and it was essential that I got my Irish characters right. I had been planning to go over for a refresher, but 2020 put paid to that. Instead Carrie read my draft, then reminded me of a few choice phrases. For decency's sake we didn't include them!

I am also grateful to my publishers and editors for coping with my inability to master hyphenation and commas, amongst everything else.

As ever, all mistakes, factual or grammatical, are completely mine.

All in all I hope that you have enjoyed reading this book as much as I have enjoyed writing it, and I thank you for your continuing support.

To keep in touch you can follow me on any of the social media platforms – I'm @lizhurleywrites – or sign up for my newsletter on my website at www.lizhurleywrites.com

If you haven't already, you can read about the other sisters if you follow these links:

A New Life for Ariana Byrne
https://books2read.com/ariana-byrne

High Heels in the Highlands
https://books2read.com/high-heels

Cornish Dreams at Cockleshell Cottage
https://books2read.com/Cornish-dreams